SEIZE THE NIGHT

"No bestselling suspense novelist creates magnetic characters as consistently as Koontz does. The wonderfully delineated loyalties among these characters will win readers' hearts. The suspense soars . . . a rousing crowd pleaser."
—*Publishers Weekly*

"Page by page, Koontz builds the tension until it is almost unbearable. Koontz is a born storyteller [and] *Seize the Night* is well-paced, full of believable dialogue in a plot almost too scary to contemplate."
—*San Francisco Examiner*

"A remarkable technical feat. The ability to articulate his scary visions in such detail and to keep the level of excitement so high, moment by moment, is a main reason for Koontz's popularity."
—*Los Angeles Times*

"A tour de force. Heavy suspense. With headlong glee, Koontz again reveals encyclopedic intelligence about how things work in the physical world—and how to bolt sentences into the moonlight."
—*Kirkus Reviews*

"*Seize the Night* is a book of bad dreams, and the author's fans are going to love it."
—*Chicago Tribune*

"One of the best fictions including surfing in its plot. Koontz has obviously been exposed to the surf culture, because he writes about surfing without committing the usual faux pas of non-surfing authors."
—*Surfing Journal*

"I write this review at 2:38 A.M. I have closed the window behind me, I'm up on the 14th floor, so I should be safe now. . . . Blame my disquiet on Dean Koontz and his new suspense novel, *Seize the Night*."
—*USA Today*

"Plenty of suspense and enough action to keep turning the pages."
—*The Blade,* Toledo

"Looking for the kind of suspense that will raise goose bumps on goose bumps? Cozy up to the latest pulse-quickener from Dean Koontz . . . full of the creepy kind of dread [his fans] have come to savor in his novels."
—*People*

"*Seize the Night* and its predecessor, *Fear Nothing,* will make a fan out of you, thanks in no small part to Koontz's terrific writing. He skillfully creates a spellbinding page-turner every time he puts his fingers to the keyboard."
—*The Sunday Star-Ledger,* Newark

"Koontz is a master of all things mysterious, and his marvelous imagination is fully at work in this novel. He not only creates a fabulous adventure with *Seize the Night,* he also offers a fairly sensitive look at relationships and creates dialogue that is real and usually pretty hilarious."
—*Milwaukee Journal Sentinel*

"This is one of the scariest, most gripping gothic techno-thrillers I have ever read. This book will leave you breathless."
—*The Providence Sunday Journal*

"Koontz is a fine writer."
—*The Detroit News-Free Press*

"As creepily suspenseful as anything Koontz has done."
—*The Flint Journal*

"An extraordinary follow-up to his terrifying *Fear Nothing*."
—*The Arizona Republic*

"As he has done time after time, the awesome Dean Koontz delivers all the nail-biting suspense and hair-raising thrills a reader could possibly request."
—*Romantic Times*

"*Seize the Night* is a story of loyalty, love and courage . . . a grand adventure that is sure to give fans of the genre a thrill."
—*McKeesport News*

"[Christopher] Snow is a strong unique character that Koontz should be proud of. . . . A zip-bang pace that doesn't let up."
—*Mostly Murder*

"This sequel to *Fear Nothing* is a stunning achievement . . . a [combination of] Edgar Allan Poe, Spielberg, and Walt Disney. The language is beautifully evocative."
—*The Advocate*, Baton Rouge

SEIZE THE NIGHT

ALSO BY DEAN KOONTZ

DEAN KOONTZ

SEIZE THE NIGHT

BANTAM BOOKS

new york toronto london sydney auckland

This edition contains the complete text
of the original hardcover edition.
NOT ONE WORD HAS BEEN OMITTED.

SEIZE THE NIGHT

A Bantam Book

PUBLISHING HISTORY
Bantam hardcover edition published January 1999
Bantam paperback edition / December 1999

ISBN 0-553-58019-1

Published simultaneously in the United States and Canada

Bantam Books are published by Bantam Books, a division of Random House, Inc. Its trademark, consisting of the words "Bantam Books" and the portrayal of a rooster, is Registered in U.S. Patent and Trademark Office and in other countries. Marca Registrada. Bantam Books, 1540 Broadway, New York, New York 10036.

PRINTED IN THE UNITED STATES OF AMERICA

OPM   20   19   18   17   16   15   14   13   12   11

This second Christopher Snow adventure
is dedicated to Richard Aprahamian
and to Richard Heller,
who bring honor to the law—
and who so far have kept me out of jail!

Friendship is precious, not only in the shade, but in the sunshine of life. And thanks to a benevolent arrangement of things, the greater part of life is sunshine.

—Thomas Jefferson

FIRST

My name is Christopher Snow. The following account is an installment in my personal journal. If you are reading it, I am probably dead. If I am not dead, then because of the reportage herein, I am now—or soon will be—one of the most famous people on the planet. If no one ever reads this, it will be because the world as we know it has ceased to exist and human civilization is gone forever. I am no more vain than the average person, and instead of universal recognition, I prefer the peace of anonymity. Nevertheless, if the choice is between Armageddon and fame, I'd prefer to be famous.

ONE

THE LOST BOYS

1

Elsewhere, night falls, but in Moonlight Bay it steals upon us with barely a whisper, like a gentle dark-sapphire surf licking a beach. At dawn, when the night retreats across the Pacific toward distant Asia, it is reluctant to go, leaving deep black pools in alleyways, under parked cars, in culverts, and beneath the leafy canopies of ancient oaks.

According to Tibetan folklore, a secret sanctuary in the sacred Himalayas is the home of all wind, from which every breeze and raging storm throughout the world is born. If the night, too, has a special home, our town is no doubt the place.

On the eleventh of April, as the night passed through Moonlight Bay on its way westward, it took with it a five-year-old boy named Jimmy Wing.

Near midnight, I was on my bicycle, cruising the residential streets in the lower hills not far from Ashdon College, where my murdered parents had once been professors. Earlier, I had been to the beach, but although there was no wind, the surf was mushy; the sloppy waves didn't make it worthwhile to suit up and float a board. Orson, a black Labrador mix, trotted at my side.

Fur face and I were not looking for adventure, merely getting some fresh air and satisfying our mutual need to be on the move. A restlessness of the soul plagues both of us more nights than not.

Anyway, only a fool or a madman goes looking for adventure in picturesque Moonlight Bay, which is simultaneously one of the quietest and most dangerous communities on the planet. Here, if you stand in one place long enough, a lifetime's worth of adventure will find you.

Lilly Wing lives on a street shaded and scented by stone pines. In the absence of lampposts, the trunks and twisted branches were as black as char, except where moonlight pierced the feathery boughs and silvered the rough bark.

I became aware of her when the beam of a flashlight swept back and forth between the pine trunks. A quick pendulum of light arced across the pavement ahead of me, and tree shadows jumped. She called her son's name, trying to shout but defeated by breathlessness and by a quiver of panic that transformed *Jimmy* into a six-syllable word.

Because no traffic was in sight ahead of or behind us, Orson and I were traveling the center of the pavement: kings of the road. We swung to the curb.

As Lilly hurried between two pines and into the street, I said, "What's wrong, Badger?"

For twelve years, since we were sixteen, "Badger" has been my affectionate nickname for her. In those days, her name was Lilly Travis, and we were in love and believed that a future together was our destiny. Among our long list of shared enthusiasms and passions was a special fondness for Kenneth Grahame's *The Wind in the Willows,* in which the wise and courageous Badger was the stalwart defender of all the good animals in the Wild Wood. "Any friend of *mine* walks where he likes in this country," Badger had promised Mole, "or I'll know the reason why!" Likewise, those who shunned me because of my rare disability, those who called me *vampire* because of my inherited lack of tolerance for more than the dimmest light, those teenage psychopaths who plotted to torture me with fists and flashlights, those who spoke maliciously of me behind my back, as if I'd *chosen* to be born with xeroderma pigmentosum—all had found themselves answering to Lilly, whose face flushed and whose heart raced with righteous anger at any exhibition of intolerance. As a young boy, out of urgent necessity, I learned to fight, and by the time I met

Lilly, I was confident of my ability to defend myself; nevertheless, she had insisted on coming to my aid as fiercely as the noble Badger ever fought with claw and cudgel for his friend Mole.

Although slender, she is mighty. Only five feet four, she appears to tower over any adversary. She is as formidable, fearless, and fierce as she is graceful and good-hearted.

This night, however, her usual grace had deserted her, and fright had tortured her bones into unnatural angles. When I spoke, she twitched around to face me, and in her jeans and untucked flannel shirt, she seemed to be a bristling scarecrow now magically animated, confused and terrified to find itself suddenly alive, jerking at its supporting cross.

The beam of her flashlight bathed my face, but she considerately directed it toward the ground the instant she realized who I was. "Chris. Oh, God."

"What's wrong?" I asked again as I got off my bike.

"Jimmy's gone."

"Run away?"

"No." She turned from me and hurried toward the house. "This way, here, look."

Lilly's property is ringed by a white picket fence that she herself built. The entrance is flanked not by gateposts but by matched bougainvillea that she has pruned into trees and trained into a canopy. Her modest Cape Cod bungalow lies at the end of an intricately patterned brick walkway that she designed and laid after teaching herself masonry from books.

The front door stood open. Enticing rooms of deadly brightness lay beyond.

Instead of taking me and Orson inside, Lilly quickly led us off the bricks and across the lawn. In the still night, as I pushed my bike through the closely cropped grass, the tick of wheel bearings was the loudest sound. We went to the north side of the house.

A bedroom window had been raised. Inside, a single lamp glowed, and the walls were striped with amber light and faint honey-brown shadows from the folded cloth of the pleated shade. To the left of the bed, Star Wars action figures stood on a set of bookshelves. As the cool night air sucked warmth from the house, one panel of the curtains was drawn across the sill, pale and fluttering like a troubled spirit reluctant to leave this world for the next.

"I thought the window was locked, but it mustn't have been," Lilly said frantically. "Someone opened it, some sonof-abitch, and he took Jimmy away."

"Maybe it's not that bad."

"Some sick bastard," she insisted.

The flashlight jiggled, and Lilly struggled to still her trembling hand as she directed the beam at the planting bed alongside the house.

"I don't have any money," she said.

"Money?"

"To pay ransom. I'm not rich. So no one would take Jimmy for ransom. It's worse than that."

False Solomon's seal, laden with feathery sprays of white flowers that glittered like ice, had been trampled by the intruder. Footprints were impressed in trodden leaves and soft damp soil. They were not the prints of a runaway child but those of an adult in athletic shoes with bold tread, and judging by the depth of the impressions, the kidnapper was a large person, most likely male.

I saw that Lilly was barefoot.

"I couldn't sleep, I was watching TV, some stupid show on the TV," she said with a note of self-flagellation, as if she should have anticipated this abduction and been at Jimmy's bedside, ever vigilant.

Orson pushed between us to sniff the imprinted earth.

"I didn't hear anything," Lilly said. "Jimmy never cried out, but I got this *feeling*. . . ."

Her usual beauty, as clear and deep as a reflection of eternity, was now shattered by terror, crazed by sharp lines of an anguish that was close to grief. She was held together only by desperate hope. Even in the dim backwash of the flashlight, I could hardly bear the sight of her in such pain.

"It'll be all right," I said, ashamed of this facile lie.

"I called the police," she said. "They should be here any second. Where *are* they?"

Personal experience had taught me to distrust the authorities in Moonlight Bay. They are corrupt. And the corruption is not merely moral, not simply a matter of bribe-taking and a taste for power; it has deeper and more disturbing origins.

No siren shrieked in the distance, and I didn't expect to hear one. In our special town, the police answer calls with utmost discretion, without even the quiet fanfare of flashing emergency lights, because as often as not, their purpose is to conceal a crime and silence the complainant rather than to bring the perpetrator to justice.

"He's only five, only five," Lilly said miserably. "Chris, what if this is that guy on the news?"

"The news?"

"The serial killer. The one who . . . burns kids."

"That's not around here."

"All over the country. Every few months. Groups of little kids burned alive. Why not here?"

"Because it isn't," I said. "It's something else."

She swung away from the window and raked the yard with the flashlight beam, as though she hoped to discover her tousle-haired, pajama-clad son among the fallen leaves and the curled strips of papery bark that littered the grass under a row of tall eucalyptus trees.

Catching a troubling scent, Orson issued a low growl and backed away from the planting bed. He peered up at the windowsill, sniffed the air, put his nose to the ground again, and headed tentatively toward the rear of the house.

"He's got something," I said.

Lilly turned. "Got what?"

"A trail."

When he reached the backyard, Orson broke into a trot.

"Badger," I said, "don't tell them Orson and I were here."

A weight of fear pressed her voice thinner than a whisper: "Don't tell who?"

"The police."

"Why?"

"I'll be back. I'll explain. I swear I'll find Jimmy. I swear I will."

I could keep the first two promises. The third, however, was something less meaningful than wishful thinking and was intended only to provide a little hope with which she might keep herself glued together.

In fact, as I hurried after my strange dog, pushing the bicycle at my side, I already believed that Jimmy Wing was lost forever. The most I expected to find at the end of the trail was the boy's dead body and, with luck, the man who had murdered him.

2

When I reached the rear of Lilly's house, I couldn't see Orson. He was so coaly black that even the light of a full moon was not sufficient to reveal him.

From off to the right came a soft *woof*, then another, and I followed his call.

At the end of the backyard was a freestanding garage that could be entered by car only from the alley beyond. A brick walkway led alongside the garage to a wooden gate, where Orson stood on his hind legs, pawing at the latch.

For a fact, this dog is radically smarter than ordinary mutts. Sometimes I suspect that he is also considerably smarter than I am.

If I didn't have the advantage of hands, no doubt I would be the one eating from a dish on the floor. He would have control of the most comfortable easy chair and the remote control for the television.

Demonstrating my single claim to superiority, I disengaged the bolt latch with a flourish and pushed open the creaking gate.

A series of garages, storage sheds, and backyard fences lay along this flank of the alley. On the farther side, the cracked and runneled blacktop gave way to a narrow dirt shoulder, which in turn led to a line of massive eucalyptuses and a weedy verge that sloped into a canyon.

Lilly's house is on the edge of town, and no one lives in

the canyon behind her place. The wild grass and scattered
scrub oaks on the descending slopes provide homes for hawks,
coyotes, rabbits, squirrels, field mice, and snakes.

Following his formidable nose, Orson urgently investi-
gated the weeds along the edge of the canyon, padding north
and then south, softly whining and grumbling to himself.

I stood at the brink, between two trees, peering down
into a darkness that not even the fat moon could dispel. No
flashlight moved in those depths. If Jimmy had been carried
into that gloom, the kidnapper must have uncanny night vision.

With a yelp, Orson abruptly abandoned his search along
the canyon rim and returned to the center of the alleyway. He
moved in a circle, as though he might start chasing his tail,
but his head was raised and he was excitedly sniffing spoor.

To him, the air is a rich stew of scents. Every dog has a
sense of smell thousands of times more powerful than yours or
mine.

The medicinal pungency of the eucalyptus trees was the
only aroma that I could detect. Drawn by another and more
suspicious scent, as if he were but a bit of iron pulled inexorably toward a powerful magnet, Orson raced north along the
alley.

Maybe Jimmy Wing was still alive.

It's my nature to believe in miracles. So why not believe
in this one?

I climbed on my bike and pedaled after the dog. He was
swift and certain, and to match his pace, I really had to make
the drive chain hum.

In block after block, only a few widely spaced security
lamps glowed at the back of the residential properties that we
passed. By habit I steered away from those radiant pools,
along the darker side of the alleyway, even though I could
have sailed through each patch of lamplight in less than a
second or two, without significant risk to my health.

Xeroderma pigmentosum—XP for those who aren't able
to tie their tongues in knots—is an inherited genetic disorder
that I share with an exclusive club of only one thousand other

Americans. One of us per 250,000 citizens. XP renders me highly vulnerable to skin and eye cancers caused by exposure to *any* ultraviolet radiation. Sunshine. Incandescent or fluorescent bulbs. The shining, idiot face of a television screen.

If I dared to spend just half an hour in summer sun, I would burn severely, though a single searing wouldn't kill me. The true horror of XP, however, is that even minor exposure to ultraviolet radiation shortens my life, because the effect is cumulative. Years of imperceptible injuries accrete until they manifest as visible lesions, malignancies. Six hundred minutes of exposure, spread one by one over an entire year, will have the same ultimate effect as ten continuous hours on a beach in brightest July. The luminosity of a streetlamp is less dangerous to me than the full ferocity of the sun, but it's not entirely safe.

Nothing is.

You, with your properly functioning genes, are able routinely to repair the injury to your skin and eyes that you unknowingly suffer every day. Your body, unlike mine, continuously produces enzymes that strip out the damaged segments of nucleotide strands in your cells, replacing them with undamaged DNA.

I must exist in shadows, while you live under exquisitely blue skies, and yet I don't hate you. I don't resent you for the freedom that you take for granted—although I do envy you.

I don't hate you because, after all, you are human, too, and therefore have limitations of your own. Perhaps you are homely, slow-witted or too smart for your own good, deaf or mute or blind, by nature given to despair or to self-hatred, or perhaps you are unusually fearful of Death himself. We all have burdens. On the other hand, if you are better-looking and smarter than I am, blessed with five sharp senses, even more optimistic than I am, with plenty of self-esteem, and if you also share my refusal to be humbled by the Reaper . . . well, then I could *almost* hate you if I didn't know that, like all of us in this imperfect world, you also have a haunted heart and a mind troubled by grief, by loss, by longing.

Rather than rage against XP, I regard it as a blessing. My passage through life is unique.

For one thing, I have a singular familiarity with the night. I know the world between dusk and dawn as no one else can know it, for I am a brother to the owl and the bat and the badger. I am at home in the darkness. This can be a greater advantage than you might think.

Of course, no number of advantages can compensate for the fact that death before the age of consent is not uncommon for those with XP. Survival far into adulthood isn't a reasonable expectation—at least not without progressive neurological disorders, such as tremors of the head and hands, hearing loss, slurred speech, even mental impairment.

Thus far I have tweaked Death's cold nose without retribution. I've also been spared all the physical infirmities that my physicians have long predicted.

I am twenty-eight years old.

To say that I am living on borrowed time would be not merely a cliché but also an understatement. My entire life has been a heavily mortgaged enterprise.

But so is yours. Eventual foreclosure awaits all of us. More likely than not, I'll receive my notice before you do, though yours, too, is in the mail.

Nevertheless, until the postman comes, be happy. There is no other rational response but happiness. Despair is a foolish squandering of precious time.

Now, here, on this cool spring night, past the witching hour but with dawn still far away, chasing my sherlock hound, believing in the miracle of Jimmy Wing's survival, I cycled along empty alleys and deserted avenues, through a park where Orson did not pause to sniff a single tree, past the high school, onto lower streets. He led me eventually to the Santa Rosita River, which bisects our town from the heights to the bay.

In this part of California, where annual rainfall averages a mere fourteen inches, rivers and streams are parched most of the year. The recent rainy season had been no wetter than usual, and this riverbed was entirely exposed: a broad expanse of powdery silt, pale and slightly lustrous in the lunar light. It was as smooth as a bedsheet except for scattered knots of dark driftwood like sleeping homeless men whose limbs were twisted by nightmares.

In fact, though it was sixty to seventy feet wide, the Santa Rosita looked less like a real river than like a man-made drainage channel or canal. As part of an elaborate federal project to control the flash floods that could swell suddenly out of the steep hills and narrow canyons at the back door of Moonlight Bay, these riverbanks had been raised and stabilized with wide concrete levees from one end of town to the other.

Orson trotted off the street, across a barren strip of land, to the levee.

Following him, I coasted between two signs, sets of which alternated with each other for the entire length of the watercourse. The first declared that public access to the river was restricted and that anti-trespassing ordinances would be enforced. The second, directed at those lawless citizens who were undeterred by the first sign, warned that high water at a storm's peak could be so powerful and fast-moving that it would overwhelm anyone who dared to venture into it.

In spite of all the warnings, in spite of the obvious turbulence of the treacherous currents and the well-known tragic history of the Santa Rosita, a thrill seeker with a homemade raft or a kayak—or even just a pair of water wings—is swept to his death every few years. In a single winter, not long ago, three drowned.

Human beings can always be relied upon to assert, with vigor, their God-given right to be stupid.

Orson stood on the levee, burly head raised, gazing east toward the Pacific Coast Highway and the serried hills beyond. He was stiff with tension, and a thin whine escaped him.

This night, neither water nor anything else moved along the moonlit channel. Not enough of a breeze slipped off the Pacific even to stir a dust ghost from the silt.

I checked the radiant dial of my wristwatch. Worried that

every minute might be Jimmy Wing's last—if, indeed, he was still alive—I nudged Orson: "What is it?"

He didn't acknowledge my question. Instead, he pricked his ears, sniffed the becalmed night almost daintily, and seemed to be transfixed by emanations of one kind or another from some quarry farther up the arid river.

As usual, I was uncannily attuned to Orson's mood. Although I possessed only an ordinary nose and mere human senses—but, to be fair to myself, a superior wardrobe and bank account—I could almost detect those same emanations.

Orson and I are closer than dog and man. I am not his master. I am his friend, his brother.

When I said earlier that I am brother to the owl, to the bat, and to the badger, I was speaking figuratively. When I say I'm the brother of this dog, however, I mean to be taken more literally.

Studying the riverbed as it climbed and dwindled into the hills, I asked, "Something spooking you?"

Orson glanced up. In his ebony eyes floated twin reflections of the moon, which at first I mistook for me, but my face is neither that round nor that mysterious.

Nor that pale. I am not an albino. My skin is pigmented, and my complexion somewhat dusky even though the sun has rarely touched me.

Orson snorted, and I didn't need to understand the language of dogs to interpret his precise meaning. The pooch was telling me that he was insulted by my suggestion that he could be so easily spooked.

Indeed, Orson is even more courageous than most of his kind. During the more than two and a half years that I've known him, from puppyhood to the present, I have seen him frightened of only one thing: monkeys.

"Monkeys?" I asked.

He chuffed, which I interpreted as *no*.

Not monkeys this time.

Not yet.

Orson trotted to a wide concrete access ramp that descended along the levee wall to the Santa Rosita. In June and

July, dump trucks and excavators would use this route when maintenance crews removed a year's worth of accumulated sediment and debris from below, restoring a flood-preventing depth to the dry watercourse before the next rainy season.

I followed the dog down to the riverbed. On the darkly mottled concrete slope, his black form was no more substantial than a shadow. On the faintly luminous silt, however, he appeared to be stone solid even as he drifted eastward like a homeward-bound spirit crossing a waterless Styx.

Because the most recent rainfall had occurred three weeks in the past, the floor of the channel wasn't damp. It was still well compacted, however, and I was able to ride the bicycle without struggle.

At least as far as the pearly moonlight revealed, the bike tires made few discernible marks in the hard-packed silt, but a heavier vehicle had passed this way earlier, leaving clear tracks. Judging by the width and depth of the tread impressions, the tires were those of a van, a light truck, or a sports utility vehicle.

Flanked by twenty-foot-high concrete ramparts, I had no view of any of the town immediately around us. I could see only the faint angular lines of the houses on higher hills, huddled under trees or partially revealed by streetlamps. As we ascended the watercourse, the townscape ahead also fell away from sight beyond the levees, as though the night were a powerful solvent in which all the structures and citizens of Moonlight Bay were dissolving.

At irregular intervals, drainage culverts yawned in the levee walls, some only two or three feet in diameter, a few so large that a truck could have been driven into them. The tire tracks led past all those tributaries and continued up the riverbed, as straight as typed sentences on a sheet of paper, except where they curved around a punctuation of driftwood.

Although Orson's attention remained focused ahead, I regarded the culverts with suspicion. During a cloudburst, torrents gushed out of them, carried from the streets and from the natural drainage swales high in the grassy eastern hills above town. Now, in fair weather, these storm drains were the subterranean lanes of a secret world, in which one might encounter exceptionally strange travelers. I half expected someone to rush at me from one of them.

I admit to having an imagination feverish enough to melt good judgment. Occasionally it has gotten me into trouble, but more than once it has saved my life.

Besides, having roamed all the storm drains large enough to accommodate a man my size, I've encountered a few peculiar tableaux. Oddities and enigmas. Sights to wring fright from even the driest rag of imagination.

Because the sun rises inevitably every day, my night life must be conducted within the town limits, to ensure that I'm always close to the safely darkened rooms of my house when dawn draws near. Considering that our community has a population of twelve thousand and a student population, at Ashdon College, of an additional three thousand, it offers a reasonably large board for a game of life; it can't fairly be called a jerkwater burg. Nevertheless, by the time I was sixteen, I knew every inch of Moonlight Bay better than I knew the territory inside my own head. Consequently, to fend off boredom, I am always seeking new perspectives on the slice of the world to which XP confines me; for a while I was intrigued by the view from below, touring the storm drains as if I were the Phantom prowling the realms beneath the Paris Opera House, though I lacked his cape, cloche hat, scars, and insanity.

Recently, I've preferred to keep to the surface. Like everyone born into this world, I'll take up permanent residence underground soon enough.

Now, after we passed another culvert without being assaulted, Orson suddenly picked up his pace. The trail had gotten hot.

As the riverbed rose toward the east, it gradually grew narrower, until it was only forty feet wide where it passed under Highway 1. This tunnel was more than a hundred feet long, and although faint silvery moonlight glimmered at the farther end, the way ahead was dauntingly dark.

Apparently, Orson's reliable nose didn't detect any danger. He wasn't growling.

On the other hand, he didn't sprint confidently into the gloom, either. He stood at the entrance, his tail still, his ears pricked, alert.

For years I have traveled the night with only a modest amount of cash for the infrequent purchases I make, a small flashlight for those rare instances when darkness might be more of an enemy than a friend, and a compact cell phone clipped to my belt. Recently, I'd added one other item to my standard kit: a 9-millimeter Glock pistol.

Under my jacket, the Glock hung in a supple shoulder holster. I didn't need to touch the gun to know that it was there; the weight of it was like a tumor growing on my ribs. Nevertheless, I slipped one hand under the coat and pressed my fingertips against the grip of the pistol as a superstitious person might touch a talisman.

In addition to the black leather jacket, I was dressed in black Rockports, black socks, black jeans, and a black long-sleeve cotton pullover. The black-on-black is not because I style myself after vampires, priests, ninja assassins, or Hollywood celebrities. In this town, at night, wisdom requires you to be well armed but also to blend with the shadows, calling as little attention to yourself as possible.

Leaving the Glock in the holster, still straddling my bike but with both feet on the ground, I unclipped the small flashlight from the handlebars. My bicycle doesn't have a headlamp. I have lived so many years in the night and in rooms lit mostly by candles that my dark-adapted eyes don't often need assistance.

The beam penetrated perhaps thirty feet into the concrete tunnel, which had straight walls but an arched ceiling. No threat lurked in the first section of that passage.

Orson ventured inside.

Before following the dog, I listened to the traffic roaring south and north on Highway 1, far above. To me, as always, this sound was simultaneously thrilling and melancholy.

I've never driven a car and probably never will. Even if I

protected my hands with gloves and my face with a mask, the ceaseless oncoming headlights would pose a danger to my eyes. Besides, I couldn't go any significant distance north or south along the coast and still return home before sunrise.

Relishing the drone of the traffic, I peered up the broad concrete buttress in which the river tunnel was set. At the top of this long incline, headlights flared off the steel guardrails that defined the shoulder of the highway, but I couldn't see the passing vehicles.

What I did see—or thought I saw—from the corner of my eye, was someone crouched up there, to the south of me, a figure not quite as black as the night around him, fitfully backlit by the passing traffic. He was on the buttress cap just this side of the guardrails, barely visible yet with an aura as menacing as a gargoyle at the corner of a cathedral parapet.

When I turned my head for a better look, the lights from a dense cluster of speeding cars and trucks caused shadows to leap like an immense flock of ravens taking flight in a lightning storm. Among those swooping phantoms, an apparently more solid figure raced diagonally downward, moving away from me and from the buttress, south along the grassy embankment.

In but a flicker of time, he was beyond the reach of the strobing headlights, lost in the deeper darkness and also blocked from view by the levee walls that towered twenty feet above me. He might be circling back to the edge of the channel, intending to enter the riverbed behind me.

Or he might not be interested in me at all. Though it would be comforting to think that galaxies revolve around me, I am not the center of the universe.

In fact, this mysterious figure might not even exist. I'd gotten such a brief glimpse of it that I couldn't be absolutely certain it was more than an illusion.

Again I reached under my coat and touched the Glock.

Orson had padded so far into the passageway beneath Highway 1 that he was almost beyond the reach of my flashlight.

After glancing at the channel behind me and seeing no

stalker, I followed the dog. Instead of riding my bike, I walked beside it, guiding it with my left hand.

I didn't like having my right hand—my gun hand—occupied with the flashlight. Besides, the light made me easy to follow and easy to target.

Although the riverbed was dry, the walls of the tunnel gave off a not unpleasant damp odor, and the cool air was scented with a trace of lime from the concrete.

From the roadbed high above, the rumble-hum of passing cars and trucks translated all the way down through layers of steel, concrete, and earth, echoing across the vault overhead. Repeatedly, in spite of the screening thrum of the traffic, I thought I heard someone stealthily approaching. Each time I swung toward the sound, the flashlight revealed only the smooth concrete walls and the deserted river behind me.

The tire tracks continued through the tunnel into another open stretch of the Santa Rosita, where I switched off the flashlight, relieved to rely on ambient light. The channel curved to the right, out of sight, leading east-southeast away from Highway 1, rising at a steeper grade than before.

Although houses still stippled the surrounding hills, we were nearing the edge of town.

I knew where we were going. I had known for some time but was disturbed by the prospect. If Orson was on the right trail and if Jimmy Wing's abductor was driving the vehicle that had left these tracks, then the kidnapper had fled with the boy into Fort Wyvern, the abandoned military base that was the source of many of Moonlight Bay's current problems.

Wyvern, which covers 134,456 acres—far more territory than our town—is surrounded by a high chain-link fence supported by steel posts sunk in concrete caissons, topped with helixes of razor wire. This barrier bisected the river, and as I rounded the curve in the channel, I saw a dark-colored Chevrolet Suburban parked in front of it, at the end of the tracks we had been following.

The truck was about sixty feet away, but I was reasonably sure no one was in it. Nevertheless, I intended to approach it with caution.

Orson's low growl indicated a wariness of his own.

Turning to the terrain we had crossed, I could see no sign of the creeping gargoyle that I had glimpsed on the east side of Highway 1. Nonetheless, I felt as though I were being watched.

I concealed my bike on the ground, behind a snarl of driftwood that had gotten its teeth into a few dead tumbleweeds.

After tucking the flashlight under my belt, at the small of my back, I drew the Glock from my holster. It is a safe-action pistol with only internal safety devices: no little levers that need thumbing to ready the gun for use.

This weapon has saved my life more than once, yet although it's a reassurance to me, I am not entirely comfortable with it. I suspect I'll never be able to handle it with complete ease. The weight and design of the piece have nothing to do with my aversion to the feel of it; this is a superb handgun. As a boy roaming the town at night, however, I was subjected to some memorable verbal and physical abuse from bullies—mostly kids but also some adults old enough to know better—and although their harassment motivated me to learn how to defend myself and taught me never to let an injustice pass without a firm response, these experiences also instilled in me a loathing of violence as an easy solution. To protect myself and those I love, I will use lethal force when I must, but I'll never enjoy it.

With Orson at my side, I approached the Suburban. No driver or passenger waited inside. The hood was still warm with engine heat; the truck had been parked here only minutes.

Footprints led from the driver's door around to the front door on the passenger's side. From there, they continued toward the nearby fence. They appeared to be similar—if not identical—to the prints in the planting bed under Jimmy Wing's bedroom window.

The silver-coin moon was rolling slowly toward the dark purse of the western horizon, but its glow remained bright enough to allow me to read the license plate on the back of the vehicle. I quickly memorized the number.

I found where a bolt cutter had been used to breach the chain-link fence. Evidently, this was accomplished some time ago, before the most recent rain, because the water-smoothed silt was not heavily disturbed, as it would have been by someone doing all that work.

Several culverts also link Moonlight Bay to Wyvern. Usually, when I explore the former army base, I enter by one of those more discreet passages, where I have used my own bolt cutter.

On this river-spanning fence—as elsewhere along the entire perimeter and throughout the sprawling grounds of Wyvern—a sign with red and black lettering warned that although this facility had been shut down at the recommendation of the Defense Base Closure and Realignment Commission, as a consequence of the end of the Cold War, trespassers would nevertheless be prosecuted, fined, and possibly imprisoned under a list of relevant federal statutes so long that it occupied the bottom third of the notice. The tone of the warning was stern, uncompromising, but I wasn't deterred by it. Politicians also promise us peace, perpetual prosperity, meaning, and justice. If their promises are ever fulfilled, perhaps then I'll have more respect for their threats.

Here, at the fence, the kidnapper's tracks were not the only marks in the riverbed. The gloom prevented me from positively identifying the new impressions.

I risked using the flashlight. Hooding it with one hand, I flicked it on for only a second or two, which was long enough for me to figure out what had happened here.

Although the breach in the fence apparently had been made well ahead of time, in preparation for the crime, the kidnapper had not left a gaping hole. He'd created a less obvious pass-through, and tonight he had needed only to pull the loosely hanging flap of chain-link out of his way. To free both hands for this task, he had put down his captive, ensuring against an escape attempt either by paralyzing Jimmy with vicious threats or by tethering the boy.

The second set of tracks was considerably smaller than the first. And shoeless. These were the prints of a child who had been snatched barefoot from his bed.

In my mind's eye, I saw Lilly's anguished face. Her husband, Benjamin Wing, a power-company lineman, had been electrocuted almost three years ago in a work-related accident. He'd been a big, merry-eyed guy, half Cherokee, so full of life that it had seemed as if he would never run short of it, and his death had stunned everyone. As strong as Lilly was, she might be broken if she had to suffer this second and even more terrible loss so soon after the first.

Although she and I had long ago ceased to be lovers, I still loved her as a friend. I prayed that I'd be able to bring her son back to her, smiling and unharmed, and see the anguish vanish from her face.

Orson's whine was filled with worry. He was quivering, eager to give pursuit.

After tucking the small flashlight under my belt once more, I peeled up the flap of fence. A soft twang of protest sang through the steel links.

I promised, "Frankfurters for the brave of heart," and Orson shot through the gap.

3

As I followed the dog into the forbidden zone, the ragged edge of one of the cut fence links snared my cap and pulled it from my head. I snatched it off the ground, dusted it against my jeans, and put it on again.

This navy-blue, billed cap has been in my possession about eight months. I found it in a strange concrete chamber, three stories underground, deep in the abandoned warrens of Fort Wyvern.

Above the visor, embroidered in red, were the words *Mystery Train.* I had no idea to whom the cap once belonged, and I didn't know the meaning of the ruby-red needlework.

This simple headgear had little intrinsic value, but of all my material possessions, it was in some ways the most precious. I had no proof that it was related to my mother's work as a scientist, to any project of which she was a part—at Fort Wyvern or elsewhere—but I remained convinced that it was. Though I already knew some of Wyvern's terrible secrets, I also believed that if I were able to discover the meaning of the embroidered words, more astonishing truths would be revealed. I had vested a lot of faith in this cap. When I wasn't wearing it, I kept it close, because it reminded me of my mother and, therefore, comforted me.

Except for the cleared area immediately beyond the breach in the chain-link, driftwood and tumbleweed and trash were piled against the sifting fence. Otherwise, the bed of the

Santa Rosita was as well made on the Wyvern side as it was on the other.

Again the only footprints were those of the kidnapper. He had resumed carrying the boy from this point.

Orson raced along the trail, and I ran close behind him. Soon we came to another access road that sloped up the north wall of the river, and Orson ascended without hesitation.

I was breathing harder than the dog when I reached the top of the levee, even though, in canine years, fur face was pretty much my age.

How fortunate I've been to live long enough to recognize the subtle but undeniable fading of my youthful stamina and spryness. To hell with those poets who celebrate the beauty and the purity of dying young, all powers intact. In spite of xeroderma pigmentosum, I'd be grateful to survive to relish the sweet decrepitude of my eightieth year, or even the delicious weakness of one whose birthday cake is ablaze with a hundred dangerous candles. We are the most alive and the closest to the meaning of our existence when we are most vulnerable, when experience has humbled us and has cured the arrogance which, like a form of deafness, prevents us from hearing the lessons that this world teaches.

As the moon hid its face behind a veil of clouds, I looked both directions along the north bank of the Santa Rosita. Jimmy and his abductor were not in sight.

Nor did I see a hunched gargoyle moving on the riverbed below or along either side of the channel. Whatever it had been, the figure from the highway embankment was not interested in me.

Without hesitation, Orson trotted toward a group of massive warehouses fifty yards from the levee. These dark structures appeared mysterious in spite of their mundane purpose and in spite of the fact that I was somewhat familiar with them.

Although enormous, these are not the only warehouses on the base, and although they would cover a few square blocks in any city, they represent an insignificant percentage of the buildings within these fenced grounds. At its peak of activity, Fort Wyvern was staffed by 36,400 active-duty personnel. Nearly thirteen thousand dependents and more than four thousand civilian personnel were also associated with the facility. On-base housing alone consisted of three thousand single-family cottages and bungalows, all of which remain standing, though in disrepair.

In a moment we were among the warehouses, and Orson's nose guided him swiftly through a maze of serviceways to the largest structure in the cluster. Like most of the surrounding buildings, this one was rectangular, with thirty-foot-high corrugated-steel walls rising from a concrete foundation to a curved metal roof. At one end was a roll-up door big enough to admit cargo-laden trucks; it was closed, but beside it, a man-size door stood wide open.

Previously bold, Orson became hesitant as he approached this entrance. The room past the threshold was even darker than the serviceway around us, which itself was illuminated only by starlight. The dog seemed not entirely to trust his nose to detect a threat in the warehouse, as if the scents on which he relied were filtered beyond detection by the very thickness of the murk inside the place.

Keeping my back to the wall, I sidled along the building to the doorway. I stopped just short of the jamb, with my pistol raised and the muzzle pointed at the sky.

I listened, holding my breath, nearly as silent as the dead—except for the faint gurgle of my stomach, which continued to work on a pre-midnight snack of jack cheese, onion bread, and jalapeño peppers. If anyone waited to ambush me just inside the entrance, he must actually have been dead, because he was even quieter than I was. Whether he was dead or not, his breath was no doubt sweeter than mine.

Though Orson was as difficult to see as a flow of ink across wet black silk, I watched as he stopped short of the entrance. After a hesitation that struck me as being full of puzzlement, he turned away from the door and ventured a few steps across the serviceway toward the next building.

He, too, was silent—no tick of claws on paving, no panting, not even any digestive noises—as though he were only the ghost of a dog. He peered intently back the way we'd come, his eyes dimly revealed by a reflection of starshine; the faint white points of his bared teeth were like the unsettling phosphorescent grin of an apparition.

I didn't feel that his hesitancy was caused by fear of what lay ahead of us. Instead, he no longer seemed to be certain where the trail led.

I consulted my wristwatch. Each faintly blinking second marked not only the passage of time but the fading of Jimmy Wing's life force. Almost certainly not taken for ransom, he had been seized to satisfy dark needs, perhaps including savageries that didn't bear consideration.

I waited, struggling to suppress my vivid imagination, but when Orson finally turned again to the open door of the warehouse without indicating any greater confidence that our quarry was inside, I decided to act. Fortune favors the bold. Of course, so does Death.

With my left hand, I reached for the flashlight tucked against the small of my back. Crouching, I entered the doorway, crossed the threshold, and scuttled quickly to the left. Even as I switched on the flash, I rolled it across the floor, a simple and perhaps foolish ruse to draw gunfire away from me.

No gunfire erupted, and when the flashlight rolled to a stop, the stillness in the warehouse was as deep as the silence of a dead planet with no atmosphere. Somewhat to my surprise, when I tried to breathe, I could.

I retrieved the flashlight. Most of the warehouse was given over to a single room of such length that the beam didn't penetrate from one end to the other; it even failed to reach halfway across the much narrower width of the building to illuminate either side wall.

As I scythed away the shadows, they regrew immediately after the beam passed, lusher and blacker than ever. At least no looming adversary was revealed.

Looking more doubtful than suspicious, Orson padded into the light and, after a hesitation, seemed to dismiss the warehouse with a sneeze. He headed toward the door.

A muffled *clang* broke the silence elsewhere in the building. The cold acoustics caused the sound to resonate along the walls of this cavernous chamber, lingering until the initial hard metallic quality softened into an eerie, whispery ringing like the voices of summer insects.

I switched off the flashlight.

In the blinding dark, I felt Orson return to my side, his flank brushing against my leg.

I wanted to *move*.

I didn't know *where* to move.

Jimmy must be near—and still alive, because the kidnapper hadn't yet reached the dark altar where he would play his ritualistic games and sacrifice the lamb. Jimmy, who was small and frightened and alone. Whose dad was dead like mine. Whose mother would be forever withered by grief if I failed her.

Patience. That is one of the great virtues God tries to teach us by refusing to show Himself in this world. Patience.

Orson and I stood still and vigilant until well after the final echo of the noise faded. Just as the subsequent silence grew long enough to make me wonder if what we'd heard had any significance, a voice arose, deep-toned and angry, as muffled as the *clang* had been. One voice. Not a conversation. A monologue. Someone talking to himself—or to a small, frightened captive who dared not reply. I couldn't make out the meaning, but the voice was as hollow and grumbly as that of a troll in a fairy tale.

The speaker was neither approaching nor retreating, and clearly he was not in this chamber with Orson and me. Before I was able to determine the direction from which the growled words came, the troll fell silent.

Fort Wyvern has been closed only nineteen months, so I haven't had time to learn each niche of it as thoroughly as I've acquainted myself with every cranny of Moonlight Bay. Thus far, I've confined most of my explorations to the more mysterious precincts of the base, where I'm most likely to encounter strange and intriguing sights. Of this warehouse, I knew only that it was like the others in this cluster: three stories high, with an open-beam ceiling, and composed of four spaces—the main room, in which we stood, one office in the far right corner, a matching room in the far left corner, and an open loft above those offices. I was sure that neither the sudden noise nor the voice had come from any of those places.

I turned in a circle, frustrated by the impenetrable darkness. It was as pitiless and unremitting as the black pall that will fall over me if, one day, cumulative light damage plants the seeds of tumors in my eyes.

A louder noise than the first, a resounding crash of metal against metal, boomed through the building, giving rise to echoes that rolled like a distant cannonade. This time I felt vibrations in the concrete floor, suggesting that the source of the disturbance might be below the main level of the warehouse.

Under certain buildings on the base lie secret realms that were apparently unknown to the vast majority of the soldiers who conducted the ordinary, reputable army business of Wyvern. Doors, once cunningly disguised, led from basements down to subbasements, to deeper cellars, to vaults far below the cellars. Many of these subterranean structures are linked to others throughout the base by staircases, elevators, and tunnels that would have been far less easy to detect before the facility, prior to abandonment, was stripped of all supplies and equipment.

Indeed, even with some of Wyvern's secrets left exposed by its departing stewards, my best discoveries would not have been possible without the aid of my clever canine companion. His ability to detect even the faintest fragrant drafts wafting through cracks from hidden rooms is as impressive as his talent for riding a surfboard, though perhaps not as impressive as his knack for occasionally wheedling a second beer from his friends, like me, who know full well that he is incapable of handling more than one.

Without question, this sprawling base harbors more installations that remain well hidden, waiting to be revealed; nevertheless, as interesting as my explorations have been, I've periodically refrained from them. When I spend too much time in the shadowland under Fort Wyvern, its disturbing atmosphere grows oppressive. I have seen enough to know that this netherworld was the site of wide-ranging clandestine operations of dubious wisdom, that numerous and diverse "black-budget" research projects were surely conducted here, and that some of those projects were so ambitious and exotic as to defy understanding based on the few enigmatic clues that were left behind.

This knowledge alone, however, isn't what makes me uncomfortable in Wyvern's underworld. More distressing is a perception—little more than an intuition but nonetheless powerful—that some of what happened here was not merely well-intentioned foolishness of a high order, not merely science in the service of mad politics, but pure wickedness. When I spend more than a couple of nights in a row under Wyvern, I'm overcome by the conviction that unknown evils were loosed in its buried warrens and that some still roam those byways, waiting to be encountered. Then it isn't fear that drives me to the surface. Rather, it's a sense of moral and spiritual suffocation—as though, by remaining too long in those realms, I will acquire an ineradicable stain on my soul.

I hadn't expected these ordinary warehouses to be so directly linked to the hobgoblin neighborhoods below ground. In Fort Wyvern, however, nothing is as simple as it first appears to be.

Now I switched on the flashlight, reasonably confident that the kidnapper—if that's who I was following—was not on this level of the building.

It seemed odd that a psychopath would bring his small victim here rather than to a more personal and private place, where he would be entirely comfortable while he fulfilled whatever perverse needs motivated him. On the other hand, Wyvern had a mysterious allure akin to that of Stonehenge, to that of the great pyramid at Giza, to that of the Mayan ruins at Chichén Itzá. Its malevolent magnetism would surely appeal to a deranged man who, as was frequently true in these cases, got his purest thrill not from molesting the innocent but from torturing and then brutally murdering them. These strange grounds would draw him as surely as would a decon-secrated church or a crumbling old house on the outskirts of town where, fifty years ago, a madman had chopped up his family with an ax.

Of course, there was always the possibility that this kid-napper was not insane at all, not a pervert, but a man working in a bizarre but nonetheless official capacity in regions of Wyvern that perhaps remained secretly active. This base, even shuttered, is a breeding ground of paranoia.

With Orson remaining close at my side, I hurried toward the offices at the far end of the main room.

The first of them proved to be what I expected. A barren space. Four plain walls. A hole in the ceiling where the fluo-rescent lighting fixture had once been mounted.

In the second, the infamous Darth Vader lay on the floor: a molded-plastic action figure about three inches tall, black and silver.

I recalled the collection of similar Star Wars toys that I'd glimpsed on the bookshelves in Jimmy's bedroom.

Orson sniffed at Vader.

"Come to the Dark Side, Luke," I murmured.

A large rectangular opening gaped in the back wall, from which a pair of elevator doors had been stripped by an army salvage crew. As a half-baked safety measure, a single two-by-six was bolted across the gap at waist height. Several elaborate steel fittings, still dangling from the wall, suggested that in the days when Fort Wyvern had served the national defense, the elevator had been concealed behind something—perhaps a slide-aside or swing-away bookcase or cabinet.

The elevator cab and lift mechanism were gone, too, and a quick use of the flashlight revealed a three-story drop. Sole access was by a maintenance ladder fixed to the shaft wall.

My quarry was probably too busy elsewhere to see the ghostly glow in the shaft. The beam soaked into the gray concrete until it was barely brighter than a séance-summoned cloud of spirit matter hovering above a knocking table.

Nevertheless, I switched off the light and jammed the

flashlight under my belt once more. Reluctantly, I returned the Glock to the holster under my coat.

Dropping to one knee, I reached tentatively into the inkiness that surrounded me, which seemed as though it could be either the dimensions of the warehouse office or billions of light-years deep, a black hole linking our odd universe to one even stranger. For a moment my heart rattled against my ribs, but then my hand found good Orson, and by smoothing his fur, I was calmed.

He put his blocky head on my raised knee, encouraging me to stroke him and to scratch his ears, one of which was pricked, the other limp.

We have been through a lot together. We have lost too many people we loved. With equal emotion, we dread being left to face life alone. We have our friends—Bobby Halloway, Sasha Goodall, a few others—and we cherish them, but the two of us share something beyond the deepest friendship, a unique relationship without which neither of us would be quite whole.

"Bro," I whispered.

He licked my hand.

"Gotta go," I whispered, and I didn't need to say that where I had to go was down.

Neither did I have to note that Orson's myriad abilities didn't include the extraordinary balance required to descend a perfectly vertical ladder, paw over paw. He has a talent for tracking, a great good heart, unlimited courage, loyalty as reliable as the departure of the sun at dusk, a bottomless capacity for love, a cold nose, a tail that can wag energetically enough to produce more electricity than a small nuclear reactor—but like every one of us, he has his limitations.

In the blackness, I moved to the hole in the wall. Blindly gripping one of the steel fittings that had secured the missing bookcase to a wall-mounted track, I pulled myself up until I was crouching with both feet on the sturdy two-by-six bolted across the opening. I reached into the shaft, fumbled for a steel rung, snared one, and swung off the two-by-six onto the service ladder.

Admittedly, I am less quiet than a cat, but by a degree that only a mouse would appreciate. I don't mean to imply that I have a paranormal ability to race across a carpet of crisp autumn leaves without raising a crackle. My stealth is largely a consequence of three things: first, the profound patience that XP has taught me; second, the confidence with which I have learned to move through the bleakest night; third, and not least important, decades spent observing the nocturnal animals and birds and other creatures with whom I share my world. Every one of them is a master of silence when it needs to be, and more often than not it desperately needs to be, because the night is a kingdom of predators, in which every hunter is also the hunted.

I descended from darkness into darkness distilled, wishing that I didn't need both hands for the ladder and could, instead, swing downward like an ape, swift and nimble, gripping with my left hand and both feet, holding the pistol ready. But then if I were an ape, I would have been too wise to put myself in this precarious position.

Before I reached the first basement, I began to wonder how my quarry had gone down the ladder while encumbered with the boy. Across his shoulder in a fireman's carry? Jimmy would have to have been bound at ankles and wrists to prevent him from making a movement, either intentionally or out of panic, that might dislodge his abductor. Even then, although the boy was small, he'd have been a considerable burden and a relentless backward drag that had to be diligently resisted every time the kidnapper moved a hand from one rung to the next.

I decided that the man I was pursuing must be as strong, agile, and confident as he was psychotic. So much for my fond hope that I was chasing a soft-bellied librarian who, dazed and confused, had been driven to this insane act by the stress of converting from the Dewey decimal system to a new computerized inventory.

Even in the lightless murk, I knew when I had reached the gap in the shaft where the basement elevator doors had once been, one floor below the warehouse office. I can't explain *how* I could know, any more than I can explain the plotline of the average Jackie Chan movie, though I love Jackie Chan movies. Perhaps there was a draft or a scent or a resonance so subtle that I was only subconsciously aware of it.

I couldn't be sure this was the level to which the kidnapper had taken the boy. He might have gone farther down.

Listening intently, hoping to hear again the troll-deep voice or another sound that would guide me, I hung like a spider on an obsessively well-organized web. I had no intention of gobbling up unwary flies and moths, but the longer I remained suspended in the gloom, the more I felt that I was not the spider, after all, not the diner but the dinner, and that a mutant tarantula as big as an elevator cab was ascending from the pit below, its sharp mandibles silently scissoring.

My dad was a professor of poetry, and throughout my childhood, he read to me from the entire history of verse, Homer to Dr. Seuss, Donald Justice to Ogden Nash, which makes him partly responsible for my baroque imagination. Blame the rest of it on that aforementioned snack of cheese, onion bread, and jalapeños.

Or blame it on the eerie atmosphere and the realities of Fort Wyvern, for here even a rational man might have legitimate reasons to entertain thoughts of giant ravenous spiders. The impossible was once made possible in this place. If the hideous arachnid in my mind's eye was the fault of just my dad and my diet, then my imagination would have conjured not a simple spider but an image of the grinning Grinch climbing toward me.

As I hung motionless on the ladder, the grinning Grinch rapidly became an inexpressibly more terrifying image than any spider could have been, until another hard crash boomed through the building, shaking me back to reality. It was identical to the first crash, which had drawn me this far: a steel door slamming in a steel frame.

The sound had come from one of the two levels below me.

Daring the maw of spider or Grinch, I went down one more story, to the next opening in the shaft.

Even as I arrived at this second subterranean floor, I heard the grumbling voice, less distinct and even less comprehensible than it had been before. Unquestionably, however, it issued from this level rather than from the final floor, at the base of the pit.

I peered toward the top of the ladder. Orson must be gazing down, as blinded to the sight of me as I was to the sight of him, sniffing my reassuring scent. Reassuring and soon ripe: I was sweating, partly from exertion and partly from anticipation of the pending confrontation.

Clinging to the ladder with one hand, I felt for the shaft opening, found it, reached around the corner, and discovered a metal handgrip on the face of the jamb, which facilitated the transition from the ladder to the threshold. No two-by-six safety barricade had been bolted across the gap at this level, and I passed easily out of the elevator shaft into the subbasement.

Out of a distillate of darkness into a reduction of darkness.

Drawing the Glock, I sidled away from the open shaft, keeping my back against the wall. The concrete felt cold even through the insulating layers of my coat and cotton pullover.

I was overcome by a prideful little flush of accomplishment, a curious if short-lived pleasure to have made it this far without detection. The flush almost at once gave way to a chill as a more rational part of me demanded to know *what the hell I was doing here.*

I seemed insanely compelled, *driven,* to travel into ever darker—impossibly bleak—conditions, to the heart of all blackness, where the darkness was as condensed as matter had been the instant before the Big Bang spewed forth the universe, and once there, beyond all hope of light, to be crushed until my shrieking spirit was pressed from my mind and from my mortal flesh like juice from a grape.

Man, I needed a beer.

Hadn't brought one. Couldn't get one.

I tried taking slow deep breaths instead. Through my mouth, to minimize the noise. Just in case the hateful troll, armed with a chain saw, was creeping closer, one gnarled finger poised over the starter button.

I am my own worst enemy. This, more than any other trait, proves my fundamental humanity.

The air didn't taste remotely as good as a cool Corona or a Heineken. It had a faintly bitter tang.

Next time I went chasing after bad guys, I'd have to bring a cooler full of ice and a six-pack.

For a while I conned myself with thoughts of all the eight-foot glassy waves waiting to be surfed, all the icy beers and the tacos and the lovemaking with Sasha that lay ahead of me, until the feeling of oppression and the claustrophobic panic gradually lifted.

I didn't fully calm down until I was able to summon a mental picture of Sasha's face. Her gray eyes as clear as rainwater. Her lush mahogany hair. The shape of her mouth curved by laughter. Her radiance.

Because I'd been cautious, the kidnapper was surely unaware that I was present, which meant he would have no reason to conduct his business without benefit of a lamp. Being unable to see his victim's terror would diminish his twisted pleasure. The absolute darkness seemed proof to me that he was not dangerously close but in another room, shut off from here but nearby.

The absence of screams must mean that the child had not yet been touched. To this predator, the pleasure of hearing would be equal to the pleasure of seeing; in the cries of his victims, he would perceive music.

If I couldn't detect the dimmest trace of the lamp by which he worked, he wouldn't be able to see mine. I fished the flashlight from under my belt and switched it on.

I was in an ordinary elevator alcove. To the right and around a corner, I found a corridor that was quite long and perhaps eight feet wide, with an ash-gray ceramic-tile floor and poured-in-place concrete walls painted pale, glossy blue. It led in one direction: under the length of the warehouse that I had recently traversed at ground level.

Not much dust had filtered down to this depth, where

the air was as still and as cool as that in a morgue. The floor was too clean to reveal footprints.

The fluorescent bulbs and diffusion panels hadn't been pulled out of the ceiling. They didn't pose any danger to me, because power was no longer supplied to any of these buildings.

On other nights, I had found that the government's salvage operation had stripped away items of value from only limited areas of the base. Perhaps, in the middle of the process, the Department of Defense accountants had decided that the effort was more expensive than the liquidation value of the salvaged goods.

To my left, the corridor wall was unbroken. Along the right side lay rooms waiting behind a series of unpainted, stainless-steel doors without markings of any kind.

Even though I was currently unable to consult with my clever canine brother, I was capable of deducing on my own that the slamming of two of these doors must have produced the crashes that had drawn me down here. The corridor was so long that my flashlight couldn't reveal the end of it. I wasn't able to see how many rooms it served, whether fewer than six or more than sixty, but I suspected that the boy and his abductor were in one of them.

The flashlight was beginning to feel hot in my hand, but I knew the heat wasn't real. The beam was not intense, and it was directed away from me; I was keeping my fingers well back from the bright lens. Nevertheless, I was so accustomed to avoiding light that, by holding this source of it too long, I began to feel something of what hapless Icarus must have felt when, flying too near the sun, he'd detected the stink of burning feathers.

Instead of a knob, the first door featured a lever, and instead of a keyhole, there was a slot for the insertion of a magnetic card. Either the electronic locks would have been disabled when the base was abandoned or they would have disengaged automatically when the power was shut off.

I put one ear to the door. There was no sound whatsoever from within.

Gingerly, I pressed down on the lever. At best I expected a thin, betraying *skreek* and at worst the "Hallelujah Chorus" from Handel's *Messiah*. Instead, the lever worked as noiselessly as if it had been installed and oiled only yesterday.

With my body, I pushed open the door, holding the Glock in one hand and the flashlight in the other.

The room was large, about forty feet wide by eighty feet long. I could only guess at the precise dimensions, because my small flashlight barely reached the width of the space and could not penetrate the entire depth.

As far as I could see, no machinery or furniture or supplies had been left behind. Most likely, everything had been hauled off to the fog-wreathed mountains of Transylvania to re-equip Victor Frankenstein's laboratory.

Strewn across the vast gray tile floor were hundreds of small skeletons.

For an instant, perhaps because of the frail-looking rib cages, I thought these were the remains of birds—which made no sense, as there is no feathered species with a preference for subterranean flight. As I played the flashlight over a few calcimine skulls and as I registered both the size of them and then the lack of wing structures, I realized that these must be the skeletons of rats. Hundreds of rats.

The majority of the skeletons lay alone, each separate from all the others, but in places there were also piles of bones, as though a score of hallucinating rodents had suffocated one another while competing for the same imaginary hunk of cheese.

Strangest of all were the *patterns* of skulls and bones that I noted here and there. These remains appeared to be curiously arranged—not as though the rats had perished at random dropping points, but as though they had painstakingly positioned themselves with an intricacy similar to the elaborate lines in a Haitian priest's voodoo *veves*.

I know all about *veves* because my friend Bobby Halloway once dated an awesomely beautiful surfer, Holly Keene, who was into voodoo. The relationship didn't last.

A *veve* is a design that represents the figure and power of an astral force. The voodoo priest prepares five large copper bowls, each containing a different substance: white flour, cornmeal, red brick powder, powdered charcoal, and powdered tannis root. He makes the sacred designs on the floor with these substances, allowing each to dribble in a measured flow from his cupped hand. He must be able to draw hundreds of complex *veves* freehand, from memory. For even the least ambitious ritual, several *veves* are needed to force the attention of the gods to the *Oumphor,* the temple, where the rites are conducted.

Holly Keene was a practitioner of good magic, a self-proclaimed *Hougnon,* rather than a black-magic *Bocor.* She said it was maximum uncool to create zombies by reanimating the dead, cast curses that transformed her enemies' beating hearts into rotting chicken heads, and stuff like that—even though, as she made clear, she could *do* those things by renouncing her *Hougnon* oath and getting a *Bocor* union card. She was basically a sweet person, if a little odd, and the only time she made me uneasy was when, with passionate advocacy, she declared that the greatest rock-'n'-roll band of all time was the Partridge Family.

Anyway, the rat bones. They must have been here a long time, because no flesh adhered to them—as far as I could see or cared to look. Some were white; others were stained yellow or rust red, or even black.

Except for a few scattered gray puffballs of hair, the rats' pelts surprisingly had not survived decomposition. This led me to wonder briefly if the creatures' bodies had been rendered elsewhere, their boiled bones later arranged here by someone with more sinister motives than those of Holly Keene, bikinied *Bocor.*

Then, under many of the skeletons, I saw that the tile floor was stained. This vile-looking residue appeared to be gummy but must have been brittle with age, because otherwise it would have lent an appalling odor to the cool dry air.

In a deeply hidden facility on these grounds, experiments in genetic engineering had been conducted—perhaps were still *being* conducted—with catastrophic results. Rats are widely used in medical research. I had no proof but plenty of reason to suppose that these rodents had been the subjects of one of those experiments, though I couldn't imagine how they had wound up here, like this.

The mystery of the *veve* rats was only one more of Fort Wyvern's virtually infinite supply of enigmas, and it had nothing to do with the more urgent mystery of Jimmy Wing's disappearance. At least I hoped it didn't. God forbid that I should open another door, farther along the hall, and discover the ritualistically arranged skeletons of five-year-old boys.

I stepped backward, out of the rodents' equivalent of the legendary elephants' graveyard, easing the door shut with a *click* so preternaturally soft that it could have been heard only by a cat on methamphetamines.

A quick arc of the flashlight, hotter than ever in my hand, revealed that the corridor was still deserted.

I moved to the next door. Stainless steel. Unmarked. Lever handle. Identical to the previous one.

Beyond was a room the size of the first, sans rat skeletons. The tile floor and painted walls gleamed as if they had been spit-polished.

I was relieved by the sight of the bare floor.

As I backed out of the second room and silently eased the door shut, the troll voice rose once more, nearer than before but still too muffled to be understood. The corridor remained deserted both ahead and behind me.

For a moment the voice grew louder and seemed to draw closer, as though the speaker was approaching a door, about to step into the hallway.

I thumbed off the flashlight.

The claustrophobic darkness closed around me again, as soft as Death's hooded robe and with pockets almost as deep.

The voice continued grumbling for several seconds—but then abruptly broke off, seemingly in mid-sentence.

I didn't hear a door open or any sound to indicate that the kidnapper had entered the hallway. Besides, light would betray him when at last he came. I was still the sole presence here—but instinct warned me that I would soon have company.

I was close to the wall, facing away from the direction I'd come, toward unexplored realms.

The extinguished flashlight was now cool in my hand, but the pistol felt hot.

The longer the quiet lasted, the more it seemed bottomless. Soon it was an abyss into which I imagined myself drifting down, down, like a deep-sea diver festooned with lead weights.

I listened so hard that I was half convinced I could feel the fine hairs vibrating in my ear canals. Yet I could hear only one sound, and it was strictly internal: the thick, liquid thud of my own heartbeat, faster than normal but not racing.

As time passed without a noise or a sudden wedge of light from an opening door farther along the corridor, the likelihood grew that in spite of what instinct told me, the troll voice had been receding rather than approaching. If the kidnapper and the boy were on the move and heading away from me, I might lose their trail if I didn't stay close behind them.

I was about to switch on the flashlight again, when a shiver of superstitious dread passed through me. If I had been in a cemetery, I would have seen a ghost skating on the moon-iced grass between tombstones. If I had been in the Northwest woods, I would have seen Big Foot shagging among the trees. If I had been in front of any garage door, I would have seen the face of Jesus or the Holy Virgin in a weather stain, warning of the Apocalypse. I was in the bowels of Wyvern, however, and unable to see any damn thing at all, so I could only *feel,* and what I felt was a presence, an aura, like a pressure, hovering, looming, what a medium or a psychic would call an *entity,* a spiritual force that could not be denied, chilling my blood and marrow.

I was in face-to-face confrontation with it. My nose was only inches from its nose, assuming it had a nose. I couldn't smell its breath, which was a good thing, as its breath must smell like rotting meat, burning sulfur, and swine manure.

Obviously, my nuclear imagination was nearing meltdown.

I told myself that this was no more real than my feverish vision of a gigantic spider in the elevator shaft.

Bobby Halloway says my imagination is a three-hundred-ring circus. Currently, I was in ring two hundred and ninety-nine, with elephants dancing and clowns cartwheeling and tigers leaping through rings of fire. The time had come to step back, leave the main tent, go buy some popcorn and a Coke, bliss out, cool down.

I was ashamed to realize that I didn't have the guts to switch on the flashlight. I was constrained by a fear of what might be eye-to-eye with me.

Though part of me wanted to believe I was suffering a runaway chain reaction of imagination, and though I probably *was* just jerking my own chain, there was good reason to be afraid. Those aforementioned experiments in genetic engineering—some designed by my mother, who had been a theoretical geneticist—had ultimately not been controllable. In spite of a high degree of biological security, a designer strain of retrovirus had gotten out of the lab. Thanks to the remarkable talents of this new bug, the residents of Moonlight Bay—and, to a lesser extent, people and animals in the wider world beyond—have been . . . changing.

So far, the changes have been disturbing, sometimes terrifying, but, with a few notable exceptions, they have been subtle enough that authorities have successfully concealed the truth about the catastrophe. Even in Moonlight Bay, at most a few hundred people know what is happening. I myself learned only a month before this April night; upon the death of my father, who knew all the dreadful details, and who revealed things to me that I now wish I didn't know. The rest of the townspeople live in happy ignorance, but they may not be out of the loop much longer, because the mutations may not remain subtle.

This was the thought that had paralyzed me when, if instinct could be trusted, I found myself facing some presence in the blind-dark passageway.

Now my heart was racing.

I was disgusted. If I didn't get control of myself, I would have to spend the rest of my life sleeping *under* my bed, just to be sure the boogeyman couldn't slip beneath the box springs while I was dreaming.

Holding the unlit flashlight in a tight circlet of thumb and forefinger, with my other three fingers extended, intending to prove to myself that this superstitious dread enjoyed no basis in fact, I reached into the tomb-perfect darkness. And touched a face.

4

The side of a nose. The corner of a mouth. My little finger slid across a rubbery lip, wet teeth.

I cried out and recoiled. As I stumbled backward, I managed to click on the flashlight.

Although the beam was pointed at the floor, the backsplash of light revealed the entity before me. It had no fangs, no eyes full of crackling hellfire, but it was composed of a substance more solid than ectoplasm. It wore chinos, what appeared to be a yellow polo-style shirt, and a pecan-brown sports jacket. Indeed, it wasn't something from beyond the grave but something from the Sears men's department.

He was about thirty years old, maybe five feet eight, as stocky as a bull standing on its hind feet in a pair of Nikes. With close-cropped black hair, eyes as mad-yellow as those of a hyena, and thick red lips, he seemed too formidable to have glided soundlessly through the seamless dark. His teeth were as small as kernels of white corn, and his smile was a cold side dish, which he served in a generous portion as he swung the club that he was holding.

Fortunately, it was a length of two-by-four rather than an iron pipe, and he was too close to execute a bone-shattering arc. Instead of recoiling farther at the sight of the club, I stepped into the guy in an attempt to minimize the impact, simultaneously trying to bring the Glock to bear on him, figuring that the very sight of it would cause him to retreat.

He swung the two-by-four not from overhead, not like a woodsman wielding an ax, but low from his side, like a golfer teeing off. It grazed my left flank and caught me under the arm. The blow wasn't devastating, but it was unquestionably more painful than Japanese-massage therapy. The flashlight flew out of my hand, tumbling end over end.

His yellow eyes flared. I knew that he had registered the pistol in my right hand and that it was an unpleasant surprise for him.

The tumbling flashlight struck the farther wall, bounced to the floor without shattering the lens, and revolved like the pointer in a game of spin the bottle, casting luminous spirals over the glossy blue walls.

Even as the flashlight clattered to the floor, my smiling assailant was winding up to take another swing, handling the two-by-four like a baseball bat this time.

Rocked by the first blow, I warned him: "Don't."

His yellow eyes revealed no fear of the gun, and the expression on his broad blunt face was pitiless fury.

I squeezed off a shot as I twisted out of his way. The club cut the air with sufficient force to have driven shards of bone and splinters of wood into my left temporal lobe if I'd not been able to dodge it, while the 9-millimeter slug ricocheted noisily but harmlessly from wall to wall of the concrete passage.

Instead of pulling the blow, he followed all the way through, allowing the momentum of the club to swivel him three hundred and sixty degrees. As the spinning flashlight slowed, the attacker's distorted silhouette pumped around the corridor, around and around, pumped like a carousel horse, and out of his own galloping shadow, he rushed at me when I stumbled backward against the featureless wall opposite the doors.

He was as condensed as a cube of squashed automobiles from a salvage-yard compactor, eyes bright but without depth, face knotted and florid with rage, smile fixed and humorless. He appeared to have been born, raised, educated, and groomed for one purpose: hammering me to pulp.

I did not like this man.

Yet I didn't want to kill him. As I said before, I'm not big on killing. I surf, I read poetry, I do some writing of my own, and I like to think of myself as a sort of Renaissance man. We Renaissance men generally don't resort to bloodshed as the first and easiest solution to a problem. We think. We ponder. We brood. We weigh the possible effects and analyze the complex moral consequences of our actions, preferring to use persuasion and negotiation instead of violence, hopeful that each confrontation will culminate in handshakes and mutual respect if not always in hugs and dinner dates.

He swung the two-by-four.

I ducked, slipped sideways.

The club cracked so hard against the wall that I could almost hear the low vibrations traveling the length of the wood. The two-by-four dropped from his numbed hands, and he cursed vehemently.

Too bad it hadn't been an iron pipe. The recoil might have been nasty enough to loosen some of his milk-white baby teeth and make him cry for mama.

"All right, that's enough," I said.

He made an obscene suggestion and, flexing his powerful hands, snatched the club off the floor, rounding on me.

He seemed to have little or no fear of the gun, probably because my reluctance to fire it, other than to squeeze off a warning shot, had convinced him that I was too chickenshit to blow him away. He didn't impress me as a particularly bright individual, and stupid people are often dangerously sure of themselves.

His body language, a sly look in his eyes, and a sudden sneer told me that he was going to feint, fake another swing with the club but not follow through. He would come at me some other way when I reacted to the false move. Perhaps he'd drive the two-by-four like a pike straight at my chest, hoping to knock me down and then smash my face.

While I like to think of myself as a Renaissance man, persuasion and negotiation were unlikely to bear fruit in this situation, and I manifestly do not like to think of myself as a *dead* Renaissance man. When he feinted, I didn't wait to see what the bastard's real plan of attack might be. With apologies to poets and diplomats and gentle persons everywhere, I pulled the trigger.

I was hoping to hit him in the shoulder or arm, though I suspect it's only in movies that you can confidently calculate to wound a man rather than kill him. In real life, panic and physics and fate screw things up. Most likely, more often than not, in spite of the best intentions, the polite wounding shot drills through the guy's brain or bounces among his ribs, off his sternum, and ends up dead-center in his heart—or kills a kindly grandmother baking cookies six blocks away.

This time, though I *wasn't* firing another warning shot, I missed his shoulder, arm, heart, brain, and everything else that would have bled. Panic, physics, fate. The bullet tore into the club, spraying his face with splinters and larger fragments of wood.

Suddenly convinced of his own mortality and perhaps recognizing the incomparable danger of confronting a marksman as poor as I am, the weasel pitched his makeshift cudgel, turned, and ran back toward the elevator alcove.

I juked when I saw he was going to throw the club, but my Big Bag of Really Smooth Moves was empty. Instead of ducking away from the club, I cunningly dodged straight into it, got rapped across the chest, and fell.

I was getting up even as I was going down, but by the time I made it to my feet again, my assailant was nearing the end of the hall. My legs were longer than his, but I wasn't going to be able to catch up with him easily.

If you're looking for someone to shoot a man in the back, I'm not your guy, regardless of the circumstances. My attacker safely turned the corner into the elevator alcove—where he switched on a flashlight of his own.

Although I needed to nail this creep, finding Jimmy Wing was an even higher priority. The boy might have been hurt and left to die.

Besides, when the kidnapper arrived at the top of the

ladder, a toothy surprise would be waiting for him. Orson wouldn't let the guy get out of the elevator shaft.

I scooped up the flashlight and hurried to the third in the line of doors along the hall. It was ajar, and I pushed it all the way open.

Of the three chambers I'd thus far explored, this was the smallest, less than half the size of the other two, so the light swept from wall to wall. Jimmy was not here.

The only item of interest was a balled-up yellow cloth about ten feet beyond the threshold. I almost ignored it, eager to try the next door along the corridor, but then I ventured inside, and with the same hand that held the gun, I plucked the rag off the floor.

It wasn't a rag, after all, but the soft cotton top from a pair of pajamas. A crew-neck pullover. About the right size for a five-year-old. Across the chest, in red and black letters, were the words *Jedi Knight*.

A sudden foreboding made my mouth go dry.

When I'd followed Orson away from Lilly Wing's house, I had already reluctantly decided that her little boy was beyond saving, but subsequently, against my better judgment, I had allowed myself to hope too much. In this uncertain space between birth and death, especially here at the end of the world in Moonlight Bay, we need hope as surely as we need food and water, love and friendship. The trick, however, is to remember that hope is a perilous thing, that it's not a steel and concrete bridge across the void between this moment and a brighter future. Hope is no stronger than tremulous beads of dew strung on a filament of spiderweb, and it alone can't long support the terrible weight of an anguished mind and a tortured heart. Because I had loved Lilly for so many years—now as a friend; in other days, more deeply than one loves even the dearest friend—I had wanted to spare her from this worst of all calamities, from the loss of a child. I had wanted this more desperately than I'd realized, and consequently I'd been running across a bridge of hope, a high arched span, which now dissolved like gossamer and directed my attention to the chasm beneath me.

Clutching the pajama top, I returned to the corridor.

I heard the boy's name, *"Jimmy,"* before I realized that I was the one who had softly spoken it.

I called to him again, not sotto voce this time but at the top of my voice.

I might as well have spoken in a murmur, because my shout drew no more response than my whisper. No surprise. I hadn't expected a reply.

Angrily, I wadded the thin pajama top and stuffed it in a coat pocket.

With the illusion of hope dispelled, I could more clearly see the truth. The boy wasn't here, not in any of the rooms along this hallway, not on the level below this one or on the level above. I'd thought it must have been difficult for the kidnapper to descend the maintenance ladder with Jimmy, but Jimmy hadn't been with him. The yellow-eyed bastard had at some point realized he was being followed by a man—and a dog. He had put Jimmy elsewhere before carrying the pajama top—which was saturated with the boy's scent—into the rat catacombs under the warehouse, hoping to mislead us.

I remembered how uncertain Orson had become after leading me so confidently to the warehouse entrance. He had wandered nervously back and forth in the serviceway, sniffing the air, as though puzzled by contradictory spoor.

After I'd entered the warehouse, Orson had remained loyally at my side as we had been drawn by the noises rising from deeper in the building. By the time I'd found the Darth Vader action figure, I'd forgotten Orson's hesitancy and had become convinced that I was close to finding Jimmy.

Now I ran toward the elevator alcove, wondering why I hadn't heard a bark or a snarl. I'd expected the kidnapper to be surprised when he found a dog waiting for him on the main level. But if he'd known that he was being tracked and had taken the trouble to use the pajama top to establish a false trail, perhaps he was prepared to deal with Orson.

When I reached the alcove, it was deserted. The shaft wasn't aglow with the kidnapper's light, which I had glimpsed just before I'd gone into the third room and found the pajama top.

I directed my flashlight up toward the warehouse, then down at the bottom of the shaft, one floor below. There was no sign of my quarry in either direction.

He might have descended. Maybe he was more familiar with this section of the Wyvern maze than I was. If he knew of a passage connecting the lowest level of the warehouse with another facility, elsewhere on the military base, he could have left by that back door.

Nevertheless, I intended to go upstairs and find Orson, whose continued silence worried me.

I could risk climbing with one hand partly encumbered, but I couldn't hold both the flashlight and the pistol and still keep my balance. The Glock wouldn't be helpful if I wasn't able to see trouble coming, so I holstered it and kept the light.

As I ascended from the second subterranean level toward the first, I became convinced that the kidnapper had not gone all the way up to the ground floor of the warehouse. He had climbed just one level, halfway. He was waiting there. I was certain of it. He was waiting there like a troll with a lemon-sour gaze. Going to ambush me as I clambered past the next entrance to the shaft. Lean out, smile to reveal all his neat doll-size teeth, and take a whack at my head with another club. Maybe he'd even discovered a better weapon this time. An iron pipe. An ax. A scuba diver's spear gun loaded with a barbed, explosive-tipped, shark-killing bolt. A tactical nuclear weapon.

I slowed and finally stopped before I reached the rectangular black hole in the shaft wall. From a few rungs below, I played the flashlight beam into the alcove, but I was at an angle that allowed me to see little more than the ceiling of that space.

Indecisive, I hung on the ladder, listening.

Finally I overcame my trepidation by reminding myself that any delay could be deadly. After all, a humongous mutant tarantula was crawling toward me from the pit below, poison dripping off its serrated mandibles, fiercely angry because it hadn't gotten me on my way *down*.

Nothing gives us courage more readily than the desire to avoid looking like a damn fool.

Emboldened, I quickly climbed past the first basement, to the main level, into the office where I had left Orson. I was neither hammered into mush by a blunt instrument nor shredded by giant arachnid jaws.

My dog was gone.

Drawing the pistol once more, I hurried from the office into the huge main room of the warehouse.

Flocks of shadows flew away from me, then circled to roost in even greater profusion at my back.

"Orson!"

When circumstances left him no alternative, he was a first-rate fighter—my brother the dog—and always reliable. He wouldn't have allowed the kidnapper to pass, at least not without extracting a painful toll. I'd seen no blood in the office, and there was none here, either.

"Orson!"

Echoes of his name rippled across the corrugated steel walls. The repetition of those two hollow syllables was reminiscent of a church bell tolling in the distance, which made me think of funerals, and in my mind rose a vivid image of good Orson lying battered and broken, a glaze of death in his eyes.

My tongue grew so thick and my throat so tight with fear that I could barely swallow.

The door by which we'd entered was wide open, just as we had left it.

Outside, the sleeping moon remained bedded down in mattresses of clouds to the west. Only stars lit the sky.

The cool clear air hung motionless, as sharp with dire promise as the suspended blade of a guillotine.

The flashlight beam revealed a discarded socket wrench that had been left behind so long ago it was orange with rust, from its ratchet handle to its business end. An empty oil can waited for wind strong enough to roll it elsewhere. A weed bristled out of a crack in the blacktop, tiny yellow flowers rising defiantly from this inhospitable compost.

Otherwise, the serviceway was empty. No man, no dog.

Whatever might lie ahead, I'd deal with it more effectively if I recovered my night vision. I switched off the light and tucked it under my belt. *"Orson!"*

I risked nothing by calling out at the top of my voice. The man I'd encountered under the warehouse already knew where I was.

"Orson!"

Possibly the dog had split shortly after I'd left him. He might have become convinced we'd followed the wrong trail. Maybe he had caught a fresh scent of Jimmy; weighing the risks of disregarding my instructions against the need to locate the missing child as quickly as possible, perhaps he had left the warehouse and returned to the hunt. He might be with the boy now, ready to confront the kidnapper when the creep showed up to collect his captive.

For a two-bit philosopher full of smug homilies about the danger of investing too much emotional capital in mere hope, I was laboring mightily to build another of those gossamer bridges.

I drew a deep breath, but before I could shout again, Orson barked twice.

At least I assumed it was Orson. For all I knew, it could have been the Hound of the Baskervilles. I wasn't able to determine the direction from which the sound had come.

I called to him once more.

No response.

"Patience," I counseled myself.

I waited. Sometimes there is nothing to be done but wait. Most times, in fact. We like to think we operate the loom that weaves the future, but the only foot on that treadle is the foot of fate.

In the distance, the dog barked again, ferociously this time.

I got a fix on the sound and ran toward it, from serviceway to serviceway, from shadow to shadow, among abandoned warehouses that loomed as massive and black and cold as temples to the cruel gods of lost religions, then into a broad paved area that might have been a parking lot or a staging area for trucks delivering freight.

I had run a considerable distance, leaving the pavement and plunging through knee-high grass lush from the recent rains, when the moon rolled over in its bed. By the light that came through the disarranged covers, I saw ranks of low structures less than half a mile away. These were the small houses once occupied by the married military personnel and their families who preferred on-base living.

Although the barking had stopped, I kept moving, certain that Orson—and perhaps Jimmy—could be found ahead. The grass ended at a cracked sidewalk. I leaped across a gutter choked with dead leaves, scraps of paper, and other debris, into a street lined on both sides with enormous old Indian laurels. Half the trees were flourishing, and the moonlit pavement under them was dappled with leaf shadows, but an equal number were dead, clawing at the sky with gnarled black branches.

The barking rose once more, closer but still not near enough to be precisely located. This time it was punctuated by yawps, yelps—and then a squeal of pain.

My heart knocked against my ribs harder than it had when I'd been dodging the two-by-four, and I was gasping for breath.

The avenue I followed led among the dreary rows of decaying, single-story houses. Branching from it was a large but orderly grid of other streets.

More barking, another squeal, then silence.

I stopped in the middle of the street, turning my head left and right, listening intently, trying to control my labored wheezing. I waited for more battle sounds.

The living trees were as still as those that were leafless and rotting.

The breath I'd outrun caught up with me quickly. But as I grew quiet, the night grew even quieter.

In its current condition, Fort Wyvern is most comprehensible to me if I think of it as a theme park, a twisted Disney-land created by Walt Disney's evil twin. Here the guiding themes are not magic and wonder but weirdness and menace, a celebration not of life but of death.

As Disneyland is divided into territories—Main Street USA, Tomorrowland, Adventureland, Fantasyland—Wyvern is composed of many attractions. These three thousand small houses and associated buildings, among which I now stood, constitute the "land" that I call Dead Town. If ghosts walked in any neighborhood of Fort Wyvern, this would be the place where they would choose to do their haunting.

No sound was louder than the moon pulling the clouds around itself once more.

5

As though I had crossed into the land of the dead without having the good manners to die first, I slowly drifted spirit-silent along the starlit street, seeking some sign of Orson. So profoundly hushed and lonely was the night, so preternaturally still, I could easily believe that mine was the only heart beating within a thousand miles.

Washed by the faint radiance of far nebulae, Dead Town appears to be merely sleeping, an ordinary suburb dreaming its way toward breakfast. The single-story cottages, bungalows, and duplexes are revealed in no detail, and the bare geometry of walls and roofs presents a deceptive image of solidity, order, and purpose.

Nothing more than the pale light of a full moon, however, is required to expose the ghost-town reality. Indeed, on some streets, a half-moon is sufficient. Rain gutters droop from rusted fasteners. Clapboard walls, once pristine white and maintained with military discipline, are piebald and peeling. Many of the windows are broken, yawning like hungry mouths, and the lunar light licks the jagged edges of the glass teeth.

Because the landscape sprinkler systems no longer function, the only trees surviving are those with taproots that have found some deep store of water that sustains them through California's long rainless summer and autumn. The shrubbery is withered beyond recovery, reduced to wicker webs and stubble. The grass grows green only during the wet winter, and by June it is as golden and crisp as wheat waiting for the thresher.

The Department of Defense doesn't have sufficient funds either to raze these buildings or to keep them in good repair against the possibility of future need, and no buyers exist for Wyvern. Of the numerous military bases closed following the collapse of the Soviet Union, some were sold off to civilian interests, transformed into tracts of houses and shopping centers. But here along California's central coast, vast reaches of open land, some farmed and some not, remain in the event that Los Angeles, like a creeping fungus, should eventually cast spoors this far north or the suburban circuitry of Silicon Valley should encroach on us from the opposite direction. Currently, Wyvern has more value to mice, lizards, and coyotes than to people.

Besides, if a would-be developer had placed an offer for these 134,456 acres, he would most likely have been rebuffed. There is reason to believe that Wyvern was never entirely vacated, that secret facilities, far beneath its increasingly weathered surface, continue to be manned and to carry out clandestine projects worthy of such fictional lunatics as Doctors Moreau and Jekyll. No press release was ever issued expressing compassionate concern for the unemployed mad scientists of Wyvern or announcing a retraining program, and since many of them resided on-base and had little community involvement, no locals wondered where they had gone. Abandonment, here, is but a refinement of the sophisticated camouflage under which this work has long been performed.

I reached an intersection, where I stopped to listen. When the restless moon rolled out of its covers yet again, I turned in a full circle, studying the ranks of houses, the lunar-resistant darkness between them, and the compartmentalized gloom beyond their windows.

Sometimes, prowling Wyvern, I become convinced that I am being watched—not necessarily stalked in a predatory way, but shadowed by someone with a keen interest in my every move. I've learned to trust my intuition. This time I felt that I was alone, unobserved.

I returned the Glock to my holster. The pattern of the grip was impressed into my damp palm.

I consulted my wristwatch. Nine minutes past one o'clock.

Moving out of the street to a leafy Indian laurel, I unclipped the phone from my belt and switched it on. I squatted with my back against the tree.

Bobby Halloway, my best friend for more than seventeen years, has several phone numbers. He has given the most private of these to no more than five friends, and he answers that line at any hour. I keyed in the number and pressed *send*.

Bobby picked up on the third ring: "This better be important."

Although I believed that I was alone in this part of Dead Town, I spoke softly: "Were you sleeping?"

"Eating kibby."

Kibby is Mediterranean cuisine: ground beef, onion, pine nuts, and herbs wrapped in a moist ball of bulgur and quickly deep-fried.

"Eating it with what?"

"Cucumbers, tomatoes, some pickled turnip."

"At least I didn't call when you were having sex."

"This is worse."

"You're way serious about your kibby."

"So entirely serious."

"I've just been radically clamshelled," I said, which is surfer lingo for being enfolded by a large collapsing wave and wiped off your board.

Bobby said, "You at the beach?"

"I'm speaking figuratively."

"Don't do that."

"Sometimes it's best," I said, meaning that someone might be tapping his phone.

"I hate this crap."

"Get used to it, bro."

"Kibby spoiler."

"I'm looking for a missing weed."

A *weed* is a small person, and the term is usually but not always used as a synonym for *grommet,* which means a preadolescent surfer. Jimmy Wing was too young to be a surfer, but he was indeed a small person.

"Weed?" Bobby asked.

"A totally small weed."

"You playing at being Nancy Drew again?"

"In Nancy work up to my neck," I confirmed.

"Kak," he said, which along this stretch of coast is not a nice thing for one surfer to call another, though I believed I detected a note of affection in his voice that was almost equal to the disgust.

A sudden flapping caused me to leap to my feet before I realized that the source of the sound was just a night bird settling into the branches overhead. A nighthawk or an oilbird, a lone nightingale or chimney swift out of its element, nothing as large as an owl.

"This is stone-dead serious, Bobby. I need your help."

"You see what you get for ever going inland?"

Bobby lives far out on the southern horn of the bay, and surfing is his vocation and avocation, his life's purpose, the foundation of his philosophy, not merely his favorite sport but a true spiritual enterprise. The ocean is his cathedral, and he hears the voice of God only in the rumble of the waves. As far as Bobby is concerned, little of real consequence ever occurs farther than half a mile from the beach.

Peering into the branches overhead, I was unable to spot the now quiet bird, even though the moonlight was bright and though the struggling laurel was not richly clothed in leaves. To Bobby, I said again, "I need your help."

"You can do it yourself. Just stand on a chair, tie a noose around your neck, and jump."

"Don't have a chair."

"Pull the shotgun trigger with your toe."

In any circumstance, he can make me laugh, and laughter keeps me sane.

An awareness that life is a cosmic joke is close to the core of the philosophy by which Bobby, Sasha, and I live. Our guiding principles are simple: Do as little harm to others as you can; make any sacrifice for your true friends; be responsible for yourself and ask nothing of others; and grab all the fun you can. Don't give much thought to yesterday, don't worry about tomorrow, live in the moment, and trust that your existence has meaning even when the world seems to be all blind chance and chaos. When life lands a hammer blow in your face, do your best to respond to the hammer as if it had been a cream pie. Sometimes black humor is the only kind we can summon, but even dark laughter can sustain.

I said, "Bobby, if you knew the name of the weed, you'd already be here."

He sighed. "Bro, how am I ever going to be a fully realized, super-maximum, jerk-off slacker if you keep insisting I have a conscience?"

"You're doomed to be responsible."

"That's what I'm afraid of."

"The furry dude is missing, too," I said, meaning Orson.

"Citizen Kane?"

Orson was named after Orson Welles, the director of *Citizen Kane,* for whose films he has a strange fascination.

I made an admission that I found difficult to voice: "I'm scared for him."

"I'll be there," Bobby said at once.

"Cool."

"Where's *there?*"

Wings thrummed, and another bird or possibly two joined the one already roosting in the laurel.

"Dead Town," I told him.

"Oh, man. You never listen."

"I'm a bad boy. Come in by the river."

"The river?"

"There's a Suburban parked there. Belongs to a mondo psycho, so be careful. The fence is cut."

"Do I have to creep or can I strut?"

"Sneaky doesn't matter anymore. Just watch your ass."

"Dead Town," he said disgustedly. "What am I going to do with you, young man?"

"No TV for a month?"

"Kak," he called me again. "Where in D Town?"

"Meet me at the movies."

He didn't know Wyvern a fraction as well as I did, but he would be able to find the movie theater in the commercial area adjacent to the abandoned houses. As a teenager, not yet so religiously devoted to the seashore that it had become his monastery, he had for a while dated a military brat who lived on-base with her parents.

Bobby said, "We'll find them, bro."

I was on a perilous emotional ledge. The threat of my own death troubles me far less than you might expect, because from the earliest days of childhood, I've lived with an awareness of my mortality that is both more acute and more chronic than what most people experience; but I'm crushed flat by the loss of someone I love. Grief is sharper than the tools of any torturer, and even the prospect of such a loss now seemed to have severed my vocal cords.

"Hang loose," Bobby said.

"I'm just about untied," I said thinly.

"That's too loose."

He hung up and so did I.

More wings beat a tattoo through the dark air, and feathers rattled leaves as another bird settled with the growing flock in the upper branches of the laurel.

None of them had yet raised a voice. The cry of the nighthawk, as it jinks through the air, snapping insects in its sharp beak, is a distinctive *peent-peent-peent*. The nightingale sings in lengthy performances, weaving harsh and sweet piping notes into enchanting phrases. Even an owl, mostly taciturn lest it alarm the rodents on which it feeds, hoots now and then to please itself or to assert its continued citizenship in the community of owls.

The quiet of these birds was eerie and disturbing, not because I believed they were gathering to peck me to pieces in an homage to the Hitchcock film, but because this sounded too much like the brief but deep stillness that often settles upon the natural world in the wake of sudden violence. When a coyote catches a rabbit and snaps its spine or when a fox bites into a mouse and shakes it to death, the dying cry of the prey, even if nearly inaudible, brings a hush to the immediate area. Though Mother Nature is beautiful, generous, and comforting, she is also bloodthirsty. The never-ending holocaust over which she presides is one aspect of her that isn't photographed for wall calendars or dwelt upon at loving length in Sierra Club publications. Every field in her domain is a killing field, so in the immediate wake of violence, her multitudinous children often fall silent, either because they have an instinctive reverence for the natural law under which they exist—or because they're reminded of the old girl's murderous personality and hope to avoid becoming the next object of her attention. Consequently, the mute birds worried me. I wondered if their silence was in witness to slaughter—and if the shed blood had been that of a small boy and a dog.

Not a peep.

I left the night shade of the Indian laurel and sought a less disturbing place, from which to make another telephone call. Except for the birds, I continued to feel that I was unobserved, yet I was suddenly uneasy about remaining in the open.

The feathered sentinels didn't leave their perches to pursue me. They didn't even rustle the leaves around them.

I was being truthful when I said that I didn't believe they were going to pull a Hitchcock; but I had not ruled out the possibility altogether. After all, in Wyvern—in all of Moonlight Bay, in fact—even a creature as unintimidating as a nightingale can be more than it seems and more dangerous than a tiger. The end of the world as we know it may lie in the breast of a chimney swift or in the blood of the tiniest mouse.

As I continued along the street, the light of the awakened moon was so bright that I cast a faint shadow, which walked neither ahead of nor behind me, but remained close by my side, as though to remind me that my four-legged brother, who usually occupied that spot, was missing.

6

Half the cottages and bungalows in Dead Town have only stoops. This was one of the other half, a bungalow enhanced by a set of brick steps leading up to a front porch.

A spider had built a web between the pilasters flanking the top of the steps. I couldn't see this construction in the dark, but it must not have been the home of a giant mutant species, because the silk-thread spokes and spirals were so fragile they dissolved around me without resistance. Some of those fine-spun filaments clung to my face, but I wiped them away with one hand as I crossed the porch, no more concerned about the destruction that I had wrought than Godzilla is concerned about the demolished skyscrapers he leaves in his wake.

Although events of recent weeks had given me a new and profound respect for many of the animals with which we share this world, I'd never be able to embrace pantheism. Pantheists regard all forms of life, even spiders and flies, with reverence, but I can't ignore the fact that spiders and flies—bugs and worms and wriggly things in general—will feed on me when I'm dead. I don't feel compelled to treat any creature as a fellow citizen of the planet, with rights equal to mine and deserving of all courtesies, if it regards me as dinner. I'm confident that Mother Nature understands my attitude and is not offended.

The front door, its peeling paint somewhat phosphorescent in the moonlight, was ajar. The corroded hinges didn't creak but rasped like the dry knuckle bones of a skeleton making a fist.

I stepped inside.

Because I had come in here for the express reason that I felt safer under a roof than in the open, I considered closing the door. Maybe the birds would suddenly shake off their eerie stupor and come shrieking after me.

On the other hand, an open door is an avenue of escape. I left it open.

Although I was wrapped by silky blackness as effective as a blindfold, I knew I was in the living room, because the hundreds of bungalows that do have porches also share exactly the same floor plan, with nothing as grand as a foyer or front hall. Living room, dining room, kitchen, and two bedrooms.

Even when well maintained, these humble homes had offered the minimum comforts to the mostly young military families who occupied them, each family residing here for only a couple of years between transfers. Now they smell of dust, mildew, dry rot, and mice.

The floors are tongue-and-groove wood covered with many coats of paint, except for linoleum in the compact kitchen. Even under a self-proclaimed master of stealth like yours truly, they squeak.

The loose boards didn't concern me. They ensured that no one could enter from the back of the bungalow and easily sneak up on me.

My eyes adapted to the gloom enough to allow me to see the front windows. Although these panes were set under the porch roof, they were visible even in the indirect moonlight: ash-gray rectangles in the otherwise pervasive blackness.

I went to the nearest of the two windows, neither of which was broken. The glass was dirty, and with a Kleenex I polished a cleaner circle in the center of it.

The front yards of these properties are not deep; between the Indian laurels, I had a view of the nearby street. I didn't expect to see a parade go past, but since I find majorettes in short skirts to be as much of a turn-on as anybody does, I thought it wise to be prepared.

I switched on my cell phone again and keyed in the number for the unlisted back line that went directly to the broadcasting booth at KBAY, the biggest radio station in Santa Rosita County, where Sasha Goodall was currently the disc jockey on the midnight-to-six airshift. She was also the general manager, but since the station had lost the military audience—and thus a portion of its ad revenue—with the closing of Fort Wyvern, she was not the only one of the surviving employees to have assumed double duty.

The back line doesn't ring in the booth but activates a flashing blue light on the wall opposite Sasha's microphone. Evidently, she wasn't doing on-air patter at the moment, because instead of leaving the call to the engineer, she herself picked it up: "Hey, Snowman."

I don't have sole possession of the back-line number, and like many privacy-minded people, I directed the phone company to prevent my number from registering on caller ID; yet even when the call doesn't come through her engineer, Sasha always knows if it's me.

"Are you spinning a tune?" I asked.

" 'A Mess of Blues.' "

"Elvis."

"Less than a minute to go."

"I know how you do that," I said.

"Do what?"

"Say, 'Hey, Snowman,' before I speak a word."

"So how do I do it?"

"Probably half the calls you ever answer directly on the back line are from me, so you *always* answer 'Hey, Snowman.' "

"Wrong."

"Right," I insisted.

"I never lie."

That was true.

"Stay with me, baby," she said, putting me on hold.

While I waited for her to come back, I could hear her

program over the phone line. She did a live public-service spot followed by a doughnut spot—recorded material at the front and back, with a live plug in the center—for a local car dealership.

Her voice is husky yet silky, soft and smooth and inviting. She could sell me a time-share condominium in Hell, as long as it came with air-conditioning.

I tried not to be entirely distracted by that voice as I listened with one ear for a creaking floorboard. Outside, the street remained deserted.

To give herself a full five minutes with me, she set up back-to-back tracks. Sinatra's "It Was a Very Good Year," followed by Patsy Cline's "I Fall to Pieces."

When she returned to me, I said, "Never heard such an eclectic program format before. Sinatra, Elvis, and Patsy?"

"It's a theme show tonight," she said.

"Theme?"

"Haven't you been listening?"

"Busy. What theme?"

" 'Night of the Living Dead,' " she said.

"Stylin'."

"Thanks. What's happening?"

"Who's your engineer this shift?"

"Doogie."

Doogie Sassman is a panoramically tattooed Harley-Davidson fanatic who weighs more than three hundred pounds, twenty-five of which are accounted for by his untamed blond hair and lush silky beard. In spite of having a neck as wide as a pier caisson and a belly on which an entire family of sea gulls could gather to groom themselves, Doogie is a babe magnet who has dated some of the most beautiful women ever to walk the beaches between San Francisco and San Diego. Although he's a good guy, with enough bearish charm to star in a Disney cartoon, Doogie's solid success with stunningly gorgeous wahines—who are not normally won over by personality alone—is, Bobby says, one of the greatest mysteries of all time, right up there with what wiped out the dinosaurs and why tornadoes always zero in on trailer parks.

I said, "Can you go canned for a couple of hours and let Doogie run the show from his control panel?"

"You want a quickie?"

"With you, I want a forever."

"Mr. Romance," she said sarcastically but with secret delight.

"We've got a friend needs hand-holding big time."

Sasha's tone grew somber. "What now?"

I couldn't lay out the situation in plain words, because of the possibility that the call was being monitored. In Moonlight Bay we live in a police state so artfully imposed that it is virtually invisible. If they were listening, I didn't want to tip them to the fact that Sasha would be going to Lilly Wing's house, because they might decide to stop her before she got there. Lilly desperately needed support. If Sasha dropped in by surprise, maybe by the back door, the cops would discover that she could stick like a five-barbed fishhook.

"Do you know . . ." I thought I saw movement in the street, but when I squinted through the bungalow window, I decided I'd seen only a moonshadow, perhaps caused by the tail of a cloud brushing across one cheek of the lunar face. "Do you know thirteen ways?"

"Thirteen ways?"

"The blackbird thing," I said, wiping at the glass again with the Kleenex. My breath had left a faint condensation.

"Blackbird. Sure."

We were talking about Wallace Stevens's poem "Thirteen Ways of Looking at a Blackbird."

My father worried about how I, limited by XP, would make it in the world without family, so he bequeathed to me a house without a mortgage and the proceeds of a huge life insurance policy. But he had given me another comforting legacy, too: a love of modern poetry. Because Sasha had acquired this passion from me, we could confound eavesdroppers as Bobby and I had done by using surfer lingo.

"There's a word you expect him to use," I said, referring to Stevens, "but it never appears."

"Ah," she said, and I knew she was following me.

A lesser poet writing thirteen stanzas relating to a blackbird would surely use the word *wing*, but Stevens never resorts to it.

"You realize who I mean?" I asked.

"Yes." She knew that Lilly Wing—once Lilly Travis—had been the first woman I had loved and the first to break my heart.

Sasha is the second woman I have loved in the most profound sense of the word, and she swears that she will never break my heart. I believe her. She never lies.

Sasha has also assured me that if I ever cheat on her, she'll use her Black & Decker power drill to put a half-inch bit *through* my heart.

I have seen the drill. The bits—an extensive set—that go with it are kept in a plastic case. On the steel shank of the half-inch auger bit, using red nail polish, she has painted my name: *Chris*. I'm pretty sure this is a joke.

She doesn't have to worry. If I ever broke her heart, I would drill my own chest and save her the trouble of having to wash her hands afterward.

Call me Mr. Romance.

"What's the hand-holding about?" Sasha asked.

"You'll find out when you get there."

"Any message?" she asked.

"Hope. That's the message. There's still hope."

I wasn't as confident as I sounded. There might be no truth in the message I'd just sent to Lilly. I'm not proud of the fact that, unlike Sasha, I sometimes lie.

"Where are you?" Sasha asked.

"Dead Town."

"Damn."

"Well, you asked."

"Always in trouble."

"My motto."

I didn't dare tell her about Orson, not even indirectly, using poetry code. My voice might crack, revealing the intensity of my anguish, which I was striving mightily to contain. If she thought he was in serious jeopardy, she would insist on coming to Wyvern to search for him.

She would have been a big help. I'd recently been surprised to discover Sasha possessed self-defense skills and weapons expertise that weren't taught in any disc-jockey school. Though she didn't look like an Amazon, she could do battle like one. She was, however, an even better friend than fighter, and Lilly Wing needed Sasha's sympathy and compassion more than I needed backup.

"Chris, you know what your problem is?"

"Too good-looking?"

"Yeah, right," she said sarcastically.

"Too smart?"

"Your problem is reckless caring."

"Then I better ask my doctor for some who-gives-a-damn pills."

"I love you for it, Snowman, but it's going to get you killed."

"This is for a friend," I reminded her, meaning Lilly Wing. "Anyway, I'll be all right. Bobby's coming."

"Ah. Then I'll start working on your eulogy."

"I'll tell him you said that."

"The Two Stooges."

"Let me guess—we're Curly and Larry."

"Right. Neither of you is smart enough to be Moe."

"Love you, Goodall."

"Love you, Snowman."

I switched off the phone and was about to turn away from the window, when I saw movement in the street again. This time it wasn't merely the shadow of a cloud gliding across a corner of the moon.

This time I saw monkeys.

I clipped the phone to my belt, freeing both hands.

The monkeys were not in a barrel and not in a pack. The correct word for monkeys traveling in a group is not *pack* or *herd*, not *pride* or *flock*, but *troop*.

Recently, I have learned a great deal about monkeys, not

only the term *troop*. For the same reason, if I were living in the Florida Everglades, I would become an expert on alligators.

Here, now, deep in Dead Town, a troop of monkeys passed the bungalow, moving in the direction I'd been headed. In the moonlight, their coats looked silvery rather than brown.

In spite of this luster, which made them more visible than they would have been otherwise, I had difficulty taking an accurate count. Five, six, eight . . . Some traveled on all fours, some were half erect; a few stood up almost as straight as a human. Ten, eleven, twelve . . .

They were not moving fast, and they repeatedly raised their heads, scanning the night ahead and on both sides, sometimes peering suspiciously back the way they had come. Although their pace and alert demeanor might signify caution or even fear, I suspected that they were not afraid of anything and that instead they were searching for something, hunting something.

Maybe me.

Fifteen, sixteen.

In a circus ring, costumed in sequined vests and red fezzes, a troop of monkeys might inspire smiles, laughter, delight. These specimens didn't dance, caper, tumble, twirl, jig, or play miniature accordions. Not one seemed interested in a career in entertainment.

Eighteen.

They were rhesus monkeys, the species most often used in medical research, and all were at the upper end of the size range for their kind: more than two feet tall, twenty-five or even thirty pounds of bone and muscle. I knew from hard experience that these particular rhesuses were quick, agile, strong, uncannily smart, and dangerous.

Twenty.

Throughout much of the world, monkeys live everywhere in the wild, from jungles to open grasslands to mountains. They are not found on the North American continent—except for these that skulk through the night in Moonlight Bay, unknown to all but a handful of the populace.

I now understood why, earlier, the birds had fallen silent in the tree above me. They had sensed the approach of this unnatural parade.

Twenty-one. Twenty-two.

The troop was becoming a battalion.

Did I mention teeth? Monkeys are omnivorous, never having been persuaded by the arguments of vegetarians. Primarily they eat fruit, nuts, seeds, leaves, flowers, and birds' eggs, but when they feel the need for meat, they munch on such savory fare as insects, spiders, and small mammals like mice, rats, and moles. Absolutely never accept a dinner invitation from a monkey unless you know precisely what's on the menu. Anyway, because they are omnivorous, they have strong incisors and pointy eyeteeth, the better to rip and tear.

Ordinary monkeys don't attack human beings. Likewise, ordinary monkeys are active in daylight and rest during the night—except for the softly furred douroucouli, an owl-eyed South American species that is nocturnal.

Those who roam the darkness in Fort Wyvern and Moonlight Bay aren't ordinary. They're hateful, vicious, psychotic little geeks. If given the choice of a plump tasty mouse sautéed in butter sauce or the chance to tear your face off for the sheer fun of it, they wouldn't even lick their lips with regret at passing up the snack.

I had tallied twenty-two individuals when the passing tide of monkey fur in the street abruptly turned, whereupon I lost count. The troop doubled back on itself and halted, its members huddling and milling together in such a conspiratorial manner that you could easily believe one of *them* had been the mysterious figure on the grassy knoll in Dallas the day Kennedy was shot.

Although they showed no more interest in this bungalow than in any other, they were directly in front of it and close enough to give me a major case of the heebie-jeebies. Smoothing the bristling hair on the nape of my neck with one hand, I considered creeping out the back of the house before they came knocking on the front door with their damn monkey-magazine subscription cards.

If I slipped away, however, I wouldn't know in which direction they had gone after breaking out of their huddle. I'd be as likely to blunder into them as to avoid them—with mortal consequences.

I had counted twenty-two, and I had missed some: There might have been as many as thirty. My 9-millimeter Glock held ten rounds, two of which I'd already expended, and a spare magazine was nestled in a pouch on my holster. Even if I were suddenly possessed by the sharpshooting spirit of Annie Oakley and miraculously made every shot count, I would still be overwhelmed by twelve of the beasts.

Hand-to-hand combat with three hundred pounds of screaming monkey menace is not my idea of a fair fight. My idea of a fair fight is one unarmed, toothless, nearsighted old monkey versus me with a Blackhawk attack helicopter.

In the street, the primates were still loitering. They were clustered so tightly that they almost appeared, in the moonlight, to be one large organism with multiple heads and tails.

I couldn't figure out what they were doing. Probably because I'm not a monkey.

I leaned closer to the window, squinting at the moonwashed scene, trying to see more clearly and to put myself in a monkey frame of mind.

Among the hey-let's-play-God crowd that worked in the deepest bunkers of Wyvern, the most exciting—and most generously funded—research had included a project intended to enhance both human and animal intelligence, as well as human agility, speed, sight, hearing, sense of smell, and longevity. This was to be accomplished by transferring selected genetic material not just from one person to another but from species to species.

Although my mother was brilliant, a genius, she was not—trust me on this—a mad scientist. As a theoretical geneticist, she didn't spend much time in laboratories. Her workplace was inside her skull, and her mind was as elaborately equipped as the combined research facilities of all the universities in the country. She kept to her office at Ashdon College, only occasionally venturing into a lab, supported by government grants, doing the heavy thinking while other scientists did the heavy lifting. She set out not to destroy humanity but to save it, and I am convinced that for a long time she didn't know the reckless and malevolent purposes to which those at Wyvern were applying her theories.

Transferring genetic material from one species into another. In the hope of creating a super race. In an insane quest for the perfect, unstoppable soldier. Smart beasts of myriad design bred for future battlefields. Weird biological weapons as tiny as a virus or as large as a grizzly bear.

Dear God.

Personally, all this makes me nostalgic for the good old days when the most ambitious big-brain types were content with dreaming up city-busting nuclear bombs, satellite-mounted particle-beam death rays, and nerve gas that causes its victims to turn inside out the way caterpillars do when cruel little boys sprinkle salt on them.

For these experiments, animals were easily obtained, because they generally can't afford to hire first-rate attorneys to prevent themselves from being exploited; but, surprisingly, human subjects were readily available, as well. Soldiers courts-martialed for particularly savage murders and condemned to life sentences were offered the choice of rotting in maximum-security military prisons or earning a measure of freedom by participating in this secret enterprise.

Then something went wrong.

Big time.

In all human endeavors, something inevitably goes woefully wrong. Some say this is because the universe is inherently chaotic. Others say this is because we are a species that has fallen from the grace of God. Whatever the reason, among humankind, for every Moe there are thousands of Curlys and Larrys.

The delivery system used to ferry new genetic material into the cells of research subjects—to insert it in their DNA chains—was a retrovirus brilliantly conceived by my mom, Wisteria Jane Snow, who somehow still had time to make terrific chocolate-chip cookies. This engineered retrovirus was designed to be fragile, crippled—that is, sterile—and benign: merely a living tool that would do exactly what was wanted of it. Once having done its job, it was supposed to die. But it soon mutated into a hardy, rapidly reproducing, infectious bug that could be passed in bodily fluids through simple skin contact, causing genetic change instead of disease. These microorganisms captured random sequences of DNA from numerous species in the lab, transporting them into the bodies of the project scientists, who for a while remained unaware that they were being slowly but profoundly altered. Physically, mentally, emotionally altered. Before they understood what was happening to them and why, some Wyvern scientists began to *change* . . . to have a lot in common with the research animals in their cages.

A couple years ago, this process suddenly became obvious when a violent episode occurred in the labs. No one has explained to me exactly what happened. People killed one another in a bizarre, savage confrontation. The experimental animals either escaped or were purposefully released by people who felt a strange kinship with them.

Among those animals were rhesus monkeys whose intelligence had been substantially enhanced. Although I'd thought intelligence was related to brain size and to the number of folds in the surface of the brain, these rhesuses didn't have enlarged craniums; except for a few telltale characteristics, they resembled ordinary members of their species.

The monkeys have been on the run ever since. They are hiding from the federal and military authorities who are quietly trying to eradicate them and all other evidence of what happened at Wyvern before the public learns that its elected officials have ensured the end of the world as we know it. Other than those involved in the conspiracy, only a handful of us know anything about these events, and if we attempt to go public, even though we possess no hard proof, they will kill us as righteously as they would waste the rhesuses.

They killed my mom. They claim that she was despondent over the way in which her work was misused, that she committed suicide by driving her car at high speed into a bridge abutment just south of town. But my mother was not a quitter. And she would never have abandoned me to face alone the nightmare world that may be coming. I believe she intended to go public, spill the truth to the media, in hope of building a consensus for a crash research program, bigger than what's buried under Wyvern, bigger than the Manhattan Project, commandeering the best genetic scientists in the world. So they pushed her through the big door and slammed it behind her. This is what I believe. I have no proof. She was my mom, however; and about some of these issues, I'll believe what I want, what I must.

Meanwhile, the contagion is spreading faster than the monkeys, and it's unlikely that the damage can be undone or even contained. Infected Wyvern personnel relocated all over the country, carrying the retrovirus with them, before anyone knew there was a problem, before a quarantine could have been effectively imposed. Genetic mutation will probably occur in all species. Perhaps the only thing in doubt is whether this will be a slow process that requires decades or centuries to unfold—or whether the terror will rapidly escalate. Thus far, the effects have been, with rare exception, subtle and not widespread, but this may be the calm before the holocaust. Those responsible are, I believe, frantically seeking a remedy, but they are also expending a lot of energy in an effort to conceal the source of the oncoming catastrophe, so no one will know who's to blame.

No one at the top of the government wants to face the public's wrath. They're not afraid of being booted out of office. Far worse than job loss might await them if the truth gets out. They might be tried for crimes against humanity. They probably justify the ongoing cover-up as necessary to avoid panic in the streets, civil disorder, and perhaps even an international quarantine of the entire North American continent, but what really concerns them is the possibility that they will be torn to pieces by angry mobs.

Perhaps a few of the creatures now milling in the street outside the bungalow were among the twelve who had escaped from the labs on that historic and macabre night of violence. Most were descendants of the escapees, bred in freedom but as intelligent as their parents.

Ordinary monkeys are chatterboxes, but I heard no sound from these thirty. They roiled together with what seemed to be increasing agitation, arms flailing, tails lashing, but if they raised their voices, the gabble wasn't audible either through the window glass or through the open front door, only a few feet away.

They were plotting something worse than monkeyshines.

Although the rhesuses are not as smart as human beings, the advantage we have isn't great enough to make me feel comfortable about playing a high-stakes game of poker with any three of them. Unless I could first get them drunk.

These precocious primates aren't the primary threat born in the laboratories at Wyvern. That honor must go, of course, to the gene-swapping retrovirus that might remake every living thing. But as villains go, the monkeys constitute a damn fine backup team.

To fully appreciate the long-term threat of these redesigned rhesuses, consider that rats are dreadful pests even though they are a tiny fraction as intelligent as we are. Scientists estimate that rodents destroy twenty percent of the food supply worldwide, in spite of the fact that we are relatively effective at exterminating colonies of them and keeping their numbers manageable. Imagine what might happen if rats were even half as smart as we are, and were able to compete on fairer footing than they now enjoy. We'd be engaged in a desperate war with them to prevent massive starvation.

Watching the monkeys in the street, I wondered if I was seeing our adversaries in some future Armageddon.

Aside from their high level of intelligence, they have another quality that makes them more formidable enemies than any rodents could be. Though rats operate entirely on instinct and have insufficient brain power to take anything personally, these monkeys hate us with a black, bitter passion.

I believe they are hostile toward humanity because we created them but did a half-assed job. We robbed them of their simple animal innocence, in which they were content.

We raised their intelligence until they became aware of the wider world and of their true place in it, but we didn't give them enough intelligence to make it possible for them to improve their lot. We made them just smart enough to be dissatisfied with the life of a monkey; we gave them the capacity to dream but didn't give them the means to fulfill their dreams. They have been evicted from their niche in the animal kingdom and cannot find a new place to fit in. Cut loose from the fabric of creation, they are unraveling, wandering, lost, full of a yearning that can never be mended.

I don't blame them for hating us. If I were one of them, I'd hate us, too.

My sympathy wouldn't save me, however, if I walked out of the bungalow and into the street, tenderly grasped a monkey paw in each of my hands, declared my outrage at the arrogance of the human species, and sang a rousing rendition of "Yes, We Have No Bananas."

In minutes, I would be reduced to kibble.

My mother's work led to the creation of this troop, which they appear to understand: They have stalked me in the past. She is dead, so they can't take vengeance on her for the anguished, outcast lives they lead. Because I'm her only child, the monkeys nurture a special animosity toward me. Perhaps they should. Perhaps their hatred of every Snow is justified. Of all people, I have no right to debate the merit of their grievance, though this doesn't mean I feel obliged to pay a price for what, with the best of motivations, my mother did.

Remaining safely unkibbled at the bungalow window, I heard what seemed to be the single reverberant toll of a large bell, followed by a clatter. I watched as the churning troop parted around an object I couldn't see. A scraping of iron on stone followed, and several individuals conspired to raise the weighty thing onto its side.

Busy monkeys prevented me from immediately getting a clear view of the item, although it appeared to be round. They began to roll it in a circle, from curb to curb and back again, some watching while others scampered beside the object, keeping it balanced on edge. In the burnishing moonlight, it initially resembled a coin so enormous that it must have fallen out of the giant's pocket from the top of Jack's beanstalk. Then I realized it was a manhole cover they had pried from the pavement.

Suddenly they were chattering and shrieking as though they were a group of exuberant children who had made a toy out of an old tire. In my experience, such playfulness was completely out of character for them. Of my previous encounters with the troop, only one had been face-to-face, and throughout that confrontation, they had acted less like children than like a pack of homicidal skinheads wired on PCP-and-cocaine cocktails.

They quickly tired of rolling the manhole cover. Then three individuals worked together to spin it, as if in fact it were a coin, and with considerable coordinated effort they eventually set it in a blur of motion.

The troop fell silent again. They gathered in a wide circle around the whirling disc, giving it space to move but watching it with great interest.

Periodically, the three who had spun the cover darted to it, one by one, judiciously applying enough force to keep it balanced and in steady motion. Their timing revealed at least a rudimentary understanding of the laws of physics and a mechanical skill that belied their ordinary appearance.

The tightly rotating disc sang roughly, its iron edge grinding against the concrete pavement. This low metallic song had become the sole sound in the night: nearly a one-note drone, oscillating only faintly over a half-tone range.

The spinning manhole cover didn't seem to provide sufficient spectacle to explain the intensity of the troop's attention. They were rapt. Almost in a trance. I found it difficult to believe that the disc, merely by chance, could have achieved the precise rotational velocity that, combined with exactly these oscillating tones, was hypnotic to monkeys.

Perhaps this wasn't a game that I was witnessing, not play but ritual, a ceremony with a symbolic significance that was clear to these rhesuses but was an impenetrable mystery to me.

Ritual and symbol not only implied abstract thinking but raised the possibility that these monkeys' lives had a spiritual dimension, that they were not just smart but capable of brooding about the origin of all things and the purpose of their existence.

This idea disconcerted me so much that I almost turned away from the window.

In spite of their hostility toward humanity and their enthusiasm for violence, I already had sympathy for these pathetic creatures, was moved by their status as outcasts with no rightful place in nature. If they indeed possess the capacity to wonder about God and about the design of the cosmos, then they may know the exquisite pain that humanity knows too well: the yearning to understand why our Creator allows us to suffer so much, the terrible unfulfilled longing to find Him, to see His face, to touch Him, and to know that He is real. If they share this quiet but profound agony with us, then I sympathize with their plight, but I also *pity* them.

And while pitying them, how can I kill them without hesitation if another confrontation requires me to do so in order to save my life or that of a friend? In one previous encounter, I've had to meet their ferocious assault with gunfire. Lethal force is easy to use when your adversary is as mindless as a shark. And you can pull the trigger without remorse when you are able to match your enemy's hatred with pure hatred of your own. Pity engenders second thoughts, hesitation. Pity may be the key to the door of Heaven, if Heaven exists, but it is not an advantage when you are fighting for your life against a pitiless opponent.

From the street came a change in the sound of the spinning iron, a greater oscillation between tones. The manhole cover had begun to lose rotational velocity.

None in the troop rushed forward to stabilize the whirligig. They watched with curious fascination as it wobbled, as its song changed to a steadily slowing *wah-waah-waaah-waaaah*.

The disc clattered to a halt, flat on the pavement, and at

the same instant the monkeys froze. A final note rang across the night, followed by silence and stillness so absolute that Dead Town might have been sealed inside a gigantic Lucite paperweight. As far as I could tell, every member of the troop gazed with magnetized eyes at the iron manhole cover.

After a while, as though waking from a deep sleep, they drifted dreamily toward the disc. They slowly circled it, hunched low with the knuckles of their forepaws grazing the pavement, examining the iron with the pensive attitude of Gypsies analyzing wet tea leaves to read the future.

A few hung back, either because something about the disc made them uneasy or because they were waiting their turn. These hesitant individuals conspicuously directed their attention toward anything *but* the manhole cover: on the pavement, on the trees that lined the street, on the star-stippled sky.

One of the beasts glanced at the bungalow in which I had taken refuge.

I didn't hold my breath or tense up, because I was confident that nothing about this structure lent it a character different from the shabby and desolate appearance of hundreds of others throughout the neighborhood. Even the open front door was not remarkable; most of these buildings were exposed to the elements.

After dwelling on the house for only a few seconds, the monkey raised its face toward the gibbous moon. Either its posture conveyed a deep melancholy—or I was overcome by sentimentality, attributing more human qualities to these rhesuses than made sense.

Then, although I hadn't moved or made a sound, the wiry beast twitched, sprang erect, lost interest in the sky, and looked again at the bungalow.

"Don't monkey with me," I murmured.

In a slow rolling gait, it moved out of the street, over the curb, and onto a sidewalk dappled with the moonshadows of laurel branches, where it halted.

I resisted the urge to back away from the window. The

darkness around me was as perfect as that in Dracula's coffin with the lid closed, and I felt invisible. The overhanging porch roof prevented moonlight from directly touching my face.

The miserable little geek appeared to be studying not just the window at which I stood but every aspect of the small house, as though it intended to locate a Realtor and make an offer for the property.

I am excruciatingly aware of the interplay of light and shadow, which, for me, is more sensuous than any woman's body. I am not forbidden to know the comfort of a woman, but I am denied all but the most meager light. Therefore, every form of illumination is imbued with a shimmering erotic quality, and I'm acutely aware of the caress of every beam. Here in the bungalow, I was confident that I was untouched, beyond anyone's ken, as much a part of the blackness as the wing is part of the bat.

The monkey advanced a few steps, onto the walkway that bisected the front yard and led to the porch steps. It was no more than twenty feet from me.

As it turned its head, I caught a glimpse of its gleaming eyes. Usually muddy yellow and as baleful as the eyes of a tax collector, they were now fiery orange and even more menacing in this poor light. They were filled with that luminosity exhibited by the eyes of most nocturnal animals.

I could barely see the creature in the laurel shadows, but the restless movement of its jack-o'-lantern eyes indicated that it was curious about something and that it still hadn't fixated specifically on my window. Maybe it had heard the peep or rustle of a mouse in the grass—or one of the tarantulas native to this region—and was hoping only to snare a tasty treat.

In the street, the other members of the troop were still engaged by the manhole cover.

Ordinary rhesuses, which live primarily by day, do not exhibit eyeshine in darkness. Members of the Wyvern troop have better night vision than other monkeys, but in my experience they aren't remotely as gifted as owls or cats. Their visual acuity is only fractionally—not geometrically—better than that of the common primates from which they were engineered. In an utterly lightless place, they are nearly as helpless as I am.

The inquisitive monkey—my own Curious George—scampered three steps closer, out of the tree shadow and into moonlight again. When it halted, it was less than fifteen feet away, within five feet of the porch.

The marginal improvement in their nocturnal sight is probably an unexpected side effect of the intelligence-enhancement experiment that spawned them, but as far as I have been able to discern, it isn't matched by improvement in their other senses. Ordinary monkeys aren't spoor-tracking animals with keen olfactory powers, like dogs, and neither are these. They would be able to sniff me out from no greater distance than I would be able to smell them, which meant from no farther than a foot or two, even though they were unquestionably a fragrant bunch. Likewise, these long-tailed terrorists don't benefit from paranormal hearing, and they are not able to fly like their screeching brethren who do dirty work for the Wicked Witch of the West. Although they are fearsome, especially when encountered in significant numbers, they aren't so formidable that only silver bullets or kryptonite will kill them.

On the sidewalk, Curious George sat on his haunches, wrapped his long arms around his torso as if comforting himself, and peered up at the moon once more. He gazed heavenward so long that he seemed to have forgotten the bungalow.

After a while, I consulted my wristwatch. I was worried that I would be trapped here, unable to meet Bobby at the movie theater.

He was also in danger of blundering into the troop. Even a man as resourceful as Bobby Halloway would not prevail if he had to face them alone.

If the monkeys didn't move on soon, I'd have to risk a call to Bobby's mobile number to warn him. I wasn't happy about the electronic tone that would sound when I switched on my cell phone. In the hush of Dead Town, that pure note would resonate like a monk breaking wind in a monastery where everyone had taken a vow of silence.

Finally, Curious George finished contemplating the medallion moon, lowered his face, and rose to his feet. He stretched his shaggy arms, shook his head, and scampered back toward the street.

Just as I let out a sigh of relief, the little freak squealed, and his shrill cry could have been interpreted only as a shriek of alarm.

As one, the troop responded, raising their heads, springing away from the iron disc that had preoccupied them, craning their necks to see what was happening.

Bleating, shrieking, scolding, gibbering, Curious George leaped into the air, leaped and leaped, tumbled and flipped and twirled and capered, beat upon the sidewalk with his fists, hissed and screeched, clawed at the air as if it were cloth that could be rended, contorted himself until he seemed to be looking up his own butt, rolled, sprang to his feet, slapped his chest with his hands, hissed and spat and sputtered, rocked and jigged, raced toward the bungalow, but exploded away from it and scurried back toward the street, keening at a pitch that ought to have cracked the concrete under him.

Regardless of how primitive their language might be, I was pretty sure I got the message.

Even though most of the troop was forty feet from the bungalow, I could see their beady shining eyes like a swarm of fat fireflies.

A few of them began to croon and hoot. Their voices were lower and softer than Curious George's caterwauling, but they didn't sound like a hospitality committee welcoming a visitor.

I drew the Glock from my shoulder holster.

Eight rounds remained in the gun.

I had the spare ten-round magazine in the holster.

Eighteen bullets. Thirty monkeys.

I had done the calculations before. I did them again. Poetry, after all, is of more interest to me than math, so there was reason to double-check my figures. They still sucked.

Curious George raced toward the house again. This time he kept coming.

Behind him, the entire troop erupted out of the street, across the lawn, straight at the bungalow. Simultaneously, as they came, they all fell into a silence that implied organization, discipline, and deadly purpose.

1

I still didn't believe the troop could have seen me, heard me, or smelled me, but they must have detected me somehow, because obviously they were not merely expressing their distaste for the undistinguished architecture of the bungalow. They were in a rage of a kind that I had seen before, a fury they reserved for humanity.

Furthermore, by their schedule, dinnertime had probably arrived. In lieu of a mouse or juicy spider, I was the meat dish, a refreshing change from their usual fare of fruits, nuts, seeds, leaves, flowers, and birds' eggs.

I turned a hundred eighty degrees from the window and headed across the living room, hands out in front of me. I was moving fast, blindly trusting in my familiarity with these houses. My shoulder clipped the casing on a doorway, and I pushed through a half-open door into the dining room.

Although the monkeys continued to restrain themselves, operating in attack-status silence, I heard the hollow thumping of their paws on the wooden floor of the porch. I hoped they would hesitate at the front entrance, tempering their rancor with caution long enough for me to put a little ground between us.

A tattered blind, though askew, covered most of the single window in the small dining room. Too little light penetrated to bring meaningful relief from the gloom.

I kept moving, because I knew that the door to the

kitchen was directly in line with the living-room door through which I had just entered. This time, passing from room to room, I didn't even knock my shoulder against the jamb.

No blinds or curtains covered the pair of windows over the sink in the kitchen. Painted with a thin wash of moonlight, they had that ghostly phosphorous glow of television screens just after you switch them off.

Under my feet, the aging linoleum popped and cracked. If any members of the troop had entered the house behind me, I couldn't hear them above the noise that I was making.

The air was thick with a foul miasma that made me want to retch. A rat or some wild animal must have died in a corner of the kitchen or in one of the cabinets, where it was now decomposing.

Holding my breath, I hurried to the back door, which featured a large pane of glass in the upper half. It was locked.

When this was a military base, personal security had been assured, and no one who lived inside the fence had reason to fear crime. Consequently, the locks were simple, keyed only from the outside.

I felt for the doorknob, which would have a lock-release button in the center. Found it. I would have turned it and torn open the door—except that the shadow of a leaping monkey flew up across the glass and fell away just as my hand closed on the cold brass.

I quietly released the knob and retreated two steps, considering my options. I could open the door and, pistol blazing, stride boldly through the murderous monkey multitudes as though I were Indiana Jones minus bullwhip and fedora, relying on sheer panache to survive. The only alternative was to remain in the kitchen and wait to see what happened next.

A monkey leaped onto the sill of one of the windows above the sink. Gripping the casing to keep its balance, it pressed against the glass, peering into the kitchen.

Because this mangy gremlin was silhouetted against moonlight, I could see no details of its face. Just its hot-ember eyes. The faint white crescent of its humorless grin.

Turning its head left and right and left again, it rolled its eyes, squinted, then went wide-eyed once more. By following its questing gaze, which roamed the kitchen, I deduced that it couldn't see me in the darkness.

Options. Stay here and be trapped. Plunge into the night only to be dragged down and savaged under the mad moon.

These weren't options, because either choice guaranteed an identical outcome. The worst kook surfer knows that whether you get sucked over the falls on a fully macking shore break or just get pitched off the board and do a faceplant in some seaweed soup, the result is the same: wipeout.

Another monkey leaped onto the sill at the second window.

Like most of us in this movie-besotted, Hollywood-corrupted world, if I succumbed to the narcissist in me and listened to my mind's ear, I could probably hear a film score underlying my every waking moment: gluey sentimental string-section indulgences when I am stricken by sadness or sorrow; tear-evoking, heart-stirring full-orchestra rhapsodies when I enjoy a triumph; droll piano riffs during my not infrequent spells of foolishness. Sasha insists that I look like the late James Dean, and even though I don't see the resemblance, I am appalled and ashamed to say that at times I take pleasure in this supposed resemblance to such a celebrated figure; indeed, it would require little effort for me to conduct periods of my life with the edgy score of *Rebel Without a Cause* swelling in my mind. At the door a moment earlier, when the monkey shadow swooped up the window: Hear the violins shriek from the shower scene in *Psycho*. Now, as I considered my next move, with monkeys closing in all around me: Imagine low, ominous, pulsing tones plucked from a bass fiddle, threaded through by a single attenuated but muted high note from a clarinet.

Although I am as capable of self-delusion as the next guy, I decided against the most cinematic of my options, electing not to swashbuckle into the night. After all, though charismatic, James Dean is no Harrison Ford. In the majority of his handful of movies, sooner or later he got the crap beaten out of him.

I quickly sidled across the floor, away from the windows, but also away from the entrance to the dining room. Within a few feet, I bumped into cabinetry.

These cabinets would match those in every house in Dead Town: plain but sturdy, with birch frames, their shiplap doors painted so often that the shallow grooves created by the overlapping joints had all but disappeared under the many coats. The work counters would be laminated with one color or another of speckled Formica.

Before any of the troop entered the kitchen from the front of the house, I needed to get off the floor. If I stood with my back to a wall, pressed into a corner, dead motionless, breathing as noiselessly as a fish passing water through its gills, I was still certain to give myself away. The linoleum was so curled and so undermined by tiny pockets of air that it would crackle and pop from any unintentional shift of weight, from no more than a heavy *thought.* The betraying sound was sure to come precisely when the monkeys were stone still and ready to hear it.

In spite of darkness so thick that it seemed viscous, and in spite of a stench of decomposition strong enough to mask any scent of me that they might otherwise detect, I didn't think I'd have much chance of escaping the troop's notice during a search of the kitchen, even if they conducted it strictly by touch. Nevertheless, I had to give it a try.

If I climbed onto the countertop, I would be restricted by the narrow space between the Formica and the upper cabinets. I'd have to lie on my left side, facing out toward the room. After drawing my knees toward my chest, curling compactly into the fetal position, so as to occupy as small a space as possible and to make myself more difficult to locate, I wouldn't be in an ideal posture to fight back if I was found by one of those walking condominiums for lice.

By body contact alone, I followed the cabinetry to the corner, where the kitchen in every one of these bungalows features a broom closet with a tall lower compartment and a single shelf at the top. If I was able to squeeze into that narrow space and close the door after me, at least I would be off the treacherous linoleum and beyond easy reach if the troop probed-poked-groped-tapped its way around the room.

At the end of the cabinet row, I discovered the broom closet where I'd expected it to be—but the door was missing. With dismay, I felt one bent and broken hinge, then the other, and patted air where the door should have been, as though just the right series of magical gestures would charm the door into existence again.

Unless the horde of monkeys that had followed Curious George onto the front porch was still huddled there, devising strategy or discussing the price of coconuts, I was nearly out of time.

My hidey-hole was suddenly more hole than hidey.

Unfortunately, no alternative presented itself.

I fished the spare magazine of ammunition from its pocket in my holster and clutched it in my left hand.

Holding the Glock ready in front of me, I eased backward into the broom closet—and wondered if the reek of death that saturated the kitchen might have its maggoty source in this cramped space. My stomach slithered like a ball of copulating eels, but nothing squished under my shoes.

The closet was just wide enough to admit me. To fit, I had to scrunch my shoulders only slightly. Although I am nearly six feet tall, I didn't have to hunch down; however, the underside of the storage shelf pressed hard enough against my *Mystery Train* cap to impress the shape of the crown button through my hair and into my scalp.

To avoid second thoughts and an attack of claustrophobia, I decided not to pass the time by listing the ways in which my hiding place was like a coffin.

As it turned out, I didn't have any time to pass. No sooner had I stashed myself in the broom closet than monkeys entered the kitchen from the dining room.

I heard them just beyond the threshold, revealed only by a barely audible conspiratorial hissing and muttering. They hesitated, apparently scoping the situation, then entered at a rush, lantern eyes aglow as they fanned out to both sides of the door, like SWAT-team cops in a TV drama.

The crackling linoleum startled them. One squeaked in surprise, and they all froze.

As far as I could determine, this first squad consisted of three members. I couldn't see anything but their shining eyes, which were revealed only during the moments when they were facing in my direction. Because they were standing still, swiveling just their heads as they surveyed the black room, I could be sure that I wasn't seeing the same pair of eyes as a single individual progressed from place to place.

I was breathing shallowly through my mouth, not solely because this method was comparatively quiet. Using my nose would result in a more sickening exposure to the vile stink. Already, a sludge of nausea oozed back and forth in my belly. Now I was beginning to be able to *taste* the foul air, which left a musty-bitter flavor on my tongue and induced a flux of sour saliva that threatened to make me gag.

After a pause to analyze the situation, the bravest of the three monkeys moved—and then went rigid when the linoleum protested noisily again.

One of its pals took a step with the same result, and it, too, halted warily.

A nerve began to twitch in my left calf. I hoped to God it wouldn't develop into a painful cramp.

Following a lengthy silence, the most timid member of the squad issued a thin whine. It sounded fearful.

Call me insensitive, call me cruel, call me a mutant-monkey hater, but under the circumstances, I was pleased by the anxiety in its voice.

Their apprehension was so palpable that if I said "Boo," they would leap, screaming, straight to the ceiling and hang there by their fingernails. Monkey stalactites.

Of course, totally pissed by that little trick, they would eventually come down again and, with the rest of the troop, tear my guts out. Which would spoil the joke.

If they were as spooked as I believed they were, they might conduct only a token search and retreat from the house, where after Curious George would be the troop's equivalent of the boy who cried wolf.

The increased intelligence conferred on these rhesuses is as much a curse as a blessing to them. With higher intelligence comes an awareness of the complexity of the world, and from this awareness arises a sense of mystery, wonder. Superstition is the dark side of wonder. Creatures with simple animal intelligence fear only real things, such as their natural predators. But those of us who have higher cognitive abilities are able to torture ourselves with an infinite menagerie of imaginary threats: ghosts and goblins and vampires and brain-eating extraterrestrials. Worse, we find it difficult *not* to dwell on the most terrifying two words in any language, even in monkey talk: *what if* . . .

I was counting on these creatures being, right now, nearly paralyzed by a daunting list of what-ifs.

One of the squad snorted as though trying to clear the stench out of its nostrils, then spat with distaste.

The wimpy one whined again.

It was answered by one of its brethren, not with another whine, but with a fierce growl that dispelled my cozy notion that all the monkeys were too spooked to linger here. The growler, at least, was not intimidated, and it sounded tough enough to ensure the discipline of the other two.

The three proceeded deeper into the kitchen, past the broom closet, and out of my line of sight. They seemed to be full of trepidation, but they were no longer inhibited by the noisy flooring.

A second squad, also composed of three members and also revealed only by their eyeshine, entered the room. They paused to survey the unpierceable darkness, and one by one they looked in my direction without any indication that they detected me.

From elsewhere in the kitchen arose the continuous crackle of the brittle linoleum. I heard a scrabbling and a thump, noises no doubt made by one of the first three monkeys as it climbed onto a counter.

The button on my cap was pressed so firmly between the crown of my head and the shelf above me that I felt as though God's thumb was thrust against my scalp in a not so subtle announcement that my number was up, my ticket punched, my dime dropped, my license to live revoked. If I could have hunched down an inch or two, the pressure would have been relieved, but I was afraid that even with the monkeys making a racket, I would still be heard as my back and shoulders slid along the walls of the narrow closet. Besides, the twitching nerve in my leg had quickly evolved into a mild cramp, as I had feared that it would; even a minor change in my position might contract the calf muscle and cause the pain to flare into intolerable agony.

A member of the second squad began to move slowly toward me, its bright eyes sliding nervously from side to side while it felt its way through the cloying murk. As the clever little beast approached, I could hear it rhythmically slapping its right hand against the wall to keep itself oriented.

In another corner of the room, rusted hinges squeaked. One of the shiplap doors banged shut, its loose joints rattling.

Evidently, they were opening the cabinets and fumbling blindly inside.

I had hoped that they would not be intelligent enough to conduct a thorough search or, conversely, that they would be too intelligent to endanger themselves by poking blindly into places where an armed man might be waiting to blast them to monkey hell. They were smart enough to be thorough, all right, but too reckless to be as cautious as the situation required. From past encounters, I had already known all this about them; but having jammed myself into the broom coffin, having regretted doing so almost as soon as I was encased, I'd been in denial.

The wall slapper was still coming toward me, no more than three feet away. Its eyes continued to blaze at the gloom on all sides of it, not just at me.

More hinges squeaked. A warped cabinet door stuttered open with some resistance, and another door banged shut.

The cramp in my calf abruptly became more severe. Hot. Sharp. I clenched my teeth to keep from groaning. I had a headache, too: The cap button felt as if it had been pressed all the way through my skull, into my brain, and had begun working its way out through my right eye. My neck ached. My scrunched shoulders didn't feel too good, either. I had a nagging pain in the small of my back, a spot of tenderness in the gum at an upper right molar, a queasy feeling that I was developing serious hemorrhoids at the tender age of twenty-eight, and was in general feeling pretty much, you know, blah.

The wall slapper stopped slapping the wall when it reached the corner and discovered the cabinetry. It was directly in front of me now.

I was almost four feet taller than this monkey, and a hundred twenty pounds heavier. Though it was unnervingly intelligent, I was a lot smarter than it. Nevertheless, I gazed down at it with dread and loathing, cringing inwardly, with no less repulsion and fear for my life than I would have felt if this had been a demon risen straight from Hell.

It is easy to make jokes about the troop when you are at a comfortable distance from them. Yet a close encounter reduces you to primal fear, fills you with a heart-chilling sense of the *alien,* and infuses the waking world with that acutely real yet simultaneously surreal atmosphere of your most horrific nightmares.

The sympathy I'd had for them earlier was still with me, markedly diminished, but I couldn't feel the pity at all. Good.

Judging by where its bright eyes were focused and by the fumbling sounds its hands made, the monkey was exploring the face frame to which the broom-closet door should have been attached.

The Glock weighed less than three pounds, but it felt as heavy as a granite gravestone. I tightened my finger on the trigger.

Eighteen rounds.

Seventeen, really.

I would have to count the shots as I squeezed them off—and save the last round for myself.

Above the other sounds in the kitchen, I heard the monkey pluck at one of the loose and broken hinges from which the broom-closet door had once hung.

The total depth of my pathetic hiding place was only two

feet, which meant I was standing mere inches from the inquisitive primate. If it reached inside, there was no chance whatsoever that it would fail to discover me. Only the terrible stench in the kitchen prevented it from smelling me.

The cramp in my left calf twisted like barbed wire through the muscle. I was afraid that my foot was going to start twitching involuntarily.

Elsewhere in the room, a cabinet door banged shut.

Then another opened with a squeak of hinges.

Linoleum crackled under small, quick feet.

A monkey spat, as though trying to rid itself of the air's foul taste.

I had the curious feeling that I was about to wake up and find myself safe in bed, beside Sasha.

My heart was racing, and now it hammered even faster when Sasha's face bloomed in my mind. The possibility that I would never hear her voice again, never hold her again, never look again into her kind eyes: This was as frightening as the likelihood that I would be torn apart by the troop. And more terrifying, still, was the thought of not being at her side to help her cope with this strange and violent new world, of leaving her alone when, at the next day's end, night returned home to Moonlight Bay once more.

Before me, the monkey remained invisible except for its luminous eyes, which seemed to grow brighter as it peered suspiciously into the broom closet. Its attention traveled upward from my feet, across my body, to my face.

Its night vision might be better than mine, but in this pure liquid blackness, which was as unrelieved as that four miles down at the bottom of the sea, I was sure that we were equally blind.

Yet our eyes locked.

We seemed to be in a staring contest, and I didn't believe that my imagination was boiling over. The creature wasn't looking at my brow or at the bridge of my nose; it was looking directly into *both* my eyes.

And it didn't look away.

Although I wasn't betrayed by eyeshine, as the monkey

was, my eyes might be serving as mirrors in which its radiant glare was dimly reflected. Perhaps it detected the merest pinpoint glimmers of its own fiery scrutiny returned to it, wasn't sure that it saw anything at all, but remained transfixed by the mystery.

I considered closing my eyes, letting the monkey's bright stare fall upon my unreflective lids. But I was afraid that I would miss its sudden blink of comprehension and would fail to shoot it before it launched itself in at me and, perhaps, bit my gun hand or climbed my body to claw and chew my face.

Meeting its gaze at this close range, with such intensity, I was surprised that my fear and thick revulsion could coexist with a mess of other powerful emotions: anger at those who had brought this new species into existence, sorrow over the hideous oncoming corruption of this beautiful world that God has given us, wonder at the inhuman but undeniable intelligence in these strange eyes. Bleak despair, too. And loneliness. And yet . . . an irrational wild hope.

Standing in my line of fire, unaware that it was vulnerably exposed to an emotional basket case with a handgun, the creature burbled softly, more like a pigeon than a rhesus. The sound had an inquisitive quality.

One of the other monkeys shrieked.

I almost fired the Glock reflexively.

Two additional voices scolded the first.

In front of me, the monkey spun away from the broom closet. It scampered deeper into the kitchen, drawn by the commotion.

In fact, the uproar indicated that all six were now gathered at the farther end of the room. I saw no shining eyes turned in my direction.

They had found something of interest. I could imagine only that it was the source of the putrid odor.

As I eased up on the trigger, I realized that a glutinous mass had risen into my throat—maybe my heart, maybe my lunch—and I had to swallow hard to get it down and to be able to breathe again.

While my eyes and the monkey's had been locked, I'd

fallen into a curious physical detachment so complete that I
had ceased to feel the spasms of pain in my cramping calf.
Now the agony returned, worse than before.

Because all the members of the search party were distracted and making noise, I exercised the cramped muscle as
best I could by shifting my weight firmly back and forth from
heel to toe of my left foot. This maneuver relieved the pain
somewhat, although not enough to ensure that I would be
able to move gracefully if one of the monkeys invited me to
waltz.

The conferring members of the search party began to
jabber in louder voices. They were excited. Although I don't
believe they have a language in remotely the sense that we do,
their bleats and hisses and growls and warbles were obviously
argumentative. They appeared to have forgotten what they
had come looking for in the first place. Easily distracted,
quick to fall into disorganization, prone to put aside mutual
interests in favor of quarreling among themselves—for the
first time, these guys seemed an awful lot like human beings.

The longer I listened to them, the more I dared to believe
that I would get out of this bungalow alive.

I was still rocking my foot, flexing and contracting my
calf, when one of the quarrelers broke away from the rest of
the search party and crossed the kitchen to the dining-room
doorway. The instant I saw its eyeshine, I stopped moving
and pretended to be a broom.

The monkey halted at the dining-room threshold and
shrieked. It seemed to be calling to other members of the
troop, who were, presumably, waiting outside on the front
porch or searching the bedrooms.

Answering voices rose at once. They grew nearer.

The prospect of sharing this small kitchen with even
more monkeys—possibly with the entire troop—punctured
my half-inflated hope of survival. As my shaky confidence
rapidly gave way to confident desperation, I examined my
options and found no new ones.

The depth of my desperation was so abyssal that I actually asked myself what the immortal Jackie Chan would do in

a situation like this. The answer was simple: Jackie would erupt out of the broom closet with an athletic leap that landed him in the very midst of the search party, drop-kick one of them between the legs, karate-chop two of them in their necks as he somersaulted to his feet, get off a cool one-liner, break the arms and legs of multiple adversaries during an astonishing pirouette of flashing fists and feet, execute a series of charming and hilarious rubber-faced expressions the likes of which no one has seen since the days of Buster Keaton and Charlie Chaplin, tap-dance across the heads of the remaining members of the troop, crash through the window above the sink, and flee to safety. Jackie Chan never gets calf cramps.

Meanwhile, *my* calf cramp had become so painful that my eyes were watering.

More monkeys entered the kitchen. They were chattering as they came, as if the discovery of any decomposing critter was the ideal occasion to call in all the relatives, open a keg of beer, and have a hootenanny.

I couldn't discern how many joined the original six searchers. Maybe two. Maybe four. Not more than five or six.

Too many.

None of the newcomers showed the least interest in my corner of the room. They joined the others around whatever fascinating mound of rotting flesh they had discovered, and the lively argument continued.

My luck wouldn't hold. At any moment they might decide to finish their inspection of the cabinets. The individual that had nearly discovered me might remember it had sensed something odd in this vicinity.

I considered slipping out of the broom closet, creeping along the wall, easing through the doorway, and taking refuge in a corner of the dining room, as far away from the main traffic pattern as I could get. Before they had entered the kitchen, the first squad of searchers must have satisfied themselves that no one was lurking in that chamber; they wouldn't thoroughly inspect the same territory again.

With my cramp, I couldn't move fast, but I could still rely on the cover of darkness, my old friend. Besides, if I had to stay where I was much longer, my nerves were going to wind so tight that I'd implode.

Just as I convinced myself that I had to move, one of the monkeys sprinted away from whatever reeking pile they had gathered to discuss, returning to the dining-room doorway. It shrieked, perhaps calling for yet additional members of the troop to come here and sniff the vile remains.

Even above the chattering and muttering of the crowd clustered around the dead thing, I could hear an answering cry from elsewhere in the bungalow.

The kitchen was only marginally less noisy than a monkey house at a zoo. Maybe the lights would come on and I'd discover myself in a Twilight Zone moment. Maybe Christopher Snow wasn't my current identity but merely the name under which I had lived in a previous life, and now I was one of *them*, reincarnated as a rhesus. Maybe we weren't in a Dead Town bungalow but were in a giant cage, surrounded by people pointing and laughing as we swung from ropes and scratched our bald butts.

As though I had tempted fate merely by thinking about the lights coming on, a glow arose toward the front of the house. I was aware of it, at first, solely because the monkey at the threshold of the dining room began to resolve out of the blackness, the way an image gradually solidifies on Polaroid film.

This development didn't alarm or even surprise the beast, so I assumed that it had called for the light.

I wasn't as sanguine about these changing circumstances as the monkey appeared to be. The shroud of darkness in which I'd been hiding was going to be stripped away.

8

Because the approaching luminosity was frost white rather than yellow and because it didn't throb like an open flame, it was most likely produced by a flashlight. The beam wasn't focused on the doorway; instead, the monkey standing there was illuminated by the indirect radiance, indicating that the source was a two- or three-battery model, not just a penlight.

Evidently, to the extent that their small hands could serve them, the members of the troop were tool users. They had either found the flashlight or stolen it—probably the latter, because these monkeys have no more respect for the law and property rights than they have for Miss Manners' rules of etiquette.

The individual at the doorway faced the steadily brightening dining room with a peculiar air of expectation, perhaps even with a degree of wonder.

At the farther end of the kitchen, out of my line of sight, the rest of the searchers had fallen silent. I suspected that their posture matched that of the rhesus I could see, that they were equally fascinated or even awed.

Since the source of the glow was surely nothing more exotic than a flashlight, I assumed that something about the bearer of the light elicited these monkeys' reverence. I was curious about that individual, but reluctant to die for the satisfaction of my curiosity.

Already, a dangerous amount of light was passing through

the doorway. Absolute darkness no longer reigned. I could make out the general shapes of the cabinets across the kitchen.

When I glanced down, I was still in shadow, but I could see my hands and the pistol. Worse, I could see my clothes and shoes, which were all black.

The cramp burned in my leg. I tried not to think about it. That was like trying not to think about a grizzly bear while it gnawed off your foot.

To clear my vision, I was now blinking away both involuntary tears of pain and a flood of cold sweat. Forget about the danger posed by the rapidly receding darkness: Soon the troop was going to be able to smell eau de Snow even over the malodor of decomposition.

The monkey at the dining-room threshold took two steps backward as the light advanced. If the beast looked in my direction, it could not fail to see me.

I was almost reduced to the childhood game of pretending with all my might to be invisible.

Then, in the dining room, the bearer of the flashlight evidently halted and turned toward something else of interest. A murmur swept through the searchers in the kitchen as the glow diminished.

Oily gloom welled out of the corners, and now I heard the sound that had captured the monkeys' attention. The drone of an engine. Perhaps a truck. It was growing louder.

From the front of the house came a cry of alarm.

In the dining room, the bearer of the light switched it off.

The search party fled the kitchen. The linoleum crackled under their feet, but they made no other sound.

From the dining room onward, they retreated with the stealth they had exhibited when originally charging the bungalow from the street.

They were so silent that I wasn't convinced they had entirely withdrawn. I half suspected they were toying with me, waiting just inside the dining-room doorway. When I limped out of the kitchen, they would swarm over me, gleefully yelling "Surprise," gouge out my eyes, bite off my lips, and conduct a fortune-telling session with my entrails.

The growl of the engine grew steadily louder, although the vehicle that produced it was still some distance away.

During all the nights I had explored Fort Wyvern's desolate precincts, I had never until now heard an engine or other mechanical sound. Generally this place was so quiet that it might have been an outpost at the end of time, when the sun no longer rose and the stars remained fixed in the heavens and the only sound was the occasional low moan of a wind from nowhere.

As I tentatively eased out of the broom closet, I remembered something Bobby had asked when I'd told him to come in by the river: *Do I have to creep or can I strut?*

I had said that sneaky didn't matter anymore. By that, I hadn't meant that he should arrive with drum and fife. I had also told him to watch his ass.

Although I had never imagined that Bobby would *drive* into Wyvern, I was more than half convinced that the approaching vehicle was his Jeep. I should have anticipated this. Bobby was Bobby, after all.

I'd first thought that the troop had reacted with fright to the engine noise, that they had fled in fear of being spotted, pursued. They spend most of their time in the hills, in the wild, coming into Moonlight Bay—on what mysterious missions I do not know—only after sundown, preferring to limit their visits to nights when they have the double cover of darkness and fog. Even then, they travel as much as possible by storm drains, parks, arroyos, dry riverbeds, vacant lots, and perhaps from tree to tree. With rare exception, they do not show themselves, and they are masters of secrecy, moving among us as covertly as termites move through the walls of our houses, as unnoticed as earthworms tunneling the ground under our feet.

Here on turf more congenial to them, however, their reaction to the sound of an engine might be bolder and more aggressive than it would have been in town. They might not flee from it. They might be drawn to it. If they followed it without showing themselves and waited for the driver to park and get out . . .

The engine roar grew steadily louder. The vehicle was in the neighborhood, probably only a few blocks away.

Abandoning caution, trying to shake the pain out of my leg as though it were a biting mongrel that could be kicked loose, I hobbled out of the kitchen and hurried blindly through the monkeyless dining room. As far as I could tell, none of the flea farms lingered in the living room, either.

At the window from which I had watched them earlier, I put my brow to the glass and saw eight or ten members of the troop in the street. They were dropping, one by one, through the open manhole, into which their comrades had apparently already vanished.

Happily, Bobby wasn't in jeopardy of having his brain scooped out and his skull turned into a flowerpot to beautify some monkey den. Not immediate jeopardy, anyway.

As fast as flowing water, the monkeys poured into the manhole, gone in a quicksilver ripple. In their wake, the tree-lined street appeared to be no more substantial than a dream-scape, a mere illusion of twisted shadows and secondhand light, and it was almost possible to believe that the troop had been as imaginary as the cast of a nightmare.

Heading for the front door, I returned the spare magazine to the pocket in my shoulder holster. I held on to the Glock.

When I reached the porch, I heard the manhole cover being slid into place. I was surprised that the monkeys were strong enough to maneuver that heavy object from the storm drain below, a tricky task even for a grown man.

The engine noise reverberated through the bungalows and trees. The vehicle was close, yet I saw no headlights.

As I reached the street, still working the last of the cramp out of my leg, the manhole cover clanked into its niche. I arrived in time to see the curved point of a steel grappling hook wiggle out of a slot in the iron, extracted from below. City street-department crews carry such implements to snare and lift these covers without having to pry them loose from the edge. The monkeys must have found or stolen the hook; hanging from the service ladder in the drain, a couple of them were able to leverage the disc into place, covering their trail.

Their use of tools had ominous implications that I was loath to consider.

Headlight beams flashed through the spaces between bungalows. The truck. It was passing on the next street parallel to this one, behind the small houses.

Although I hadn't seen any details of the vehicle, I was sure Bobby had arrived. The pitch of the engine was similar to that of his Jeep, and it was speeding toward the commercial district of Dead Town, where we were supposed to meet.

I headed in that direction as the roar of the truck rapidly diminished. The pain was gone from my calf, but the nerve continued to flutter, leaving my left leg weaker than my right. With the cramp threatening to recur, I didn't even try to run.

From above came the shearing sound of wings, cutting the air into scimitar shapes. I looked up, ducking defensively, as a flock of birds made a low pass, in tight formation, and vanished into the night ahead.

Their speed and the darkness prevented me from identifying their species. This might have been the mysterious crew that had roosted in the tree under which I'd placed my call to Bobby.

When I reached the end of the block, the birds were flying in a circle over the intersection, as if marking time until I caught up with them. I counted ten or twelve, more than had kept watch over me from the Indian laurel.

Their behavior was peculiar, but I didn't feel that they intended any harm.

Even if I was wrong and they posed a danger to me, there was no way to avoid them. If I changed my route, they could easily follow.

As they passed across the face of the descendent moon, traveling more slowly than before, I saw them clearly enough to identify them tentatively as nighthawks. Because they live by my schedule, I am familiar with this species, also known as nightjars, which encompasses seventy varieties, including the whippoorwill.

Nighthawks feed on insects—moths, flying ants, mosquitoes, beetles—and dine while on the wing. Snatching tidbits from the air, they jink this way and that, exhibiting a singular swooping-darting-twisting pattern of flight that, as much as anything, identifies them.

The full moon provides them with the ideal circumstances for a banquet, because in its radiance, flying insects are more visible. Ordinarily, nighthawks are ceaselessly active in these conditions, their harsh churring calls cutting the air as they feast.

The lunar lamp above, currently unobstructed by clouds, ensured good hunting, yet these birds were not inclined to take advantage of the ideal conditions. Acting counter to instinct, they squandered the moonlight, flying monotonously in a circle that was approximately forty feet in diameter, around and around over the intersection. For the most part, they proceeded in single file, though three pairs flew side by side, none feeding or issuing a single cry.

I crossed the intersection and kept going.

In the distance, the sound of the engine abruptly cut off. If it was Bobby's Jeep, he must have arrived at our rendezvous point.

I was a third of the way into the subsequent block when the flock followed. They passed overhead at a higher altitude than previously but low enough to cause me to tuck my head down.

When I arrived at another intersection, they had again formed a bird carousel, minus calliope, circling thirty feet overhead. Although any attempt to take a count would have resulted in more vertigo than waits in a bottle of tequila, I was sure the number of nighthawks had grown.

Over the next two blocks, the size of the flock swelled until it wasn't necessary to take a count to verify the increase. By the time I reached the three-way intersection in which this street ended, at least a hundred birds were circling quietly above. For the most part, they were now grouped in pairs, and there were two layers to this flying feathered ring, one about five to ten feet higher than the other.

I stopped, gazing up, transfixed.

Thanks to the circus between my ears, I can seize upon

the smallest disquieting observation and from it extrapolate a terror of cataclysmic proportions. Yet, though the birds unnerved me, I still didn't believe they were a threat.

Their unnatural behavior was ominous without implying aggression. This aerial ballet, humdrum in its pattern yet inexpressibly graceful, conveyed a mood as clear and unmistakable as any ballet ever performed by dancers on a stage, as affecting as any piece of music ever meant to touch the heart—and the mood here was sorrow. Sorrow so poignant that it pinched my breath and made me feel as though something more bitter than blood were pumping through my veins.

To poets but also to those whose stomachs curdle at the mention of poetry, birds in flight usually evoke thoughts of freedom, hope, faith, joy. The thrum of these pinions, however, was as bleak as the keening of an arctic wind coming across a thousand miles of barren ice; it was a forlorn sound, and in my heart it coalesced into an icy weight.

With the exquisite timing and choreography that suggests psychic connections among the members of a flock, the double ring of birds fluidly combined into a single ascending spiral. They rose like a coil of dark smoke, around and up and up through the flue of the night, across the pocked moon, becoming steadily less visible against the stars, until at last they dissipated like mere fumes and soot across the rooftop of the world.

All was silent. Windless. Dead.

This behavior of the nighthawks had been unnatural, certainly, but not a meaningless aberration, not a mere curiosity. There was calculation—therefore meaning—in their air show.

The puzzle resisted an easy solution.

Actually, I wasn't sure I wanted to fit all the pieces together. The resultant picture was not likely to be comforting. The birds themselves posed no threat, but their bizarre performance couldn't be construed as a good thing.

A sign. An omen.

Not the kind of omen that makes you want to buy a lottery ticket or take a quick trip to Vegas. Certainly not an omen that would make you decide to commit more of your net worth to the stock market. No, this was an omen that might inspire you to move to rural New Mexico, up into the fastness of the Sangre de Cristo mountains, as far from civilization as you could get, with a hoard of food, twenty thousand rounds of ammunition—and a prayer book.

I returned the pistol to the holster under my jacket.

Suddenly I was tired, drained.

I took a few deep breaths, but each inhalation was as stale as the air I exhaled.

When I wiped a hand across my face, hoping to slough off my weariness, I expected my skin to be greasy. Instead, it was dry and hot.

I found a penny-size tender spot just below my left cheekbone. Gently massaging it with a fingertip, I tried to remember whether I had knocked against anything during the night's adventures.

Any pain without apparent cause is a possible early signal of a forming lesion, of the cancer that I have thus far remarkably escaped. If the suspect blemish or tenderness occurs on my face or hands, which are exposed to light even though sheathed in sunscreen, the chances of malignancy are greater.

Lowering my hand from my face, I reminded myself to live in the moment. Because of XP, I was born with no future, and in spite of my limitations, I live a full life—perhaps a better one—by concerning myself as little as possible with what tomorrow may bring. The present is more vivid, more precious, more fulfilling, if you understand that it is all you have.

Carpe diem, said the poet Horace, more than two thousand years ago. Seize the day. And trust not in tomorrow.

Carpe noctem works as well for me. I seize the night, wringing from it all that it has to offer, and I refuse to dwell on the fact that eventually the darkness of all darknesses will wring the same from me.

9

The solemn birds had cast down a dreary mood, like feathers molting from their wings. I walked determinedly out of that fallen plumage, heading toward the movie theater where Bobby Halloway was waiting.

The sore spot on my cheek might never develop into a lesion or a blister. Its value, as a source of worry, had been solely to distract me from the more terrible fear that I was reluctant to face: The longer Jimmy Wing and Orson were missing, the greater the likelihood they were dead.

Bordering the northern edge of Dead Town's residential district is a park with handball courts at one end and tennis courts at the other. In the middle are acres of picnic grounds shaded by California live oaks that have fared well since the base closure, a playground with swings and jungle gyms, an open-air pavilion, and an enormous swimming pool.

The large oval pavilion, where bands once played on summer nights, is the only ornate structure in Wyvern: Victorian, with an encircling balustrade, fluted columns, a deep cornice enhanced by elaborate millwork, and a fanciful roof that drops from finial to eaves in shingled scallops reminiscent of the swags of a circus tent. Here, under strings of colored Christmas lights, young men had danced with their wives—and then gone off to bloody deaths in World War II, the Korean War, Vietnam, and lesser skirmishes. The lights still dangle from rafter to rafter, unplugged and sheathed in dust, and often it seems that if you squint your eyes just slightly on moonlit nights like this, you can see the ghosts of martyrs to democracy dancing with the spirits of their widows.

As I strode through the tall grass, past the community swimming pool, where the chain-link fence sagged around the entire perimeter and was completely broken down in a few spots, I increased my pace, not solely because I was anxious to get to the movie house. Nothing has happened here to make me fearful of the place, but instinct tells me not to linger near this concrete-walled swamp. The pool is nearly two hundred feet long and eighty feet wide, with a lifeguard platform in the center. Currently, it was two-thirds full of collected rain. The black water would be black in daylight, too, because it was thickened with rotting oak leaves and other debris. In this fetid sludge, even the moon lost its silver purity, leaving a distorted, bile-yellow reflection like the face of a goblin in a dream.

Although I remained at a distance, I could smell the reeking slough. The stench wasn't as bad as that in the bungalow kitchen, but it was pretty close.

Worse than the odor was the aura of the pool, which could not be perceived by the usual five senses but which was readily apparent to an indescribable sixth. No, my overactive imagination wasn't overacting. This is, at all times, an undeniably real quality of the pool: a subtle but cold squirming energy from which your mind shrinks, an evil mojo that slithers across the surface of your soul with all the tactility of a ball of worms writhing in your hand.

I thought I heard a splash, something breaking the surface of the sludge, followed by an oily churning, as if a swimmer were doing laps. I assumed these noises *were* the products of my imagination, but nevertheless, as the swimmer stroked closer to my end of the pool, I broke into a run.

Beyond the park lies Commissary Way, along the north side of which stand the enterprises and institutions that, in addition to those in Moonlight Bay, once served Wyvern's thirty-six thousand active-duty personnel and thirteen thousand of their dependents. The commissary and the movie theater anchor opposite ends of the long street. Between them are a barbershop, a dry cleaner, a florist, a bakery, a bank, the enlisted men's club, the officers' club, a library, a game arcade, a kindergarten, an elementary school, a fitness center, and additional shops—all empty, their painted signs faded and weathered.

These one- and two-story buildings are plain but, precisely because of their simplicity, pleasing to the eye: white clapboard, painted concrete blocks, stucco. The utilitarian nature of military construction combined with Depression-era frugality—which guided every project in 1939, when the base was commissioned—could have resulted in an ugly industrial look. But the army architects and construction crews had made an effort to create buildings with some grace, relying on only such fundamentals as harmonious lines and angles, rhythmic window placement, and varying but complementary roof lines.

The movie theater is as humble as the other buildings, and its marquee rests flat against the front wall, above the entrance. I don't know what film last played here or the names of the actors who appeared in it. Only three black plastic letters remain in the tracks where titles and cast were announced, forming a single word: WHO.

In spite of the absence of concluding punctuation, I read this enigmatic message as a desperate question referring to the genetic terror spawned in hidden laboratories somewhere on these grounds. *Who am I? Who are you? Who are we becoming? Who did this to us? Who can save us?*

Who? Who?

Bobby's black Jeep was parked in front of the theater. The vinyl roof and walls were not attached to the frame and roll bars, so the vehicle was open to the night.

As I approached the Jeep, the moon sank behind the clouds in the west, so close to the horizon now that it was unlikely to reappear, but even from a block away, I could clearly see Bobby sitting behind the steering wheel.

We are the same height and weight. Although my hair is blond and his is dark brown, although my eyes are pale blue and his are so raven black they have blue highlights, we can pass for brothers. We have been each other's closest friend since we were eleven, and so perhaps we have grown alike in many ways. We stand, sit, and move with the same posture and at the same pace; I think this is because we have spent so much time surfing, in sync with the sea. Sasha insists we have "catlike grace," which I think flatters us too much, but however catlike we may or may not be, neither of us drinks milk from a saucer or prefers a litter box to a bathroom.

I went to the passenger side, grabbed the roll bar, and swung into the Jeep without opening the low door. I had to work my feet around a small Styrofoam cooler on the floor in front of the seat.

Bobby was wearing khakis, a long-sleeve white cotton pullover, and a Hawaiian shirt—he owns no other style—over the thin sweater.

He was drinking a Heineken.

Although I had never seen Bobby drunk, I said, "Hope you're not too mellow."

Without looking away from the street, he said, "Mellow isn't like dumb or ugly," meaning the word *too* should never be used to modify it.

The night was pleasantly cool but not crisp, so I said, "Flow me a Heinie?"

"Go for it."

I fished a bottle out of the ice in the cooler and twisted off the cap. I hadn't realized how thirsty I was. The beer washed the lingering bitterness out of my mouth.

Bobby glanced at the rearview mirror for a moment, then returned his attention to the street in front of us.

Braced between the seats, aimed toward the rear of the Jeep, was a pistol-grip, pump-action shotgun.

"Beer and guns," I said, shaking my head.

"We're obviously not Amish."

"You come in by the river like I said?"

"Yeah."

"How'd you drive through the fence?"

"Cut the hole bigger."

"I expected you to walk in."

"Too hard to carry the cooler."

"I guess we might need the speed," I conceded, considering the size of the area to be searched.

He said, "You smell maximum real, bro."

"Worked at it."

From the rearview mirror dangled a bright-yellow air freshener shaped like a banana. Bobby slipped it off the mirror and hung it from my left ear.

Sometimes he is too funny for his own good. I wouldn't reward him with a laugh.

"It's a banana," I said, "but it smells like a pine tree."

"That old American ingenuity."

"Nothing like it."

"We put men on the moon."

"We invented chocolate-flavored breakfast cereal."

"Don't forget plastic vomit."

"Funniest gag *ever*," I said.

Bobby and I solemnly clinked bottles in a patriotic toast and took long swallows of beer.

Although I was, on one level, frantic to find Orson and Jimmy, on the surface I fell into the languid tempo by which Bobby lives. He is so laid back that if he visited someone in a hospital, the nurses might mistake him for a patient in a coma, shuck him out of his Hawaiian shirt, and slide him into a backless bed gown before he could correct their misapprehension. Except when he's rocking through epic surf, getting totally barreled in an insanely hollow wave, Bobby values tranquility. He responds better to easy and indirect conversation than to any expression of urgency. During our seventeen-year friendship, I've learned to value this relaxed approach, even if it doesn't come naturally to me. Calm is essential to prudent action. Because Bobby acts only after contemplation, I've never known him to be blindsided by anyone or anything. He may look relaxed, even sleepy at times, but like a Zen master, he is able to make the flow of time slow down while he considers how best to deal with the latest crisis.

"Bitchin' shirt," I said.

He was wearing one of his favorite antique shirts: a brown Asian landscape design. He has a couple hundred in his collection, and he knows every detail of their histories.

Before he could reply, I said, "Made by Kahala about 1950. Silk with coconut-shell buttons. Same shirt John Wayne wore in *Big Jim McLain*."

He was silent long enough for me to have repeated all the shirt data, but I knew he'd heard me.

He took another pull at his bottle of beer. Finally: "Have you for real developed an interest in aloha threads, or are you just mocking me?"

"Just mocking you."

"Enjoy yourself."

As he studied the rearview mirror again, I said, "What's that in your lap?"

"I'm just way happy to see you," he said. Then he held up a serious handgun. "Smith & Wesson Model 29."

"This is definitely not a barn raising."

"Exactly what is it?"

"Somebody took Lilly Wing's boy."

"Who?"

"Some abb," I said, meaning an abnormal type, a sleazeball.

"Woofy," he said, which is Australian surfer lingo for waves contaminated by a sewage spill, but which has evolved other, related meanings, none positive.

I said, "Boosted Jimmy right out of his bedroom, through a window."

"So Lilly called you?"

"I was just in the wrong place at the wrong time, biking by right after the abb did the deed."

"How'd you get from there to here?"

"Orson's nose."

I told him about the abb, the kidnapper, whom I'd encountered under the warehouse.

He frowned. "You said yellow eyes?"

"Yellow-brown, I guess."

"Shine-in-the-dark yellow?"

"No. Brownish yellow, burnt amber, but the natural color."

Recently, we'd encountered a couple of men in whom radical genetic changes had occurred, guys in the process of becoming something more or less than human, who appeared for the most part normal but whose *otherness* was betrayed by brief but detectable flashes of animal eyeshine. These people are driven by strange, hateful needs, and they are capable of extreme violence. If Jimmy was in the hands of one of these, then the list of outrages to which he might be subjected was even longer than the savageries that a standard-issue sociopath might have in mind.

"You recognize this abb?" I asked Bobby.

"You say about thirty, black hair, yellow eyes, built like a fireplug?"

"Neat little baby teeth."

"Not my type."

"I never saw him before, either," I said.

"Twelve thousand people in town."

"And this isn't a dude who's a beachhead," I said, meaning we wouldn't have seen him hanging out with surfers. "So he could still be local and we wouldn't know."

For the first time all night, a breeze sprang up, a gentle onshore flow that brought to us a faint but bracing scent of the sea. In the park across the street, the oaks became conspiratorial, plotting together in whispers.

Bobby said, "Why did this abb bring Jimmy here of all places?"

"Maybe privacy. To do his thing."

"I'd like to do my thing, Cuisinart the creep."

"Plus the weirdness of this place probably feeds his dementia."

"Unless it's more directly connected to Wyvern."

"Unless. And Lilly's worried about the guy on the news."

"What guy?"

"Kidnaps kids, locks them away. When he gets three or five or whatever from one community, then he burns them all at once."

"Stuff like this is why I don't listen to news these days."

"You've never listened to news."

"I know. But I used to have different reasons." Looking around at the night, Bobby said, "So where would they be now?"

"Anywhere."

"Maybe this is more 'anywhere' than we can handle."

He hadn't looked at the rearview mirror recently, so I turned in my seat to check things out behind us.

Bobby said casually, "Saw a monkey on the way in."

Taking the air freshener off my ear and looping its string over the mirror again, I said, "Just one? I didn't know they traveled alone."

"Me neither. I turned a corner in Dead Town, and there it was, running across the street, caught in the headlights. This little freakin' dude. Not your ordinary evolutionary link, missing or otherwise."

"Different?"

"Maybe four feet tall."

Apparently, there were refrigeration coils in my spine.

All the rhesuses we had seen thus far had been about two feet tall. They were trouble enough. At four feet, they would constitute a different magnitude of threat.

"Major head," Bobby said.

"What?"

"Four feet tall, big head."

"How big?"

"I didn't try to measure it for a hat."

"Give me a guess."

"Maybe as big as yours or mine."

"On a four-foot body."

"Top-heavy. And misshapen."

"Grisly," I said.

"Hard-core grisly."

Bobby leaned forward over the steering wheel, squinting through the windshield.

About a block away, something was moving. About the size of a monkey. Slowly and fitfully approaching.

Putting one hand on the shotgun, I said, "What else?"

"That's all I saw, bro. It was way fast."

"Something new."

"Maybe soon there's gonna be a bunch of that."

"Tumbleweed," I said, identifying the approaching object.

Neither of us relaxed.

With the moon down, it was easy to imagine that the park across the street was swarming with phantasmagorical figures under—and high in—the massive oaks.

When I described my encounter with the gang that had almost caught me in the bungalow, Bobby said, "Thirty? Man, they're busy breeders."

I told him about their use of the flashlight and the man-hole hook.

"Next," he said, "they'll be driving cars, trying to date our women."

He finished his beer and handed the empty bottle to me, which I planted upside down in the ice chest.

From somewhere along the street came a soft, rhythmic creaking. It was probably just one of the shop signs swinging on its mountings, disturbed by the breeze.

"So Jimmy could be anywhere in Wyvern," Bobby said. "What about Orson?"

"The last I heard him barking, I think it was coming from here in Dead Town somewhere."

"Here on Commissary Way or over in the houses?"

"I don't know. Just this direction."

"Lot of houses over there." Bobby looked toward the residential streets on the far side of the park.

"Three thousand."

"Say like four minutes a house . . . Take us nine or ten days, searching around the clock, to go through all of 'em. And you don't do day work."

"Orson's probably not in any of the houses."

"But we have to start somewhere. So where?"

I didn't have an answer. Besides, I didn't trust myself to speak without my voice cracking.

"You think Orson is with Jimmy? We find one, we find both?"

I shrugged.

"Maybe this is one time we should tell Ramirez what we know," Bobby suggested.

Manuel Ramirez was the current chief of police in Moonlight Bay. He had once been a good man, but like all the cops in town, he had been co-opted by higher authorities.

"Maybe," Bobby said, "in this case, Manuel's interests are the same as ours. He's got the manpower for a search."

"He's not just corrupted by the feds," I said. "He's becoming."

Becoming. That's the word some of the genetically afflicted use to describe the physical, mental, and emotional changes that are taking place in them—but only once those changes have passed the subtle stage and reached a crisis.

Bobby was surprised. "He tell you he's becoming?"

"He says he isn't. But there's something wrong with him. I don't trust Manuel."

"Hell, I don't entirely trust me," Bobby said, which put into words our greatest fear—that we might not merely become infected with the retrovirus but that we might start becoming something less than human without being aware of the changes taking place.

I sucked down the last of the Heineken, jammed the empty bottle into the ice chest.

"We gotta find Orson," I said.

"We will."

"Crucial, bro."

"We will."

Orson is no ordinary dog. My mother brought him home from the Wyvern lab when he was a puppy. Until recently, I didn't realize where fur face had come from or how special he was, because my mom didn't tell me and because Orson was good at keeping his secrets. The intelligence-enhancement experiments were conducted on monkeys and on hardcase lifers transferred from military prisons, but also on dogs, cats, and other animals. I've never given Orson an IQ test; pencils aren't designed for paws, and because he lacks the complex larynx of a human being, he isn't capable of speech. He understands everything, however, and in his own way he makes himself understood. He is smarter than the monkeys.

I suspect he possesses human-level intelligence. At least.

Earlier, I suggested that the monkeys hate us because we gave them the ability to dream but not the means to fulfill their dreams, leaving them lost outside the natural order. But if this explains their hostility and thirst for violence, why should Orson, who is also outside the natural order, be so affectionate and good-hearted?

He is trapped in a body that serves his enhanced intelligence less well than the monkeys' bodies serve them. He has no hands, as they have, and his vision is comparatively weak, as is that of any domesticated breed of canine.

The monkeys have the communal comfort of the troop, but Orson endures in a terrible solitude. Though more dogs as smart as Orson might have been created, I've yet to encounter another. Sasha, Bobby, and I love him, but we are too little comfort, because we can never truly share his point of view, his experience. Because he is, at least for now, a singularity, Orson lives with a profound loneliness that I can perceive but never fully comprehend, loneliness that is with him even when he is among his friends.

Maybe his basic doggie nature explains why he doesn't share the monkeys' hatred and rage. I think dogs were put in this world to remind humanity that love, loyalty, devotion, courage, patience, and good humor are the qualities that, with honesty, are the essence of admirable character and the very definition of a life well lived.

In good Orson I see the hopeful side of my mother's work, the real potential of science to bring light into an often dark world, to lift us up, to stir the spirit and to remind us that the universe is a place of wonder and infinite potential.

She did, in fact, hope to accomplish great things. She aligned herself with a biological-weapons project solely because this was the only way to obtain the high level of funding needed to realize her design for a gene-splicing retrovirus, which she believed could be used to cure many illnesses and inherited disorders—not least of all, my XP.

You see, my mom didn't destroy the world without good reason. She did it trying to help me. Because of me, all of nature is now poised on the brink. Maternal love became the wellspring of ultimate terror.

So . . . you want to talk about *your* conflicted feelings for your mother?

Orson and I are her sons. I am the fruit of her heart and womb. Orson is the fruit of her mind, but she created him as surely as she created me. We are brothers. Not just figuratively. We are bound not by blood but by our mother's passions, and in that sense we share one heart.

If anything were to happen to Orson, a part of me would die—the purer part, the better part—and die forever.

"Gotta find him," I repeated.

"Faith, bro," Bobby said.

He reached for the key in the ignition, but before he could switch on the engine, a sound arose, louder than the soft million-tongue flutter of leaves in the breeze, swelling by the second.

Bobby put one hand on the Smith & Wesson in his lap.

I didn't draw my pistol because I knew what I was hearing. The beating of wings. Many wings.

Like wind-torn shingles from Heaven's roof, the voiceless flock came out of the night, tumbling down in a clatter and whirl of wings more than half a block away, then flying parallel to the pavement, following the street, streaking in our direction. The hundred birds I'd seen earlier were surely part of this apparition, but another hundred had joined them, perhaps two hundred.

Bobby decided against the revolver and snatched the shotgun from between the seats.

"Ice it down," I told him.

He gave me an odd look. Usually, he's the one advising *me* to stay cool.

Seventeen years of friendship ensure that he takes me

seriously, but he chambered a round in the shotgun nevertheless.

Spread the width of the street, the flock swept over us, no more than six feet above our heads. I had the sense that they were flying with astonishing precision, arranged in formations so orderly as to be uncanny. An aerial view of the entire swarm might reveal patterns intriguing because of their unnatural degree of complex order—but also disturbing because they would seem simultaneously meaningful and indecipherable.

Bobby ducked, but I gazed up into the dark churning cloud of wings and feathered breasts, trying to determine if there were species other than nighthawks in these multitudes. The poor light and the blur of movement made it difficult to conduct even a cursory census.

By the time the last of the enormous flock soared past, not a single bird had dived at us or shrieked. Their passing had such an otherworldly quality that I almost felt as though I had been hallucinating, but a sprinkling of feathers in the Jeep and along the blacktop confirmed the reality of the experience.

Even as the last small bits of fluffy down descended on the breeze, Bobby threw open the driver's door and scrambled from the Jeep. He was still gripping the shotgun when he turned to stare after the departing flock, although he was holding the weapon in one hand now, muzzle pointed at the pavement, with no intention of using it.

I got out of the Jeep, too, and watched as the birds swooped up from the end of the street, arcing high across a sea of stars, disappearing into the blackness between those distant suns.

"Totally awesome," Bobby said.

"Yeah."

"But . . ."

"Yeah."

"Feels a little sharky, too."

I knew what he meant. This time the birds radiated more than the sorrow that I had felt before. Although the flock's choreography had been breathtaking, even exhilarating, and although their amazing conspiracy of silence seemed to express and to inspire an odd sort of reverence, something dangerous lay under their performance, the same way that a sun-spangled blue sea could look so totally sacred even while great whites churned in a feeding frenzy just under the surface. This felt a little sharky.

Although the nighthawks had climbed out of sight, Bobby and I stood staring at the constellation into which they had vanished, as if we were in full-on early Spielberg, waiting for the mother ship to appear and bathe us in white light only slightly less intense than God sheds.

"Saw it before," I told him.

"Bogus."

"True."

"Insane."

"Maximum."

"When?"

"On my way here," I said. "Just the other side of the park. But the flock was smaller."

"What're they doing?"

"I don't know. But here they come again."

"I don't hear them."

"Me neither. Or see 'em. But they're coming."

He hesitated, then slowly nodded and said, "Yeah," when he felt it, too.

Stars over stars under stars. A larger light that might have been Venus. One, two, three closely grouped flares as small meteors hit the atmosphere and were incinerated. A small winking red dot moving east to west, perhaps an airliner sailing along the interface between our sea of air and the airless sea between worlds.

I was almost prepared to question my instinct, when, at last, the flock returned from the same part of the sky into which it had risen out of sight. Incredibly, the birds swept down into the street and past us in a helix, corkscrewing along Commissary Way, boring through the night in a *whirr* of wings.

This exhibition, this incredible stunt, was so thrilling that inevitably it inspired wonder, and in wonder is the seed of joy. I felt my heart lift at this amazing sight, but my exhilaration was constrained by the continuing perception of a *wrongness* in the birds' behavior that was separate from the charming novelty of it.

Bobby must have felt the same way, because he couldn't sustain the brief laugh of delight with which he first greeted the sight of the spiraling flock. His smile dried out as his laugh withered, and he turned to stare after the departing nighthawks with a cracking expression that was becoming less grin than grimace.

Two blocks away, the birds twisted up into the sky, like the withdrawing funnel of a fading tornado.

Their aerobatics had required strenuous effort; the beating of their wings had been so furious that even as the drumlike pounding diminished, I could *feel* the reverberations of it in my ears, in my heart, in my bones.

The birds soared out of sight once more, leaving us with just the whisper of the onshore breeze.

"It's not over," Bobby said.

"No."

Quicker than before, the birds returned. They didn't reappear from the point at which they had vanished; instead, they came from high over the park. We heard them before we saw them, and the sound that heralded their approach was not the drumming of wings but an unearthly shrieking.

They had broken their vow of silence, exploded it. Screeching, churring, whistling, screaking, shrilling, cricking, they *hurtled* down out of the stars. Their tuneless skirling was sharp enough to make my ears sting as though lanced, and the note of misery was so piercing that my soul seemed to shrivel around the cold shank of this wounding sound.

Bobby didn't even begin to raise the shotgun.

I didn't reach for my pistol, either.

We both knew the birds weren't attacking. No anger resonated in their cries, only a wretchedness, a desolation so deep and bleak that it was beyond despair.

Plummeting behind this blood-freezing wail, the birds appeared. They engaged in none of their previous aerobatics, forsaking even a simple formation, swarming gracelessly. Only speed mattered to them now, because speed alone served their purpose, and they dived, wings back, using gravity like a sling-shot.

With a purpose that neither Bobby nor I foresaw, they shrieked across the park, across the street, and rocketed unchecked into the face of a two-story building three doors from the movie theater in front of which we stood. They hit the structure with such brutal force that the *pock-pock-pock* of their bodies smashing against the stucco sounded like relentless automatic-weapons fire; combined with their shrill cries, this barrage nearly drowned out the brittle ringing of the shattered window glass.

Horrified, sickened, I turned away from the carnage and leaned against the Jeep.

Considering the speed of the flock's kamikaze descent, the hard rattle of death could not have continued for more than seconds, but minutes seemed to pass before the terrible noise ceased. The quiet that followed was heavy with catastrophic import, like the hush in the wake of a bomb blast.

I closed my eyes—but opened them again when a replay of the flocks' suicidal plunge was projected vividly onto the backs of my eyelids.

All of nature was on the brink. I had known that much for the past month, since I'd learned what had happened in the hidden labs of Wyvern. Now the perilous ledge on which the future stood seemed narrower than I had thought, the height of the cliff far greater than it had seemed a moment ago, and the rocks below more jagged than my worst imaginings.

With my eyes open, into my mind came a photographic memory of my mother's face. So wise. So kind.

The image of her blurred. Everything around me blurred for a moment, the street and the movie theater.

I took a shallow breath, which entered my chest with an

ache, then a deeper breath that hurt less, and I wiped my eyes with the back of one jacket sleeve.

My heritage requires me to bear witness, and I can't shirk that responsibility. The light of the sun is denied to me, but I must not avoid the light of truth, which also burns but anneals rather than destroys.

I turned to look at the silenced flock.

Hundreds of small birds littered the sidewalk. Only a few wings shuddered feebly with rapidly fading life. Most of them had hit so hard that their fragile skulls had shattered and their necks had broken on impact.

Because they appeared to be ordinary nighthawks, I wondered what internal change had swept through these birds. Although invisible to the unassisted eye, the difference was evidently so substantive that they believed continued existence to be intolerable.

Or perhaps their kamikaze flight had not been a conscious act. Perhaps it had resulted from a deterioration of their directional instincts or mass blindness, or dementia.

No. Remembering their elaborate aerobatics, I had to assume that the change was more profound, more mysterious, and more disturbing than mere physical dysfunction.

Beside me, the engine of the Jeep turned over, caught, roared, and then idled as Bobby let up on the accelerator.

I hadn't been aware of him getting behind the steering wheel.

"Bro," he said.

Although not directly related to the disappearance of Orson or to the kidnapping of Jimmy Wing, the flock's self-destruction added urgency to the already pressing need to find the dog and the boy.

For once in his life, Bobby appeared to feel the solvent of time passing through him and swirling away, carrying with it some dissolved essence, like water into a drain.

He said, "Let's cruise," with a solemn expression in his eyes that belied the laid-back tone of his voice and the casualness of his language.

I climbed into the Jeep and yanked the door shut.

The shotgun was propped between the seats again.

Bobby switched on the headlights and pulled away from the curb.

As we approached the mounded birds, I saw that no wing fluttered any longer, except from the ruffling touch of the gentle breeze.

Neither Bobby nor I had spoken of what we'd witnessed. No words seemed adequate.

Passing the site of the carnage, he kept his eyes on the street ahead, not glancing even once at the dead flock.

I, on the other hand, couldn't look away—and turned to stare back after we had passed.

In my mind's ear, the music came from a piano with only black keys, jangling and discordant.

Finally I turned to face forward. We drove into the fearsome brightness of the Jeep headlamps, but regardless of our speed, we remained always in the dark, hopelessly chasing the light.

10

Dead Town could have passed for a neighborhood in Hell, where the condemned were subjected not to fire and boiling oil but to the more significant punishment of solitude and an eternity of quiet in which to contemplate what might have been. As if we were engaged in a supernatural rescue mission to extract two wrongfully damned souls from Hades, Bobby and I searched the streets for any sign of my furry brother or Lilly's son.

With a powerful handheld spotlight that Bobby plugged into the cigarette lighter, I probed between houses lined up like tombstones. Through cracked or partially broken-out windows, where the reflection of the light glowed like a spirit face. Along bristling brown hedgerows. Among dead shrubs from which leaped bony shadows.

Though the light was directed away from me, the backwash was great enough to be troublesome. My eyes quickly grew tired; they felt strained, grainy. I would have put on my sunglasses, which on some occasions I wear even at night, but a pair of Ray-Bans sure as hell wouldn't facilitate the search.

Cruising slowly, surveying the night, Bobby said, "What's wrong with your face?"

"Sasha says nothing."

"She needs an emergency transfusion of good taste. What're you picking?"

"I'm not picking."

"Didn't your mom ever teach you not to pick at yourself?"

"I'm poking."

While with my right hand I held the pistol-grip spotlight, with my left I'd been unconsciously fingering the sore spot on my face, which I had first discovered a little earlier in the night.

"You see a bruise here?" I asked, indicating the penny-size tenderness on my left cheek.

"Not in this light."

"Sore."

"Well, you've been knocking around."

"This is the way it'll start."

"What?"

"Cancer."

"Probably a pimple."

"First a soreness, then a lesion, and then, because my skin has no defense against it . . . rapid metastasis."

"You're a one-man party," Bobby said.

"Just being realistic."

Turning right into a new street, Bobby said, "What good did being realistic ever do anyone?"

More shabby bungalows. More dead hedgerows.

"Got a headache, too," I said.

"You're giving *me* a full-on skull-splitter."

"One day maybe I'll get a headache that never goes away, from neurological damage caused by XP."

"Dude, you've got more psychosomatic symptoms than Scrooge McDuck has money."

"Thanks for the analysis, Doctor Bob. You know, you've never cut me any slack in seventeen years."

"You never need any."

"Sometimes," I said.

He drove in silence for half a block and then said, "You never bring me flowers anymore."

"What?"

"You never tell me I'm pretty."

I laughed in spite of myself. "Asshole."

"See? You're way cruel."

Bobby stopped the Jeep in the middle of the street.

I looked around alertly. "Something?"

"If I was wrapped in neoprene, man, I wouldn't have to stop," he said, neoprene meaning the wet suit that a surfer wears when the water temp is too nipple for him to hit the waves in only a pair of swimming trunks.

During a long session in cold water, while sitting in the line waiting for a set of glassy, pumping monoliths, surfers from time to time relieve themselves right in their wet suits. The word for it is *urinophoria,* that lovely warm sensation that lasts until the constant but gradual flush of seawater rinses it away.

If surfing isn't the most romantic, glamorous sport *ever,* then I don't know what is. Certainly not golf.

Bobby got out of the Jeep and stepped to the curb, with his back to me. "I hope this bladder pressure doesn't mean I've got cancer."

"You already made your point," I said.

"This bizarre urge to relieve myself. Man, it's . . . it's mondo malignant."

"Just hurry up."

"I probably held it too insanely long, and now I've got uric-acid poisoning."

I had switched off the spotlight. I put it down and picked up the shotgun.

Bobby said, "My kidneys will probably implode, my hair'll fall out, my nose'll drop off. I'm doomed."

"You are if you don't shut up."

"Even if I don't die, what wahine is going to want to date a bald, noseless guy with imploded kidneys?"

The engine noise, the headlights, and the spotlight might have brought us unwanted attention if anyone or anything hostile was in the neighborhood. The troop had hidden at the sound of the Jeep when Bobby had first driven into Wyvern, but perhaps they had done some reconnaissance since then; in which case they were aware that we were only two and that even with guns we were not necessarily a match for a horde of peevish primates. Worse, maybe they realized that one of us was Christopher Snow, son of Wisteria Snow, who perhaps was known to them as Wisteria von Frankenstein.

Bobby zipped up and returned safely to the Jeep. "That's the first time anyone's been prepared to lay down covering fire for me while I peed."

"De nada."

"You feeling better, bro?"

He knew me well enough to understand that my apparent attack of hypochondria was actually unexpressed anxiety for Orson.

I said, "Sorry for acting like a wanker."

Releasing the hand brake, shifting the Jeep into drive, he said, "To wank is human, to forgive is the essence of Bobbyness."

As we rolled slowly forward, I put down the shotgun and picked up the spotlight again. "We're not going to find them like this."

"Better idea?"

Before I could respond, something screamed. The cry was eerie but not entirely alien; worse, it was a disturbing hybrid of the familiar and the unknown. It seemed to be the wail of an animal, yet it had a too-human quality, a forlorn note full of loss and yearning.

Bobby braked again. "Where?"

I had already switched on the spotlight and aimed it across the street, toward where I thought the scream had originated.

The shadows of balusters and roof posts stretched to follow the beam of light, creating the illusion of movement across the front porch of a bungalow. The shadows of bare tree limbs crawled up a clapboard wall.

"Geek alert," Bobby said, and pointed.

I swung the spotlight where he indicated, just in time to catch something racing through tall grass and disappearing behind a long, four-foot-high boxwood hedge that separated the front lawns of four bungalows from the street.

"What is it?" I asked.

"Maybe—what I told you about."

"Big Head?"

"Big Head."

During long hot months without water, the hedge had died, and the quenching rains of the recent winter had not been able to revive it. Although not a lick of green could be seen, a dense snarl of brittle branching remained, with wads of brown leaves lodged here and there like bits of half-masticated meat.

Bobby kept the Jeep in the middle of the street but drove slowly forward, parallel to the hedge.

Even stripped of new growth, the dead boxwood was so mature that its spiny skeleton effectively screened the creature crouched beyond it. I didn't think I was going to be able to pick out the beast at all, but then I spotted it because, although it was a shade of brown similar to the woody veil in front of it, the softer lines of its body contrasted with the jagged patterns of the bare hedge. Through the interstices in the many layers of boxwood bones, I fixed the beam on our quarry, revealing no details but getting a glimpse of eyeshine as green as that of certain cats.

This thing was too big to be any cat other than a mountain lion.

It was no mountain lion.

Found, the creature bleated again and raced along the shielding deadwood with such speed that I couldn't keep the light trained on it. A break in the hedgerow allowed a walkway to connect a bungalow with the street, but Big Head—or Big Foot, or the wolfman, or the Loch Ness monster in drag, or whatever the hell this was—crossed the gap fast, an instant ahead of the light. I didn't get a look at anything but its shaggy ass, and not even a clear view of that, though a clear view of its ass might not have been either informative or gratifying.

All I had were vague impressions. The impression that it ran half erect like a monkey, shoulders sloped forward and head low, the knuckles of its hands almost dragging the ground. That it was a lot bigger than a rhesus. That it might

have been even taller than Bobby had guessed, and that if it
rose to its full height, it would be able to peer at us over the
top of the four-foot hedge and stick its tongue out at us.

I swept the spotlight back and forth but couldn't locate
the critter along the next section of boxwood.

"Running for it," Bobby said, braking to a full stop,
rising half out of his seat, pointing.

When I shifted my focus beyond the hedgerow, I saw a
shapeless figure loping across the yard, away from the street,
toward the corner of the bungalow.

Even when I held the spotlight high, I couldn't get an
angle on the fast-moving beast, whose disappearing act was
abetted by the intervening branches of a laurel and by tall
grass.

Bobby dropped back into his seat, swung toward the
hedgerow, threw the Jeep into four-wheel drive, and tramped
on the accelerator.

"Geek chase," he said.

Because Bobby lives for the moment and because he ex-
pects ultimately to be mulched by something more immediate
than melanoma, he maintains the deepest tan this side of a
skin-cancer ward. By contrast, his teeth and his eyes glow as
white as the plutonium-soaked bones of Chernobyl wildlife,
which usually make him look dashing and exotic and full of
Gypsy spirit, but which now made him look more than a little
like a grinning madman.

"Way stupid," I protested.

"Geek, geek, geek chase," he insisted, leaning into the
steering wheel.

The Jeep jumped the curb, flashed under the low-hanging
branches of two flanking laurels, and crashed through the
boxwood hard enough to rattle the bottles of beer in the
slush-filled cooler, spitting broken hedge branches behind it.
As we crossed the lawn, a raw, sweet, green odor rose from the
crushed grass under the tires, which was lush from the winter
rains.

The creature had disappeared around the side of the bungalow even as we were blasting through the hedge.

Bobby went after it.

"This has nothing to do with Orson or Jimmy," I shouted over the engine roar.

"How do you know?"

He was right. I didn't know. Maybe there was a connection. Anyway, we didn't have any better leads to follow.

As he swung the Jeep between two bungalows, he said, "*Carpe noctem*, remember?"

I had recently told him my new motto. Already, I regretted having revealed it. I had the feeling that it was going to be quoted to me, at inopportune moments, until it had less appeal than a mutton milkshake.

About fifteen feet separated the bungalows, and there were no shrubs in this narrow sward. The headlights would have revealed the critter if it was here; but it was gone.

This vanishment didn't give Bobby second thoughts. Instead, he pressed harder on the accelerator.

We rocketed into the backyard in time to see our own private Sasquatch as it sprang across a picket fence and disappeared into the next property, once more revealing no more of itself than a fleeting glimpse of its hirsute buttocks.

Bobby wasn't any more intimidated by the line of spindly wooden pickets than he had been by the hedgerow. Speeding toward it, he laughed and said, "Skeggin'," meaning *having big-time fun*, which most likely comes from *skeg*, the name for the rudderlike fin on the underside of a surfboard, which allows you to steer and do cool maneuvers.

Although Bobby is laid back and tranquility-loving, ranking as high in the annals of slackerhood as Saddam Hussein ranks in the Insane Dictator Hall of Fame, he's another dude altogether, a huge macking tsunami, once he's committed himself to a line of action. He will sit on a beach for hours, studying wave conditions, looking for sets that will push him to and maybe past his personal threshold, oblivious even to the passing contents of bun-floss bikinis, so focused and patient that he makes one of those Easter Island stone heads seem positively jittery, but when he sees what he needs and paddles his board out to the lineup, he doesn't wallow there like a buoy; he becomes a true raging slashmaster, ripping the waves, domesticating even the hugest thunder crushers, going for it so totally that if any shark mistook him for chum, he'd flip it upside down and ride it like a longboard.

"Skeggin', my ass," I said as we hit the fence.

Weathered white pickets exploded over the hood of the Jeep, rattled across the windshield, clattered against the roll bar, and I was sure that one of them would ricochet at precisely the right angle to skewer one of my eyes and make brain shish kebab, but that didn't happen. Then we were crossing the rear lawn of the house that faced out on the next street in the grid.

The yard we had left behind was smooth, but this one was full of troughs and mounds and chuckholes, over which we rollicked with such exuberance that I had to clamp one hand on my cap to keep it from flying off.

In spite of the serious risk of biting all the way through my tongue if we suddenly bottomed out too hard, I said, in a stutter worthy of Porky Pig, "You see it?"

"On it!" he assured me, though the headlights were arcing up and down so radically with the wildly bucking Jeep that I didn't believe he could see anything smaller than the house around which he was steering us.

I'd switched off the spotlight, because I wasn't illuminating anything except my knees and various galactic nebulae, and if I threw up in my lap, I didn't care to scrutinize the mess under a high beam.

The terrain between bungalows was as rugged as the backyard, and the ground in front of the house proved to be no better. If someone hadn't been burying dead cows on this property, then the gophers must be as big as Holsteins.

We rocked to a halt before reaching the street. There were no hedgerows to hide behind, and the trunks of the Indian laurels weren't thick enough to entirely conceal a bulimic supermodel, let alone Sasquatch.

I switched on the spotlight and swept it left and right along the street. Deserted.

"I thought you were on it," I said.

"Was."

"Now?"

"Not."

"So?"

"New plan," he said.

"I'm waiting."

"*You're* the planning dude," Bobby said, shifting the Jeep into park.

Another weird scream—like fingernails scraping on a chalkboard, the dying wail of a cat, and the sob of a terrified child all woven together and re-created on a malfunctioning synthesizer by a musician whacked on crystal meth—brought us out of our seats, not merely because it was eerie enough to snap our veins like rubber bands, but because it came from behind us.

I was not aware of pulling my legs up, swiveling, gripping the roll bar, and standing on my seat. I must have done so, and with the swift grace of an Olympic gymnast, because that was where I found myself as the scream reached a crescendo and abruptly cut off.

Likewise, I wasn't consciously aware of Bobby grabbing the shotgun, flinging open his door, and leaping out of the Jeep, but there he was, holding the 12-gauge Mossberg, facing back the way we had come.

"Light," he said.

The spotlight was still in my hand. I clicked it on even as he spoke.

No missing link loomed behind the Jeep.

The knee-deep grass swooned as a bare whisper of wind romanced it. If any predator had been trying to squirm toward us, using the grass as cover, it would have disturbed the courtly patterns drawn by the gentle caress of the breeze, and it would have been easy to spot.

The bungalow was one of those that lacked a porch, fronted only by two steps and a stoop, and the door was closed. The three windows were intact, and no boogeyman glowered at us from behind any of those dusty panes.

Bobby said, "It sounded right here."

"Like right under my butt."

He had a solid grip on the shotgun. Looking around at the night, as creeped out as I was by the deceptive peacefulness of it, he said, "This sucks."

"It sucketh," I agreed.

A look of high suspicion crimped his face, and he backed slowly away from the Jeep.

I didn't know if he had glimpsed something under the vehicle or if he was just operating on a hunch.

Dead Town was even more silent than its name implied. The faint breeze was expressive but mute.

Still standing on the passenger seat, I glanced down along the side of the Jeep, at the lazily undulating blades of grass. If some foul-tempered freak erupted from beneath the vehicle, it could climb the door and be at my neck before I would be able to locate either a crucifix or an even halfway attractive necklace of garlic.

I needed only one hand for the spotlight. I slipped the Glock out of my shoulder holster.

When Bobby had backed off three or four steps from the Jeep, he knelt on one knee.

To throw a little light where he needed to peek, I held the spotlight out of the Jeep and directed the beam toward the undercarriage on my side, hoping to backlight whatever might be hiding there.

In the classic, wary half-kneel of the experienced monster hunter, Bobby tilted his head and slowly lowered it to peer under the Jeep.

"Nada," he said.

"Zip?"

"Zero."

"I was stoked," I said.

"I was pumped."

"Ready to kick ass."

We were lying.

As Bobby rose to his feet, another scream tore the night: the same scraping-fingernails-dying-cat-sobbing-child-malfunctioning-synthesizer wail that had made us jump like light-ning-struck cats only moments ago.

This time I had a better fix on the source of the scream, and I shifted my attention to the bungalow roof, where the spotlight revealed Big Head. There was no question now: This was the creature that Bobby had called Big Head, because its head was undeniably big.

It was crouched at one end of the roof, right on the peak, maybe sixteen feet above us, like Kong on the Empire State Building but re-created in a direct-to-video flick that lacked the budget for a larger set, fighter planes, or even a damsel in peril. With its arms covering its face as though the sight of us hideous human beings frightened and disgusted it, Big Head studied Bobby and me with radiant green eyes, which we could see through the gap between its crossed arms.

Even though the beast's face was covered, I could discern that the head was disproportionately large for the body. I also suspected that it was malformed. Malformed not just by human standards but surely by the standards of monkey beauty, as well.

I couldn't determine whether it had been spawned primarily from a rhesus or from another primate. It was covered in matted fur not unlike that of a rhesus, with long arms and hunched shoulders that were definitely simian, although it appeared to be stronger than any mere monkey, as formidable as a gorilla though otherwise nothing like one. You wouldn't have required my hyperactive imagination to wonder if, in certain aspects of the creature, you were glimpsing a spectrum of species so broad that the genetic sampling had extended beyond the warm-blooded classes of vertebrates to include reptilian traits—and worse.

"Extreme geek-a-mo," Bobby said as he edged back to the Jeep.

"Major geekster," I agreed.

On the roof, Big Head turned its face skyward, as if studying the stars, still concealing its features behind the mask of its arms.

Suddenly I found myself identifying with this creature. Its

posture, its very attitude, told me that it was covering its face out of embarrassment or shame, that it didn't want us to see what it looked like because it knew we would find it repulsive, which meant that it must *feel* repulsive. Perhaps I was able to interpret its behavior and intuit its feelings because I'd lived twenty-eight years as an outsider. I'd never felt the need to hide my face, but as a small child I'd known the pain of being an outcast when cruel kids called me Nightcrawler, Dracula, Ghoul Boy, and worse.

Echoing in my mind was my own voice from a moment ago—*major geekster*—and I winced. Our pursuit of this creature reminded me of the way bullies had chased me when I'd been a boy. Even when I had learned to defend myself and fight back, they were sometimes not dissuaded, willing to risk a drubbing merely for the chance to harass and torment me. Of course, with Orson and Jimmy in peril, Bobby and I had good reason to follow any lead. We hadn't been motivated by meanness; but what troubled me, in retrospect, was the strange dark wild delight with which we had mounted the chase.

The stargazer shifted its attention from the heavens and peered down at us again, still hiding its face.

I directed the spotlight onto the asphalt shingles near the creature's feet, letting the backwash illuminate it rather than directly assaulting it with the beam.

My discretion didn't encourage Big Head to lower its arms. It did, however, issue a sound unlike the previous screams, one at odds with its fierce appearance: a cross between the cooing of pigeons and the more guttural purr of a cat.

Bobby tore his attention away from the beast long enough to conduct a three-hundred-sixty-degree sweep of the neighborhood around us.

I, too, had been stricken by the nape-crinkling feeling that Big Head might be distracting us from a more immediate threat.

"Super placid," Bobby reported.

"For now."

Big Head's cooing-purring grew louder and then became a fluent series of exotic sounds, simple and rhythmic and patterned, but not like mere animal noises. These were modulated groups of syllables, full of inflection, delivered with urgency and emotion, and it was no stretch to think of them as *words.* If this speech wasn't complex enough to be defined as a language in the sense that English, French, or Spanish is a language, it was at least a primitive attempt to convey meaning, a language in the making.

"What's it want?" Bobby asked.

His question, whether he realized it or not, arose from the perception that the creature was not just chattering at us but *speaking* to us.

"No clue," I said.

Big Head's voice was neither deep nor menacing. Although as strange as a bagpipe employed by a reggae band, it was pitched like that of a child of nine or ten, not entirely human but halfway there, edgy, eerily lilting without being musical, with a pleading note that aroused sympathy in spite of the source.

"Poor sonofabitch," I said, as it fell silent again.

"You serious?"

"Sorrowful damn thing."

Bobby studied this Quasimodo in search of a bell tower and finally allowed, "Maybe."

"Certified sorrowful."

"You want to go up on the roof, give it a big hug?"

"Later."

"I'll turn on the Jeep's radio. You can go up there and ask it to dance, make it feel attractive."

"I'll pity it from afar."

"Typical man. You talk a good game of compassion, but you can't play it."

"I'm afraid of rejection."

"You're afraid of commitment."

Turning away from us, Big Head dropped its arms from its face. On all fours, straddling the ridgeline, it raced across the bungalow roof.

"Keep the light on it!" Bobby said.

I tried, but the creature moved quicker than a striking snake. I expected it to launch itself off the roof and straight at us or disappear across the peak and down the far slope, but it traveled the length of the ridgeline and sprang without hesitation into the fifteen-foot gap between this bungalow and the next. With catlike poise, it landed atop the neighboring house, where it reared onto its hind legs, cast a green-eyed glance back at us, then dropped low, sprinted from gable to gable, leaped to a third roof, crossed over that ridgeline, and disappeared onto the back of the house.

During its swift flight, captured repeatedly by the spotlight beam but for only an instant at a time, the creature's face had been less than half revealed in kaleidoscopic glimpses. I was left with impressions rather than clear images. The back of its skull seemed to be elongated, and like a cowl, its forehead appeared to overhang its large sunken eyes. The lumpish face might have been distorted by excrescences of bone. To an even greater degree than the head was disproportionate to the body, the mouth appeared too large for the head. Cracking its steam-shovel jaws, the creature revealed an abundance of sharp curved teeth more wicked-looking than Jack the Ripper's cutlery collection.

Bobby gave me a chance to reconsider my assessment of Big Head. "Sorrowful?"

"I still think so."

"You're nothing but cardiac muscle, dude."

"Lub-dub."

"Anything moves that fast, teeth that big—its diet isn't just fruits, vegetables, and whole grains."

I switched off the handheld spot. Although the beam had been directed away from me, I was groggy from a surfeit of light. I had not seen much, yet I'd seen too much.

Neither of us suggested going on another Big Head hunt. Surfers don't trade bite for bite with sharks; when we see enough fins, we get out of the water. Considering this creature's speed and agility, we wouldn't have a chance of catching it, anyway, not on foot or in the Jeep, and even if we did find and corner it, we weren't prepared to capture or kill it.

"Supposing we don't just want to sit here sucking down beer and trying to forget we saw anything," Bobby wondered as he got behind the wheel.

"Suppose."

"Then what was that thing?"

Settling into the passenger seat again, working my feet around the beer cooler, I said, "Could be an offspring of the original troop that escaped from the lab. There might be bigger, stranger mutations occurring in the new generation."

"We've seen beaucoup offspring before. And you saw a bunch earlier tonight, right?"

"Yeah."

"They look like normal monkeys."

"Yeah."

"This was awesomely not normal."

I knew now what Big Head was, where it had come from, but I wasn't ready to tell Bobby quite yet. Instead, I said, "This is the street where they trapped me in the bungalow."

Assessing the sameness of the houses around us, he said, "You can tell one of these streets from another?"

"Mostly."

"Then you're spending a seriously psychotic amount of time here, bro."

"Nothing hot on TV."

"Try stamp collecting."

"Couldn't handle the excitement."

As Bobby drove off the rutted lawn and over the curb, into the street, I holstered the 9-millimeter Glock and told him to turn right.

Two blocks later, I said, "Stop. Here. This is where they were spinning the manhole cover."

"If they take over the world, they'll probably make that an Olympic event."

"At least it's more exciting than synchronized swimming."

As I got out of the Jeep, he said, "Where you going?"

"Pull forward and park with one wheel on the manhole. I don't think they're still here. They've moved on. But just in case, I don't want them coming up behind us while we're inside."

"Inside what?"

I walked in front of the vehicle and directed Bobby until he stopped with the right front tire squarely atop the manhole cover.

He switched off the engine and, with the shotgun, got out of the Jeep.

The weak onshore breeze grew a little stronger, and the clouds in the west, which had swallowed the moon, were gradually expanding eastward, devouring the stars.

"Inside what?" Bobby repeated.

I pointed to the bungalow where I'd squeezed into the broom closet to hide from the troop. "I want to see what was rotting in the kitchen."

"Want to?"

"Need to," I said, heading toward the bungalow.

"Perverse," he said, falling in beside me.

"The troop was fascinated."

"We want to lower ourselves to monkey level?"

"Maybe this is important."

He said, "My belly's full of kibby and beer."

"So?"

"Just a friendly warning, bro. Right now I've got a low puke threshold."

11

The front door of the bungalow was open, as I had left it. The living room still smelled of dust, mildew, dry rot, and mice; in addition, there was now a lingering odor of mangy monkey.

My flashlight, which I'd not dared to use here before, revealed a series of three-inch-long, yellowish-white cocoons fixed in the angle where the back wall met the ceiling, home to developing moths or butterflies, or perhaps egg cases spun by an exceptionally fertile spider. Lighter rectangles on the discolored walls marked where pictures had once hung. The plaster wasn't as fissured as you would expect in a house that was more than six decades old and that had been abandoned for nearly two years, but a web of fine cracks gave the walls the appearance of eggshells beginning to give way to hatching entities.

On the floor, in a corner, was a child's red sock. It couldn't have anything to do with Jimmy, because it was caked with dust and had been here for a long time.

As we crossed to the dining-room door, Bobby said, "Got a new board yesterday."

"The world's ending, you go shopping."

"Friends at Hobie made it for me."

"Hot?" I asked as I led him into the dining room.

"Haven't ridden it yet."

In one corner, at the ceiling, was a cluster of cocoons similar to those in the previous room. They were also big, each three to four inches long and, at the widest point, approximately the diameter of plump frankfurters.

Outside of this bungalow, I had never seen anything quite like these silken constructs. I moved directly under them, fixing them with the light.

"Not uncreepy," Bobby said.

Within a couple of the cocoons were dark shapes, curled like question marks, but they were so heavily swaddled in flossy filaments that I could make out no details of them.

"See anything moving?" I asked.

"No."

"Me neither."

"Might be dead."

"Yeah," I said, though I wasn't convinced. "Just some big, dead, half-made moths."

"Moths?"

"What else?" I asked.

"Huge."

"Maybe new moths. A new, bigger species. Becoming."

"Bugs? Becoming?"

"If people, dogs, birds, monkeys . . . why not bugs?"

Frowning, Bobby thought about that. "Probably wouldn't be smart to buy any more wool sweaters."

A cold quiver of nausea wound through me as I realized that I'd been in these rooms in absolute darkness, unaware of the fat cocoons overhead. I'm not entirely sure why I found this thought so deeply disturbing. After all, it wasn't likely that I'd been in danger of being pinned to the wall by some bug and imprisoned in a suffocating cocoon of my own. On the other hand, this was Wyvern, so perhaps I'd been in precisely such danger.

Partly, the nausea was caused by the stench wafting from the kitchen. I'd forgotten how fiercely ripe it was.

Holding the shotgun in his right hand, covering his nose and mouth with his left, Bobby said, "Tell me the stink doesn't get worse than this."

"It doesn't get worse than this."

"But it does."

"Oh, yeah."

"Let's be quick."

Just as I moved the flashlight away from the cocoons, I thought I saw one of the dark, curled forms writhe inside its silken sac.

I focused the beam on the cluster again.

None of the mystery bugs moved.

Bobby said, "Jumpy?"

"Aren't you?"

"As a toad."

We ventured into the kitchen, where the linoleum cracked and popped underfoot and where the reek of decomposition was as thick in the air as a cloud of vaporized, rancid cooking oil in the kitchen of a greasy-spoon restaurant.

Before searching for the source of the stench, I directed the light overhead. The upper cabinets hung under a soffit, and in the angle where the soffit met the ceiling, there were more cocoons than in the previous two rooms combined. Thirty or forty. Most were in the three-to-four-inch range, though a few were half again as large. Another twenty were nestled around the boxy fluorescent fixture in the center of the ceiling.

"Not good," Bobby said.

I lowered the flashlight and at once discovered the source of the putrescent smell. A dead man was sprawled on the floor in front of the sink.

At first I thought he must have been killed by whatever made the cocoons. I expected to see a wad of spun silk in his open mouth, yellowish-white sacs bulging from his ears, wispy filaments trailing from his nose.

The cocoons, however, had nothing to do with it. This was a suicide.

The revolver lay on his abdomen, where recoil and death spasm had tossed it, and the swollen index finger of his right hand was still hooked through the trigger guard. Judging by the wound in his throat, he'd put the muzzle under his chin and fired one round straight up into his brain.

Entering the lightless kitchen earlier in the night, I had

gone directly to the back door, where I'd halted with my hand on the knob when a monkey shadow leaped up the glass. Approaching the door and backing away from it, I must have come within inches of stepping on this corpse.

"This what you expected?" Bobby asked, voice muffled by the hand with which he was trying to filter the sickening odor.

"No."

I didn't know what I'd expected, but I was sure this wasn't the worst thing that had been lurking in the deepest cellars of my imagination. When I'd first seen the cadaver, I'd been relieved—as though subconsciously I had envisioned a specific and far worse discovery than this, an ultimate horror that now I would not have to confront.

Dressed in generic white athletic shoes, chinos, and a red-and-green plaid shirt, the dead man was flat on his back, his left arm at his side, the palm turned up as though seeking alms. He appeared to have been fat, because his clothes were stretched taut over parts of his body, but this was the result of swelling from bacterial-gas formation.

His face was bloated, opaque eyes bulging from the sockets, swollen tongue protruding between grimacing lips and bared teeth. Purge fluid—produced by decomposition and often mistaken for blood by the inexperienced—was draining from the mouth and nostrils. Pale green with areas of greenish black, the flesh was also marbleized by hemolysis of veins and arteries.

Bobby said, "Must've been here—what?—a week, two weeks?"

"Not that long. Maybe three or four days."

The weather had been mild for the past week, neither warm nor chilly, which would have allowed decomposition to proceed at a predictable pace. If the man had been dead much longer than four days, the flesh would have been not pale green but green-black, with patches that were entirely black. Vesicle formation, skin slippage, and hair slippage had occurred but were not yet extreme, enabling me to make an educated guess as to the date of the suicide.

"Still walking around with *Forensic Pathology* in your head," Bobby said.

"Still."

My education in death dated to the year I was fourteen. By the time they enter their teens, most boys have a morbid fascination with gruesome comic books, horror novels, and monster movies. Adolescent males measure progress toward manhood by their ability to tolerate the worst gross-outs, those sights and ideas that test courage, the balance of the mind, and the gag reflex. In those days, Bobby and I were fans of H. P. Lovecraft, of the biologically moist art of H. R. Giger, and of low-budget Mexican horror movies full of gore.

We outgrew this fascination to an extent that we didn't outgrow other aspects of our adolescence, but in those days I explored death further than did Bobby, progressing from bad movies to the study of increasingly clinical texts. I learned the history and techniques of mummification and embalming, the lurid details of epidemics like the Black Death that killed half of Europe between 1348 and 1350.

I realize now that by immersing myself in the study of death, I had hoped to accept my mortality. Long before adolescence, I knew that each of us is sand in an hourglass, steadily running out of the upper globe into the stillness of the globe below, and that in my particular hourglass, the neck between these spheres is wider than in most, the fall of sand faster. This was a heavy truth to have been carried by one so young, but by becoming a graveyard scholar, I meant to rob death of its terror.

In recognition of the steep mortality rate of people with XP, my special parents had raised me to play rather than work, to have fun, to regard the future not with anxiety but with a sense of mystery. From them, I learned to trust God, to believe I was born for a purpose, to be joyful. Consequently, Mom and Dad were disturbed by my obsession with death, but because they were academics with a belief in the liberating power of knowledge, they didn't hamper my pursuit of the subject.

Indeed, I relied on Dad to acquire the book that completed my death studies: *Forensic Pathology*, published by Elsevier in a series of thick volumes written for law-enforcement professionals involved in criminal investigations. This grisly tome, generously illustrated with victim photographs that will chill the hottest heart and instill pity in all but the coldest, is not on the shelves of most libraries and is not knowingly provided to children. At fourteen, with a life expectancy thought to be—at that time—no greater than twenty, I could have argued that I was not a child but already past middle age.

Forensic Pathology covers the myriad ways we perish: disease, death by fire, death by freezing, by drowning, by electrocution, by poisoning, by starvation, by suffocation, by strangulation, death from gunshot wounds, from blunt-instrument trauma, from pointed and sharp-edged weapons. By the time I finished this book, I'd outgrown my fascination with death . . . and my fear of it. The photos depicting the indignity of decomposition proved that the qualities I cherish in the people I love—their wit, humor, courage, loyalty, faith, compassion, mercy—are not ultimately the work of the flesh. These things outlast the body; they live on in the memories of family and friends, live on forever by inspiring others to be kind and loving. Humor, faith, courage, compassion—these don't rot and vanish; they are impervious to bacteria, stronger than time or gravity; they have their genesis in something less fragile than blood and bone, in a soul that endures.

Though I believe that I'll live beyond this life and that those I love will be where I go next, I *do* still fear that they will depart ahead of me, leaving me alone. Sometimes I wake from a nightmare in which I'm the sole living person on earth; I lie in bed, trembling, afraid to call out for Sasha or to use the telephone, fearful that no one will answer and that the dream will have become reality.

Now, here, in the bungalow kitchen, Bobby said, "Hard to believe he could be this far gone in three or four days."

"Exposed to the elements, complete skeletonization can occur in two weeks. Eleven or twelve days under the right circumstances."

"So at any time . . . I'm two weeks from being bones."

"It's a quashing thought, isn't it?"

"Major quash."

Having seen more than enough of the dead man, I directed the flashlight at the items that he evidently had arranged on the floor around himself before pulling the trigger. A California driver's license with photo identification. A paperback Bible. An ordinary white business envelope on which nothing was written or typed. Four snapshots in a neatly ordered row. A small ruby-red glass of the type that usually contains votive candles, though no candle was in this one.

Learning to live with nausea, trying to will myself to recall the scent of roses, I crouched for a closer look at the driver's-license photo. In spite of the decomposition, the cadaver's face had sufficient points of similarity to the face on the license to convince me that they were the same.

"Leland Anthony Delacroix," I said.

"Don't know him."

"Thirty-five years old."

"Not anymore."

"Address in Monterey."

"Why'd he come here to die?" Bobby wondered.

In hope of finding an answer, I turned the light on the four snapshots.

The first showed a pretty blonde of about thirty, wearing white shorts and a bright yellow blouse, standing on a marina dock against a backdrop of blue sky, blue water, and sailboats. Her gamine smile was appealing.

The second evidently had been taken on a different day, in a different place. This same woman, now in a polka-dot blouse, and Leland Delacroix were sitting side by side at a redwood picnic table. His arm was around her shoulders, and she was smiling at him as he faced the camera. Delacroix appeared to be happy, and the blonde looked like a woman in love.

"His wife," Bobby said.

"Maybe."

"She's wearing a wedding ring in the picture."

The third snapshot featured two children: a boy of about

six and an elfin girl who could have been no older than four. In swimsuits, they stood beside an inflatable wading pool, mugging for the camera.

"Wanted to die surrounded by memories of his family," Bobby suggested.

The fourth snapshot seemed to support that interpretation. The blonde, the children, and Delacroix stood on a green lawn, the kids in front of their parents, posed for a portrait. The occasion must have been special. Even more radiant here than in the other photos, the woman wore a summery dress and high heels. The little girl flashed a gap-toothed smile, clearly delighted by her outfit of white shoes, white socks, and a frilly pink dress flaring over petticoats. So freshly scrubbed and combed that you could almost smell the soap, the boy wore a blue suit, white shirt, and red bow tie. In an army uniform and an officer's cap—his rank not easy to determine, perhaps a captain—Delacroix was the definition of pride.

Precisely because the subjects were so visibly happy in these shots, the effect of the photos was inexpressibly sad.

"They're standing in front of one of these bungalows," Bobby noted, indicating the background of the fourth snapshot.

"Not one of them. *This* one."

"How can you tell?"

"Gut feeling."

"So they lived here once?"

"And he came back to die."

"Why?"

"Maybe . . . this was the last place he was ever happy."

Bobby said, "Which also means this was where it all started going wrong."

"Not just for them. For all of us."

"Where do you think the wife and kids are?"

"Dead."

"Gut feeling again?"

"Yeah."

"Me too."

Something glittered inside the small red votive-candle glass. I prodded it with the flashlight, tipping it over. A woman's wedding and engagement rings spilled out onto the linoleum.

These items were all Delacroix had left of his beloved wife, other than a few photographs. Perhaps I was reaching too far for meaning, but I thought he had chosen the votive-candle holder to contain the rings because this was a way of saying that the woman and the marriage were sacred to him.

I looked again at the photograph that had been taken in front of the bungalow. The elfin girl's wide smile, with one missing tooth, was a heartbreaker.

"Jesus," I said softly.

"Let's split, bro."

I didn't want to touch these objects the deceased had arranged around himself, but the contents of the envelope might be important. As far as I could see, it wasn't contaminated with blood or other tissue. When I picked it up, I could discern by touch that it didn't hold any paper documents.

"Audiotape cassette," I told Bobby.

"A little death music?"

"Probably his last testament."

In ordinary times, before a slow-motion Armageddon was unleashed in Wyvern's labs, I would have called the cops to report finding a dead body. I would not have removed anything from the scene, even though the death had every appearance of being a suicide rather than a homicide.

These are not ordinary times.

As I rose to my feet, I slipped the envelope—and tape—into an inside jacket pocket.

Bobby's attention snapped to the ceiling, and he took a two-hand grip on the shotgun.

I followed his gaze with the flashlight.

The cocoons appeared unchanged, so I said, "What?"

"Did you hear something?"

"Like?"

He listened. Finally he said, "Must've been in my head."

"What did you hear?"

"Me," he said cryptically, and without further explanation, he moved toward the dining-room door.

I felt bad about leaving the late Leland Delacroix here, especially as I wasn't sure that I would report his suicide to the authorities even anonymously. On the other hand, this was where he had wanted to be.

On the way across the dining room, Bobby said, "This baby's eleven feet long."

Overhead, the clustered cocoons remained quiescent.

"What baby?" I asked.

"My new surfboard."

Even a longboard is rarely more than nine feet. An eleven-foot monster with cool airbrush art was usually a wallhanger, produced to lend atmosphere to a theme restaurant.

"Decor?" I asked.

"No. It's a tandem board."

In the living room, the cocoons were as we had last seen them. Bobby cast wary glances upward as he went to the front door.

"Twenty-five inches wide, five inches thick," he said.

Maneuvering a surfboard that size, even with two hundred fifty or three hundred pounds aboard, required talent, coordination, and belief in a benign, ordered universe.

"Tandem?" I said, switching off the flashlight as we crossed the front porch. "Since when have you traded wave thrashing for cab driving?"

"Since never. But a little tandem might be sweet."

If he was going to do some tandem riding, he must have a partner in mind, a particular wahine. Yet the only woman he loves is a surfer and painter named Pia Klick, who has been meditating in Waimea Bay, Hawaii, trying to find herself, for almost three years, since leaving Bobby's bed one night for a walk on the beach. Bobby didn't know she was lost until she called from an airliner on her way to Waimea to say the search for herself had begun. She is as kind, gentle, and intelligent as anyone I have ever known, a talented and successful artist. Yet she believes that Waimea Bay is her spiritual home—not Oskaloosa, Kansas, where she was born and raised; not Moonlight Bay, where she fell in love with Bobby—and lately she claims that she is the incarnation of Kaha Huna, the goddess of surfing.

These were strange times even before the catastrophe in the Wyvern labs.

We stopped at the foot of the porch steps and took slow deep breaths to purge ourselves of the reek of death, which seemed to have permeated us as though it were a marinade in which we had been steeping. We also took advantage of the moment to survey the night before venturing farther into it, looking for Big Head, the troop, or a new threat that even I, in full hyperdrive of the imagination, could not envision.

Rolling off the loom of the Pacific, two strata of cross-woven clouds, as twilled as gabardine, now dressed more than half the sky.

"Could get a boat," Bobby said.

"What kind of boat?"

"We could afford whatever."

"And?"

"Stay at sea."

"Extreme solution, bro."

"Sail by day, party by night. Drop anchor off deserted beaches, catch some tasty tropical waves."

"You, me, Sasha, and Orson?"

"Pick up Pia at Waimea Bay."

"Kaha Huna."

"Won't hurt to have a sea goddess aboard," he said.

"Fuel?"

"Sail."

"Food?"

"Fish."

"Fish can carry the retrovirus, too."

"Then find a remote island."

"How remote?"

"The sphincter of nowhere."

"And?"

"Grow our own food."

"Farmer Bob."

"Minus the bib overalls."

"Shitkicker chic."

"Self-sufficiency. It's possible," he insisted.

"So is killing a grizzly bear with a spear. But you get in a pit with a spear, put the bear in there with some tortillas, and that bear is going to have Bobby tacos for dinner."

"Not if I take a class in bear killing."

"So before you set sail, you're going to spend four years at a good college of agriculture?"

Bobby sucked in a breath deep enough to ventilate his upper intestine, and blew it out. "All I know is, I don't want to end up like Delacroix."

"Everyone ever born into this world ends up like Delacroix," I said. "But it's not an end. It's just an exit. To what comes next."

He was silent a moment. Then: "I'm not sure I believe in that like you do, Chris."

"So you believe you can ride through the end of the world by growing potatoes and broccoli on an uncharted tropical island somewhere east of Bora Bora, where there's both insanely fertile soil and mondo glassy surf—but you find it hard to believe in an afterlife?"

He shrugged. "Most days, it's easier to believe in broccoli than in God."

"Not for me. I hate broccoli."

Bobby turned toward the bungalow. His face crinkled as if he could still detect a trace of decomposing Delacroix. "This here is one evil piece of real estate, bro."

Imaginary mites crawled between the layers of my skin as I remembered the pendulant cocoons, and I had to agree with him: "Bad mojo."

"Looks super-burnable."

"Whatever they are, I doubt the cocoons are only in this one bungalow."

In their sameness and orderly placement, the houses of Dead Town suddenly seemed less like man-made structures and more like the mounds of termite colonies or hives.

"Burn this one for starters," Bobby insisted.

Hissing in the knee-high grass, ticking-clicking in the dead twigs of the withered shrubbery, buzzing and rasping in the leaves of the Indian laurels, the breeze mimicked a multitude of insect sounds, as though mocking us, as though predicting the inevitability of a future inhabited solely by six-, eight-, and hundred-legged beings.

"Okay," I said. "We'll burn the place."

"Too bad we don't have a nuke."

"But not now. It'll draw cops and firemen from town, and we don't want them in our way. Besides, there's not a lot of the night left. We've got to get moving."

As we followed the walkway toward the street, he said, "Where?"

I had no idea how to search more effectively for Jimmy Wing and Orson in the vastness of Fort Wyvern, so I didn't respond to his question.

The answer was tucked under the passenger-side windshield wiper on the Jeep. I saw it as I was rounding the front of the vehicle. It looked like a parking ticket.

I plucked the item from under the rubber blade and switched on the flashlight to examine it.

When I got into the passenger seat, Bobby leaned over to study my discovery. "Who put it there?"

"Not Delacroix," I said, surveying the night, once more overcome by the feeling that I was being watched.

I was holding a four-inch-square, laminated security badge designed to be pinned to a shirt or to a coat lapel. The photograph on the right half was of Delacroix, although this was a different picture from the one on the driver's license we had found beside his body. He was wide-eyed in this shot, startled, as though he had foreseen his suicide in the flash of the camera. Under the photo was the name *Leland Anthony Delacroix*. Listed on the left of the badge were his age, height, weight, eye color, hair color, and social security number. At the top were the words *initialize on entry*. Printed across the entire face of the badge, in a three-dimensional hologram that did not obscure the photograph or the information under it, were three transparent, pale-blue capital letters: DOD.

"Department of Defense," I said, because my mom had possessed a DOD security clearance, although I'd never seen a badge like this in her possession.

" 'Initialize on entry,' " Bobby said thoughtfully. "Bet there's a microchip implanted in this."

He's computer literate, but I never will be. I have no need for a computer, and with my biological clock ticking faster than yours, I have no time for one. Besides, while wearing heavy-duty sunglasses, I can't easily read a monitor. Sitting for long sessions in front of a screen, you are bathed in low-level UV radiation no more dangerous to you than a spring rain; because of my susceptibility to cumulative damage, however, exposure to those emissions is liable to transform me into one giant lumpy melanoma of such peculiar squishy dimensions that I'll never be able to find clothes that are both comfortable and stylish.

Bobby said, "When he enters the facility, they initialize the microchip in the badge, you know?"

"No."

"Initialize—clear the memory on the microchip. Then every time he passes through a doorway, maybe the chip in the badge responds to microwave transmitters in the threshold, recording where he went and how long he stayed in each place. Then when he leaves, the data is downloaded into his file."

"You creep me out when you talk computer."

"I'm still the same full-on jerk-off, bro."

"I get evil-twin vibes."

"There's just one Bobby," he assured me.

I glanced at the bungalow where we had found Delacroix, half expecting to see eerie lights beyond the windows, frenzied bug-wing shadows flitting up the walls, and a shambling cadaver crossing the porch.

Snapping a finger against the badge, I said, "Tracking every step he makes even after they let him through the front door—that's maximum-paranoid security."

"This must've been on the floor beside the corpse with

the other stuff. Somebody went in the bungalow ahead of us, took it, and put it here. Why?"

The answer was to be found in the line at the bottom of the badge. *Project Clearance: MT.*

Bobby said, "You think this ID got him into the labs where they were doing these genetic experiments, the very place where the shit hit the fan?"

"Maybe. MT. Mystery Train?"

Bobby glanced at the words embroidered on my cap, then at the badge again. "Nancy Drew would be proud."

I switched off the flashlight. "I think I know where he wants us to go."

"Where who wants us to go?"

"Whoever left this under the wiper."

"Which is who?"

"I don't have *all* the answers, bro."

"Yet you're positive there's an afterlife," he said as he started the engine.

"The big answers I have. It's just some of the little ones that elude me."

"Okay, where are we going?"

"The egg room."

"So now we're in a Batman movie, and you're the Riddler?"

"It's not in Dead Town. It's in a hangar on the north side of the base."

"Egg room."

"You'll see."

"He's not our friend," Bobby said.

"He who?"

"Whoever left that badge, bro, he's no friend of ours. We don't have friends in this place."

"I'm not so sure of that."

As he released the hand brake and shifted into drive, he said, "Could be a trap."

"Probably not. He could've disabled the Jeep and been laying for us right here when we came out of the bungalow, if all he wanted was to waste us."

Driving out of Dead Town, Bobby said, "Still could be a trap."

"Okay, maybe."

"That doesn't bother you like it does me, 'cause you've got God and an afterlife and choirs of angels and palaces of gold in the sky, but all I've got is broccoli."

"Better think about that," I agreed.

I consulted my watch. Dawn was no more than two hours away.

As dark and mottled as a strange fungus, spongy masses of clouds had spread far into the east, leaving only a narrow band of clean sky in which the bright stars looked cold and even farther away than they actually were.

For more than two years, Wisteria Jane Snow's gene-swapping retrovirus had been loose in the wider world beyond the laboratory. During that time, the destruction of the natural order had progressed almost as lazily as big fluffy snow-flakes drifting out of a windless winter sky, but I suspected that at last the blizzard was at hand, the avalanche.

12

The hangar rises like a temple to some alien god with a wrathful disposition, surrounded on three sides by smaller service buildings that could pass for the humble dwellings of monks and novitiates. It is as long and wide as a football field, seven stories high, with no windows other than a line of narrow clerestory panes just below the spring line of the arched Quonset-style roof.

Bobby parked in front of a pair of doors at one end of the building, switching off the engine and headlights.

Each door is twenty feet wide and forty high. Set in upper and lower tracks, they were motor-driven, but the power to operate them was disconnected long ago.

The daunting mass of the building and the enormous steel doors make the place as forbidding as the fortress that might stand at the gap between this world and Hell to keep the demons from getting out.

Taking a flashlight from under his seat, Bobby said, "This place is the egg room?"

"Under this place."

"I don't like the look of it."

"I'm not asking you to move in and set up housekeeping."

Getting out of the Jeep, he said, "Are we near the airfield?"

Fort Wyvern, which was established as both a training

and a support facility, boasts runways that can accommodate large jets and those giant C-13 transports that are capable of carrying trucks, assault vehicles, and tanks.

"Airfield's half a mile that way," I said, pointing. "They didn't service aircraft here. Unless maybe choppers, but I don't think that's what this place was about, either."

"What *was* it about?"

"Don't know."

"Maybe it's where they held bingo games."

In spite of the negative aura around the building, in spite of the fact that we had perhaps been induced here by persons unknown and possibly hostile, I didn't feel as though we were in imminent danger. Anyway, Bobby's shotgun would stop any assailant a lot faster than my 9-millimeter. Leaving the Glock holstered, carrying only the flashlight, I led the way to a man-size door set in one of the larger portals.

"Big surf coming," Bobby said.

"Guess or fact?"

"Fact."

Bobby earns a living by analyzing weather-satellite data and other information to predict surf conditions worldwide, with a high degree of accuracy. His enterprise, Surfcast, provides information daily to tens of thousands of surfers through subscriptions to a bulletin sent by fax or E-mail, and through a 900 number that draws more than eight hundred thousand calls a year. Because his lifestyle is simple and his corporate offices are funky, no one in Moonlight Bay realizes that he is a multimillionaire and the richest man in town. If they knew, it would matter more to them than it does to Bobby. To him, wealth is having every day free to surf; everything else that money can buy is no more than an extra spoon of salsa on the enchilada.

"Gonna be minimum ten-foot corduroy to the horizon," Bobby promised. "Some sets of twelve, pumping all day and night, every boardhead's dream."

"Don't like this onshore flow," I said, raising a hand in the breeze.

"I'm talking the day after tomorrow. Strictly offshore by

then. Gonna be waves so scooped out, you'll feel like the last pickle in the barrel."

The hollow channel in a breaking wave, scooped to the max by a perfect offshore wind, is called a barrel, and surfers live to ride these tubes all the way through and out the collapsing end before being clamshelled. You don't get them every day. They are a gift, sacred, and when they come, you ride them until you're surfed out, until your legs are rubber and you can't stop the muscles in your stomach from fluttering, and then you flop on the sand and wait to see if you'll expire like a beached fish or, instead, go scarf down two burritos and a bowl of corn chips.

"Twelve-footers," I said wistfully as I opened the man-size entrance in the forty-foot-high door. "*Double* overhead corduroy."

"Churning out of a storm north of the Marquesas Islands."

"Something to live for," I said as I crossed the threshold into the hangar.

"That's why I mention it, bro. Boardhead motivation to get out of here alive."

Even two flashlights could not illuminate this cavernous space on the main floor of the hangar, but we could see the overhead tracks on which a mobile crane—long since dismantled and hauled away—had traveled from one end of the building to the other. The massiveness of the steel supports under these rails indicated that the crane had lifted objects of tremendous weight.

We stepped over inch-thick steel angle plates, still anchored to the oil- and chemical-stained concrete, upon which heavy machinery had once been mounted. Deep and curiously shaped wells in the floor, which must have housed hydraulic mechanisms, forced us to follow an indirect path to the far end of the hangar.

Bobby cautiously checked out each hole as though he expected something to be crouching in it, waiting to spring up and bite off our heads.

As our flashlight beams swept over the crane tracks and

their supporting structures, complex shadows and flares of light were flung off steel rails and beams, thrown to the walls and to the high curved ceiling, where they formed faint, constantly changing hieroglyphics that flickered ahead of us but quickly vanished, unreadable, into the darkness that crept at our heels.

"Sharky," Bobby said softly.

"Just wait." Like him, I spoke only slightly above a whisper, not so much for fear of being overheard as because this place has the same subduing effect as do churches, hospitals, and funeral parlors.

"You been here alone?"

"No. Always with Orson."

"I'd expect *him* to have more sense."

I led him to an empty elevator shaft and a wide set of stairs in the southwest corner of the hangar.

As in the warehouse where I'd encountered the *veve* rats and the thug with the two-by-four, access to the floors below had surely been concealed. The vast majority of the personnel who had worked in the hangar—good men and women who had served their country well and with pride—must have been oblivious of the infernal regions under their feet.

The false walls or the devices that had concealed entrance to the lower floors had been stripped away during deconstruction. Although the stairhead door was removed, a steel jamb was left untouched at the upper landing.

Past the threshold, our flashlights revealed dead pill bugs on the concrete steps, some crushed and some as whole and round as buckshot.

There were also the impressions of shoes and paws in the dust. These overlaid tracks were both ascending and descending.

"Me and Orson," I said, identifying the prints. "From previous visits."

"What's below?"

"Three subterranean levels, each bigger than the hangar itself."

"Massive."

"Mucho."

"What did they do down there?"

"Bad stuff."

"Don't get so technical on me."

The maze of corridors and rooms under the hangar has been stripped to the bare concrete. Even the air-filtration, plumbing, and electrical systems have been torn out: every length of duct, every pipe, every wire and switch. Many structures in Wyvern remain untouched by salvagers. Usually, wherever salvage was pursued, the operation was conducted with an eye for the most valuable items that could be removed with the least effort. The hallways and rooms under this hangar, however, were scraped out so thoroughly that you might suspect this was a crime scene from which the guilty made a Herculean effort to eradicate every possible clue.

As we descended the stairs side by side, a flat metallic echo of my voice bounced immediately back to me at some points, while at other places the walls absorbed my words as effectively as the acoustical material that lines the broadcasting booth from which Sasha spins night music at KBAY.

I said, "They scoured away virtually every trace of what they were doing here—every trace but one—and I don't think they were just concerned about protecting national security. I think . . . it's just a feeling, but judging by the way they totally gutted these three floors, I sense they were afraid of what happened here . . . but not *just* afraid. Ashamed of it, too."

"Were these some of the genetic labs?"

"Can't have been. That requires absolute biological isolation."

"So?"

"There would be decontamination chambers everywhere—between suites of labs, at every elevator entrance, at every exit from the stairwell. Those spaces would still be identifiable for what they were, even after everything was torn out of them."

"You have a knack for this detective crap," Bobby said as

we reached the bottom of the second flight of steps and kept going.

"Awesomely smooth deductive reasoning," I admitted.

"Maybe I could be your Watson."

"Nancy Drew didn't work with Watson. That was Holmes."

"Who was Nancy's right-hand dude?" Bobby wondered.

"Don't think she had one. Nancy was a lone wolfette."

"One tough bitch, huh?"

"That's me," I said. "There's only one room down here that might have been a decon chamber . . . and it's full-on weird. You'll see."

We didn't speak further as we proceeded to the deepest of the three subterranean levels. The only sounds were the soft scrape of our rubber shoe soles on the concrete and the crunch of dead pill bugs.

In spite of the pistol-grip shotgun he carried, Bobby's relaxed demeanor and the easy grace with which he descended the stairs would have convinced anyone else that he was carefree. To some degree, he *was* enjoying himself. Bobby pretty much always enjoys himself, in all but the most extreme situations. But I'd known him so long that I—and perhaps only I—could tell that he was not, at this moment, free of care. If he was humming a song in his mind, it was moodier than a Jimmy Buffett tune.

Until a month ago, I hadn't been aware that Bobby Halloway—Huck Finn without the angst—could be either rattled or spooked. Recent events had revealed that even this natural-born Zen master's heart rate could occasionally exceed fifty-eight beats per minute.

I wasn't surprised by his edginess, because the stairwell was sufficiently cheerless and oppressive to give the heebie-jeebies to a Prozac-popping nun with an attitude as sweet as marzipan. Concrete ceiling, concrete walls, concrete steps. An iron pipe, painted black and fixed to one wall, served as a handrail. The dense air itself seemed to be turning to concrete, for it was cold, thick, and dry with the scent of lime that leached from the walls. Every surface absorbed more light than it reflected, and so in spite of our two flashlights, we wound downward in gloom, like medieval monks on our way to say prayers for the souls of dead brethren in the catacombs under a monastery.

The atmosphere would have been improved even by a single sign featuring a skull and crossbones above huge red letters warning of deadly levels of radioactivity. Or at least some gaily arranged rat bones.

The final basement in this facility—where no dust has yet settled and no pill bugs have ventured—has a peculiar floor plan, beginning with a wide corridor, in the form of an elongated oval, that extends around the entire perimeter, rather like a racetrack. A series of rooms, of different widths but identical depths, open off one side of this corridor—occupying the infield of the track—and through some of them you can reach a second oval corridor, which is concentric with the first; not as wide or as long as the first, it is nonetheless enormous. This smaller racetrack rings a single central chamber: the egg room.

The smaller corridor dead-ends at a connecting module through which you can enter the innermost sanctum. This transitional space is a ten-foot-square chamber accessed through a circular portal five feet in diameter. Inside this cubicle, to the left, another circular portal of the same size leads into the egg room. I believe these two openings were once fitted with formidable steel hatches, like those in the bulkheads between watertight compartments in a submarine or like bank-vault doors, and that this connecting module was, in fact, an airlock.

Although I am certain that these were not biological-research labs, one of the functions of the airlock might have been to prevent bacteria, spores, dust, and other contaminants from being carried into or out of the chamber that I call the egg room. Perhaps those personnel going to and from that inner sanctum were subjected to powerful sprays of sterilizing solution as well as to microbe-killing spectrums of ultraviolet radiation.

My hunch, however, is that the egg room was pressurized

and that this airlock served the same purpose as one aboard a spaceship. Or perhaps it functioned as a decompression chamber of the type deep-sea divers resort to when at risk of the bends.

In any event, this transitional chamber was designed either to prevent something from getting into the egg room—or to prevent something from getting out.

Standing in the airlock with Bobby, I trained my flashlight on the raised, curved threshold of the inner portal and swept it around the entire rim of this aperture to reveal the thickness of the egg-room wall: five feet of poured-in-place, steel-reinforced concrete. The entryway is so deep, in fact, that it is essentially a five-foot-long tunnel.

Bobby whistled softly. "Bunker architecture."

"No question, it's a containment vessel. Meant to restrain something."

"Like what?"

I shrugged. "Sometimes gifts are left for me here."

"Gifts? You found that cap here, right? Mystery Train?"

"Yeah. It was on the floor, dead center of the egg room. I don't think I found it, exactly. I think it was left there to be found, which is different. And on another night, while I was in the next room, someone left a photograph of my mother here in the airlock."

"Airlock?"

"Doesn't it seem like one?"

He nodded. "So who left the photo?"

"I don't know. But Orson was with me at the time, and he didn't realize someone had entered this space behind us."

"And he's got the nose of noses."

Warily, Bobby directed his flashlight through the first circular hatchway, into the corridor along which we had just come. It was still deserted.

I went through the inner portal, the short tunnel, crouching because only someone under five feet could pass this way without stooping.

Bobby followed me into the egg room, and for the first time in our seventeen years of friendship, I saw him stricken with awe. He turned slowly in a circle, sweeping his flashlight across the walls, and though he tried to speak, he couldn't initially produce a sound.

This ovoid chamber is a hundred twenty feet long and slightly less than sixty feet in diameter at its widest point, tapering toward each end. The walls, ceiling, and floor are curved to form a single continuous plane, so you seem to be standing in the empty shell of an enormous egg.

All surfaces are coated in a milky, vaguely golden, translucent substance that, judging by the profile around the entry hatchway, is nearly three inches thick and is bonded so securely to the concrete that the two appear to be fused.

The beams of our flashlights shimmered over this highly polished coating, but they also penetrated the exotic material, quivering and flickering to the depths of it, flaring off whorls of glittering golden dust that were suspended like miniature galaxies within. The substance was highly refractive, but light did not shatter through it in hard prismatic lines as it might through crystal; rather, buttery bright currents, as warm and sinuous as candle flames seduced by a draft, flowed and rippled through the thick, glossy surface plating, imparting to it the appearance of a liquid, purling away from us into the farther, darker corners of the room, there to dissipate like pulses of heat lightning behind summer thunderheads. Gazing down at the floor, I could almost believe that I was standing on a pool of pale-amber oil.

Marveling at the unearthly beauty of this spectacle, Bobby walked farther into the room.

Although this lustrous material appears to be as slick as wet porcelain, it is not at all slippery. In fact, at times—but not always—the floor seems to grip at your feet, as if it is gluey or exerts a mild magnetic attraction even on objects that contain no iron.

"Strike it," I said softly.

My words spiraled along the walls and ceiling and floor, and a cascade of whispery echoes returned to my ears from more than one direction.

Bobby blinked at me.

"Go ahead. Go on. With the barrel of the shotgun," I prompted. "Strike it."

"It's glass," Bobby protested.

The extended sibilant at the end of his second word returned to us in a wash of echoes as susurrant as gently foaming surf.

"If it's glass, it's not breakable."

Hesitantly, he gave the floor near his feet a gentle tap with the muzzle of the shotgun.

A quiet ringing, like chimes, seemed to arise simultaneously from every corner of the huge chamber, then faded into a silence that was curiously pregnant with suspense, as if the bells had announced the approach of some power or person of great import.

"Harder," I said.

When he rapped the steel barrel harder against the floor, the ringing was louder and of a different character, like that of tubular bells: euphonious, charming, yet as strange as any music that might be performed on a world at some far end of the universe.

As the sound drained into another suspenseful silence, Bobby squatted in order to smooth one hand across the floor where he had rapped the shotgun barrel.

"Not chipped."

I said, "You can bang on it with a hammer, scrape at it with a file, chop at it with an ice pick, and you won't leave the slightest scratch."

"You tried all that?"

"And a hand drill."

"You're a destructive imp."

"It runs in my family."

Pressing his hand to the floor at a few different points around him, Bobby said, "It's slightly warm."

Even on hot summer nights, the deep concrete structures of Fort Wyvern are as cool as caverns, cool enough to serve as wine cellars, and the chill sinks deeper into your bones the longer you haunt these places. All other surfaces within these warrens, other than those in this ovoid room, are cold to the touch.

"The stuff is always warm," I said, "yet the room itself isn't warm, as if the heat doesn't translate to the air. And I don't see how this material could retain heat more than eighteen months after they abandoned this place."

"You can almost feel . . . an energy in it."

"There's no electrical power here, no gas. No furnaces, no boilers, no generators, no machinery. All stripped away."

Bobby rose from a squat and walked deeper into the chamber, playing his flashlight over the floor, walls, and ceiling.

Even with two flashlights and the unusually high refractivity of the mysterious material, shadows ruled the room. Tracers, blooms, girandoles, pinwheels, lady ferns, and fireflies of light swarmed across the curving surfaces, mostly in shades of gold and yellow but some red and others sapphire, fading to oblivion in far dark corners, like fireworks licked up and swallowed by a night sky, dazzling but illuminating little.

Bobby said wonderingly, "It's as big as a concert hall."

"Not really. But it seems even bigger than it is because of how every surface curves away from you."

As I spoke, a change occurred in the acoustics of the chamber. The whispery echoes of my words faded away, swiftly became inaudible, and then my words themselves diminished in volume. The air felt as if it had thickened, transmitting sound less efficiently than before.

"What's happening?" Bobby asked, and his voice, too, sounded suppressed, muffled, as though he were speaking from the other end of a bad telephone connection.

"I don't know." Although I raised my voice almost to a shout, it remained muffled, precisely as loud as when I'd spoken in a normal tone.

I would have thought I was imagining the increased density of the air if I hadn't suddenly begun experiencing difficulty breathing. Although not suffocating, I was afflicted severely enough to have to concentrate to draw and expel breath. I was swallowing reflexively with each inhalation; the air was virtually a liquid that I had to force down. Indeed, I could feel it sliding along my throat like a drink of cold water. Each shallow breath felt heavy in my chest, as if it had more substance than ordinary air, as though my lungs were filling with fluid, and the moment I completed each inhalation, I was overwhelmed by a frantic urge to get this stuff out, to eject it, convinced that I was drowning in it, but each exhalation had to be forced, almost as if I were regurgitating.

Pressure.

In spite of my rising panic, I remained clearheaded enough to figure out that the air was not being alchemized into a liquid but that, instead, the air pressure was drastically increasing, as if the depth of the earth's atmosphere above us were doubling, tripling, and pushing down on us with crushing force. My eardrums fluttered, my sinuses began to throb, I felt phantom fingertips pressing hard against my eyeballs, and at the end of each inhalation, my nostrils pinched shut.

My knees began to quiver and then buckle. My shoulders bent under an invisible weight. Straight as plumb bobs, my arms were hanging at my sides. My hands could no longer grip the flashlight, and it clattered to the floor at my feet. It bounced silently on the glassy surface, for now there was no sound whatsoever, not even the flutter of my eardrums or the thud of my own heart.

Abruptly, all returned to normal.

The pressure lifted in an instant.

I heard myself gasping for air. Bobby was gasping, too.

He had dropped his flashlight but had managed to hold tight to the shotgun.

"Shit!" he said explosively.

"Yeah."

"Shit."

"Yeah."

"What was that?"

"Don't know."

"Ever happen before?"

"No."

"Shit."

"Yeah," I said, reveling in the ease with which I could draw cool, deep breaths.

Though our flashlights were at rest on the floor, an increasing number of Roman candles and pinwheels and serpents and sparklers and spirals of light spread across the floor and up the walls.

"This place isn't shut down," Bobby said.

"But it is. You saw."

"Nothing's what it seems in Wyvern," he said, quoting me.

"Every room we passed, every hallway—stripped, abandoned."

"What about the two floors above this?"

"Just bare rooms."

"And there's nothing below?"

"No."

"There's something."

"Not that I've found."

We picked up our flashlights, and as the beams moved across the floors and walls, the flamboyant eruptions of light in the deep glassy surface multiplied threefold, fourfold: a dazzling profusion of fiery blooms. We might have been in a Fourth of July extravaganza, suspended from a hot-air balloon, with barrages of rockets bursting around us, whiz-bangs and cracker bonbons and fountains and fizgigs, but all silent, all marvelous glistering light and no bang, yet so reminiscent of Independence Day displays that you could almost smell the saltpeter and the sulfur and the charcoal, almost hear a stirring John Philip Sousa march, almost taste hot dogs with mustard and chopped onions.

Bobby said, "Something's still happening."

"Split?"

"Wait."

He studied the ceaselessly changing and increasingly colorful patterns of light as though they held a meaning as explicit as that in a paragraph of prose on a printed page, if only he could learn to read them.

Although I doubted that the astonishingly luminous re-

fractive bursts were casting off any more UV rays than the
flashlight beams that produced them, I was not accustomed to
such brightness. Radiant whorls and drizzles and rivulets
streamed across my exposed face and hands, a storm of scintil-
lant tattoos, and even if this rain of light was washing a little
death into me, the spectacle was irresistible, exhilarating. My
heart was racing, powered partly by fear but mostly by wonder.

Then I saw the door.

I was turning, so enthralled by the carnival of light
around me that my gaze traveled past the door, distracted by
the pyrotechnics, before I realized what I had seen. Massive,
five feet in diameter, of matte-finish steel, surrounded by a
polished-steel architrave: It was similar to what you would
expect to see at the entrance to a bank vault, and no doubt it
established an airtight seal.

Startled, I swung back toward the door—but it was gone.
Through a pandemonium of gazelle-quick lights and pursuing
shadows, I saw that the circular hole in the wall was as it had
been when we entered through it: open, with a dark concrete
tunnel beyond, leading to what had once been an airlock.

I took a couple of steps toward the opening before I
realized that Bobby was speaking to me. As I turned toward
him, I glimpsed the door again, this time from the corner of
my eye. But when I looked directly at the damn thing, it
wasn't there.

"What's happening?" I asked nervously.

Bobby had extinguished his flashlight. He pointed at
mine. "Douse it."

I did as he asked.

The fireworks in the glassy surface of the room should
have at once vanished into absolute darkness. Instead, colorful
star shells and chrysanthemums and glittering pinwheels continued to arise within this magical material, swarmed around
the chamber, casting off a farrago of lights and shadows, and
then faded away as new eruptions replaced them.

"It's running by itself," Bobby said.

"Running?"

"The process."

"What process?"

"The room, the machine, the process, whatever it is."

"It can't be running by itself," I insisted, in full-on denial of what was happening around me.

"The beam energy?" he wondered.

"What?"

"The flashlight beams?"

"Can you be any more obscure?"

"Way more, bro. But I mean, that's what must've powered it up. The energy in the flashlight beams."

I shook my head. "Doesn't make sense. That's almost no energy at all."

"This stuff soaked in the light," he insisted, sliding one foot back and forth on the radiant floor, "spun it into more power, used what it absorbed to generate more energy."

"How?"

"Somehow."

"That's not science."

"I've heard worse on *Star Trek*."

"It's sorcery."

"Science or sorcery, it's real."

Even if what Bobby said was true—and obviously there was at least some truth in it—the phenomenon was not perpetually self-sustaining. The number of bright eruptions began to decline, as did both the richness of the colors and the intensity of the lights.

My mouth had gone so dry that I needed to work up some saliva before I could say, "Why didn't this happen before?"

"Were you ever here with two flashlights?"

"I'm a one-flashlight guy."

"So maybe there's a critical mass, a critical amount of energy input, needed to start it."

"Critical mass is two lousy flashlights?"

"Maybe."

"Bobby Einstein." With my concern not in the least allayed by the subsidence of the light show, I looked toward the exit. "Did you see that door?"

"What door?"

"Totally massive vault, like a blast door in a nuclear-missile silo."

"Are you feeling that beer?"

"It was there and not there."

"The door?"

"Yeah."

"This isn't a haunted house, bro."

"Maybe it's a haunted laboratory."

I was surprised that the word *haunted* felt so right and true, resonating loudly in the tuning fork of instinct. This wasn't the requisite decaying house of many gables and creaking floorboards and inexplicable cold drafts, but I sensed unseen presences nonetheless, malevolent spirits pressing against an invisible membrane between my world and theirs, the air of expectancy preceding the imminent materialization of a hateful and violent entity.

"The door was there and not there," I insisted.

"It's almost a Zen koan. What's the sound of one hand clapping? Where does a door lead if it's there and not there?"

"I don't think we have time for meditation just now."

Indeed, I was overcome by the feeling that time was running out for us, that a cosmic clock was rapidly ticking toward the stop point. This premonition was so powerful that I almost bolted for the exit.

All that kept me in the egg room was the certainty that Bobby would not follow me if I left. He was not interested in politics or the great cultural and social issues of our times, and nothing could rouse him from his pleasant life of sun and surf except a friend in need. He didn't trust those he called *people with a plan,* those who believed they knew how to make a better world, which seemed always to involve telling other people what they should do and how they should think. But the cry of a friend would bring him instantly to the barricades, and once committed to the cause—in this case, to finding Jimmy Wing and good Orson—he would neither surrender nor retreat.

Likewise, I could never leave a friend behind. Our convictions and our friends are all we have to get us through times of trouble. Friends are the only things from this damaged world that we can hope to see in the next; friends and loved ones are the very light that brightens the Hereafter.

"Idiot," I said.

"Asshole," Bobby said.

"I wasn't talking to you."

"I'm the only one here."

"I was calling myself an idiot. For not getting out of here."

"Oh. Then I retract the asshole remark."

Bobby switched on his flashlight, and immediately the silent fireworks dazzled across the lining of the egg room. They didn't well up slowly but began at the peak of intensity that they had previously achieved by degrees.

"Turn on your light," Bobby said.

"Are we really dumb enough to do this?"

"Way more than dumb enough."

"This place has nothing to do with Jimmy and Orson," I said.

"How do you know?"

"They're not here."

"But something here may help us find them."

"We can't help them if we're dead."

"Be a good idiot and turn on your light."

"This is nuts."

"Fear nothing, bro. *Carpe noctem.*"

"Damn," I said, hung with my own noose.

I switched on my flashlight.

13

A riot of fiery lights erupted within the translucent walls around us, and it was easy to imagine that we were in the canyons of a great city stricken by insurrection, bomb throwers and arsonists on every side, blazing rioters ignited by their own torches and now running in terror through the night, cyclones of tempestuous fire whirling along avenues where the pavement was as molten as lava, tall buildings with orange flames seething from the high windows, smoldering chunks of parapets and cornices and ledges trailing comet tails of sparks as they crashed into the streets.

Yet at the same time, with the slightest shift of perspective, it was also possible to see this panoramic cataclysm not primarily as a series of bright eruptions but as a shadow show, because for every Molotov-cocktail flash, for every roiling mass of hot napalm, for every luminous trail that reminded me of tracer bullets, there was a dark shape in motion, begging interpretation as do the faces and figures in clouds. Ebony capes billowed, black robes swirled, sable serpents coiled and struck, shadows swooped like angry ravens, flocks of crows dived and soared overhead and underfoot, armies of charred skeletons marched with a relentless scissoring of sharp black bones, midnight cats crouched and pounced, sinuous whips of darkness lashed through the balefires, and iron-black blades slashed.

In this pandemonium of light and darkness, wholly encapsulated by a chaos of spinning flames and tumbling shadows, I was becoming increasingly disoriented. Though I stood still, with my feet widely planted for balance, I felt as if I were moving, twirling like poor Dorothy aboard the Kansas-to-Oz Express. Forward, behind, right, left, up, down—all rapidly became more difficult to define.

Again, from the corner of my eye, I glimpsed the door. When I looked more directly, it was still there, formidable and gleaming.

"Bobby."

"I see it."

"Not good."

"Not a real door," he concluded.

"You said the place wasn't haunted."

"Mirage."

The storm of light and shadow gained velocity. It seemed to be escalating toward an ominous crescendo.

I was afraid that the furious motion, the increasingly spiky and disturbing patterns in the walls, foretold an onrushing event that would translate all this energy into sudden violence. This ovoid room was so strange that I was unable to imagine the nature of the threat rushing at us, couldn't guess even the direction from which it might come. For once, my three-hundred-ring imagination failed me.

The vault door was hinged on this side; therefore, it would swing inward. There was no lock wheel to disengage the ring of thick bolts that were currently seated in holes around the jamb, so the door could be opened only from the short tunnel between this room and the airlock, from the other side, which meant we were trapped here.

No. Not trapped.

Striving to resist a surging claustrophobia, I assured myself that the door wasn't real. Bobby was right: It was a hallucination, an illusion, a mirage.

An apparition.

My perception of the egg room as a haunted place grew harder to shake off. The luminous forms raging through the walls suddenly seemed to be tortured spirits in a dervish dance of anguish, frantic to escape damnation, as though all around me were windows with views of Hell.

As my heart pumped nearly hard enough to blow out my carotid arteries, I told myself that I was seeing the egg room not as it was at this moment but as it had been before the industrious gnomes of Wyvern had stripped it—and the entire facility around it—to the bare concrete. The massive vault door had been here then; but it was not here now, even though I could see it. The door had been dismantled, hauled away, salvaged, melted down, and recast into soup ladles, pinballs, and orthodontic braces. Now it was purely apparitional, and I could walk through it as easily as I had walked through the spiderweb at the top of the porch steps of the bungalow in Dead Town.

Not intending to leave, wishing merely to test the mirage hypothesis, I headed toward the exit. In two steps, I was reeling. I almost collapsed, facedown, in a free fall that would have broken my nose and cracked enough teeth to make a dentist smile. Regaining my balance at the penultimate moment, I spread my legs wide and planted my feet hard against the floor, as though trying to make the rubber soles of my shoes grip as firmly as a squid's suckers.

The room was not moving, even if it felt like a ship wallowing in rough seas. The movement was a subjective perception, a symptom of my increasing disorientation.

Staring at the vault door in a futile attempt to *will* it out of existence, trying to decide whether I should drop to my knees and crawl, I registered an odd detail of its design. The door was suspended on one long barrel hinge that must have been eight or ten inches in diameter. The knuckles of the barrel, which would move around the center pin—the pintle—when the door was pushed open or drawn shut, were exposed in most hinges, but not in this one. The knuckles were covered by a solid length of armoring steel, and the head of the pintle was recessed in this shield, as though to hamper anyone who might try to get through the locked door from this side by prying or hammering at the elements of the hinge. If the door could have swung outward, they would not have put the hinge inside the egg room, but because the walls were five feet thick, the door at this end of the entry tunnel could only swing inward. This ovoid chamber and the adjoining airlock might have been designed to contain a greater number of atmospheres of pressure and possible biological contaminants; but all evidence supported the conclusion that it had also been constructed with the intention, at least under certain circumstances, of imprisoning someone.

Thus far, the kaleidoscopic displays in the walls had not been accompanied by sound. Now, though the air remained dead calm, there arose a hollow and mournful moaning of wind, as it might strike the ear when blowing off barren alkaline flats.

I looked at Bobby. Even through the tattoos of light and shadow that melted across his face, I could see that he was worried.

"You hear that?" I asked.

"Treacherous."

"Fully," I agreed, not liking the sound any more than he did.

If this noise was a hallucination, as the door apparently was, at least we shared it. We could enjoy the comfort—cold as it might be—of going insane together.

The unfelt wind grew louder, speaking with more than one voice. The hollow wail continued, but with it came a rushing sound as of a northwester blowing through a grove of trees in advance of rain, fierce and full of warnings. Groaning, gibbering, soughing, keening. And the lonely tuneless whistling of a blustery winter storm playing rain gutters and downspouts as though they were icy flutes.

When I heard the first words in the choir of winds, I thought that I must be imagining them, but they swiftly grew louder, clearer. Men's voices: half a dozen, maybe more. Tinny, hollow, as if spoken from the far end of a long steel pipe. The words came in clusters separated by bursts of static, issuing from walkie-talkies or perhaps a radio.

". . . here somewhere, right here . . ."

". . . *hurry, for Christ's sake!*"

". . . *give . . . don't . . .*"

". . . *gimme cover, Jackson, gimme cover . . .*"

The rising cacophony of wind was almost as disorienting as the stroboscopic lights and the shadows that kited like legions of bats in a feeding frenzy. I couldn't discern from which direction the voices came.

". . . *group . . . here . . . group and defend.*"

". . . *position to translate . . .*"

". . . *group, hell . . . move, haul ass.*"

". . . *translate now!*"

". . . *cycle, cycle it . . .*"

Ghosts. I was listening to ghosts. They were dead men now, had been dead since before this facility had been abandoned, and these were the last words they had spoken immediately before they perished.

I didn't know exactly what was about to happen to these doomed men, but as I listened, I had no doubt that some terrible fate had overcome them, which was now being replayed on some spiritual plane.

Their voices grew more urgent, and they began to speak over one another:

". . . *cycle it!*"

". . . *hear 'em? Hear 'em coming?*"

". . . *hurry . . . what the hell . . .*"

". . . *wrong . . . Jesus . . . what's wrong?*"

They were shouting now, some hoarse and others shrill, every voice raw with panic:

"*Cycle it open! Cycle it!*"

"*Get us out!*"

"*Oh, God, God, oh, God!*"

"*GET US OUT OF HERE!*"

Instead of words in the wind, there were screams such as I had never heard before and hoped never to hear again, the cries of men dying but not dying quickly or mercifully, shrieks that conveyed the intensity of their prolonged agony but that also expressed a chilling depth of despair, as though their anguish was as much spiritual as physical. Judging by their screams, they weren't just being killed; they were being butchered, torn apart by something that knew where the soul inhabits the body. I could hear—or, more likely, imagined I could hear—a mysterious predator clawing the spirit out of the flesh and greedily devouring this delicacy before feeding on the mortal remains.

My heart was pounding so fiercely that my vision throbbed when I looked at the door again. From the design of that armored hinge, a frightening truth could be deduced, but because of the distracting bedlam of sound and light, it remained frustratingly just beyond my grasp.

If the barrel of the hinge had been left unshielded, you would still have needed an array of heavy-duty power tools, diamond-tipped drill bits, and a lot of time to fracture those knuckles and jack out the pintle—

In every surface of the room, the war between light and darkness raged more furiously, battalions of shadows clashing with armies of light in ever more frenzied assaults, to the harrowing shriek-hiss-whistle of the unfelt winds and the ceaseless, ghastly screaming.

—and even if the hinge could be broken, the vault door would be held in place, because the bolts that secured it were surely snugged into evenly spaced holes around the entire circumference of the steel jamb rather than along one arc of it—

The screaming. The screaming seemed to have substance, pouring into me through my ears until I was filled to bursting with it and could contain no more. I opened my mouth as if to let the dark energy of those ghostly cries pass out of me.

Struggling to concentrate, squinting to focus more clearly on the door, I realized that a team of professional safecrackers would probably never get through that barrier without explosives. For the purpose of containing mere men, therefore, this door was absurdly overdesigned.

At last the fearsome truth came within my grasp. The purpose of the redundantly armored door was to contain something in addition to men or atmosphere. Something bigger, stronger, more cunning than a virus. Some damn thing around which my usually vivid imagination was unable to wrap itself.

Switching off my flashlight, turning away from the vault door, I called to Bobby.

Mesmerized by the fireworks and the shadow show, buffeted by the wind noises and the screams, he didn't hear me, although he was only ten feet away.

"Bobby!" I shouted.

As he turned his head to look at me, the wind abruptly matched sound with force, gusting through the egg room, whipping our hair, flapping my jacket and Bobby's Hawaiian shirt. It was hot, humid, redolent of tar fumes and rotting vegetation.

I couldn't identify the source of the gale, because this chamber had no ventilation ducts in its walls, no breaches whatsoever in its seamless glassy surface, except for the circular exit. If the steel cork plugging that hole were, in fact, nothing but a mirage, perhaps these gusts could have been coming through the tunnel linking the egg room to the airlock, blowing through the nonexistent door; however, the wind blustered from all sides, rather than from one direction.

"Your light!" I shouted. "Shut it off!"

Before Bobby could do as I wanted, the reeking wind brought with it another manifestation. A figure came *through* the curved wall, as if five feet of steel-reinforced concrete were no more substantial than a veil of mist.

Bobby clutched the pistol-grip shotgun with both hands, dropping his flashlight without switching it off.

The spectral visitor was startlingly close, less than twenty feet from us. Because of the swarming lights and shadows, which served as continually changing camouflage, I couldn't at first see the intruder clearly. Glimpsed in flickering fragments, it looked manlike, then more like a machine, and then, crazily, like nothing else but a lumbering rag doll.

Bobby held his fire, perhaps because he still believed that

what we were seeing was illusionary, either ghost or hallucination, or some strange combination of the two. I suppose I was clinging desperately to the same belief, because I didn't back away from it when it staggered closer to us.

By the time it had taken three uncertain steps, I could see clearly enough to identify it as a man in a white vinyl, airtight spacesuit. More likely, the outfit was an adapted version of the standard gear that NASA had developed for astronauts, intended primarily not to shield the wearer from the icy vacuum of interplanetary space but rather to protect him from deadly infection in a biologically contaminated environment.

The large helmet featured an oversize faceplate, but I wasn't able to see the person beyond, because reflections of the whirling light-and-shadow show streamed across the Plexiglas. On the brow of the helmet was stenciled a name: HODGSON.

Perhaps because of the fireworks, more likely because he was blinded by terror, Hodgson didn't react as if he saw Bobby and me. He entered screaming, and his voice was by far the loudest of those still borne on the foul wind. After staggering a few steps away from the wall, he turned to face it, holding up both hands to ward off an attack by something that was invisible to me.

He jerked as if hit by multiple rounds of high-caliber gunfire.

Though I'd heard no shots, I ducked reflexively.

When he fell to the floor, Hodgson landed on his back. He was propped halfway between a prone and a sitting position by the air tank and by the briefcase-size waste-purification-and-reclamation system strapped to his back. His arms fell limp at his sides.

I didn't need to examine him to know he was dead. I had no idea what might have killed him, and I didn't have enough curiosity to risk investigating.

If he'd already been a ghost, how could he die again?

Some questions are better left unanswered. Curiosity is one of the engines of human achievement, but it's not much of a survival mechanism if it motivates you to see what the back side of a lion's teeth look like.

Crouching, I scooped up Bobby's flashlight and clicked it off.

An immediate drop in the ferocity of the wind seemed to support the theory that even the minimal energy input from the beams of our flashlights had triggered all this bizarre activity.

The stench of steaming tar and rotting vegetation was also fading.

Rising to my feet again, I glanced at the door. It was still there. Huge and shiny. Too real.

I wanted to get out, but I didn't head for the exit. I was afraid it would actually be there when I reached it, whereupon this waking dream might become a waking nightmare.

In every surface, the pyrotechnics continued undiminished. Previously, when we'd doused the flashlights, this extraordinary spectacle had been self-perpetuating for a short while, and it would probably power itself even longer this time.

I regarded the walls, the floor, and the ceiling with suspicion. I expected another figure to coalesce out of the bright, ceaselessly changing cyclorama, something more threatening than the man in the bio-secure gear.

Bobby was approaching Hodgson. Apparently, the disorienting effect of the light show did not affect his equilibrium as it did mine.

"Bro," I warned.

"Cool."

"Not."

He had the shotgun. He believed it was protection.

I, on the other hand, figured that the weapon was potentially as dangerous as the flashlights. Any lead pellets not stopped by the target would most likely ricochet from wall to ceiling to floor to wall with deadly velocity. And every time a bit of lead shot struck any surface in the chamber, the kinetic energy of the impact might be absorbed by that glassy material, further powering these weird phenomena.

The wind subsided to a breeze.

Carnivals and catastrophes still glittered and blazed through every curving surface of the room, Ferris wheels of rotating blue lights and orange-red spouts like volcanic eruptions.

The vault door appeared dauntingly solid.

No ghost had ever looked as real as the body in the spacesuit. Not Jacob Marley rattling his chains at Scrooge, not the Ghost of Christmas Future, not the White Lady of Avenel, not Hamlet's dad, certainly not Casper.

I was surprised to find my balance restored. Maybe the brief disruption of equilibrium hadn't been a reaction to the spinning lights and shadows, but had been merely another transient effect similar to the pressure that, earlier, had muffled our voices and made breathing difficult.

The hot breeze—and the stink it carried—disappeared. The air was cool and calm once more. The sound of the winds began to fade, as well.

Next, perhaps, the spacesuited man on the floor would dissolve into a twist of icy vapor that would rise and vanish like a wraith returning to the spirit world where it belonged. Soon. Before we had to take a close look at it. Please.

Certain that Bobby couldn't be persuaded to retreat, I followed him toward Hodgson's body. He was deep into the same stoked, gonzo mind-set with which he surfed twenty-foot, fully macking behemoths: a maximum kamikaze commitment as total as his more characteristic slacker indifference. When he was on this board, he would ride it all the way to the end of the barrel—and one day straight out of this life.

Because the lights in the walls were contained within the surface layer of glassy material and shed only a small fraction of their illuminating power into the egg room itself, Hodgson wasn't well revealed.

"Flashlight," Bobby said.

"Not smart."

"That's me."

Reluctantly, steeling myself to take a close look at the back side of the aforementioned lion's teeth, I stepped cautiously to the right of the body as Bobby moved less cautiously to the left. I switched on one flashlight and played it over the far too solid ghost. Initially the beam jiggled because my hand was shaking, but I quickly steadied it.

The Plexiglas in the helmet was tinted. The single flashlight was not powerful enough to let us see either Hodgson's face or his condition.

He—or possibly she—was as still and silent as a headstone, and whether a ghost or not, he seemed indisputably dead.

On the breast of his pressure suit was an American-flag patch, and immediately below the flag was a second patch, featuring a speeding locomotive, an image clearly from the Art Deco period of design, which evidently had been adapted to serve as the logo for this research project. Although the image was bold and dynamic, without any element of mystery, I was willing to bet my left lung that this identified Hodgson as a member of the Mystery Train team.

The only other distinguishing features on the front of the suit were six or eight holes across the abdomen and chest. Recalling how Hodgson had turned to face the wall out of which he had appeared, how he had held his hands up defensively, and how he had jerked as if hit by automatic-weapons fire, I at first assumed that these punctures were bullet holes.

On closer inspection, however, I realized that they were too neat to be gunshot wounds. High-velocity lead slugs would have torn the material, leaving rips or starburst punctures rather than these round holes, each as large as a quarter, which looked as though they had been die cut or even bored with a laser. Aside from the fact that we had heard no gunfire, these were far too large to be entry wounds; any caliber of ammunition capable of punching holes that big would have passed directly through Hodgson, killing Bobby or me, or both of us.

I could see no blood.

"Use the other flash," Bobby said.

Silence had replaced the last murmuring voices of the wind.

Explosive scripts of bright, meaningless calligraphy continued to scroll through the walls, perhaps marginally less dazzling than they had been a minute ago. Experience suggested that this phenomenon, too, was about to wind down, and I was reluctant to stimulate it again.

"Just once, quick, for a clearer look," he urged.

Against all instincts, I did as Bobby wanted, crouching over the cumbersomely attired figure for a better view.

The tinted Plexiglas still partially obscured what lay beyond, but at once I understood why, with the single flashlight, we hadn't been able to see poor Hodgson's face: Hodgson no longer *had* a face. Inside the helmet was a wet churning mass that seemed to be feeding voraciously on the remaining substance of the dead man: a sickening pale tangle of seething, squirming, slithering, jittering things that looked somewhat soft-bodied like worms but were not worms, that also looked somewhat chitinous like beetles but were not beetles, a greasy white colony of something unnameable that had invaded his suit and overwhelmed him with such rapidity that he had died no less abruptly than if he had been shot straight through the heart. And now these twitching *things* responded to the flashlight beam by surging against the inner surface of the Plexiglas faceplate, teeming with obscene excitement.

Bolting to my feet, reeling backward, I thought I saw movement in some of the holes in the abdomen and chest of Hodgson's violated pressure suit, as though the things that had killed him were going to boil out of those punctures.

Bobby split without firing the shotgun, which he might easily have done, out of shock and terror. Thank God he didn't pull the trigger. A shotgun blast or two—or ten—wouldn't wipe out even half the hellacious swarm in Hodgson's pressure suit, but it would probably pump them into an even greater killing frenzy.

As I ran, I switched off the flashlights, because the fireworks in the walls were gaining speed and power once more.

Although Bobby had been farther from the exit than I was, he got there ahead of me.

The vault door was as solid as a damn vault door.

What I'd seen from a distance was confirmed close up: There was no wheel or other release mechanism to disengage the lock bolts.

14

Back toward the center of the room, about forty feet away from the vault door, Hodgson's pressure suit was where we had left it. Because it hadn't collapsed upon itself like a deflated balloon, I assumed that it was still filled out by the nightmare colony and by the remaining odds and ends of Hodgson on which those squirming things were feeding.

Bobby tapped the barrel of the shotgun against the door. The sound was as real as steel striking steel.

"Mirage?" I suggested, tossing his deficient explanation back at him as I shoved one flashlight under my belt and jammed the other into a jacket pocket.

"It's bogus."

In reply, I slapped my hand against the door.

"Bogus," he insisted. "Check your watch."

I was less interested in the time than in whether anything might be coming out of Hodgson's pressure suit.

With a shudder, I realized that I was brushing at the sleeves of my jacket, wiping at the back of my neck, scrubbing the side of my face, trying to rid myself of crawling things that weren't really there.

Motivated by a vivid memory of the squirming horde inside the helmet, I hooked my fingers in a groove along the edge of the door and pulled. I grunted, cursed, and pulled harder, as though I might actually be able to move a few tons of steel by tapping the store of energy I'd laid up from a breakfast of crumb cake and hot chocolate.

"Check your watch," Bobby repeated.

He had rucked back the sleeve of his cotton pullover to look at his own watch. This surprised me. He had never before worn a timepiece, and now he had one just like mine.

When I consulted the luminous digital readout on the oversize face of my wristwatch, I saw *4:08 P.M.* The correct time, of course, was short of four o'clock in the morning.

"Mine, too," he said, showing me that our watches agreed.

"Both wrong?"

"No. That's what time it is. Here. Now. In this place."

"Witchy."

"Pure Salem."

Then I registered the date in a separate window below the digital time display. This was the twelfth of April. My watch claimed it was *Mon Feb 19.* So did Bobby's.

I wondered what year the watch would reveal if its date window had been four digits wider. Somewhere in the past. A memorably catastrophic afternoon for the big-brow scientists on the Mystery Train team, an afternoon when the feces hit the flabellum.

The speed and brightness of the spiraling-bursting-streaming lights in the walls were slowly but noticeably diminishing.

I looked toward the bio-secure suit, which had proved no more secure against hostile organisms than a porkpie hat and a fig leaf, and I saw that whatever inhabited it was moving, churning restlessly. The arms flopped limply against the floor, and one leg twitched, and the entire body quivered as though a powerful electric current was passing through it.

"Not good," I decided.

"It'll fade."

"Oh, yeah?"

"The screams did, the voices, the wind."

I rapped my knuckles against the vault door.

"It'll fade," Bobby insisted.

Though the light show was diminishing, Hodgson—rather, the Hodgson suit—was becoming more active. It drummed the heels of its boots against the floor. It bucked and thrashed its arms.

"Trying to get up," I said.

"Can't hurt us."

"You serious?" My logic seemed unassailable: "If the vault door is real enough to keep us in here, then that thing's real enough to cause us major grief."

"It'll fade."

Apparently not having been informed that all its efforts were pointless, due to its impending fade, the Hodgson suit thrashed and bucked and rocked until it rolled off its air tank and onto its side. I was looking at the dark faceplate again, and I could feel something staring back at me from the other side of that tinted Plexiglas, not simply a mass of worms or beetles, stupidly churning, but a cohesive and formidable entity, a malevolent consciousness, as curious about me as I was terrified of it.

This was not my feverish imagination at work.

This was a perception as unambiguous and valid as the chill I would have felt if I'd held an ice cube to the nape of my neck.

"It'll fade," Bobby repeated, and the thin note of dread in his voice revealed that he, too, was aware of being observed.

I was not comforted by the fact that the Hodgson thing was forty feet away from us. I wouldn't have felt safe if the distance had been forty *miles* and if I'd been studying this spastic apparition through a telescope.

The pyrotechnics had lost perhaps a third of their power.

The door was still cold and hard under my hand.

As the light show proceeded toward a final flourish, visibility declined, but even in the slowly deepening gloom, I could see the Hodgson thing rolling off its side, lying facedown on the floor, and then struggling to get to its hands and knees.

If I'd correctly interpreted the gruesome sight I'd glimpsed through the faceplate, hundreds or even thousands of individual creatures infested the pressure suit, flesh-eating multitudes that constituted a nest or hive. A colony of beetles might operate under a sophisticated structure of divisional labor, maintain a high degree of social order, and work together to survive and prosper; but even if Hodgson's skeleton remained to provide an armature, I couldn't believe that the colony would be able to form itself into a manlike shape and function with such superb coordination, interlocked form, and strength that it could walk around in a spacesuit, climb steps, and drive heavy machinery.

The Hodgson thing rose to its feet.

"Nasty," Bobby murmured.

Under the flat of my damp palm, I felt a short-lived vibration pass through the vault door. More peculiar than a vibration. More pronounced. It was a faint, undulant . . . tremor. The door didn't simply hum with it; the steel *quivered* briefly, for a second or two, as though it were not steel at all, as though it were gelatin, and then it became solid—and seemingly impregnable—once more.

The thing in the pressure suit swayed like a toddler unsure of its balance. It slid its left foot forward, hesitated, and dragged its right foot after the left. The scraping of its boots against the glassy floor produced only a whispery sound.

Left foot, right foot.

Coming toward us.

Perhaps more of Hodgson survived than just his skeleton. Maybe the colony had not completely devoured the man, had not even killed him, but had bored into him, nestling deep into his flesh and bones, into his heart and liver and brain, establishing a hideous symbiotic relationship with his body, while taking firm control of his nervous system from the brain to the thinnest efferent fiber.

As the fireworks in the walls darkened into amber and umber and blood red, the Hodgson thing slid its left foot forward, hesitated, then dragged its right. The old Imhotep two-step, invented by Boris Karloff in 1932.

Under my hand, the vault door quivered again and suddenly turned *mushy*.

I gasped when a painful coldness, sharper than needles, pierced my right hand, as if I had plunged it into something considerably more frigid than ice water. From wrist to fingertips, I appeared to be one with the vault door. Although the egg-room light was rapidly fading, I could see that the steel had become semitransparent; like a lazy whirlpool, circular currents were turning within it. And in the gray substance of the vault door were the paler gray shapes of my fingers.

Startled, I yanked my hand out of the door—and had no sooner extracted it than the steel regained its solidity.

I remembered how the door had first been visible only out of the corner of my eye, not when I looked directly. It had acquired substance by degrees, and it was likely to dematerialize not in a wink but in installments.

Bobby must have seen what had happened, because he took a step backward, as though the steel might suddenly become a whirling vortex and suck him out of this place into oblivion.

If I hadn't extracted my hand in time, would it have broken off at the joining point, leaving me with a neatly severed but spurting stump? I didn't need to know the answer. Let it be a question for the ages.

The chill had left my hand the instant that I'd withdrawn it from the door, but I was still gasping, and between each convulsive breath, I heard myself repeating the same four-letter word, as if I had been stricken by a terminal case of Tourette's syndrome and would spend the rest of my life unable to stop shouting this single obscenity.

Advancing through dim bloody light and legions of leaping shadows, like an astronaut returned from a mission to Planet Hell, the Hodgson thing had crossed half the original distance between us. It was twenty feet away, relentlessly dragging itself forward, obviously not offended by my language, driven by a hunger almost as palpable as the stench of hot tar and rotting vegetation that earlier had been borne on the wind from nowhere.

In frustration, Bobby struck the door with the shotgun barrel. That steel plug tolled like a bell.

He didn't even bother to point the weapon at the Hodgson thing. Evidently, he, too, had reached the conclusion that the impact of stray buckshot against the walls of the chamber might energize the place and leave us trapped here longer.

The light show ended, and over us fell absolute darkness.

If I could have stilled my storming heart and held my breath, I might have been able to hear the whispery slippage of rubber boot soles over the glassy floor, but I was a one-man percussion section. I probably couldn't have detected the sound of the Hodgson thing's approach if it had been beating a bass drum.

When the luminous phenomenon in the walls had been extinguished, surely the phantasmagoric engine had shut down altogether, surely we had come all the way back to reality, surely the Hodgson thing had ceased to exist as abruptly as it had appeared, surely—

Again, Bobby struck the vault door with the shotgun. It didn't toll this time. The tone was flat, less reverberant than before, as if he had slammed a hammer into a block of wood.

Maybe the door was changing, in the process of dematerializing, but it was still blocking the exit. We couldn't risk trying to leave until we were certain we wouldn't be passing through it while it was in a state of flux and possibly capable of taking some molecules from our bodies with it when it vanished for good.

I wondered what would happen if the Hodgson thing had a firm grip on me when its very substance began to transform. If, for even a moment, my hand had become one with the steel of the vault door, perhaps part of me would become one with the pressure suit and with the squirming entity inside the suit: a close, too-personal encounter that might destroy my sanity even if, miraculously, I survived with no physical damage.

Blackness pressed liquidly against my open eyes, as if I were deep underwater. Although I strained to catch the slightest sign of the approaching figure, I was as sightless here as I'd been in the corridor outside the room where I'd found the *veve* rats.

Inevitably, I recalled the kidnapper with the white-corn teeth, whose face I'd touched in the blinding dark.

As then, I now sensed a presence looming before me, and with more reason than I'd had previously.

After all that had happened in this Mystery Train terminal, this antechamber to Hell, I was no longer inclined to discount my fears as the product of a hyperactive imagination. This time I didn't reach out to prove to myself that my darkest suspicions were groundless, because I knew that my fingertips would slide down the smooth curve of the Plexiglas faceplate.

"Chris!"

I jerked in surprise before I comprehended that the voice was Bobby's.

"Your watch," he said.

The radiant readouts were visible even in this soot-thick murk. The green numbers in those displays were changing, counting forward so rapidly that many hours were falling behind us in a fraction of a second. The letters in the day and month windows were passing in a blur of continuously changing abbreviations.

Time past was giving way to time present.

Hell, in truth I didn't know exactly *what* was happening here. Maybe I didn't understand this situation at all, and maybe a bend in the fabric of time had nothing to do with what we'd witnessed. Maybe we were entirely delusional because someone had spiked our beer with LSD. Maybe I was at home, snug in bed, asleep and dreaming. Maybe up was down, in was out, black was white. I knew only that whatever was happening now felt *right,* felt a lot better than would a sudden embrace from the thing in Hodgson's suit.

If, in fact, we had been more than two years in the past, if we were now racing forward to the April night on which we had begun this bizarre adventure, I thought I ought to have felt some change within myself—a singing in my bones, a fever from the friction of the frantically passing hours, a sense of growing back to my real age, *something.* But a descent on a slow elevator would have had a greater physical effect than this express ride along the rails of time.

On my wristwatch, the month suddenly stopped at *Apr.* A second later, the day and date froze, and immediately thereafter, the time display registered a clear, steady 3:58 *A.M.*

We were home, minus Toto.

"Cool," Bobby said.

"Sweet," I agreed.

The big question was whether we had a fellow traveler with us, a wormy-faced companion in a pressure suit, like nothing Auntie Em or anyone else in Kansas had ever seen.

Logic argued that the Hodgson thing was lost in the past.

It might be delusional, however, to assume that logic applied within this singular situation.

I withdrew the flashlight from under my belt.

Didn't want to switch it on.

Switched it on.

The Hodgson thing wasn't face-to-face with me, as I had feared. A quick sweep of the light revealed that Bobby and I were alone—at least in that portion of the egg room into which the flashlight beam would reach.

The vault door was gone. I couldn't see it either when I looked directly at the exit tunnel or when I relied on my peripheral vision.

Apparently, the room had become so sensitized to light that once again, generated by the single beam, faint luminous whorls began to pulse and wheel in the floor, walls, and ceiling.

I immediately switched off the flashlight and jammed it under my belt.

"Go," I urged.

"Going."

As darkness descended once more, I heard Bobby scrambling over the raised threshold, feeling his way forward through the short, five-foot-high tunnel.

"Clear," he said.

Crouching, I followed him into what had once been the airlock.

I didn't turn on the flashlight again until we were out of the airlock and in the corridor, where not one stray beam could find its way back to the glassy material that lined the egg room.

"Told you it would fade," Bobby said.

"Why do I ever doubt you?"

Neither of us spoke another word all the way up through the three stripped subterranean floors of the facility, through the hangar, to the Jeep, which stood under a sky from which clotting clouds had purged all stars.

15

We drove southwest across Fort Wyvern, through Dead Town, past the warehouses where I had confronted the kidnapper, switching off the headlights as we reached the Santa Rosita, down the access ramp along the levee wall, onto the dry riverbed, obeying not a single stop sign along the way, ignoring every posted speed limit, with a loaded shotgun in a moving vehicle, a concealed weapon in my shoulder holster even though I possessed no license to carry, a cooler of beer between my feet, trespassing in flagrant violation of the federal government's Defense Base Closure and Realignment Act, while holding numerous politically incorrect attitudes, of which a few might well be against the law. We were two Clydes without a Bonnie.

Bobby had so expanded the gap in the river-spanning fence that we drove through with room to spare. He parked immediately outside the grounds of the military base, and together we got out of the Jeep and lowered the flaps of chain-link, which he had rolled up and hooked to the top of the fence.

A close inspection would reveal the breach. From a distance greater than fifteen feet, however, the violation of the fence could not be seen.

We didn't want to announce that we had trespassed. Without doubt we would soon be returning by this same route, and we would need easy access.

The tire tracks leading through the fence betrayed us, but there wasn't a way to erase them quickly and effectively. We had to hope that the breeze would become a wind and obliterate our trail.

In a few hours, we had seen more than we could process, analyze, and apply to our problem—things that we ardently wished we'd never seen. We would have preferred to avoid another sortie onto the base, but until we found Jimmy Wing and Orson, duty required us to revisit this nest of nightmares.

We were leaving now because we were temporarily at a dead end, not sure where to continue the search, and we had to strategize. Besides, more than two of us would be needed to comb even the known warrens of Wyvern.

In addition, dawn was little more than an hour away, and I had not worn my Elephant Man cloak, with hood and veil.

The Suburban, which the kidnapper had parked at the fence, was gone. I was not surprised to see that it was missing. Fortunately, I had memorized the license-plate number.

Bobby drove to the snarl of driftwood and tumbleweed that lay sixty feet from the fence. I retrieved my bicycle from concealment and loaded it into the back of the Jeep.

Passing through the dark tunnel under Highway 1, without headlights, Bobby accelerated. Engine noise, like barrages from ack-ack guns, rattled back to us from the concrete walls.

I remembered the mysterious figure that I had seen earlier on the sloping buttress at the west end of this passage, and my tension grew rather than diminished as the farther end became the nearer end. When we raced into the open, I tensed, half expecting an assault, but nothing was waiting for us.

A hundred yards west of the highway, Bobby braked to a halt and switched off the engine.

We had not spoken since the corridor outside the egg room. Now he said, "Mystery Train."

"All aboard."

"Name of a research project, huh?"

"According to Leland Delacroix's security badge." I fished that object from a jacket pocket, fingering it in the dark, thinking about the dead man surrounded by photographs of his family, the wedding ring in a votive-candle holder.

"So the Mystery Train project was what gave us the troop, the retrovirus, all these mutations. Your mom's little tea-and-doomsday society."

"Maybe."

"I don't think so."

"Then what?"

"She was a theoretical geneticist, right?"

"My mom, apprentice god."

"Virus designer, creature creator."

"Medically valuable little creatures, benign viruses," I said.

"Except for one."

"Your folks are no prize," I reminded him.

With a note of insincere pride, he said, "Hey, they would've destroyed the world long before your mom ever did, if they'd just been given a fair chance."

They owned the only newspaper in the county, the *Moonlight Bay Gazette,* and their religion was politics; their god was power. They were people with a plan, with an unlimited faith in the righteousness of their beliefs. Bobby didn't share their spooky vision of utopia, so they had written him off ten years ago. Apparently, utopia requires the absolute uniformity of thought and purpose exhibited by bees in a hive.

"The point is," he said, "that wacko palace of the weird back there . . . They weren't doing biological research, bro."

"Hodgson was in an airtight suit, not tennis shorts," I reminded him. "He was in typical bio-secure gear. To protect him from being infected by something."

"Totally obvious, yeah. But you said yourself, the place wasn't built for mucking around with germs."

"Not laid out for essential sterilization procedures," I agreed. "No decontamination modules, except maybe for that one airlock. And the floor plan is too open for high-security bio labs."

"That madhouse, that hyped-up lava lamp, wasn't a lab."

"The egg room."

"Call it what you want. It was never a lab with Bunsen burners, petri dishes, and cages full of cute little white mice with scalp scars from brain surgery. You know what that was, bro. We both know."

"I've been brooding about it."

"That was transport," Bobby said.

"Transport."

"They pumped mondo energy into that room, maybe a nuke's worth of energy, maybe more, and when it was fully powered, really revving, it took Hodgson somewhere. Hodgson and a few others. We heard them screaming for help."

"Took them where?"

Instead of answering me, he said, *"Carpe cerevisi."*

"Meaning?"

"Seize the beer."

I took an icy bottle from the cooler and passed it to him, hesitated, and then opened a beer for myself.

"Not wise to drink and drive," I reminded him.

"It's the Apocalypse. No rules."

After taking a long swallow, I said, "I bet God likes beer. Of course, He'd have a chauffeur."

The twenty-foot-high levee walls rose on both sides of us. The low and starless sky appeared to be as hard as iron, pressing down like a kettle lid.

"Transport where?" I asked.

"Remember your wristwatch."

"Maybe it needs repair."

"Mine went nuts, too," he reminded me.

"Since when do you wear a watch, anyway?"

"Since, for the first time in my life, I started feeling time running out," he said, referring not solely to his own mortality but to the fact that time was running out for all of us, for the entire world as we knew it. "Watches, man, I hate them, hate everything they stand for. Evil mechanisms. But lately I start wondering what time it is, though I never used to care, and if I can't find a clock, I get way itchy. So now I wear a watch, and I'm like the rest of the world, and doesn't that suck?"

"It sucketh."

"Like a tornado."

I said, "Time was screwed up in the egg room."

"The room was a time machine."

"We can't make that assumption."

"I can," he said. "I'm an assumption-making fool."

"Time travel is impossible."

"Medieval attitude, bro. Impossible is what they once said about airplanes, going to the moon, nuclear bombs, television, and cholesterol-free egg substitutes."

"For the sake of argument, let's suppose it's possible."

"It *is* possible."

"If it's just time travel, why the pressurized suit? Wouldn't time travelers want to be discreet? They'd be super-conspicuous unless they traveled back to a Star Trek convention in 1980."

"Protection against unknown disease," Bobby said. "Maybe an atmosphere with less oxygen or full of poisonous pollutants."

"At a Star Trek convention in 1980?"

"You know they were going to the future."

"I don't know, and neither do you."

"The future," Bobby insisted, the beer having given him absolute confidence in his powers of deduction. "They figured they needed the protection of the spacesuits because . . . the future might be radically different. Which it evidently is."

Even without the kiss of the moon, a faint silvery blush lent visibility to the riverbed silt. Nevertheless, the April night was deep.

Way back in the seventeenth century, Thomas Fuller said that it is always darkest just before the dawn. More than three hundred years later, he was still right, though still dead.

"How far in the future?" I wondered, almost able to smell the hot, rancid air that had blown through the egg room.

"Ten years, a century, a millennium. Who cares? No matter how far they went, something totally quashed them."

I recalled the ghostly, radio-relayed voices in the egg room: the panic, the cries for help, the screams.

I shuddered. After another pull at my beer, I said, "The thing . . . or things in Hodgson's suit."

"That's part of our future."

"Nothing like that exists on this world."

"Not yet."

"But those things were so strange. . . . The entire ecological system would have to change. Change drastically."

"If you can find one, ask a dinosaur whether it's possible."

I had lost my taste for the beer. I held the bottle out of the Jeep, turned it upside down, and let it drain.

"Even if it was a time machine," I argued, "it was dismantled. So Hodgson showing up the way he did, out of nowhere, and the vault door reappearing . . . everything that happened to us . . . *How* could it have happened?"

"There's a residual effect."

"Residual effect."

"Full-on, totally macking residual effect."

"You take the engine out of a Ford, tear apart the drive train, throw away the battery—no residual effect can cause the damn car to just drive itself off to Vegas one day."

Gazing at the dwindling, vaguely luminous riverbed as if it were the course of time winding into our infinitely strange future, Bobby said, "They tore a hole in reality. Maybe a hole like that doesn't mend itself."

"What does that mean?"

"What it means," he said.

"Cryptic."

"Styptic."

Perhaps his point was that his explanation might be cryptic, yes, but at least it was a concept we could grasp and to which we could cling, a familiar idea that kept our sanity from draining away, just as the alum in a styptic pencil could stop the blood flowing from a shaving cut.

Or perhaps he was mocking my tendency—acquired from the poetry in which my father had steeped me—to assume that everyone spoke in metaphor and that the world was always more complex than it appeared to be, in which case he had chosen the word solely for the rhyme.

I didn't give him the satisfaction of asking him to elucidate *styptic*. "They didn't know about this residual effect?"

"You mean the big-brain wizards running the project?"

"Yeah. The people who built it, then tore it down. If there was a residual effect, they'd blow in the walls, fill the ruins with a few thousand tons of concrete. They wouldn't just walk away and leave it for assholes like us to find."

He shrugged. "So maybe the effect didn't manifest until they were long gone."

"Or maybe we were hallucinating everything," I suggested.

"Both of us?"

"Could be."

"Identical hallucinations?"

I had no adequate answer, so I said, "Styptic."

"Elliptic."

I refused to think about that one. "If the Mystery Train was a time-travel project, it didn't have anything to do with my mother's work."

"So?"

"So if it didn't have anything to do with Mom, why did someone leave this cap for me in the egg room? Why did they leave her photo in the airlock on a different night? Why did someone put Leland Delacroix's security badge under the windshield wiper and send us there tonight?"

"You're a regular question machine."

He finished his Heineken, and I shoved our empty bottles into the cooler.

"Could be that we don't know half of what we think we know," Bobby said.

"Like?"

"Maybe everything that went wrong at Wyvern went wrong in the genetic-engineering labs, and maybe your mom's theories were entirely what led to the mess we're in now, just like we've been thinking. Or maybe not."

"You mean my mother didn't destroy the world?"

"Well, we can be pretty sure she helped, bro. I'm not saying your mom was a nobody."

"*Gracias.*"

"On the other hand, maybe she was only part of it, and maybe even the lesser part."

After my father's death from cancer a month earlier—a cancer I now suspect didn't have a natural cause—I had found his handwritten account of Orson's origins, the intelligence-enhancement experiments, and my mother's slippery retrovirus. "You read what my dad wrote."

"Possibly he wasn't clued in to the whole story."

"He and Mom didn't keep secrets from each other."

"Yeah, sure, one soul in two bodies."

"That's right," I said, prickling at his sarcasm.

He glanced at me, winced, and returned his attention to the riverbed ahead. "Sorry, Chris. You're totally right. Your mom and dad weren't like mine. They were way . . . special. When we were kids, I used to wish we weren't just best friends. Used to wish we were brothers so I could live with your folks."

"We *are* brothers, Bobby."

He nodded.

"In more important ways than blood," I said.

"Don't set off the maudlin alarm."

"Sorry. Been eating too much sugar lately."

There are truths about which Bobby and I never speak, because all words are inadequate to describe them, and to speak of them would be to diminish their power. One of these truths is the profound depth and sacred nature of our friendship.

Bobby moved on: "What I'm saying is, maybe your mom didn't know the full story, either. Didn't know about the Mystery Train project, which might be as much or more at fault than she was."

"Cozy idea. But how?"

"I'm not Einstein, bro. I just drained my brain."

He started the engine and drove downriver, still leaving the headlights off.

I said, "I think I know what Big Head might be."

"Enlighten me."

"It's one of the second troop."

The first troop had escaped the Wyvern lab on that violent night well over two years ago, and they had proved so elusive that every effort to locate and eradicate them had failed. Desperate to find the monkeys before their numbers drastically increased, the project scientists had released a second troop to search for the first, figuring that it would take a monkey to find a monkey.

Each of these new individuals carried a surgically implanted transponder, so it could be tracked and ultimately destroyed along with whatever members of the first troop it found. Although these new monkeys were supposedly unaware that they had been put through this surgery, once set loose they had chewed the transponders out of one another, setting themselves free.

"You think Big Head was a monkey?" he asked with disbelief.

"A radically redesigned monkey. Maybe not entirely a rhesus. Maybe some baboon in there."

"Maybe some crocodile," Bobby said sourly. He frowned. "I thought the second troop was supposed to be a lot better engineered than the first. Less violent."

"So?"

"Big Head didn't look like a pussycat. That thing was designed for the battlefield."

"It didn't attack us."

"Only because it was smart enough to know what the shotgun could do to it."

Ahead was the access ramp down which I had traveled on my bike earlier in the night, with Orson padding at my side. Bobby angled the Jeep toward it.

Recalling the sorry beast on the bungalow roof and the way it had hidden its face behind its crossed arms, I said, "I don't think it's a killer."

"Yeah, all those teeth are just for opening canned hams."

"Orson has wicked teeth, and he's no killer."

"Oh, you've convinced me, you absolutely have. Let's invite Big Head for a pajama party. We'll make huge bowls of popcorn, order in a pizza, put one another's hair up in curlers, and talk about boys."

"Asshole."

"A minute ago, we were brothers."

"That was then."

Bobby drove up the ramp to the top of the levee, between the signs warning about the dangers of the river during storms, across the barren strip of land to the street, where at last he switched on the headlights. He headed toward Lilly Wing's house.

"I think Pia and I are going to be together again," Bobby said, referring to Pia Klick, the artist and love of his life, who believes that she is the reincarnation of Kaha Huna, the goddess of surf.

"She says Waimea is home," I reminded him.

"I'm going to work some major mojo."

Mother Earth was busily rotating us toward dawn, but the streets of Moonlight Bay were so deserted and silent it was easy to imagine that it was, like Dead Town, inhabited only by ghosts and cadavers.

"Mojo? You're into voodoo now?" I asked Bobby.

"Freudian mojo."

"Pia's way too smart to fall for it," I predicted.

Although she had been acting flaky for the past three years, ever since she had gone to Hawaii to find herself, Pia was no dummy. Before Bobby ever met her, she had graduated *summa cum laude* from UCLA. These days, her hyperrealist paintings sold for big bucks, and the pieces she wrote for various art magazines were perceptive and brilliantly composed.

"I'm going to tell her about my new tandem board," he said.

"Ah. The implication being there's some wahine you're riding it with."

"You need a reality transfusion, bro. Pia can't be manipulated like that. What I tell her is—I got the tandem board, and I'm ready whenever she is."

Since Pia's meditations had led her to the revelation that she was the reincarnation of Kaha Huna, she had decided that it would be blasphemous to have carnal relations with a mere mortal man, which meant that she would have to live the rest of her life in celibacy. This had demoralized Bobby.

An elusive squiggle of hope appeared with Pia's subsequent realization that Bobby was the reincarnation of Kahuna, the Hawaiian god of the surf. A creation of modern surfers, the Kahuna legend is based on the life of an ancient witch doctor no more divine than your local chiropractor. Nevertheless, Pia says that Bobby, being Kahuna, is the one man on earth with whom she could make love—although in order for them to pick up where they left off, he must acknowledge his true immortal nature and embrace his fate.

A new problem arose when, either out of pride in being just mortal Bobby Halloway or out of pure stubbornness, of which he has some, Bobby refused to agree that he was the one and true god of the surf.

Compared to the difficulties of modern romance, the problems of Romeo and Juliet were piffling.

"So you're finally going to admit you're Kahuna," I said, as we drove through pine-flanked streets into the higher hills of town.

"No. I'll play it mysterious. I won't say I'm *not* Kahuna. Be cool. Wrap myself in enigma when she raises the subject, and let her make what she wants of that."

"Not good enough."

"There's more. I'll also tell her about this dream where I saw her in an awesomely beautiful gold-and-blue silk *holoku,* levitating over these tasty, eight-foot, glassy waves, and in the dream she says to me, *Papa he'e nalu*—Hawaiian for *surfboard.*"

We were in a residential neighborhood two blocks south of Ocean Avenue, the main east-west street in Moonlight Bay, when a car turned the corner at the intersection ahead, approaching us. It was a basic, late-model, Chevrolet sedan, beige or white, with standard California license plates.

I closed my eyes to protect them from the oncoming headlights. I wanted to duck or slide down in the seat to shield my face from the light, but I could have done nothing more calculated to call attention to myself other than, perhaps, whipping out a paper bag and pulling it over my head.

As the Chevy was passing us, its headlights no longer a danger, I opened my eyes and saw two men in the front, one in the backseat. They were big guys, dressed in dark clothes, as expressionless as turnips, all interested in us. Their night-of-the-living-dead eyes were flat, cold, and disturbingly direct.

For some reason, I thought of the shadowy figure I had seen on the sloping buttress, above the tunnel that led under Highway 1.

After we were past the Chevy, Bobby said, "Legal muscle."

"Professional trouble," I agreed.

"They might as well have had it stenciled on their foreheads."

Watching their taillights in the side mirror, I said, "They don't seem to be after us, anyway. Wonder what they're looking for."

"Maybe Elvis."

When the Chevy didn't double back and follow us, I said, "So you're gonna tell Pia that in this dream of yours, she's levitating over some waves, and she says, *Papa he'e nalu*."

"Right. In the dream, she tells me to get a tandem board we can ride together. I figured that was prophetic, so I got the board, and now I'm ready."

"What a crock," I said, by way of friendly criticism.

"It's true. I had the dream."

"No way."

"Way. In fact, I had it three nights in a row, which weirded me out a little. I'll tell her all that, and let her interpret it any way she wants."

"While you play mysterious, not admitting to being Kahuna but exhibiting godlike charisma."

He looked worried. Braking at a stop sign after having ignored all those before it, he said, "Truth. You don't think I can pull it off?"

When it comes to charisma, I have never known anyone like Bobby: The stuff pours off him in such copious quantity that he positively wades in it.

"Bro," I said, "you have so much charisma that if you wanted to form a suicide cult, you'd have people signing up by the thousands to jump off a cliff with you."

He was pleased. "Yeah? You're not spinning me?"

"No spin," I assured him.

"*Mahalo.*"

"You're welcome. But one question."

As he accelerated away from the stop sign, he said, "Ask."

"Why not just tell Pia that you've decided you're Kahuna?"

"I can't lie to her. I *love* her."

"It's a harmless lie."

"Do you lie to Sasha?"

"No."

"Does she lie to you?"

"She doesn't lie to anyone," I said.

"Between a man and woman in love, no lie is small or harmless."

"You keep surprising me."

"My wisdom?"

"Your mushy little teddy-bear heart."

"Squeeze me, and I sing 'Feelings.' "

"I'll take your word for it."

We were only a few blocks from Lilly Wing's house.

"Go in by the back, through the alley," I directed.

I wouldn't have been surprised to find a police patrol car or another unmarked sedan full of granite-eyed men waiting for us, but the alleyway was deserted. Sasha Goodall's Ford Explorer stood in front of Lilly's garage door, and Bobby parked behind it.

Beyond the windbreak of giant eucalyptuses, the wild canyon to the east lay in unrelieved blackness. Without the lamp of the moon, anything might have been out there: a bottomless abyss rather than a mere canyon, a great dark sea, the end of the earth and a yawning infinity.

As I got out of the Jeep, I remembered good Orson investigating the weeds along the verge of the canyon, urgently seeking Jimmy. His yelp of excitement when he caught the scent. His swift and selfless commitment to the chase.

Only hours ago. Yet ages ago.

Time seemed out of joint even here, far beyond the walls of the egg room.

At the thought of Orson, a coldness closed around my heart, and for a moment I couldn't breathe.

I recalled waiting by candlelight beside my father in the cold-holding room at Mercy Hospital, two years ago this past January, waiting with my mother's body for the hearse that would take her to Kirk's Funeral Home, feeling as though my own body had been broken beyond repair by the loss of her, almost afraid to move or even to speak, as though I might fly apart like a hollow ceramic figurine struck with a hammer. And my father's hospital room only a month ago. The terrible night he died. Holding his hand in mine, leaning over the bed railing to hear his final whispered words—*Fear nothing, Chris. Fear nothing.*—and then his hand going slack in mine. I had kissed his forehead, his rough cheek. Because I myself am a walking miracle, still healthy and whole with XP at the age of twenty-eight, I believe in miracles, in the reality of them and in our need for them, and so I held fast to my dead father's hand, kissed his beard-stubbled cheek, still hot with fever, and waited for a miracle, all but demanded one. God help me, I expected Dad to pull a Lazarus on me, because the pain of losing him was too fierce to bear, the world unthinkably hard and cold without him, and I could not be expected to endure it, must be granted mercy, so although I have been blessed with numerous miracles in my life, I was greedy for one more, one more. I prayed to God, begged Him, bargained with Him, but there is a grace in the natural order of things that is more important than our desires, and at last I'd had to accept that grace, as bitter as it seemed at the time, and reluctantly I'd released my father's lifeless hand.

Now I stood breathless in the alley, pierced again by the fear that I would be required to outlive Orson, my brother, that special and precious soul, who was even more an outsider in this world than I was. If he should die alone, without the hand of a friend to comfort him, without a soothing voice telling him that he was loved, I would be forever haunted by—ruined by—the thought of his solitary suffering and despair.

"Bro," Bobby said, putting one hand on my shoulder and squeezing gently. "Gonna be all right."

I hadn't spoken a word, but Bobby seemed to know what fears had rooted me to the alleyway blacktop as I stared into the forbidding blackness of the canyon beyond the eucalyptus trees.

Breath returned to me in a rush, and with it came a dangerously fierce hope, one of those seizures of hope so intense it can break your heart if it goes unfulfilled, a hope that was really a mad and unreasonable *conviction*, which I had no right to indulge here at the end of the world: We would find Jimmy Wing, and we would find Orson, untouched and alive, and those who had meant to harm them would rot in Hell.

16

Through the wooden gate, along the narrow brick walkway, into the backyard where the aroma of jasmine was as thick as incense, I worried about how I was going to convey to Lilly Wing even a small measure of my newfound faith that her son would be discovered alive and unharmed. I had little to tell her that would support such an optimistic conclusion. In fact, if I recounted a fraction of what Bobby and I had seen in Fort Wyvern, Lilly would lose hope altogether.

Bright lights were on toward the front of the Cape Cod bungalow. In expectation of my return, only faint candlelight flickered beyond the kitchen windows at the rear.

Sasha was waiting for us at the top of the back-porch steps. She must have been in the kitchen when she heard the Jeep pulling behind the garage.

The mental image of Sasha that I carry with me is idealized—yet each time I see her, after an absence, she is lovelier than my most flattering recollection. Although my vision had adapted to the dark, the light was so poor that I could not see the arrestingly clear gray of her eyes, the mahogany shade of her hair, or the faintly freckled glow of her skin. Nevertheless, she shone.

We embraced, and she whispered, "Hey, Snowman."

"Hey."

"Jimmy?"

"Not yet," I said, matching her whisper. "Now Orson's missing."

Her embrace tightened. "In Wyvern?"

"Yeah."

She kissed my cheek. "He's not just all heart and wagging tail. He's tough. He can take care of himself."

"We're going back for them."

"Damn right, and me with you."

Sasha's beauty is not just—or even primarily—physical. In her face, I also see her wisdom, her compassion, her courage, her eternal glory. This other beauty, this spiritual beauty—which is the deepest truth of her—sustains me in times of fear and despair, as other truths might sustain a priest enduring martyrdom under the hand of a tyrant. I see nothing blasphemous in equating Sasha's grace with the mercy of God, for the one is a reflection of the other. The selfless love that we give to others, to the point of being willing to sacrifice our lives for them—as Sasha would give hers for me, as I would give mine for her—is all the proof I need that human beings are not mere animals of self-interest; we carry within us a divine spark, and if we choose to recognize it, our lives have dignity, meaning, hope. In Sasha, this spark is bright, a light that heals rather than wounds me.

When she hugged Bobby, who was carrying the shotgun, Sasha whispered, "Better leave that out here. Lilly's shaky."

"Me too," Bobby murmured.

He put the shotgun on the porch swing. The Smith & Wesson revolver was tucked under his belt, concealed by his Hawaiian shirt.

Sasha was wearing blue jeans, a sweater, and a roomy denim jacket. When we embraced, I'd felt the concealed handgun in her shoulder holster.

I had the 9-millimeter Glock.

If my mother's gene-swapping retrovirus had been vulnerable to gunfire, it would have met its match in us, the end of the world would have been canceled, and we would have been at a beach party.

"Cops?" I asked Sasha.

"They were here. Gone now."

"Manuel?" I asked, meaning Manuel Ramirez, the acting chief of police, who had been my friend before he had been co-opted by the Wyvern crowd.

"Yeah. When he saw me walk through the door, he looked like he was passing a kidney stone."

Sasha led us into the kitchen, where such a hush prevailed that our soft footsteps were, comparatively, as loud and as rude as clog dancing in a chapel. Lilly's anguish cast a shroud over this humble house, no less tangible than a velvet pall on a casket, as though Jimmy had already been found dead.

Out of respect for my condition, the only light came from the digital clock on the oven, from the blue gas flame under the teakettle on one of the cooktop burners, and from a pair of fat, yellow candles. The candles, which were set in white saucers on the dinette table, emitted a vanilla fragrance that was inappropriately festive for this dark place and these solemn circumstances.

One side of the table was adjacent to a window, allowing space for three chairs. In the same jeans and flannel shirt she'd been wearing earlier, Lilly sat in the chair facing me.

Bobby remained by the door, watching the backyard, and Sasha went to the stove to check the teakettle.

I pulled out a chair and sat directly across the table from Lilly. The candles in the saucers were between us, and I pushed them to one side.

Lilly was sitting forward on her chair, her arms on the pine table.

"Badger," I said.

Brow furrowed, eyes narrowed, lips pressed tightly together, she gazed at her clasped hands with such fierce attention that she seemed to be trying to read the fate of her child in the sharp points of her knuckles, in the patterns of bones and veins and freckles, as if her hands were tarot cards or *I Ching* sticks.

"I'll never stop," I promised her.

From the subdued nature of my entrance, she already

knew that I hadn't found her son, and she didn't acknowledge me.

Recklessly, I promised her: "We're going to regroup, get more help, go back out there and find him."

At last she raised her head and met my eyes. The night had aged her mercilessly. Even by the flattering light of candles, she looked gaunt, worn, as if she'd been beaten by many cruel years rather than by a few dark hours. Through a trick of light, her blond hair seemed white. Her blue eyes, once so radiant and lively, were dark now with sorrow, fear, and rage.

"My phone doesn't work," Lilly said in an emotionless and quiet voice, her calm demeanor belied by the powerful emotions in her eyes.

"Your phone?" At first I assumed that her mind had broken under the weight of her fear.

"After the cops were gone, I called my mom. She remarried after Dad died. Three years after. Lives in San Diego. My call couldn't be completed. An operator broke in. Said long-distance service was disrupted. Temporarily. Equipment failure. She was lying."

I was struck by the odd and utterly uncharacteristic patterns of her speech: the clipped sentences, staccato cadences. She seemed to be able to speak only by concentrating on small groups of words, succinct bits of information, as if afraid that while delivering a longer sentence, her voice would break and, in breaking, would set loose her pent-up feelings, reducing her to uncontrollable tears and incoherence.

"How do you know the operator was lying?" I prodded when Lilly fell silent.

"Wasn't even a real operator. You could tell. Didn't have the lingo right. Didn't have the voice. Tone of voice. Didn't have the attitude. They sound alike. They're trained. This one was jive."

The movement of her eyes matched the rhythms of her speech. She looked at me repeatedly but each time quickly looked away; laden with guilt and a sense of inadequacy, I assumed that she couldn't bear the sight of me because I'd failed her. Once she'd shifted her attention from her clasped hands, she was unable to focus on anything for more than a second or two, perhaps because every object and surface in the kitchen summoned memories of Jimmy, memories that would shatter her self-control if she dared to dwell on them.

"So I tried a local call. To Ben's mother. My late husband's mother. Jimmy's grandma. She lives across town. Couldn't get a dial tone. Now the phone is dead. No phone at all."

From the far end of the kitchen came the clink of china, then the rattle of spoons as Sasha searched through the flatware in a drawer.

Lilly said, "The cops weren't cops, either. Looked like cops. Uniforms. Badges. Guns. Men I've known all my life. Manuel. He looks like Manuel. Doesn't act like Manuel anymore."

"What was different?"

"They asked a few questions. Scribbled some notes. Made a plaster impression of the footprint. Outside Jimmy's window. Dusted for fingerprints, but not everywhere they should have. It wasn't real. Wasn't thorough at all. They didn't even find the crow."

"Crow?"

"They didn't . . . care somehow," she continued, as if she hadn't heard my question, was struggling to understand their indifference. "Lou, my father-in-law, used to be a cop. He was thorough. And he cared. What's he have to do with this, anyway? He was a *good* cop. A kind man. You always knew he cared. Not like . . . *them*."

I turned to Sasha for some illumination about the crow and Louis Wing. She nodded, which I took to mean that she understood and would clue me in later if Lilly, in her distress, didn't make the connections for me.

Playing devil's advocate, I said to Lilly, "The police have to be detached, impersonal, to do their job right."

"It wasn't that. They'll look for Jimmy. They'll investigate. They'll try. I think they will. But they were also . . . managing me."

"Managing?"

"They said not to talk. Not to anyone. For twenty-four hours. Talking jeopardizes the investigation. Child abductions scare the public, see? Cause panic. Police phones ring off the hook. They spend all their time calming people. Can't put full resources into finding Jimmy. Bullshit. I'm not stupid. I'm coming apart here, coming apart . . . but not stupid." She almost lost her composure, took a deep breath, and finished in the same controlled, flat voice: "They just want to shut me up. Shut me up for twenty-four hours. And I don't know why."

I understood Manuel's motivation for seeking her silence. He needed to buy time until he could determine whether this was a conventional crime or one connected to events at Wyvern, because he was diligent about concealing the latter. Right now he was hoping that the kidnapper was a common variety of sociopath, a pedophile or satanic cultist, or someone with a grudge against Lilly. But the perpetrator might be one of those who were becoming, a man whose DNA was so disturbed by an aggressive infection of the retrovirus that his psychology was deteriorating, his sense of humanity dissolving in an acid of utterly alien urges and needs, compulsions darker and stranger than even the worst of bestial desires. Or maybe there was another connection to Wyvern, because these days so much that went wrong in Moonlight Bay could be traced to those haunted grounds beyond the chain-link and razor wire.

If Jimmy's kidnapper was one of the becoming, he'd never stand trial. If captured, he would be taken to the deeply hidden genetics labs in Fort Wyvern if they were, as we suspected, still operating, or he would be transported to a similar and equally secret facility elsewhere, to be studied and tested, as part of the desperate search for a cure. In that event, Lilly would be pressured to accept an officially concocted story of what had happened to her son. If she couldn't be persuaded, if she couldn't be threatened, then she would be killed or rail-roaded into the psychiatric ward at Mercy Hospital, in the name of national security and the public welfare, though in truth she would be sacrificed for no reason other than to protect the political eminences who had brought us to this brink.

Sasha came to the table with a cup of tea, which she placed in front of Lilly. On the saucer was a wedge of lemon. Beside the cup, she put a cream-and-sugar set on a matching china tray, with a small silver spoon for the sugar.

Instead of grounding us in reality, these domestic details gave a dreamlike quality to the proceedings. If Alice, the White Rabbit, and the Mad Hatter had joined us at the table, I would not have been surprised.

Apparently, Lilly had asked for tea, but now she seemed barely aware that it had been put before her. The power of her repressed emotions was growing so visible that she wouldn't be able to maintain her composure much longer, yet for the moment she continued to speak in an uninflected drone: "Phone's dead. Okay. What if I drive to my mother-in-law's? To tell her about Jimmy. Will I be stopped? Stopped on the way? Advised to be silent? For Jimmy's sake? And if I won't stop? If I won't be silent?"

"How much has Sasha told you?" I asked.

Lilly's eyes fixed on mine, then moved at once away. "Something happened at Wyvern. Something strange. Bad. In some way it affects us. Everyone in Moonlight Bay. They're trying to keep it quiet. It might explain Jimmy's disappearance. Somehow."

I turned to look at Sasha, who had retreated to the farther side of the kitchen. "That's all?"

"Isn't she in greater danger if she knows more?" Sasha asked.

"Definitely," Bobby said from his watch position at the rear door.

Considering the depth of Lilly's distress, I agreed that it was not wise to tell her every detail of what we knew. If she understood the apocalyptic threat looming over us, over all humanity, she might lose her last desperate faith that she would see her little boy alive again. I would never be the one who robbed her of that remaining hope.

Besides, I detected a dusting of gray in the night beyond

the kitchen windows, a precursor of dawn so subtle that anyone without my heightened appreciation for shades of darkness was not likely to notice. We were running out of time. Soon I would have to hide from the sun, which I preferred to do in the well-prepared sanctuary of my own home.

Lilly said, "I deserve to know. To know everything."

"Yes," I agreed.

"Everything."

"But there's not enough time now. We—"

"I'm scared," she whispered.

I pushed aside her cup of tea and reached across the table with both hands. "You aren't alone."

She looked at my hands but didn't take them, perhaps because she was afraid that by putting her hands in mine, she would lose her grip on her emotions.

Keeping my hands on the table, palms up, I said, "Knowing more now won't help you. Later, I'll tell you everything. Everything. But now . . . If whoever took Jimmy has nothing to do with . . . the mess at Wyvern, Manuel will try hard to bring him back to you. I know he will. But if it *is* related to Wyvern, then none of the police, Manuel included, can be trusted. Then it's up to us. And we've got to assume it *will* be up to us."

"This is so wrong."

"Yes."

"Crazy."

"Yes."

"So wrong," she repeated, and her flat voice was increasingly eerie. Her effort to maintain her composure left her face clenched as tight as a fist.

I couldn't bear the sight of her in such acute pain, but I did not avert my gaze. When she was able to look at me, I wanted her to see the commitment in my eyes; perhaps she could take some comfort from it.

"You've got to stay here," I said, "so we'll know where to get hold of you if . . . when we find Jimmy."

"What hope do you have?" she said, and though her voice remained flat, a flutter passed through it. "You against

. . . who? The police? The army? The government? You against all of them?"

"It isn't hopeless. Nothing's hopeless in this world—unless we want it to be. But, Lilly . . . you've got to stay here. Because if this isn't about Wyvern, isn't connected, then the police might need your help. Or might bring you good news. Even the police."

"But you shouldn't be alone," Sasha said.

"When we leave," Bobby said, "I'll bring Jenna here." Jenna Wing was Lilly's mother-in-law. "Would that be okay?"

Lilly nodded.

She was not going to take my hands, so I folded them on the table, as hers were folded.

I said, "You asked what they could do if you decided not to be silent, not to play this their way. Anything. That's what they can do." I hesitated. Then: "I don't know where my mother was going on the day she died. She was driving out of town. Maybe to break this conspiracy wide open. Because she knew, Lilly. She knew what had happened at Wyvern. She never got where she was going. Neither would you."

Her eyes widened. "The accident, the car crash."

"No accident."

For the first time since I'd sat across the table from her, Lilly met my eyes and held my gaze for longer than two or three words: "Your mother. Genetics. Her work. That's how you know so much about this."

I didn't take the opportunity to explain more to Lilly, for fear she might reach the correct conclusion that my mother was not merely a righteous whistle-blower, that she was among those fundamentally responsible for what had gone wrong at Wyvern. And if what happened to Jimmy was related to the Wyvern cover-up, Lilly might take the next step in logic, concluding that her son was in jeopardy as a direct result of my mother's work. While this was probably true, she might leap thereafter into the realm of the illogical, assume that I was one of the conspirators, one of the enemy, and withdraw from me. Regardless of what my mother could have done, I was Lilly's friend and her best hope of finding her child.

"Your best chance, Jimmy's best chance, is to trust us. Me, Bobby, Sasha. Trust us, Lilly."

"There's nothing I can do. Nothing," she said bitterly.

Her clenched face changed, though it didn't relax with relief at being able to share this burden with friends. Instead, the wretched twist of pain that distorted her features drew tighter, into a hard knot of anger, as she was overcome by a simultaneously dispiriting and infuriating recognition of her helplessness.

When her husband, Ben, died three years ago, Lilly had left her job as a teacher's aide, because she couldn't support Jimmy on that income, and she had risked the life-insurance money to open a gift shop in an area of the harbor popular with tourists. With hard work, she made the business viable. To overcome loneliness and grief at the loss of Ben, she filled her spare hours with Jimmy and with self-education: She learned to lay bricks, installing the walkways around her bungalow; she built a fine picket fence, stripped and refinished the cabinets in her kitchen, and became a first-class gardener, with the best landscaping in her neighborhood. She was accustomed to taking care of herself, to coping. Even in adversity, she had always before remained an optimist; she was a doer, a fighter, all but incapable of thinking of herself as a victim.

Perhaps for the first time in her life, Lilly felt entirely helpless, pitted against forces she could neither fully understand nor successfully defy. This time self-reliance was not enough; worse, there seemed to be no positive action that she could take. Because it was not in her nature to embrace victimhood, she could not find solace in self-pity, either. She could only wait. Wait for Jimmy to be found alive. Wait for him to be found dead. Or, perhaps worst of all, wait all her life without knowing what had happened to him. Because of this intolerable helplessness, she was racked equally by anger, terror, and a portentous grief.

At last she unclasped her hands.

Her eyes blurred with tears that she struggled not to shed.

Because I thought she was going to reach out to me, I reached toward her again.

Instead, she covered her face with her hands and, sobbing, said, "Oh, Chris, I'm so ashamed."

I didn't know whether she meant that her helplessness shamed her or that she was ashamed of losing control, of weeping.

I went around the table and tried to pull her into my arms.

She resisted for a moment, then rose from her chair and hugged me. Burying her face against my shoulder, voice raw with anguish, she said, "I was so . . . oh, God . . . I was so cruel to you."

Stunned, confused, I said, "No, no. Lilly, Badger, no, not you, not ever."

"I didn't have . . . the guts." She was shaking as if in the thrall of a fever, words stuttering out of her, teeth chattering, clutching at me with the desperation of a lost and terrified child.

I held her tight, unable to speak because her pain tore at me. I remained baffled by her declaration of shame; yet, in retrospect, I believe an understanding was beginning to come to me.

"All my big talk," she said, her voice becoming even less clear, distorted by a choking remorse. "Just talk. But I wasn't . . . couldn't . . . when it counted . . . couldn't." She gasped for breath and held me tighter than ever. "I told you the difference didn't matter to me, but in the end it did."

"Stop," I whispered. "It's all right, all right."

"Your difference," she said, but by now I knew what she meant. "Your difference. In the end it mattered. And I turned away from you. But here you are. Here you are when I need you."

Bobby moved from the kitchen onto the back porch. He wasn't investigating a suspicious noise, and he wasn't stepping outside to give us privacy. His slacker indifference was a shell inside which was concealed a snail-soft sentimental Bobby

Halloway that he thought was unknown to everyone, even to me.

Sasha started to follow Bobby. When she glanced at me, I shook my head, encouraging her to stay.

Visibly discomfited, she busied herself by brewing another serving of tea to replace the one that had cooled, untouched, in the cup on the table.

"You never turned away from me, never, never," I told Lilly, holding her, smoothing her hair with one hand, and wishing that life had never brought us to a moment where she felt compelled to speak of this.

For four years, beginning when we were sixteen, we hoped to build a life together, but we grew up. For one thing, we realized that any children we conceived would be at too high a risk of XP. I've made peace with my limitations, but I couldn't justify creating a child who would be burdened with them. And if the child was born without XP, he—or she—would be fatherless at a young age, for I wasn't likely to survive far into his teenage years. Though I would have been content to live childless with Lilly, she longed to have a family, which was natural and right. She struggled, too, with the certainty of being a young widow—and with the awful prospect of the increasing physical and neurological disorders that were likely to plague me during my final few years: slurred speech, hearing loss, uncontrollable tremors of the head and the hands, perhaps even mental impairment.

"We both knew it had to end, both of us," I told Lilly, which was true, because belatedly I'd recognized the horrendous obligation that I would eventually become to her, all in the name of love.

To be honest, I might selfishly have seduced her into marriage and allowed her to suffer with me during my eventual descent into infirmity and disability, because the comfort and companionship she could have provided would have made my decline less frightening and more tolerable. I might have closed my mind to the realization that I was ruining her life in order to improve mine. I am not adequate material for sainthood; I am not selfless. She had voiced the first doubts, tentative and apologetic; listening to her, over a period of weeks, I'd reluctantly arrived at the realization that although she would make any sacrifice for me—and though I wanted to let her make those sacrifices—what love she still had for me after my death would inevitably be corroded with resentment and with a justified bitterness. Because I am not going to have a long life, I have a deep and thoroughly selfish need to want those who have known me to keep me alive in memory. And I am vain enough to want those memories to be cherished, to be full of affection and laughter. Finally I had understood that, for my sake as much as Lilly's, we had to forgo our dream of a life together—or risk watching the dream devolve into a nightmare.

Now, with Lilly in my arms, I realized that because she had been the first to express doubts about our relationship, she felt the full responsibility for its collapse. When we'd ceased to be lovers and decided to settle for friendship, my continued longing for her and my melancholy about the end of our dream must have been dismally apparent, because I'd been neither kind enough nor man enough to spare her from them. Unwittingly, I had sharpened the thorn of guilt in her heart, and eight years too late, I needed to heal the wound that I had caused.

When I began to tell her all this, Lilly attempted to protest. By habit, she blamed herself, and over the years she had learned to take a masochistic solace in her imagined culpability, which she was now reluctant to do without. Earlier, I'd incorrectly believed that her inability to meet my eyes resulted from my failure to find Jimmy; like her, I'd been quick to torture myself with blame. This side of Eden, whether we realize it or not, we feel the stain on our souls, and at every opportunity, we try to scrub it away with steel-wool guilt.

I held fast to this dear woman, talking her into accepting exoneration, trying to make her see me for the needy fool that I am, insisting that she understand how close I had come, eight years ago, to manipulating her into sacrificing her future for me. Diligently, I tarnished the shining image she held of me. This was one of the most difficult things I've ever had to do . . . because as I held her and quieted her tears, I realized how much I still cherished her, treasured her, and how desperately I wanted her to think only well of me, though we would never be lovers again.

"We did what was right. Both of us. If we hadn't made the decision we made eight years ago," I concluded, "you wouldn't have found Ben, and I would never have found Sasha. Those are precious moments in our lives—your meeting Ben, my meeting Sasha. Sacred moments."

"I love you, Chris."

"I love you, too."

"Not like I once loved you."

"I know."

"Better than that."

"I know," I said.

"Purer than that."

"You don't need to say this."

"Not because it makes me feel rebellious and noble to love you with all your troubles. Not because you're different. I love you because you're who you are."

"Badger?" I said.

"What?"

I smiled. "Shut up."

She let out a sound that was more laugh than sob, though it was composed of both. She kissed me on the cheek and settled into her chair, weak with relief but also still weak with fear for her missing son.

Sasha brought a fresh cup of tea to the table, and Lilly took her hand, held it tightly. "Do you know *The Wind in the Willows*?"

"Didn't until I met Chris," Sasha said, and even in the dim and fluttering candlelight, I saw the tracks of tears on her face.

"He called me Badger because I stood up for him. But he's my Badger now, your Badger. And you're his, aren't you?"

"She swings a hell of a mean cudgel," I said.

"We're going to find Jimmy," Sasha promised her, relieving me of the terrible weight of repeating that impossible promise, "and we're going to bring him home to you."

"What about the crow?" Lilly asked Sasha.

From a pocket, Sasha produced a sheet of drawing paper, which she unfolded. "After the cops left, I searched Jimmy's bedroom. They hadn't been thorough. I thought we might find something they overlooked. This was under one of the pillows."

When I held the paper to the candlelight, I saw an ink sketch of a bird in flight, side view, wings back. Beneath the bird was a neatly hand-lettered message: *Louis Wing will be my servant in Hell.*

"What does your father-in-law have to do with this?" I asked Lilly.

Fresh misery darkened her face. "I don't know."

Bobby stepped inside from the porch. "Got to split, bro."

By now the coming dawn was evident to all of us. The sun had not yet appeared above the eastern hills, but the night was doing a fade, from blackest soot to gray dust. Beyond the windows, the backyard was no longer a landscape in shades of black but a pencil sketch.

I showed him the drawing of the crow. "Maybe this isn't about Wyvern, after all. Maybe someone has a grudge against Louis."

Bobby studied the paper, but he wasn't convinced that this proved the kidnapping was merely a crime of vengeance. "Everything goes back to Wyvern, one way or another."

"When did Louis leave the police department?" I asked.

Lilly said, "He retired about four years ago, a year before Ben died."

"And before everything went wrong at Wyvern," Sasha noted. "So maybe this *isn't* connected."

"It's connected," Bobby insisted. He tapped one finger against the crow. "It's too radically weird not to be connected."

"We should talk to your father-in-law," I told Lilly.

She shook her head. "Can't. He's in Shorehaven."

"The nursing home?"

"He's had three strokes over the past four months. The third left him in a coma. He can't talk to anyone. They don't expect him to live much longer."

When I looked at the ink sketch again, I understood that Bobby's "radically weird" had referred not only to the hand-lettered words but also to the crow itself. The drawing had a malevolent aura: The wing feathers bristled; the beak was open as if to let out a shriek; the talons were spread and hooked; and the eye, though merely a white circle, seemed to radiate evil, fury.

"May I keep this?" I asked Lilly.

She nodded. "It feels dirty. I don't want to touch it."

We left Lilly there with a cup of tea and with hope that, if it could have been measured, might not have equaled the volume of juice she could squeeze from the lemon wedge on her saucer.

Descending the porch steps, Sasha said, "Bobby, you better bring Jenna Wing back here as quick as you can."

I gave him the sketch of the crow. "Show her this. Ask her if she remembers any case Louis worked on . . . anything that might explain this."

As we crossed the backyard, Sasha took my hand.

Bobby said, "Who's spinning music when you're here?"

"Doogie Sassman's covering for me," she said.

"Mr. Harley-Davidson, the man-mountain love machine," Bobby said, leading us along the brick walk beside the garage. "What program format does he favor—head-banging heavy metal?"

"Waltzes," Sasha said. "Fox-trots, tangos, rumbas, cha-chas. I've warned him he has to stick with the tune sheet I gave him, 'cause otherwise, he'd just play dance music. He loves ballroom dancing."

Pushing open the gate, Bobby stopped, turned, and stared at Sasha in disbelief. To me, he said, "You knew this?"

"No."

"Ballroom dancing?"

Sasha said, "He's won some prizes."

"Doogie? He's as big as a Volkswagen Beetle."

"The old Volkswagen Beetle or the new one?" I asked.

"The new one," Bobby said.

"He's a big guy, but he's very graceful," Sasha said.

"He has a tight turning radius," I told Bobby.

The thing that happens so easily among us, the thing that makes us so close, was happening again. The groove or rhythm or mood or whatever it is we so routinely fall into with one another—we were falling into it again. You can handle anything, including the end of the world as we know it, if at your side are friends with the proper attitude.

Bobby said, "I thought Doogie hangs out in biker bars, not ballrooms."

"For fun, he's a bouncer in a biker bar two evenings a week," Sasha said, "but I don't think he hangs out there otherwise."

"For fun?" Bobby said.

"He enjoys breaking heads," Sasha said.

"Who doesn't," I said.

As we followed Bobby into the alleyway, he said, "The dude is a way skilled audio engineer, rides a Harley like he came out of the womb on it, dates awesome women who make any Ms. Universe look like the average resident of an oyster shell, fights drunken psycho bikers for fun, wins prizes for ballroom dancing—this sounds like a bro we want with us when we go back to Wyvern."

I said, "Yeah, my big worry has been what we'll do if there's a tango competition."

"Exactly." To Sasha, Bobby said, "You think he'd be up for it?"

She nodded. "I think Doogie's always up for everything."

I expected to find a police cruiser or an unmarked sedan behind the garage, and unamused authority figures waiting for us. The alley was deserted.

A pale gray swath of sky outlined the hills to the east. The breeze raised a chorus of whispers from the windbreak of eucalyptus trees along the canyon crest, as if warning me to hurry home before the morning found me.

"And Doogie has all those tattoos," I said.

"Yeah," Bobby said, "he's got more tattoos than a drunken sailor with four mothers and ten wives."

To Sasha, I said, "If you're getting into any hostile situation, and it involves a super-huge guy covered with tattoos, you want him on your side."

"It's a fundamental rule of survival," Bobby agreed.

"It's discussed in every biology textbook," I said.

"It's in the Bible," Bobby said.

"Leviticus," I said.

"It's in Exodus, too," Bobby said, "and Deuteronomy."

Alerted by movement and by a glimpse of eyeshine, Bobby snapped the shotgun into firing position, I drew the Glock from my shoulder holster, Sasha pulled her revolver, and we swung toward the perceived threat, forming a manic tableau of paranoia and rugged individualism that would have been perfection if we'd just had one of those pre-Revolutionary War flags that featured a coiled serpent and the words *Don't Tread on Me*.

Twenty feet north of us, along the eastern side of the alley, making no sound to compete with the soughing of the wind, coyotes appeared among the trunks of the eucalyptus trees. They came over the canyon crest, through the bunchgrass and wild flax, between bushy clumps of goatsbeard.

These prairie wolves, smaller than true wolves, with narrower muzzles and lighter variegated coats, possess much of the beauty and charm of wolves, of all dogs. Even in their benign moments, however, after they have hunted and fed to contentment, when they are playing or sunning in a meadow, they still look dangerous and predatory to such an extent that they are not likely to inspire a line of cuddly stuffed toys, and if one of them is chosen as the ideal photogenic pet by the next resident of 1600 Pennsylvania Avenue, we can be reasonably sure that the Antichrist has his finger on the nuclear trigger.

Slinking out of the canyon, among the trees, into the alley in the earliest ashen light of this cloud-shrouded morning, the coyotes looked post-apocalyptic, like the hellish hunters in a world long past its doomsday. Heads thrust forward, yellow eyes glowing in the gloom, ears pricked, jaws cracked in humorless serrated grins, they arrived and gathered and turned to face us in dreamlike silence, as though they had escaped from a Navajo mystic's peyote-inspired vision.

Ordinarily, coyotes travel overland in single file, but these came in a swarm, and once in the alleyway, they stood flank-to-flank, closer than any canine pack, huddling together rather like a colony of rats. Their breath, hotter than ours, smoked in the coolish air. I didn't attempt to count them, but they numbered more than thirty, all adults, no pups.

We could have tried to get into Sasha's Explorer and pull the doors shut, but we all sensed that any sudden movement from us or any show of fear might invite a vicious assault. The most we dared to do was slowly reverse a step or two, until our backs were to some degree protected by the pair of parked vehicles.

Coyote attacks on adult human beings are rare but not unknown. Even in hunting pairs or in a pack, they will stalk and chase down a man or woman only if desperate with hunger because a drought has lowered the population of mice, rabbits, and other small wildlife. Young children, left unattended in a park or in a backyard adjacent to open range, are more often seized and savaged and dragged away, but these incidents are also rare, especially considering the vast expanses of territory that human beings and coyotes inhabit together throughout the West.

I was most worried not by what coyotes might usually do, but by the perception that these were not *ordinary* animals. They could not be expected to behave as usual for their kind; the danger was in their difference.

Although all their heads were turned in our direction, I didn't feel we were the primary focus of their attention. They seemed to be raptly gazing past us, toward something in the distance, though for its eight- or ten-block length, the alley was quiet and deserted.

Abruptly, the pack moved.

Although living in families, coyotes are nonetheless fierce individualists, driven by personal needs, insights, moods.

Their independence is evident even when they hunt together, but this pack moved with uncanny coordination, with the instinctive synchronization of a cruising school of piranhas, as though they shared one mind, one purpose.

Ears laid back flat against their skulls, jaws cracked wide as if to bite, heads lowered, hackles raised, shoulders hunched, tails tucked in and held low, the coyotes raced in our direction but not directly toward us. They kept to the east half of the alley, most of them on the blacktop but some on the dusty verge, gazing past us and straight ahead, as if focused intently on prey that was invisible to human eyes.

Neither Bobby nor I came close to firing on the pack, because we were at once reminded of the behavior of the flock of nighthawks in Wyvern. At first the birds seemed to have gathered with malicious intent, then for the purpose of celebration, and in the end their only violent impulse was to self-destruction. With these coyotes, I didn't sense the bleak aura of sorrow and despair that had radiated from the nighthawks; I didn't feel they were searching for their own final solution to whatever fever gripped them. They appeared to be a danger to someone or something, but not to us.

Sasha held her revolver in a two-hand grip as the pack streamed toward us. But as they began to pass without turning a single yellow eye in our direction and without issuing one bark or snarl, she slowly lowered the weapon until the muzzle was aimed at the pavement near her feet.

These predators, breath steaming from their mouths, appeared ectoplasmic here on the cusp of dawn. If not for the slap of paws on blacktop and a musky odor, they might have been only ghosts of coyotes, engaged in one last haunt during the final minutes of this spirit-friendly night, before making their way back to the rough fields and vales in which their moldering bones awaited them.

As the final ranks of the pack poured past us, we turned to stare after the swift procession. They dwindled into the distance, chased by the gray light from the east, as though following the night toward the western horizon.

Quoting Paul McCartney—after all, she was a songwriter as well as a deejay—Sasha said, "Baby, I'm amazed."

"I've got a lot to tell you," I said. "We've seen way more than this tonight, stranger stuff."

"A catalog of the mondo weird," Bobby assured her.

In the darker distance, the coyotes seemed to shimmer out of existence, though I suspect that they slipped from the alleyway, over the canyon crest, returning to the deeper realms from which they had ascended.

"We haven't seen the last of them," Sasha predicted, and her voice was shaded by a disquieting note of precognition.

"Maybe," I said.

"Definitely," she insisted with quiet conviction. "And the next time they come around, they'll be in an uglier mood."

Breaking open the shotgun and shaking the shell from the chamber into the palm of his hand, Bobby said, "Here comes the sun."

He was not to be taken literally; the day was overcast. The relentless morning slowly stripped off the black hood of the night and turned its dead, gray face upon us.

A solid cloud cover affords me no substantial protection against the destructive force of the sun. Ultraviolet light penetrates even black thunderheads, and while the burn may build more slowly than on a searingly bright day, the irreparable damage to my skin and eyes nevertheless accumulates. Sunscreen lotions protect well against the less serious forms of skin cancer, but they have little or no ability to prevent melanoma. Consequently, I have to seek shelter from even a daytime sky as gray-black as the char and ashes in the cold bowl of Satan's pipe after he's smoked a handful of souls.

To Bobby, I said, "We're no good without a little sleep. Grab some mattress time, then meet Sasha and me at my house between noon and one o'clock. We'll put together a plan and a search party."

"You can't go back to Wyvern till sundown, but maybe some of us ought to get moving sooner," he said.

"I'm for that. But there's no point in quartering off Wyvern and searching every foot of it. That would take too long, forever. We'd never find them in time," I said, leaving unspoken the thought that we might already be too late. "We don't go back until we've got the tracker we need."

"Tracker?" Sasha asked, fitting her revolver into the holster under her denim jacket.

"Mungojerrie," I said, tucking away my 9-millimeter.

Bobby blinked. "The cat?"

"He's more than a cat," I reminded Bobby.

"Yeah, but—"

"And he's our only hope."

"Cats can track?"

"I'm sure this one can."

Bobby shook his head. "I'm never gonna be at home in this brave new smart-animal world, bro. It's like I'm living in a maximum-wacky Donald Duck cartoon, but one where, between the laughs, dudes get their guts ripped out."

"The world according to Edgar Allan Disney," I said. "Anyway, Mungojerrie hangs out around the marina. Pay a visit to Roosevelt Frost. He should know how to find our tracker."

Out of the pool of shadows in the canyon east of us, the eerie ululant cries of coyotes rose, a sound like no other on earth, like the tormented and hungry voices that banshees would have if banshees existed.

Sasha put her right hand under her jacket, as if she might draw her revolver again.

Such a frenzied choir of coyotes is a common sound at night, usually signifying that a hunt has reached its bloody end, that some prey as large as a deer has been brought down by the pack, or that the full moon is exerting its peculiar pull, but you rarely hear such a chilling chorus on this side of the sunrise. As much as anything that we had yet experienced, this sinister serenade, which escalated in volume and passion, filled me with foreboding.

"Sharky," Bobby said.

"White pointers," I said, which is surfer lingo for great whites, the most dangerous of all sharks.

I climbed into the passenger seat of the Explorer, and by

the time Sasha started the engine, Bobby pulled past us in his Jeep, heading for Jenna Wing's house across town.

I didn't expect to see him for at least seven hours, but here at the dawn of April 12, we didn't realize that we were entering a day of epic bad news. The nasty surprises were coming at us like a long series of triple overhead monoliths churned up by a typhoon in the far Pacific.

17

Sasha parked the Explorer in the driveway, because my father's car was in the garage, as were boxes of his clothing and his personal effects. The day would come, with his death far enough in the past, when I would not feel that disposing of his belongings would diminish him in my memory. I was not at that day yet.

In this matter, I know I'm being illogical. My memories of my dad, which give me sustaining strength every day, are not related to what clothes he wore on any particular occasion, to his favorite sweater or his silver-rimmed reading glasses. His *things* do not keep him vivid in my mind; he stays with me because of his kindness, his wit, his courage, his love, his joy in life. Yet twice in the three weeks since I've packed up his clothes, I've torn open one of the boxes in the garage simply to have a look at those reading glasses, at that sweater. In such moments I can't escape the truth that I'm not coping as well as I pretend to be. The cataract of grief is a longer drop than Niagara, and I guess I've not yet reached the river of acceptance at the bottom.

When I got out of the Explorer, I didn't hurry into the house, though the grizzled morning was now almost fully upon us. The day did little to restore the color that the night had stolen from the world; indeed, the smoky light seemed to deposit an ash-gray residue on everything, muting tones, dulling shiny surfaces. The cumulative UV damage I would sustain in this shineless sunshine was a risk worth taking to spend one minute admiring the two oaks in the front yard.

These California live oaks, beautifully crowned and with great canopies of strong black limbs, tower over the house, shading it in every season, because unlike eastern oaks, they don't drop their leaves in winter. I have always loved these trees, have climbed high into them on many nights to get closer to the stars, but lately they mean more to me than ever because they remind me of my parents, who had the strength to make the sacrifices in their own lives required to raise a child with my disabilities and who gave me the shade to thrive.

The weight of this leaden dawn had pressed all the wind out of the day. The oaks were as monolithic as sculpture, each leaf like a petal of cast bronze.

After a minute, calmed by the deep stillness of the trees, I crossed the lawn to the house.

This Craftsman-period structure features stacked ledger stone and weather-silvered cedar under a slate roof, with deep eaves and an expansive front porch, all modern lines yet natural and close to the earth. It is the only home I've ever known, and considering both the average life span of an XPer and my talent for getting my ass in a sling, it's no doubt where I'll live until I die.

Sasha had unlocked the front door by the time I got there, and I followed her into the foyer.

All the windows are covered with pleated shades throughout the daylight hours. Most of the lights feature rheostats, and when we must turn them on, we keep them dim. For the most part, I live here in candlelight filtered through amber or rose glass, in a soft-edged shadowy ambience that would meet with the approval of any medium who claims to be able to channel the spirits of the dead.

Sasha settled in a month previous, after Dad's death, moving out of the house provided for her as part of her compensation as general manager of KBAY. But already, during daylight hours, she moves from room to room guided largely by the faint sunshine pressing against the lowered window shades.

She thinks my shrouded world calms the soul, that life in the low illumination of Snowland is soothing, even romantic. I agree with her to an extent, though at times a mild claustrophobia overcomes me and these ever-present shadows seem like a chilling preview of the grave.

Without touching a light switch, we went upstairs to my bathroom and took a shower together by the lambent glow of a decorative glass oil lamp. This tandem event wasn't as much fun as usual, not even as much fun as riding two on a surfboard, because we were physically weary, emotionally exhausted, and worried about Orson and Jimmy; all we did was bathe, while I gave Sasha a seriously condensed version of my pursuit of the kidnapper, the sighting of Big Head, Delacroix, and the events in the egg room.

I phoned Roosevelt Frost, who lives aboard *Nostromo,* a fifty-six-foot Bluewater coastal cruiser berthed in the Moonlight Bay marina. I got an answering machine and left a message asking him to come to see me as soon after twelve o'clock as was convenient and to bring Mungojerrie if possible.

I also called Manuel Ramirez. The police operator said that he was currently out of the office, and at my request, she switched me to his voice mail.

After reciting the license number of the Suburban, which I had memorized, I said, "That's what Jimmy Wing's kidnapper was driving. If you care, give me a call after noon."

Sasha and I were turning back the covers on the bed in my room when the doorbell rang. Sasha pulled on a robe and went to see who had come calling.

I slipped into a robe, too, and padded barefoot to the head of the stairs to listen.

I took the 9-millimeter Glock with me. Moonlight Bay wasn't as full of mayhem as Jurassic Park, but I wouldn't have been entirely surprised if the doorbell had been rung by a velociraptor.

Instead, it was Bobby, six hours early. When I heard his voice, I went downstairs.

The foyer was dimly lighted, but above the Stickley-style table, the print of Maxfield Parrish's *Daybreak* glowed as though it were a window on a magical and better world.

Bobby looked grim. "I won't take long. But you have to know about this. After I took Jenna Wing to Lilly's, I swung by Charlie Dai's house."

Charlie Dai—whose birth name in correct Vietnamese order was Dai Tran Gi, before he Americanized it—is the associate editor and senior reporter at the *Moonlight Bay Gazette*, the newspaper owned by Bobby's parents. The Halloways are estranged from Bobby, but Charlie remains his friend.

"Charlie can't write about Lilly's boy," Bobby continued, "at least not until he gets clearance, but I thought he ought to know. In fact . . . I figured he might already know."

Charlie is among the handful in Moonlight Bay—a few hundred out of twelve thousand—who know that a biological catastrophe occurred at Wyvern. His wife, Dr. Nora Dai—formerly Dai Minh Thu-Ha—is now a retired colonel; while in the army medical corps, she commanded all medical services at Fort Wyvern for six years, a position of great responsibility on a base with more than fifty thousand population. Her medical team had treated the wounded and the dying on the night when some researchers in the genetics lab, having reached a crisis in the secret process of becoming, surprised their associates by savagely assaulting them. Nora Dai knew too much, and within hours of those strange events, she and Charlie were confronted with accusations that their immigration documents, filed twenty-six years ago, were forged. This was a lie, but unless they assisted in suppressing the truth of the Wyvern disaster and its aftermath, they would be deported without notice, and without standard legal procedures, to Vietnam, from which they would never be able to return. Threats were also made against the lives of their children and grandchildren, because those who have orchestrated this cover-up do not believe in half measures.

Bobby and I don't know why his parents have allowed the *Gazette* to be corrupted, publishing a carefully managed version of the local news. Perhaps they believe in the rightness of the secrecy. Perhaps they don't understand the true horror of what's happened. Or maybe they're just scared.

"Charlie's been muffled," Bobby said, "but he's still got ink in his veins, you know, he still hears things, gathers news whether he's allowed to write all of it up or not."

"He's as stoked on the page as you are on the board," I said.

"He's a total news rat," Bobby agreed.

He was standing near one of the sidelights that flank the front door: rectangular geometric stained-glass windows with red, amber, green, and clear elements. No blinds cover these panes, because the deep overhang of the porch and the giant oaks prevent direct sunlight from reaching them. Bobby glanced through one of the clearer pieces of glass in the mosaic, as if he expected to see an unwelcome visitor on the front porch.

"Anyway," he continued, "I figured if Charlie had heard about Jimmy, he might know something we don't, might've picked up something from Manuel or someone, somewhere. But I wasn't ready for what the dude told me. Jimmy was one of three last night."

My stomach clenched with dread.

"Three children kidnapped?" Sasha asked.

Bobby nodded. "Del and Judy Stuart's twins."

Del Stuart has an office at Ashdon College, is for the record an employee of the Department of Education but is rumored to work for an obscure arm of the Department of Defense or the Environmental Protection Agency, or the Federal Office of Doughnut Management, and he probably spreads the rumors himself to deflect speculation from possibilities closer to the truth. He refers to himself as a *grant facilitator*, a term that feels as deceptive as calling a hit man an *organic waste disposal specialist*. Officially, his job is to keep outgoing paperwork and incoming funds flowing for those professors who are engaged in federally financed research. There is reason to believe that most such research at Ashdon involves the development of unconventional weapons, that the college has become the summer home of Mars, the god of war, and that Del is the liaison between the discreet funding sources of black-budget weapons projects and the academics who thrive on their dole. Like Mom.

I had no doubt that Del and Judy Stuart were devastated by the disappearance of their twins, but unlike poor Lilly Wing, who was an innocent and unaware of the dark side of Moonlight Bay, the Stuarts were self-committed residents of Satan's pocket and understood that the bargain they had made required them to suffer even this terror in silence. Consequently, I was amazed that Charlie had learned of these abductions.

"Charlie and Nora Dai live next door to them," Bobby explained, "though I don't think they barbecue a lot together. The twins are six years old. Around nine o'clock last night, Judy is tucking the weeds in for the night, she hears a noise, and when she turns around, there's a stranger right behind her."

"Stocky, close-cropped black hair, yellow eyes, thick lips, seed-corn teeth," I said, describing the kidnapper I'd encountered under the warehouse.

"Tall, athletic, blond, green eyes, puckered scar on his left cheek."

"New guy," Sasha said.

"Totally new guy. He's got a chloroform-soaked rag in one hand, and before Judy realizes what's happening, the dude is all over her like fat on cheese."

"Fat on cheese?" I asked.

"That was Charlie's expression."

Charlie Dai, God love him, writes excellent newspaper copy, but though English has been his first language for twenty-five years, he has not fully gotten a grip on conversational usage to the degree that he has mastered formal prose. Idiom and metaphor often defeat him. He once told me that an August evening was "as hot as three toads in a Cuisinart," a comparison that left me blinking two days later.

Bobby peered through the stained-glass window once more, gave the day world a longer look than he had before, then returned his attention to us: "When Judy recovers from the chloroform, Aaron and Anson—the twins—are gone."

"Two abbs suddenly start snatching kids on the same night?" I said skeptically.

"There's no coincidence in Moonlight Bay," Sasha said.

"Bad for us, worse for Jimmy," I said. "If we're not dealing with typical pervs, then these geeks are acting out twisted needs that might have nothing to do with any abnormal psychology on the books, because they're way beyond abnormal. They're becoming, and whatever it is they're becoming is driving them to commit the same atrocities."

"Or," Bobby said, "it's even stranger than two dudes regressing to swamp monsters. The abb left a drawing on the twins' bed."

"A crow?" Sasha guessed.

"Charlie called it a raven. Same difference. A raven sitting on a stone, spreading its wings as if to take flight. Not the same pose as in the first drawing. But the message was pretty much the same. 'Del Stuart will be my servant in Hell.' "

"Does Del have any idea what it means?" I asked.

"Charlie Dai says no. But he thinks that Del recognized Judy's description of the kidnapper. Maybe that's why the guy let her get a look at him. He wanted Del to know."

"But if Del knows," I said, "he'll tell the cops, and the abb is finished."

"Charlie says he didn't tell them."

Sasha's voice was laden with equal measures of disbelief and disgust. "His kids are abducted, and he hides information from the cops?"

"Del's deep in the Wyvern mess," I said. "Maybe he has to keep his mouth shut about the abb's identity until he gets permission from his boss to tell the cops."

"If they were my kids, I'd kick over the rules," she said.

I asked Bobby if Jenna Wing had been able to make anything of the crow and the message left under Jimmy's pillow, but she had been clueless.

"I've heard something else, though," Bobby said, "and it makes this whole thing even more of a mind-bender."

"Like?"

"Charlie says, about two weeks ago, school nurses and county health officials conducted an annual checkup on every kid in every school and preschool in town. The usual eye exams, hearing tests, chest X-rays for tuberculosis. But this time they took blood samples, too."

Sasha frowned. "Drew blood from all those kids?"

"A couple school nurses felt parents ought to give permission before blood samples were taken, but the county official overseeing the program flushed them away with a load of woofy about there's been a low-level hepatitis outbreak in the area that could become epidemic, so they need to do preventive screening."

As I did, Sasha knew what inference Bobby had drawn from this news, and she wrapped her arms around herself as if chilled. "They weren't screening those kids for hepatitis. They were screening them for the retrovirus."

"To see how widely distributed the problem is in the community," I added.

Bobby had arrived at a further and more disturbing inference: "We know the big brains are burning up gray cells around the clock, searching for a cure, right?"

"Ears smoking," I agreed.

"What if they've discovered that a tiny percentage of infected people have a natural defense against the retrovirus?"

"Maybe in some people the bug isn't able to unload the genetic material it's carrying," Sasha said.

Bobby shrugged. "Or whatever. Wouldn't they want to study those who're immune?"

I was sickened by where this was leading. "Jimmy Wing, the Stuart twins . . . maybe their blood samples revealed they have this antibody, enzyme, mechanism, whatever it is."

Sasha didn't want to go where we were going. "For research, they wouldn't need the kids. Just tissue samples, blood samples, every few weeks."

Reluctantly, remembering these were people who had once worked with Mom, I said, "But if you have no moral compunctions, if you used human subjects before, like they used condemned prisoners, then it's a lot easier just to snatch the kids."

"Less to explain," Bobby agreed. "No chance the parents won't cooperate."

Sasha spat out a word I'd never heard her use before.

"Bro," Bobby said, "you know, in car-engine design, in airplane-engine design, there's this engineering term, something called *test to destruction.*"

"I know where you're going with this. Yeah, I'm pretty sure in some biological research there's something similar. Testing the organism to see how much it can take of one thing or another, before it self-destructs."

Sasha spat out the same word, which I had now heard her use before, and she turned her back to us, as if to hear *and* see us discussing this was too disturbing.

Bobby said, "Maybe a quick way to understand why a particular subject—why one of these little kids—has immunity from the virus is to keep infecting him with it, megadoses of infection, and study his immune response."

"Until finally they kill him? Just kill him?" Sasha asked angrily, turning to us again, her lovely face so drained of blood that she appeared to be halfway through applying the makeup for a mime performance.

"Until finally they kill him," I confirmed.

"We don't know this is what they're doing," Bobby said in an attempt to console her. "We don't know jack. It's just a half-assed theory."

"Half-assed, half-smart," I said with dismay. "But what does the damn crow have to do with all this?"

We stared at one another.

None of us had an answer.

Bobby peered suspiciously through the stained-glass window again.

I said, "Bro, what is it? Did you order a pizza?"

"No, but the town's crawling with anchovies."

"Anchovies?"

"Fishy types. Like the zombie club we saw last night, coming back from Wyvern to Lilly's house. The dead-eyed dudes in the sedan. I've seen more of them. I get the feeling something's coming down, something super-humongous."

"Bigger than the end of the world?" I asked.

He gave me an odd look, then grinned. "You're right. Can't go down from here. Where do we have to go but up?"

"Sideways," Sasha said somberly. "From one kind of hell into another."

To me, Bobby said, "I see why you love her."

I said, "My own private sunshine."

"Sugar in shoes," he said.

I said, "One hundred twenty pounds of walking honey."

"One hundred twelve," she said. "And forget what I said about you two being Curly and Larry. That's an insult to Larry."

"Curly and Curly?" Bobby said.

"She thinks she's Moe," I said.

Sasha said, "I think I'm going to bed. Unless, Bobby, you have more bad news that'll keep me from sleeping."

He shook his head. "That's the best I can do."

Bobby left.

After locking the front door, I watched through the stained-glass window until he got into his Jeep and drove away.

Parting from a friend makes me nervous.

Maybe I'm needy, neurotic, paranoid. Under the circumstances, of course, if I *weren't* needy, neurotic, and paranoid, I'd obviously be psychotic.

If we were always conscious of the fact that people precious to us are frighteningly mortal, hanging not even by a thread but by a wisp of gossamer, perhaps we would be kinder to them and more grateful for the love and friendship they give us.

Sasha and I went upstairs to bed. Lying side by side in the dark, holding hands, we were silent for a while.

We were scared. Scared for Orson, for Jimmy, for the Stuarts, for ourselves. We felt small. We felt helpless. So, of course, for a few minutes we rated our favorite Italian sauces.

Pesto with pine nuts almost won, but we mutually agreed on Marsala before falling into a contented silence.

Just when I thought she had drifted into sleep, Sasha said, "You hardly know me, Snowman."

"I know your heart, what's in it. That's everything."

"I've never talked about my family, my past, who I was and what I did before I came to KBAY."

"Are you going to talk about that now?"

"No."

"Good. I'm wiped out."

"Neanderthal."

"You Cro-Magnons all think you're so superior."

After a silence, she said, "Maybe I'll never talk about the past."

"You mean, even like about yesterday?"

"You really don't feel a need to know, do you?"

I said, "I love the person you are. I'm sure I'd also love the person you were. But it's who you are that I have now."

"You never prejudge anyone."

"I'm a saint."

"I'm serious."

"So am I. I'm a saint."

"Asshole."

"Better not talk that way about a saint."

"You're the only person I've ever known who *always* judges people solely on their actions. And forgives them when they screw up."

"Well, me and Jesus."

"Neanderthal."

"Careful now," I warned. "Better not risk divine punishment. Lightning bolts. Boils. Plagues of locusts. Rains of frogs. Hemorrhoids."

"I'm embarrassing you, aren't I?" she asked.

"Yes, Moe, you are."

"All I'm saying is, *this* is your difference, Chris. This is the difference that makes you special. Not XP."

I was silent.

She said, "You're desperately searching for some smart remark that'll get me to call you an asshole again."

"Or at least a Neanderthal."

"This is your difference. Sleep tight."

She let go of my hand and rolled onto her side.

"Love you, Goodall."

"Love you, Snowman."

In spite of the blackout blinds and the overlapping drapes, faint traces of light defined the edges of the windows. Even this morning's overcast heavens had been beautiful. I yearned to go outside, stand under the daytime sky, and look for faces, forms, and animals in the clouds. I yearned to be free.

I said, "Goodall?"

"Hmmm?"

"About your past."

"Yeah?"

"You weren't a hooker, were you?"

"Asshole."

I sighed with contentment and closed my eyes.

Worried as I was about Orson and the three missing children, I didn't expect to sleep well, but I slept the dreamless sleep of a clueless Neanderthal.

When I woke five hours later, Sasha wasn't in bed. I dressed and went looking for her.

In the kitchen, a note was fixed with a magnet to the door of the refrigerator: *Out on business. Back soon. For God's sake, don't eat those cheese enchiladas for breakfast. Have bran flakes. Moe.*

While the leftover cheese enchiladas were heating in the oven, I went into the dining room, which is now Sasha's music room, since we eat all our meals at the kitchen table. We have moved the dining table, chairs, and other furniture into the garage so the dining room can accommodate her electronic keyboard, synthesizer, sax stand with saxophone, clarinet, flute, two guitars (one electric, one acoustic), cello and cellist's stool, music stands, and composition table.

Similarly, we converted the downstairs study into her

workout room. An exercise bicycle, rowing machine, and rack of hand weights ring the room, with plush exercise mats in the center. She is deep into homeopathic medicine; consequently, the bookshelves are filled with neatly ordered bottles of vitamins, minerals, herbs—plus, for all I know, powdered wing of bat, eye-of-toad ointment, and iguana-liver marmalade.

Her extensive book collection lined the living room at her former place. Here it is shelved and stacked all over the house.

She is a woman of many passions: cooking, music, exercise, books, and me. Those are the ones I know about. I would never ask her to rank her passions in order of importance. Not because I'm afraid I'd come in fifth of the major five. I'm happy to be fifth, to have any ranking at all.

I circled the dining room, touching her guitars and cello, finally picking up her sax and blowing a few bars of "Quarter Till Three," the old Gary U.S. Bonds hit. Sasha was teaching me to play. I wouldn't claim that I wailed, but I wasn't bad.

In truth, I didn't pick up the sax to practice. You might find this romantic or disgusting, depending on your point of view, but I picked up the sax because I wanted to put my mouth where her mouth had been. I'm either Romeo or Hannibal Lecter. Your call.

For breakfast I ate three plump cheese enchiladas with a third of a pint of fresh salsa and washed everything down with an ice-cold Pepsi. If I live long enough for my metabolism to turn against me, I might one day regret never having learned to eat for any reason but the sheer fun of it. Currently, however, I am at that blissful age when no indulgence can alter my thirty-inch waistline.

In the upstairs guest bedroom that served as my study, I sat at my desk in candlelight and spent a couple of minutes looking at a pair of framed photographs of my mom and dad. Her face was full of kindness and intelligence. His face was full of kindness and wisdom.

I have rarely seen my own face in full light. The few times I've stood in a bright place and confronted a mirror, I've not seen anything in my face that I can understand. This disturbs me. How can my parents' images shine with such virtues and mine be enigmatic?

Did their mirrors show them mysteries?

I think not.

Well, I take solace from the realization that Sasha loves me—perhaps as much as she loves cooking, perhaps even as much as she loves a good aerobic workout. I wouldn't risk suggesting that she values me as much as she does books and music. Though I hope.

In my study, among hundreds of volumes of poetry and reference books—my own and my father's collections combined—is a thick Latin dictionary. I looked up the word for *beer*.

Bobby had said, *Carpe cerevisi*. Seize the beer. *Cerevisi* appeared to be correct.

We had been friends for so long that I knew Bobby had never sat through a class in Latin. Therefore, I was touched. The apparent effort that he had taken to mock me was a sign of true friendship.

I closed the dictionary and slid it aside, next to a copy of the book I had written about my life as a child of darkness. It had been a national best-seller about four years ago, when I'd thought I knew the meaning of my life, prior to my discovery that my mother, out of fierce maternal love and a desire to free me from my disability, had inadvertently made me the poster child for doomsday.

I hadn't opened this book in two years. It should have been on one of the shelves behind my desk. I assumed Sasha had been looking at it and neglected to put it back where she'd found it.

Also on the desk was a decorative tin box painted with the faces of dogs. In the center of the lid are these lines from Elizabeth Barrett Browning:

> *Therefore to this dog will I,*
> *Tenderly not scornfully,*
> *Render praise and favor:*
> *With my hand upon his head,*

*Is my benediction said
Therefore and forever.*

This tin box was a gift from my mother, given to me on the day that she brought Orson home. I keep special biscuits in it, which he particularly enjoys, and from time to time I give him a couple, not to reward him for a trick learned, because I don't teach him tricks, and not to enforce any training, but he needs no training, but simply because the taste of them makes him happy.

When my mother brought Orson to live with us, I didn't know how special he was. She kept this secret until long after her death, until after my father's death. When she gave me the box, she said, "I know you'll give him love, Chris. But also, when he needs it—and he *will* need it—take pity on him. His life is no less difficult than yours."

At the time, I assumed she meant nothing more than that animals, like us, are subject to the fear and suffering of this world. Now I know there were deeper and more complex layers of meaning in her words.

I reached toward the tin, intending to test its weight, because I wanted to be certain that it was filled with treats for Orson's triumphant return. My hand began to shake so badly that I left the box untouched.

I folded my hands, one over the other, on the desk. Staring down at the hard white points of my knuckles, I realized that I had assumed the very pose in which I'd first seen Lilly Wing when Bobby and I returned from Wyvern.

Orson. Jimmy. Aaron. Anson. Like the barbed points on a razor-wire fence, their names spiraled through my mind. The lost boys.

I felt an obligation to all of them, a fierce sense of duty, which wasn't entirely explicable—except that in spite of my good fortune in parents and in spite of the riches of friendship that I enjoyed, I was the ultimate lost boy, myself, and to some extent would be lost until the day I passed out of my darkness in this world into whatever light waits beyond.

Impatience abraded my nerves. In conventional searches

for lost hikers, for small aircraft downed in mountainous terrain, and for boats at sea, search parties break from dusk to dawn. We were limited, instead, to the dark hours, not merely by my XP but by our need to gather our forces and to act in utmost secrecy. I wondered whether the members of conventional search parties checked their watches every two minutes, chewed their lips, and went slightly screwy with frustration while waiting for first light. My watch crystal was etched with eye tracks, my lip was shaggy with shredded skin, and I was half nuts by 12:45.

Shortly before one o'clock, as I was diligently ridding myself of the second half of my sanity, the doorbell rang.

With the Glock in hand, I went downstairs. Through one of the stained-glass sidelights, I saw Bobby on the front porch. He was turned half away from the door, staring back toward the street, as though looking for a police surveillance team in one of the parked cars or for a school of anchovies in a passing vehicle.

As he stepped inside and I closed the door behind him, I said, "Bitchin' shirt."

He was wearing a red and gray volcanic-beach scene with blue ferns, which looked totally cool over a long-sleeve black pullover.

"Made by Iolani," I said. "Coconut-husk buttons, 1955."

Instead of commenting on my erudition with even as little as a roll of the eyes, he headed for the kitchen, saying, "I saw Charlie Dai again."

The kitchen was brightened only by the ashen face of the day pressed to the window blinds, by the digital clocks on the ovens, and by two fat candles on the table.

"Another kid is gone," Bobby said.

I felt a tremor in my hands once more, and I put the Glock on the kitchen table. "Who, when?"

Snatching a Mountain Dew from the refrigerator, where the standard light had been replaced with a lower-wattage, pink-tinted bulb, Bobby said, "Wendy Dulcinea."

"Oh," I said, and wanted to say more but couldn't speak.

Wendy's mother, Mary, is six years older than I am; when I was thirteen, my parents paid her to give me piano lessons, and I had a devastating crush on her. At that time, I was functioning under the delusion that I would one day play rock-'n'-roll piano as well as Jerry Lee Lewis, be a keyboard-banging maniac who could make those ivories smoke. Eventually my parents and Mary concluded—and persuaded me—that the likelihood of my becoming a competent pianist was immeasurably less than the likelihood of me levitating and flying like a bird.

"Wendy's seven." Bobby said. "Mary was taking her to school. Backed the car out of the driveway. Then realized she'd forgotten something in the house, went in to get it. When she came back two minutes later, the car was gone. With Wendy."

"No one saw anything?"

Bobby chugged the Mountain Dew: enough sugar to induce in him a diabetic coma, enough caffeine to keep a long-haul trucker awake through a five-hundred-mile run. He was legally wiring himself for the ordeal ahead.

"No one saw or heard anything," he confirmed. "Neighborhood of the blind and deaf. Sometimes I think there's something going around more contagious than your mom's bug. We've got an epidemic of the shut-up-hunker-down-see-hear-smell-speak-no-evil influenza. Anyway, the cops found Mary's car abandoned in the service lane behind the Nine Palms Plaza."

Nine Palms was a shopping center that lost all the tenants when Fort Wyvern closed and took with it the billion dollars a year that it had pumped into the county economy. These days the shop windows at Nine Palms are boarded over, weeds bristle from cracks in the blacktop parking lot, and six of the namesake palms are withered, brown, and so dead that they have been abandoned by tree rats.

The chamber of commerce likes to call Moonlight Bay the Jewel of the Central Coast. The town remains charming, graced with fine architecture and lovely tree-lined streets, but the economic scars of Wyvern's closure are visible everywhere. The jewel is not as bright as it once was.

"They searched all the empty shops in Nine Palms," Bobby said, "afraid they'd find Wendy's body, but she wasn't there."

"She's alive," I said.

Bobby looked at me pityingly.

"They're all alive," I insisted. "They have to be."

I wasn't speaking from reason now. I was speaking from my belief in miracles.

"Another crow," Bobby said. "Mary called it a blackbird. It was left on the car seat. In the drawing, the bird is diving for prey."

"Message?"

" 'George Dulcinea will be my servant in Hell.' "

Mary's husband was Frank Dulcinea. "Who the hell is George?"

"Frank's grandfather. He's dead now. Used to be a judge in the county court system."

"Dead how long?"

"Fifteen years."

I was baffled and frustrated. "If this abb is kidnapping for vengeance, what's the point of nabbing Wendy to get even with a man who's been dead fifteen years? Wendy's great-grandfather was gone long before she was even born. He never knew her. How could you get satisfaction from taking vengeance on a dead man?"

"Maybe it makes perfect sense if you're an abb," Bobby said, "with a screwed-up brain."

"I guess."

"Or maybe this whole crow thing is just cover, to make everyone think these kids were snatched by your standard-issue pervert, when maybe they're really being caged in a lab somewhere."

"Maybe, maybe, you're full of too damn many maybes," I said.

He shrugged. "Don't look to me for wisdom. I'm just a

wave-thrashing boardhead. This killer you mentioned. The guy in the news. He leave crows like this?"

"Not that I've read."

"Serial killers, don't they sometimes leave things like this?"

"Yeah. They're called *signatures*. Like a writer's byline. Taking credit for the work."

I checked my wristwatch. Sunset would arrive in about five hours. We would be ready to go back to Wyvern by then. And even if we were not ready, we would go.

TWO

NEVERLAND

18

With a second bottle of Mountain Dew in hand, Bobby sat on the cellist's stool, but he didn't pick up the bow.

In addition to all the instruments and the composition table, the former dining room contained a music system with a CD player and an antiquated audiotape deck. In fact, there were two decks, which allowed Sasha to duplicate tapes of her own recordings. I powered up the equipment, which added as much feeble illumination to the room as the dreary daylight that seeped in at the edges of the blinds.

Sometimes, after composing a tune, Sasha is convinced that she has unwittingly plagiarized another songwriter. To satisfy herself that her work is original, she spends hours listening to cuts from which she suspects she has borrowed, until finally she's willing to believe that her creation has, after all, sprung solely from her own talent.

Her music is the only thing about which Sasha exhibits more than a healthy measure of self-doubt. Her cooking, her literary opinions, her lovemaking, and all the other things she does so wonderfully are marked by a wholesome confidence and by no more than a useful amount of second-guessing. In her relationship to her music, however, she is sometimes a lost child; when she's stricken by this vulnerability, I want more than ever to put my arm around her and to comfort her—though this is when she's most likely to reject comforting and to rap me across the knuckles with her flute, her scaling ruler, or another handy music-room weapon.

I suppose every relationship can be enriched by a small measure of neurotic behavior. I certainly contribute a half cup of my own to our recipe.

Now I slipped the tape into the player. It was the cassette I'd found in the envelope beside Leland Delacroix's reeking corpse in the bungalow kitchen in Dead Town.

I turned the chair away from the composition table and, sitting down, used the remote control to switch on the cassette player.

For half a minute, we heard only the hiss of unrecorded magnetic tape passing over the playback head. A soft click and a new hollow quality to the hiss marked the beginning of the recording, which at first consisted only of someone—I assumed it was Delacroix—taking deep, rhythmic breaths, as if engaged in some form of meditation or aromatherapy.

Bobby said, "I was hoping for revelation, not respiration."

The sound was utterly mundane, with not the least inflection of fear or menace, or any other emotion. Yet the fine hairs stirred on the nape of my neck, as though these exhalations were actually coming from someone standing close behind me.

"He's trying to get a grip on himself," I said. "Deep, even breaths to get a grip on himself."

A moment later, my interpretation proved true when the breathing suddenly grew ragged, then desperate. Delacroix broke down and began to weep, tried to get a grip on himself, but choked on his pain, and let loose with great trembling sobs punctuated by wordless cries of despair.

Although I'd never known this man, listening to him in such violent throes of misery was disturbing. Fortunately, it didn't last long, because he switched off the recorder.

With another soft click, the recording began again, and though Delacroix's self-control was tenuous, he managed to speak. His voice was so thick with emotion that sometimes his speech slurred, and when he seemed in danger of breaking down completely, he paused either to take deep breaths or to drink something, presumably whiskey.

"*This is a warning. A testament. My testament. A warning to the world. I don't know where to begin. Begin with the worst. They're dead, and I killed them. But it was the only way to save them. The only way to save them. You have to understand . . . I killed them because I loved them. God help me. I couldn't let them suffer, be used. Be used. God, I couldn't let them be used that way. There was nothing else I could do. . . .*"

I remembered the snapshots arranged beside Delacroix's corpse. The elfin, gap-toothed little girl. The boy in the blue suit and red bow tie. The pretty blonde with the appealing smile. I suspected that these were the people who, to be saved, were killed.

"*We all developed these symptoms, just this afternoon, Sunday afternoon, and we were going to go to the doctor tomorrow, but we didn't make it that far. Mild fever. Chills. And every once in a while this . . . fluttering . . . this odd fluttering in the chest . . . or sometimes the stomach, in the abdomen, but then the next time in the neck, along the spine . . . this fluttering like maybe a twitching nerve or maybe heart palpitations or . . . no, nothing like that. God, no, nothing I can explain . . . not severe . . . subtle . . . a subtle fluttering but so . . . disturbing . . . nausea . . . couldn't eat much. . . .*"

Delacroix paused again. Got control of his breathing. Took a swallow of whatever he was drinking.

"*Truth. Got to tell the truth. Wouldn't have gone to the doctor tomorrow. Would've had to call Project Control. Let them know it isn't over. Even more than two years later, it isn't over. I knew. I knew somehow it wasn't over. All of us feeling the same way, and not like anything we'd felt before. Jesus, I knew. I was too scared to face it, but I knew. I didn't know what, but I knew something, knew it was Wyvern coming back to me somehow, some way, Jesus, Wyvern coming back to get me after all this time. Maureen was putting Lizzie to bed, tucking her in bed . . . and suddenly Lizzie started . . . she was . . . she started screaming. . . .*"

Delacroix swallowed more of his drink. He banged the glass down as though it was empty.

"I was in the kitchen, and I heard my Lizzie . . . my little Lizzie so scared, so . . . screaming. I ran . . . ran in there, into the bedroom. And she was . . . she . . . convulsions . . . thrashing . . . thrashing and kicking . . . flailing with her little fists. Maureen couldn't control her. I thought . . . convulsions . . . afraid she was biting her tongue. I held her . . . held her down. While I got her mouth open, Maureen folded a sock . . . going to use it . . . a pad to keep Lizzie from biting herself. But there was something . . . something in her mouth . . . not her tongue, something in her throat . . . this thing coming up her throat, something alive in her throat. And . . . and then . . . then she had her eyes tight shut . . . but then . . . but she opened them . . . and her left eye was bright red . . . bloodshot . . . and something was alive in her eye, too, some damn wriggling thing in her eye. . . ."

Sobbing, Delacroix switched off the recorder. God knows how long the poor man required to get control of himself. Of course, there was no lengthy blank section of tape, just another soft click as Delacroix hit the *record* button and continued:

"I run to our bedroom, to get . . . get my revolver . . . and coming back, passing Freddie's room, I see him . . . he's standing by his bed. Freddie . . . eyes wide . . . afraid. So I tell him . . . tell him, get in bed and wait for me. In Lizzie's room . . . Maureen has her back against the wall, hands pressed to her temples. Lizzie . . . she's still . . . oh, she's thrashing . . . her face . . . her face all swollen . . . twisted . . . the whole bone structure . . . not even Lizzie anymore. . . . There's no hope now. This was that damn place, the other side, coming through, like Lizzie was a doorway. Coming through. Oh, Jesus, I hate myself. I hate myself. I was part of it, I opened the door, opened the door between here and that place, helped make it possible. I opened the door. And now here is Lizzie . . . so I have to . . . so I . . . I shot . . . shot her . . . shot her twice. And she's dead, and so still on the bed, so small and still . . . but I don't know if something is alive in

her, alive in her though she isn't anymore. And Maureen, she has . . . she has both hands to her head . . . and she says, 'The fluttering,' and I know she means it's inside her head now, because I feel it, too, a fluttering along my spine . . . fluttering in sympathy with . . . with whatever was in Lizzie, is in Lizzie. And Maureen says . . . the most amazing . . . she says the most amazing thing . . . she says, 'I love you,' because she knows what's happening, I've told her about the other side, the mission, and now she knows somehow I've been infected all along, everything dormant for more than two years, but I'm infected, and now them, too, I've ruined us all, damned us all, and she knows. She knows what I . . . what I've done to them . . . and now what I have to do . . . so she says, 'I love you,' which is giving me permission, and I tell her I love her, too, so much, love her so much, and I'm sorry, and she's crying, and then I shoot her once . . . once, quick, my sweet Maureen, don't let her suffer. Then I . . . oh, I go . . . I go back down the hall . . . I go to Freddie's room. He's on his back in bed, sweating, hair soaked with sweat, and holding his belly with both hands. I know he feels the fluttering . . . fluttering in his tummy . . . because I feel it now in my chest and in my left biceps, like in a vein, and of all places in my testicles, and now along my spine again. I tell him I love him, and I tell him to close his eyes . . . close his . . . close his eyes . . . so I can make him feel better . . . and then I don't think I can do it, but I do it. My son. My boy. Brave boy. I make him feel better, and when I fire the shot, all the fluttering in me stops, just stops completely. But I know it's not over. I'm not alone . . . not alone in my body. I feel . . . passengers . . . something . . . a heaviness in me . . . a presence. Quiet. It's quiet but not for long. Not for long. I've reloaded the revolver."

Delacroix switched off the recorder, pausing to get a grip on his emotions.

With the remote control, I stopped the tape. The late Leland Delacroix wasn't the only one who needed to compose himself.

Without comment, Bobby got up from the cellist's stool and went into the kitchen.

After a moment, I followed him.

He was emptying his unfinished bottle of Mountain Dew into the sink, flushing it away with cold water.

"Don't turn it off," I said.

While Bobby threw the empty soda bottle in the trash can and opened the refrigerator, I went to the sink. I cupped my hands under the faucet, and for at least a minute, I splashed cold water on my face.

After I dried my face on a couple of paper towels, Bobby handed a bottle of beer to me. He had one, too.

I wanted to have a clear head when we returned to Wyvern. But after what I'd heard on the tape, and considering what else remained to be heard, I could probably have downed a six-pack without effect.

" 'That damn place, the other side,' " Bobby said, quoting Leland Delacroix.

"It's wherever Hodgson went in his spacesuit."

"And wherever he came back from when we saw him."

"Did Delacroix just go nuts, hallucinate everything, kill his family for no reason?"

"No."

"You think the thing he saw in his daughter's throat, in her eye—that was real?"

"Totally."

"Me too. Things we saw in Hodgson's suit . . . could that be what the fluttering is about?"

"Maybe that. Maybe something worse."

"Worse," I said, trying not to imagine it.

"I got the feeling—wherever the other side is, it's a real zoo over there."

We returned to the dining room. Bobby to the stool. Me to the chair by the composition table. After a moment of reluctance, I started the tape.

By the time Delacroix had begun to record again, his demeanor had changed. He wasn't as emotional as he had been. His voice broke now and then, and he needed to pause to collect himself from time to time, but for the most part, he was striving to soldier through what needed to be said.

"In the garage I keep gardening supplies, including a gallon of Spectracide. Bug killer. I got the can and emptied it on the three bodies. I don't know if that makes sense. Nothing was . . . moving in them. In the bodies, I mean. Besides, these aren't insects. Not like we think of insects. We don't even know what they are. Nobody knows. Lots of big theories. Maybe they're something . . . metaphysical. Do you think? I siphoned some gasoline out of the car. I have a couple gallons here in another can. I'll use the gasoline to start the fire before . . . before I finish myself. I'm not going to leave the four of us for overeducated janitors at Project Control. They'll just do something stupid. Like bag us and do autopsies. And spread this damn thing. I'll call the Control number after I go down to the corner and mail this tape to you, before I set the fire and . . . kill myself. I'm all quiet inside right now. Very quiet inside. For now. How long? I want to believe that—"

Delacroix halted in mid-sentence, held his breath as though he were listening for something, and then shut off the recorder.

I stopped the tape. "He didn't mail the cassette to anyone."

"Changed his mind. What does he mean—something metaphysical?"

"That was my next question," I said.

When Delacroix returned to the recorder, his voice was heavier, slower, leaden, as though he had fallen past fear, dropped below grief, and was speaking from a pit of despair.

"Thought I heard something in one of the bedrooms. Imagination. The bodies are . . . where I left them. Very still. Very still. Just my imagination. And now I realize you don't even know what this is about. I started this all wrong. There's so much to tell you, if you're going to be able to blow this wide open, but there's so little time. Okay. What you've got to know, the bones of it, is that there was a secret project at Fort Wyvern. The code name was Mystery Train. Because they thought they were making a magical mystery tour. Morons. Megalomaniacs. Me among them. Nightmare Train would have been a better name for it. Hellbound Train—that would've been better yet. And me happy

*to climb on board with the rest of 'em. I don't deserve any praise,
big brother. Not me. So . . . here are the key personnel. Not
everyone. Just the ones I knew, or as many as I remember right
now. Several are dead. Many are alive. Maybe one of the living
will talk, one of the upper-tier bastards who would know a lot
more than I do. They all must be scared, and some of them must
have guilty consciences. You're good at finding the whistle-blow-
ers."*

Delacroix proceeded to list over thirty people, identifying
each man or woman as either a civilian scientist or a military
officer: Dr. Randolph Josephson, Dr. Sarabjit Sanathra, Dr.
Miles Bennell, General Deke Kettleman. . . .

My mother was not among them.

I recognized only two names. The first was William
Hodgson, who was no doubt the poor devil we encountered
in the bizarre episode in the egg room. The second was Dr.
Roger Stanwyk, who lived with his wife, Marie, on my street,
just seven houses east of mine. Dr. Stanwyk, a biochemist,
had been one of my mother's many colleagues, associated
with the genetic experiments at Wyvern. If the Mystery Train
wasn't the project that grew from my mother's work, then Dr.
Stanwyk had been collecting more than one paycheck and had
done more than his fair share to destroy the world.

Delacroix's voice grew softer and his speech slower during
recitation of the last six or eight names, and the final name
almost seemed as though it would stick to his tongue and
remain unrevealed. I wasn't sure if he had reached the end of
his list or had stopped without finishing it.

He was silent for half a minute. Then, with his voice
abruptly energized, he rattled out what seemed to be a few
sentences in a foreign language before switching off the recorder.

I stopped the tape and looked at Bobby. "What was
that?"

"Wasn't pig Latin."

I reversed the tape, and we listened again.

This wasn't any language I could identify, and though,
for all I knew, Delacroix might have been spewing gibberish, I

was convinced that it had meaning. It had the cadence of speech, and although no word was recognizable, I found it curiously familiar.

After the thick, slow, depressed voice in which Delacroix had recited the names of people involved in the Mystery Train project, he imbued these sentences with evident emotion, perhaps even passion, which seemed a further indication that he was speaking with purpose and meaning. On the other hand, those in seizures of religious joy, who speak in tongues, also exhibit great emotion, but there is no evident meaning in the tongues they speak.

When Leland Delacroix began to record again, his voice revealed a numbing and dangerous depression: so flat as to be virtually devoid of inflection, so soft that it was barely more than a whisper, the essence of hopelessness.

"There's no point in making this tape. You can't do anything to change what's happened. There's no going back. Everything's out of balance now. Veils ripped. Realities intersecting."

Delacroix fell silent, and there was only the faint background hiss and pop of the tape.

Veils ripped. Realities intersecting.

I glanced at Bobby. He seemed as clueless as I was.

"Temporal relocator. That's what they called it."

I looked at Bobby again, and he said, with grim satisfaction, "Time machine."

"We sent test modules through, instrument packages. Some came back. Some didn't. Intriguing but mysterious data. Data so strange the argument was for a far future terminus, a lot farther than anyone expected. How far forward these packages went, no one could say or wanted to guess. Videocams were included in later tests, but when they came back, the tape counters were still at zero. Maybe they taped . . . then, coming back, they rewound, erased. But finally we got visuals. The instrument package was supposed to be mobile. Like the Mars rovers. This one must've been hung up on something. The package itself didn't move, but the videocam panned back and forth across the same narrow wedge of sky, framed by overhanging trees. There were eight hours of tape, back and forth, eight hours and not one

cloud. The sky was red. Not streaky red like a sky at sunset. An even shade of red, as the sky we know is an even shade of blue, but with no increase or diminishment of light, none at all, over eight hours."

Delacroix's low, leaden voice faded to silence, but he didn't turn off the recorder.

After a long pause, there was the sound of chair legs scraping-stuttering across a tile floor, probably a kitchen floor, followed by heavy footsteps fading as Delacroix left the room. He dragged his feet slightly, physically weighed down by his extreme depression.

"Red sky," Bobby said thoughtfully.

A still and awful red, I thought uneasily, remembering the line from Coleridge's *The Rime of the Ancient Mariner,* a favorite poem of mine when I was a young boy of nine or ten, in love with terror and with the idea of remorseless fate. These days, it held no special appeal—for the very reasons that I had liked it so much then.

We listened to the silence on the tape for a while, and then we could hear Delacroix's voice in the distance, evidently coming from another room.

I cranked up the volume, but I still couldn't make out what the man was saying.

"Who's he talking to?" Bobby wondered.

"Himself, maybe."

"Maybe to his family."

His dead family.

Delacroix must have been roaming, because his voice rose and fell independent of my use of the volume control.

At one point he cruised past or through the kitchen, and we could hear him clearly enough to determine that he was speaking in that strange language again. He was ranting with considerable emotion, not in the flat dead voice he had last used when sitting at the recorder.

Eventually he fell silent, and a short while later, he came back to the recorder. He switched it off, and I suspected that he rewound it to see where he had interrupted himself. When he began to record again, his voice was low, sluggish, once more crushed flat by depression.

"Computer analysis revealed that the red sky was an accurate color. Not an error in the video system. And the trees that framed the view of the sky . . . they were gray and black. Not in shadow. That was the true color. Of the bark. The leaves. Mostly black mottled with gray. We called them trees not because they looked like trees as we know them, but because they were more analogous to trees than to anything else. They were sleek . . . succulent . . . less like vegetation than like flesh. Maybe some form of fungus. I don't know. Nobody knew. Eight hours of unchanging red sky and the same black trees—and then something in the sky. Flying. This thing. Flying low. So fast. Only a few frames of it, the image blurred because of its speed. Enhanced it, of course. With the computers. It still wasn't entirely clear. Clear enough. There were lots of opinions. Lots of interpretations. Arguments. Debates. I knew what it was. I think most of us knew, on some deep level, the moment we saw it enhanced. We just couldn't accept it. Psychological block. We argued our way right through the truth, until the truth was behind us and we didn't have to see it anymore. I deluded myself, like all the rest, but I don't delude myself anymore."

He settled into silence. A gurgle and splash indicated that he was pouring something out of a bottle into a glass. He took a drink of it.

In silence, Bobby and I sucked at our beers.

I wondered if you could get beer in this world of the red sky and the fleshy black trees. Although I like a beer occasionally, I would have no difficulty living without it. Now, however, this bottle of Corona in my hand was the avatar of all the countless humble pleasures of daily life, of all that could be lost through human arrogance, and I held fast to it as though it were more precious than diamonds, which in one sense it was.

Delacroix began to speak in that incomprehensible tongue again, and this time he murmured the same few words over and over, as though chanting in a whisper. As before, though I couldn't understand one word, there was a familiarity in these syllables and in the cadence of his speech that sent a corkscrew chill through the hollows of my spine.

"He's drunk or kooking out," Bobby said. "Maybe both."

When I began to worry that Delacroix would not continue with his revelations, he switched to English.

"Should never have sent a manned expedition across. Wasn't on the schedule. Not for years, maybe not ever. But there was another project at Wyvern, one of many others, where something went wrong. I don't know what. Something big. Most of the projects, I think . . . they're just money-burning machines. But something went too right in this one. The top brass were scared shitless. Lot of pressure came down on us, pressure for the Mystery Train to speed up. They wanted a good look at the future. To see whether there was any future. They didn't quite put it that way, but everyone involved with the train thought that was their motivation. To see whether this screwup on the other project was going to have major consequences. So against everyone's better judgment, or almost everyone's, we put together the first expedition."

Another silence.

Then more rhythmic, whispery chanting.

Bobby said, "There's your mom, bro. The 'other project,' the one that got the top brass scared about the future."

"So she wasn't part of the Mystery Train."

"The train was just . . . reconnaissance. Or that's all it was meant to be. But something went way wrong there, too. In fact, maybe what went wrong with the train was the worse of the two."

I said, "What do you think was on that videotape? The flying thing, I mean."

"I'm hoping the man is gonna tell us."

The whispering continued for a minute or more, and in the middle of it, Delacroix hit the *stop* button.

When he resumed recording, he was in a new location. The sound quality wasn't as good as before, and there was a steady background noise.

"Car engine," Bobby said.

Engine noise, a faint whistle of wind, and the hum of tires racing over pavement: Delacroix was on the move.

His driver's license had given an address in Monterey, a couple hours up the coast. He must have left his family's bodies there.

A whispering arose. Delacroix was talking to himself in such a low voice that we could barely discern he was speaking in the unknown language. Gradually, the muttering faded away.

After a silence, when he began to speak louder and in English, his voice wasn't as clear as we would have liked. The microphone wasn't as close to his mouth as it should have been. The recorder was either on the seat beside him or, more likely, balanced on the dashboard.

His depression had given way to fear again. He spoke faster, and his voice frequently cracked with anxiety.

"I'm on Highway 1, driving south. I sort of remember getting in the car but not . . . not driving this far. I poured gasoline over them. Set them on fire. I half remember doing it. Don't know why I didn't . . . why I didn't kill myself. Took the rings off her finger. Brought some pictures from the album. It didn't want me to. I took the time . . . anyway. And the recorder. It didn't want me to. I guess I know where I'm going. I guess I know, all right."

Delacroix wept.

Bobby said, "He's losing control."

"But not the way you mean."

"Huh?"

"He's not losing his mind. He's losing control to . . . something else."

As we listened to Delacroix weep, Bobby said, "You mean losing control to . . . ?"

"Yeah."

"To whatever was fluttering."

"Yeah."

"Everyone died. Everyone on the first expedition. Three men, one woman. Blake, Jackson, Chang, and Hodgson. And only one

came back. Only Hodgson came back. Except it wasn't Bill Hodgson in the suit."

Delacroix cried out with sudden pain, as if he'd been stabbed.

The tortured cry was followed by an astonishing spell of violent cursing: every obscenity I had ever heard or read, plus others that either weren't part of my education or were invented by Delacroix, a vile torrent of rapid-fire vulgarities and blasphemies. This stream of raw filth was venomously ejected, snarled and shouted with a fury so blazing that I felt seared even when exposed to only the recording of it.

Evidently, Delacroix's vocal outburst was accompanied by erratic driving. His cursing was punctuated by the blaring horns of passing cars and trucks.

The cursing sputtered to a stop. The last of the horns faded. For a while Delacroix's raggedly drawn breaths were the loudest sounds on the tape. Then:

"Kevin, maybe you remember, you once told me that science alone couldn't give us meaningful lives. You said science would actually make life unlivable if it ever explained everything to us and robbed the universe of mystery. We desperately need our mystery, you said. In the mystery is the hope. That's what you believe. Well, what I saw over on the other side. . . . Kevin, what I saw over there is more mystery than a million years of scientists can explain. The universe is stranger than we ever conceived . . . and yet, at the same time, it's eerily like our most primitive concepts of it."

He drove in silence for a minute or so and then began to murmur to himself in that cryptic language.

Bobby said, "Who's Kevin?"

"His brother? Earlier, he referred to him as 'big brother.' I think Kevin might be a reporter somewhere."

Still speaking what was gibberish to us, Delacroix shut off the recorder. I was afraid this was the last piece of an incomplete testament, but then he returned.

"Pumped cyanide gas into the translation capsule. That didn't kill Hodgson, or what had come back in Hodgson's place."

"Translation capsule," Bobby said.

"The egg room," I guessed.

"We pumped all the atmosphere out. The capsule was a giant vacuum tube. Hodgson was still alive. Because this isn't life . . . not as we think of life. This is anti-life. We kept the capsule operative, powered it to a new cycle, and Hodgson, or whatever it was, went back where it came from."

He switched off the recorder. Only four entries remained in his testament, and each was spoken in a more confused, fearful voice. I sensed that these were Delacroix's few fitful moments of coherence.

"Eight of us on the second expedition. Four came back alive. Me among them. Not infected. The doctors declared us free of all infection. But now . . ."

Followed by:

". . . infected or possessed? Virus? Parasite? Or something more profound? Am I just a carrier . . . or a doorway? Is something in me . . . or coming through me? Am I . . . being unlocked . . . opened . . . opened like a door?"

Then, with decreasing coherence:

". . . never went forward . . . went sideways. Didn't even realize there was a sideways. Because we all long ago . . . we stopped thinking about . . . stopped believing in a sideways. . . ."

Finally:

". . . will have to abandon the car . . . walk in . . . but not where it wants me to go. Not to the translation capsule. Not if I can help it. The house. To the house. Did I tell you they all died? The first expedition? When I pull the trigger . . . will I be closing the door . . . or opening it to them? Did I tell you what I saw? Did I tell you who I saw? Did I tell you about their suffering? Do you know what flies and crawls? Under that red sky? Did I tell you? How did I get . . . here? Here?"

The last words on the tape were not in English.

I raised the bottle of Corona to my mouth and discovered that I had already emptied it.

Bobby said, "So this place with the red sky, the black trees—is it your mom's future, bro?"

"Sideways, Delacroix said."

"But what does that mean?"

"I don't know."

"Did *they* know?"

"Doesn't sound like they did," I said, pressing the *rewind* button on the remote.

"I'm having some quashingly funky thoughts."

"The cocoons," I guessed.

"Whatever spun the cocoons—did they come out of Delacroix?"

"Or through him, like he said. Like he was a doorway."

"Whatever that means. And either way, does it matter? Out of or through, it's the same to us."

"I think if his body hadn't been there, the cocoons wouldn't be there, either," I said.

"Gotta get some angry villagers together and march up to the castle with torches," he said, his tone of voice more serious than the words he had chosen to express himself.

As the tape rewound and clicked to a stop, I said, "Should we take the responsibility on this one? We don't know enough. Maybe we should tell someone about the cocoons."

"You mean like authority types?"

"Like."

"You know what they'll do?"

"Screw up," I said. "But at least it won't be us screwing up."

"They won't burn 'em all. They'll want samples for study."

"I'm sure they'll take precautions."

Bobby laughed.

I laughed, too, with as much bitterness as amusement. "Okay, sign me up for the march on the castle. But Orson and the kids come first. Because once we light that fire, we won't be as free to move around Wyvern."

I inserted a blank cassette into the second deck.

Bobby said, "Making a dupe?"

"Can't hurt." When the machines started working, I turned to him. "Something you said earlier."

"You expect me to remember all the crap I say?"

"In that bungalow kitchen, with Delacroix's body."

"I can smell it vividly."

"You heard something. Looked up at the cocoons."

"Told you. Must've been in my head."

"Right. But when I asked you what you heard, you said, 'Me.' What'd you mean by that?"

Bobby still had some beer. He drained the remaining contents of his bottle. "You were putting the cassette in your pocket. We were ready to leave. I thought I heard somebody say *stay*."

"Somebody?"

"Several somebodies. Voices. All speaking at once, all saying *stay, stay, stay*."

"Maurice Williams and the Zodiacs."

"So you're studying to be a jock at KBAY. The thing is . . . then I realized the voices were all my voice."

"All your voice?"

"Hard to explain, bro."

"Evidently."

"For eight, ten seconds I could hear them. But even later . . . I felt they were still talking, just at lower volume."

"Subliminal?"

"Maybe. Something way creepy."

"Voices in your head."

"Well, they weren't telling me to sacrifice a virgin to Satan or assassinate the pope."

"Just *stay, stay, stay*," I said. "Like a thought loop."

"No, these were like real voices on a radio. At first I thought they were coming . . . from somewhere in the bungalow."

"You panned your flashlight over the ceiling," I reminded him. "The cocoons."

The faint glow from the audio equipment was reflected in his eyes. He didn't look away from me, but he didn't say anything.

I took a deep breath. "Because I've been wondering. After I called you from Dead Town, I started to feel vulnerable out in the open. So before I called Sasha, I decide to go into a bungalow, where I wouldn't be so exposed."

"Out of all those houses, why did you pick that one? With Delacroix's body in the kitchen. With the cocoons."

"That's what I've been wondering," I said.

"You hear voices, too? Saying, *Come in, Chris, come in, sit down, come in, be neighborly, we'll be hatching soon, come in, join the fun.*"

"No voices," I said. "At least not any I was aware of. But maybe it wasn't by chance I chose that house. Maybe I was drawn to that place instead of the one next door."

"Psychic hoodoo?"

"Like the songs that sea nymphs sing to lure unwary sailors to destruction."

"These aren't sea nymphs. These are bugs in cocoons."

"We don't know they're bugs," I said.

"I'm way sure they aren't puppy dogs."

"I think maybe we got out of that bungalow just in time."

After a silence, he said, "It's crap like this that takes all the fun out of the end of the world."

"Yeah, I'm starting to feel like a piece of chum in a school of hammerheads."

The tape was duped. I took the copy to the composition table and, picking up a felt-tip pen, said, "What's a good neo-Buffett song title?"

"Neo-Buffett?"

"It's what Sasha's writing these days. Jimmy Buffett. Tropical bounce, parrothead worldview, fun in the sun—but with a darker edge, a concession to reality."

" 'Tequila Kidneys,' " he suggested.

"Good enough."

I printed that title on the label and inserted the cassette into an empty slot in the rack where Sasha stored her compositions. There were scores of cassettes that looked just like it.

"Bro," Bobby said, "if it ever comes to that, you would blow my head off, wouldn't you?"

"Anytime."

"Wait for me to ask."

"Sure. And you me?"

"Ask, and you're dead."

"The only fluttering I feel is in my stomach," I said.

"I figure that's normal right now."

I heard a hard snap and a series of clicks, followed by the same sounds again—then the unmistakable creak of the back door opening.

Bobby blinked at me. "Sasha?"

I went into the candlelit kitchen, saw Manuel Ramirez in his uniform, and knew the sounds I'd heard had been from a police lock-release gun. He was standing at the kitchen table, staring down at my 9-millimeter Glock, to which he had gone directly, in spite of the dim light. I had put the pistol on the table when Bobby's news about Wendy Dulcinea's kidnapping had left me shaky.

"That door was locked," I said to Manuel, as Bobby entered the kitchen behind me.

"Yeah," Manuel said. He indicated the Glock. "You buy this legally?"

"My dad did."

"Your dad taught poetry."

"It's a dangerous profession."

"Where'd he buy this?" Manuel asked, picking up the pistol.

"Thor's Gun Shop."

"You have a receipt?"

"I'll get it."

"Never mind."

The door between the kitchen and the downstairs hall swung inward. Frank Feeney, one of Manuel's deputies, hesitated on the threshold. For an instant, in his eyes, I thought I saw a veil of yellow light billow like curtains at a pair of windows, but it was gone before I could be sure that it had been real. "Found a shotgun and a .38 in Halloway's Jeep," Feeney said.

"You boys belong to a right-wing militia or something?" Manuel asked.

"We're going to sign up for a poetry class," Bobby said. "You have a search warrant?"

"Tear a paper towel off that roll," the chief said. "I'll write one out for you."

Behind Feeney, at the far end of the hall, in the foyer, backlit by the stained-glass windows, was a second deputy. I couldn't see him well enough to know who he was.

"How'd you get in here?" I asked.

Manuel stared at me long enough to remind me that he was not a friend of mine anymore.

"What's going on?" I demanded.

"A massive violation of your civil rights," Manuel said, and his smile had all the warmth of a stiletto wound in the belly of a corpse.

19

Frank Feeney had a serpent's face, one without fangs but with no need of fangs because he exuded poison from every pore. His eyes had the fixed, cold focus of a snake's eyes, and his mouth was a slit from which a forked tongue could have flicked without causing a start of surprise even in a stranger who'd just met him. Before the mess at Wyvern, Feeney had been the rotten apple on the police force, and he was still sufficiently toxic to cast a thousand Snow Whites into comas with a glance.

"You want us to search the place for more weapons, Chief?" he asked Manuel.

"Yeah. But don't trash it too much. Mr. Snow, here, lost his father a month ago. He's an orphan now. Let's show him some pity."

Smiling as if he had just spied a tender mouse or a bird's egg that would satisfy his reptilian hunger, Feeney turned and swaggered down the hallway toward the other deputy.

"We'll be confiscating all firearms," Manuel told me.

"These are legal weapons. They weren't used in the commission of any crime. You don't have any right to seize them," I protested. "I know my Second Amendment rights."

To Bobby, Manuel said, "You think I'm out of line, too?"

"You can do what you want," Bobby said.

"Your boardhead buddy here is smarter than he looks," Manuel told me.

Testing Manuel's self-control, trying to determine if there were any limits to the lawlessness in which the police were willing to engage, Bobby said, "An ugly, psychotic asshole with a badge can *always* do what he wants."

"Exactly," Manuel said.

Manuel Ramirez—neither ugly nor psychotic—is three inches shorter, thirty pounds heavier, twelve years older, and noticeably more Hispanic than I am; he likes country music, while I'm born for rock-'n'-roll; he speaks Spanish, Italian, and English, while I'm limited strictly to English and a few comforting mottoes in Latin; he's full of political opinions, while I find politics boring and sleazy; he's a great cook, but the only thing I can do well with food is eat it. In spite of all these differences and many others, we once shared a love of people and a love of life that made us friends.

For years he had worked the graveyard shift, the top cop of the night, but since Chief Lewis Stevenson died one month ago, Manuel had been head of the department. In the night world where I had met him and become his friend, he was once a bright presence, a good cop and a good man. Things change, especially here in the new Moonlight Bay, and although he now works the day, he has given his heart to darkness and is not the person I once knew.

"Anyone else here?" Manuel asked.

"No."

I heard Feeney and the other deputy talking in the foyer—and then footsteps on the stairs.

"Got your message," Manuel told me. "The license number."

I nodded.

"Sasha Goodall was at Lilly Wing's house last night."

"Maybe it was a Tupperware party," I said.

Breaking the magazine out of the Glock, Manuel said, "You two showed up just before dawn. You parked behind the garage and came in the back way."

"We needed some Tupperware," Bobby said.

"Where were you all night?"

"Studying Tupperware catalogs," I said.

"You disappoint me, Chris."

"You think I'm more the Rubbermaid type?"

Manuel said, "I never knew you to be a smartass."

"I'm a man of countless facets."

A subdued response to his questioning would be interpreted as fear, and any show of fear would invite harsher treatment. We both knew that the perverse martial law in force during this emergency had never been legally declared, and though it was unlikely that any authority would ever hold Manuel or his men accountable for high crimes or misdemeanors, he couldn't be certain there would be no consequences for his illegal acts. Besides, he'd once been a by-the-book lawman, and beneath all his self-justification, he still had a conscience. Wiseass remarks were my way—and Bobby's way—of reminding Manuel that we knew as well as he did that his authority was now mostly illegitimate and that pushed too hard, we would resist it.

"Don't *I* disappoint you, too?" Bobby asked.

"I've always known what *you* are," Manuel said, dropping the pistol magazine into one of his pockets.

"Likewise. You should change brands of face makeup. Shouldn't he change brands of makeup, Chris?"

"Something that covers better," I said.

"Yeah," Bobby said to Manuel, "I can still see the three sixes on your forehead."

Without responding, Manuel tucked my Glock under his belt.

"Did you check out the license number?" I asked him.

"Useless. The Suburban was stolen earlier in the evening. We found it abandoned this afternoon, near the marina."

"Any leads?"

"None of this is your business. I've got two things to say to you, Chris. Two reasons I'm here. Stay out of this."

"Is that number one?"

"What?"

"Is that number one of the two? Or is that bonus advice?"

"Two things we can remember," Bobby said. "But if there's a lot of bonus advice, we'll have to take notes."

"Stay out of this," Manuel repeated, speaking to me and ignoring Bobby. There was no unnatural luminosity in his eyes, but the hard edge in his voice was as chilling as animal eyeshine. "You've used up all the get-out-of-jail-free cards you had any right to expect from me. I mean it, Chris."

A crash came from upstairs. A heavy piece of furniture had been tipped over.

I started toward the hall door.

Manuel stopped me by drawing his billy club and slamming it hard against the table. The rap was as loud as a gunshot. He said, "You heard me tell Frank not to trash the place too much. Just relax."

"There aren't any more guns," I said angrily.

"Poetry lover like you might have a whole arsenal. For public safety, we have to be sure."

Bobby was leaning against the counter near the cooktop, arms crossed on his chest. He appeared to be entirely resigned to our powerlessness, willing to ride out this episode, so totally chilled that he might as well have had lumps of coal for eyes and a carrot for a nose. This pose no doubt deceived Manuel, but I knew Bobby so well that I could see he was like a dry-ice bomb about to achieve blast pressure. The drawer immediately to his right contained a set of knives, and I was sure that he had chosen his position with the cutlery in mind.

We couldn't win a fight here, now, and the important thing was to remain free to find Orson and the missing kids.

When the sound of shattering glass came from upstairs, I ignored it, reined in my anger, and said tightly to Manuel, "Lilly lost her husband. Now, maybe, her only child. Doesn't that reach you? You of all people?"

"I'm sorry for her."

"That's all?"

"If I could bring her boy back, I would."

His choice of words chilled me. "That sounds like he's already dead—or somewhere you can't go to get him."

With none of the compassion that once had been the essence of Manuel, he said, "I told you—stay out of it."

Sixteen years ago, Manuel's wife, Carmelita, died giving

birth to their second child. She had been only twenty-four. Manuel, who never remarried, raised a daughter and son with much love and wisdom. His boy, Toby, has Down's syndrome. As much as anyone and more than some people, Manuel knows suffering; he understands what it means to live with hard responsibilities and limitations. Nevertheless, though I searched his eyes, I couldn't see the compassion that had made him a first-rate father and policeman.

"What about the Stuart twins?" I asked.

His round face, designed more for laughter than for anger, usually a summer face, was now full of winter and as hard as ice.

I said, "What about Wendy Dulcinea?"

The extent of my knowledge angered him.

His voice remained soft, but he tapped the end of the billy club against his right palm: "You listen to me, Chris. Those of us who know what's happened—we either swallow it or we choke on it. So just relax and swallow it. Because if you choke on it, then no one is going to be there to apply the Heimlich maneuver. You understand?"

"Sure. Hey, I'm a bright guy. I understand. That was a death threat."

"Nicely delivered," Bobby noted. "Creative, oblique, no jarring histrionics—although the bit of business with the club is a cliché. Psychotic-Gestapo-torturer shtick from a hundred old movies. You'll be a more credible fascist without it."

"Screw you."

Bobby smiled. "I know you dream about it."

Manuel appeared to be one more exchange away from wading into Bobby with the club.

Stepping in front of Bobby so that the two of them wouldn't be face-to-face, and hoping miraculously to raise guilt from Manuel's graveyard conscience, I said, "If I try to go public, try to mess where I'm not supposed to mess, who puts the bullet in the back of my head, Manuel? You?"

A look of genuine hurt passed across his features, but it only briefly softened his expression. "I couldn't."

"Very broly of you." *Broly* is surfer lingo for *brotherly*.

"I'll be so much less dead if it's one of your deputies who pulls the trigger instead of you."

"This isn't easy for either of us."

"Seems easier for you than me."

"You've been protected because of who your mother was, what she achieved. And because you were . . . once a friend of mine. But don't push your luck, Chris."

"Four kids snatched in twelve hours, Manuel. Is that the going exchange rate? Four other kids for one Toby?"

Admittedly, I was cruel to accuse him of sacrificing the lives of other children for his son, but there was truth in this cruelty.

His face darkened like settled coals, and in his eyes was the livid fire of hatred. "Yeah. I have a son that I'm responsible for. And a daughter. My mother. A family I'm responsible for. It's not as easy for me as it is for a smartass loner like you."

I was sickened that, once friends, we had come to this.

The entire police department of Moonlight Bay had been co-opted by those higher authorities responsible for concealing the terrors spawned at Wyvern. The cops' reasons for cooperating were numerous: fear foremost; misguided patriotism; wads of hundred-dollar bills in prodigious quantities that only black-budget projects can provide. Furthermore, they had been impressed into the search for the troop of rhesuses and human subjects that escaped the lab more than two years ago, and on that night of violence, most had been bitten, clawed, or otherwise infected; they were in danger of becoming, so they agreed to be participants in the conspiracy, with the hope of being first in line for treatment if a cure for the retrovirus was discovered.

Manuel couldn't be bought with mere money. His patriotism was not of the misguided variety. Sufficient fear can bring any man to heel, but it wasn't fear that had corrupted Manuel.

The research at Wyvern had led to catastrophe, but also to positive discoveries. Evidently, some experiments have resulted in genetic treatments that are promising.

Manuel sold his soul for the hope that one of those experimental treatments would transform Toby. And I suspect he dreams of his son achieving intellectual *and* physical transformation.

The intellectual growth might well be possible. We know that some of the Wyvern work included intelligence-enhancement research and that there were startling successes, as witness Orson.

"How's Toby doing?" I asked.

As I spoke, I heard a stealthy but telltale sound behind me. A drawer sliding open. The knife drawer.

When I had interposed myself between Bobby and Manuel, I'd meant only to defuse the escalating tension between them, not to provide cover for Bobby to arm himself. I wanted to tell him to chill out, but I didn't know how to do so without alerting Manuel.

Besides, there are occasions when Bobby's instincts are better than mine. If he thought this situation was inevitably leading to violence, perhaps he was right.

Apparently, my question about Toby had masked the sound of the drawer, because Manuel gave no indication of having heard it.

A fierce pride, both touching and terrifying, couldn't drive out his anger; the two emotions were darkly complementary. "He's reading. Better. Faster. More comprehension. Doing better at math. And what's wrong with that? Is that a crime?"

I shook my head.

Although some people make fun of Toby's appearance or shun him, he's the image of gentleness. With his thick neck, rounded shoulders, short arms, and stocky legs, he reminds me of the good gnomes from the adventure stories that delighted me in childhood. His sloped and heavy brow, low-set ears, and soft features, and the inner epicanthic folds of his eyes, give him a dreamy aspect that matches his sweet and gentle personality.

In spite of his burdens, Toby has always been happy and content. I worry that the Wyvern crowd will raise his intelligence far enough to leave him dissatisfied with his life—but not far enough to give him an average IQ. If they steal his innocence and curse him with a self-awareness that leaves him anguished, trapping him between livable identities, they will destroy him.

I know all about unfulfillable longing, the fruitless yearning to be what one can never be.

And although I find it difficult to believe that Toby could be genetically engineered into a radically new appearance, I fear that if any such attempt were made, he might become something he wouldn't be able to bear seeing in the mirror. Those who don't perceive beauty in the face of a Down's-syndrome person are blind to all beauty or are so fearful of *difference* that they must at once turn away from every encounter with it. In every face—in even the plainest and the most unfortunate countenances—there is some precious aspect of the divine image of which we are a reflection, and if you look with an open heart, you can see an awesome beauty, a glimpse of something so radiant that it gives you joy. But will this radiance remain in Toby if he is redesigned by Wyvern scientists, if a radical physical transformation is attempted?

"He's got a future now," Manuel said.

"Don't throw your boy away," I pleaded.

"I'm lifting him up."

"He won't be your boy anymore."

"He'll finally be what he was meant to be."

"He already was what he was meant to be."

"You don't know the pain," Manuel said bitterly.

He was speaking about his own pain, not Toby's. Toby is at peace with the world. Or was.

I said, "You always loved him for what he was."

His voice was sharp and tremulous. "In *spite* of what he was."

"That's not fair to yourself. I know how you've felt about him all these years. You've treasured him."

"You don't know shit about how I felt, not *shit*," he said, and he poked the air in front of me with the club, as if driving home his point.

With sorrow as heavy as a rock on my chest, I said, "If that's true, if I didn't understand how you felt about Toby, then I didn't know you at all."

"Maybe you didn't," he said. "Or maybe you can't bear to think Toby could end up with a more normal life than yours. We all like to have someone to look down on—don't we, Chris?"

My heart contracted as if around a thorn. The ferocity of his anger revealed such profound terror and pain that I couldn't bear to respond to this mean-spirited accusation. We had been friends too long for me to hate him, and I was overcome only by pity.

He was mad with hope. In reasonable measure, hope sustains us. In great excess, it distorts perceptions, dulls the mind, corrupts the heart to no less an extent than does heroin.

I don't believe I've misunderstood Manuel all these years. High on hope, he has forgotten what he loved and, instead, loves the ideal more than the reality, which is the cause of all the misery that the human species creates for itself.

Descending footsteps sounded on the stairs. I looked toward the hall as Feeney and the other deputy appeared in the foyer. Feeney went into the living room, the other man into the study, where they switched on the lights and dialed up the rheostats.

"What's the second thing you came here to tell me?" I asked Manuel.

"They're going to get control of this."

"Of what?"

"This plague."

"With what?" Bobby asked. "A bottle of Lysol?"

"Some people are immune."

"Not everyone," Bobby said as glass shattered in the living room.

Manuel said, "But the immune factor has been isolated. Soon there'll be a vaccine, and a cure for those already infected."

I thought of the missing children, but I didn't mention them. "Some people are still becoming," I said.

"And we're learning there's only so much change they're able to tolerate."

I strove to resist the flood of hope that might have swept me away. "Only so much? How much?"

"There's a threshold. . . . They become acutely aware of the changes taking place in them. Then they're overcome by fear. An intolerable fear of themselves. Hatred of themselves. The self-hatred escalates until . . . they psychologically implode."

"Psychological implosion? What the hell does that mean?" Then I understood. "Suicide?"

"Beyond suicide. Violent . . . frenzied self-destruction. We've seen . . . a number of cases. You understand what this means?"

I said, "When they self-destruct, they're no longer carriers of the retrovirus. The plague is self-limiting."

Judging by the sound, Frank Feeney was smashing a small table or chair against one of the living-room walls. I guessed that the other deputy was sweeping Sasha's bottles of vitamins and herbs off the shelves in the study. They were dutifully teaching us a lesson—and respect for the law.

"Most of us will get through this all right," Manuel said.

But who among us will not? I wondered.

"Animals, too," I said. "They self-destruct."

He regarded me with suspicion. "We're seeing indications. What have you seen?"

I thought of the birds. The *veve* rats, which had been dead a long time. The pack of coyotes no doubt were nearing the threshold of tolerable change.

"Why're you telling me this?" I asked.

"So you'll stay the hell out of the way. Let the right people manage this situation. People who know what they're doing. People with credentials."

"The usual big brains," Bobby said.

Manuel poked the club in our direction. "You may think you're heroes, but you'll just be getting in the way."

"I'm no hero," I assured him.

Bobby said, "Me, hell, I'm just a surf-smacked, sun-fried, beer-whacked boardhead."

Manuel said, "There's too much at stake here for us to allow anyone to have an agenda of his own."

"What about the troop?" I asked. "The monkeys haven't self-destructed."

"They're different. They were engineered in the lab, and they are what they are. They are what they were made to be, what they were *born* to be. They can still *become* if they're vulnerable to the mutated virus, but maybe they aren't susceptible. After this is all over, once people are vaccinated and this outbreak self-limits, we'll track them down and wipe them out."

"Not much luck at that so far," I reminded him.

"We've been distracted by the bigger problem."

"Yeah," Bobby said. "Destroying the world is ass-busting work."

Ignoring him, Manuel said, "Once we get the rest of this cleaned up, then the troop . . . their days are numbered."

Lights flared in the adjacent dining room, where Feeney had proceeded from the living room, and I moved away from the brightness that fell through the connecting doorway.

The second deputy appeared at the hallway door, and he was not anyone I had seen before. I thought I knew all the police in town, but perhaps the financiers behind the Wyvern wizards had recently provided the funding for a larger force.

"Found some boxes of ammo," the new guy said. "No weapons."

Manuel called to Frank, who appeared in the dining-room doorway and said, "Chief?"

"We're done here," Manuel said.

Feeney looked disappointed, but the new man turned away from the kitchen and immediately headed along the hall toward the front of the house.

With startling speed, Manuel lunged toward Bobby, swinging the baton at his head. Equally quick, Bobby ducked.

The club carved the air where Bobby had been, and cracked loudly against the side of the refrigerator.

Bobby came up under the baton, right in Manuel's face, and I thought he was embracing him, which was weird, but then I saw the gleam of the butcher knife, the point against Manuel's throat.

The new deputy had raced back to the kitchen, and both he and Frank Feeney had drawn their revolvers, holding the weapons in two-hand grips.

"Back off," Manuel told his deputies.

He backed off, too, easing away from the point of the knife.

For a crazy moment I thought Bobby was going to shove the huge blade into him, though I know Bobby better than that.

Remaining wary, the deputies retreated a step or two, and they relaxed their arms from a ready-fire position, although neither man holstered his weapon.

The spill of light through the dining-room door revealed more of Manuel's face than I cared to see. It had been torn by anger and then knitted together by more anger, so the stitches were too tight, pulling his features into strange arrangements, both eyes bulging, but the left eye more than the right, nostrils flaring, his mouth a straight slash on the left but curving into a sneer on the right, like a portrait by Picasso in a crappy mood, all chopped into cubes, geometric slabs that didn't quite fit together. And his skin was no longer a warm brown but the color of a ham that had been left far too long in the smokehouse, muddy red with settled blood and too much hickory smoke, dark and marbled.

Manuel seethed with a hatred so intense that it couldn't have been engendered solely by Bobby's smartass remarks. This hatred was aimed at me, too, but Manuel couldn't bring himself to strike me, not after so many years of friendship, so he wanted to hurt Bobby because that would hurt me. Maybe some of his wrath was directed at himself, because he had flushed away his principles, and maybe we were seeing sixteen years of pent-up anger at God for Carmelita's dying in childbirth and for Toby's being born with Down's syndrome, and I think-feel-*know* that some of this was fury he could not—would not, dared not—admit feeling toward Toby, dear Toby, whom he loved desperately but who had so severely limited his life. After all, there's a reason they say that love is a two-edged sword, rather than a two-edged Wiffle bat or a two-edged Fudgsicle, because love is sharp, it pierces, and love is a needle that sews shut the holes in our hearts, that mends our souls, but it can also cut, cut deep, wound, kill.

Manuel was struggling to regain control of himself, aware that we were all watching him, that he was a spectacle; but he was losing the struggle. The side of the refrigerator was scarred where he had hammered the billy club into it, but an assault on an appliance, even a major appliance, didn't provide the satisfaction he needed, didn't relieve the pressure still building in him. A couple minutes earlier, I had thought of Bobby as a dry-ice bomb at the critical-evaporation point, but now it was Manuel who exploded, not at Bobby or at me, but at the glass panels in the four doors of a display cabinet, bashing each pane with the baton, and then he tore open one of the doors and, with the stick, swept out the Royal Worcester china, the Evesham set of which my mother had been so fond. Saucers, cups, bread plates, salad plates, a gravy boat, a butter dish, a sugar-and-cream set crashed onto the countertop and from there to the floor, porcelain shrapnel pinging off the dishwasher, singing off chair legs and cabinetry. The microwave oven was next to the display cabinet, and he hammered the club into it, once, twice, three times, four times, but the view window was evidently made of Plexiglas or something, because it didn't shatter, though the club switched on the oven and programmed the timer, and if we'd had the foresight to put a bag of Orville Redenbacher's finest in the microwave earlier, we could have enjoyed popcorn by the time Manuel had worked off his rage. He plucked a steel teapot off the stove and pitched it across the room, grabbed the toaster and threw it to the floor even as the teapot was still bouncing around—*tonk, tonk, tonk*—with the manic energy of a battered icon in a video game. He kicked the toaster, and it

tumbled across the floor, squeaking as though it were a terrified little dog, trailing its cord like a tail, and then he was
done.

He stood in the center of the kitchen, shoulders slumped,
head thrust forward, eyelids as heavy as if he had just woken
from a deep sleep, mouth slack, breathing heavily. He looked
around as though slightly confused, as though he were a bull
wondering where the hell that infuriating red cape had gone.

Throughout Manuel's destructive frenzy, I expected to
see the demonic yellow light shimmer through his eyes, but I
never caught a glimpse of it. Now there was smoldering anger
in his gaze, and confusion, and a wrenching sadness, but if he
was becoming something less than human, he wasn't far
enough devolved to exhibit eyeshine.

The nameless deputy watched cautiously through eyes as
dark as the windows in an abandoned house, but Frank Feeney's eyes were brighter than those of Halloween pumpkins,
full of fiery menace. Although this uncanny glimmer was not
constant, coming and going and coming again, the savagery
that it betokened burned as steady as a watch fire. Feeney was
backlit by the dining-room chandelier, and with his face in
shadows, his eyes at times glowed as if the light from the next
room were passing straight through his skull and radiating
from his sockets.

I had been afraid that Manuel's violence would trigger
outbursts in the deputies, that all three men were becoming,
and that a rapidly accelerating dementia would seize them,
whereupon Bobby and I would be surrounded by the high-
biotech equivalent of a pack of werewolves in the grip of
bloodlust. Because we had foolishly neglected to acquire necklaces of wolfsbane or silver bullets, we would be forced to
defend ourselves with my mother's tarnished sterling tea service, which would have to be unpacked from a box in the
pantry and perhaps even polished with Wright's silver cream
and a soft cloth to be sufficiently lethal.

Now it appeared that Feeney was the only threat, but a
werewolf with a loaded revolver is a lycanthrope of a different
caliber, and one like him could be as deadly as an entire pack.

He was shaking, glistening with sweat, inhaling with a coarse rasp, exhaling with a thin and eager whine of need. In his excitement, he had bitten his lip, and his teeth and chin were red with his own blood. He held the gun with both hands, aiming it at the floor, while his mad eyes seemed to be looking for a target, his attention flicking from Manuel to me, to the second deputy, to Bobby, to me, to Manuel again, and if Feeney decided that we were all targets, he might be able to kill the four of us even as he was cut down by his fellow officers' return fire.

I realized that Manuel was talking to Feeney and to the other deputy. The pounding of my heart had temporarily deafened me. His voiced faded in: ". . . we're done here, we're finished, finished with these bastards, come on, Frank, Harry, come on, that's it, come on, these scumbags aren't worth it, let's go, back to work, out of here, come on."

Manuel's voice seemed to soothe Feeney, like the rhythmic lines of a prayer, a litany in which his responses were recited silently rather than spoken. The balefire continued to pass in and out of his eyes, though it was absent more than not and dimmer than it had been. He broke his two-hand grip on the revolver, holding it in his right hand, and then finally holstered it. Blinking in surprise, he tasted blood, blotted his lips on his hand, and stared uncomprehendingly at the red smear across his palm.

Harry, the second deputy, to whom Manuel had at last given a name, was already to the foyer by the time Frank Feeney stepped out of the kitchen and entered the hall. Manuel followed Feeney, and I found myself following Manuel, though at a distance.

They had lost their Gestapo aura. They looked weak and weary, like three boys who had been playing cops with great exuberance but were now tuckered out, dragging their butts home to have some hot chocolate and take a nap, and then maybe put on new costumes and play pirates. They seemed to be as lost as the kidnapped children.

In the foyer, as Frank Feeney followed Harry X onto the front porch, I said to Manuel, "You see it, don't you?"

At the door he stopped and turned to face me, but he didn't respond. He was still angry, but he also looked stricken. By the second, his rage swam deeper, and his eyes were pools of sorrow.

With light entering the foyer from outside, from the study, and from the living room, I felt more vulnerable here than under the gun and the yellow stare of Feeney in the kitchen, but there was something I needed to say to Manuel.

"Feeney," I said, though Feeney wasn't the unfinished business between us. "You see that he's becoming? You aren't in denial about that, are you?"

"There's a cure. We'll have it soon."

"He's on the edge. What if you don't have a cure soon enough?"

"Then we'll deal with him." He realized he was still holding the billy club. He slipped it through a loop on his belt. "Frank is one of ours. We'll give him peace in our own way."

"He could have killed me. Me, Bobby, you, all of us."

"Stay out of this, Snow. I won't tell you again."

Snow. Not Chris anymore. Trashing a guy's house is dotting the final *i* and crossing the final *t* in *finito.*

"Maybe this kidnapper is that guy on the news," I said.

"What guy?"

"Snatches kids. Three, four, five little kids. Burns them all at once."

"That's not what's happening here."

"How can you be sure?"

"This is Moonlight Bay."

"Not all bad guys are bad just because they're becoming."

He glared at me, taking my observation personally.

I got to the unfinished business: "Toby's a great kid. I love him. I worry about what's happening. There's such a terrible risk. But in the end, Manuel, I hope everything turns out with him like you think it will. I really do. More than anything."

He hesitated, but then said, "Stay out of this. I mean it, Snow."

For a moment I watched him walk away from my vandalized house into a world that was even more broken than my mother's china. There were two patrol cars at the curb, and he got into one of them.

"Come back anytime," I said, as if he could hear me. "I've still got drinking glasses you can smash, serving dishes. We'll have a couple beers, you can bash the hell out of the TV, or take an ax to the better pieces of furniture, pee on the carpet if you want. I'll make a cheese dip, it'll be fun, it'll be festive."

As sullen and gray and dark as the afternoon was, it nonetheless stung my eyes. I closed the door.

When a loved one dies—or as in this case is lost to me for another reason—I invariably make a joke of the pain. Even on the night that my much-loved father succumbed to cancer, I was doing mental stand-up riffs about death, coffins, and the ravages of disease. If I drink too deeply of grief, I'll find myself in the cups of despair. From despair, I'll sink into self-pity so deep that I'll drown. Self-pity will encourage too much brooding about whom I've lost, what I've lost, the limitations with which I must always live, the restrictions of my strange nightbound existence . . . and finally I'll risk becoming the freak that childhood bullies called me. It strikes me as blasphemous not to embrace life, but to embrace it in dark times, I have to find the beauty concealed in the tragic, beauty which in fact is always there, and which for me is discovered through humor. You may think me shallow or even callous for seeking the laughter in loss, the fun in funerals, but we can honor the dead with laughter and love, which is how we honored them in life. God must have meant for us to laugh through our pain, because He stirred an enormous measure of absurdity into the universe when He mixed the batter of creation. I'll admit to being hopeless in many respects, but as long as I have laughter, I'm not without hope.

I quickly scanned the study to see what damage had been done, switched off the light, and then followed the same routine at the entrance to the living room. They had caused less destruction than Beelzebub on a two-day vacation from Hell, but more than the average poltergeist.

Bobby had already turned off the lights in the dining room. By candlelight, he was addressing the mess in the kitchen, sweeping shattered china into a dustpan and emptying the pan into a large garbage bag.

"You're very domestic," I said, assisting with the cleanup.

"I think I was a housekeeper to royalty in a previous life."

"What royalty?"

"Czar Nicholas of Russia."

"That ended badly."

"Then I was reincarnated as Betty Grable."

"The movie star?"

"The one and only, dude."

"I loved you in *Mother Wore Tights*."

"*Gracias*. But it's way good to be male again."

Tying shut the first garbage bag as Bobby opened another, I said, "I should be pissed off."

"Why? Because I've had all these fabulous lives, while you've just been you?"

"He comes here to kick my ass because he really wants to kick his own."

"He'd have to be a contortionist."

"I hate to say this, but he's a moral contortionist."

"Dude, when you're angry, you sure do get foul-mouthed."

"He knows he's taking an unconscionable risk with Toby, and it's eating him alive, even if he won't admit it."

Bobby sighed. "I feel for Manuel. I do. But the dude scares me more than Feeney."

"Feeney's becoming," I said.

"No shit. But Manuel scares me because he's become what he's become *without* becoming. You know?"

"I know."

"You think it's true—about the vaccine?" Bobby asked, returning the battered toaster to the counter.

"Yeah. But will it work the way they think it will?"

"Nothing else did."

"We know the other part is true," I said. "The psychological implosion."

"The birds."

"Maybe the coyotes."

"I'd feel totally super-mellow about all this," Bobby said, returning the butcher knife to the cutlery drawer, "if I didn't know your mom's bug is only part of the problem."

"Mystery Train," I said, remembering the thing or things inside Hodgson's suit, Delacroix's body, the testament on the audiotape, and the cocoons.

The doorbell rang, and Bobby said, "Tell them if they want to come in here and bust things up, we have new rules. A hundred-dollar cover charge, and everyone wears neckties."

I went into the foyer and peered through one of the clearer panes in a stained-glass sidelight.

The figure at the door was so big that you might have thought one of the oak trees had pulled up its roots, climbed the steps, and rung the bell to request a hundred pounds of fertilizer.

I opened the door and stepped back from the light to let our visitor enter.

Roosevelt Frost is tall, muscular, black, and dignified enough to make the carved faces on Mount Rushmore look like the busts of sitcom stars. Entering with Mungojerrie, a pale gray cat, nestled in the crook of his left arm, he nudged the door shut behind them.

In a voice remarkable for its deep tone, its musicality, and its gentleness, he said, "Good afternoon, son."

"Thank you for coming, sir."

"You've gotten yourself in trouble again."

"That's always a good bet with me."

"Lots of death ahead," he said solemnly.

"Sir?"

"That's what the cat says."

I looked at Mungojerrie. Draped comfortably over Roosevelt's huge arm, he appeared to be boneless. The cat was so limp that he might have been a stole or a muffler if Roosevelt had been a man given to wearing stoles and mufflers, except that his green feline eyes, flecked with gold, were alert, riveting, and filled with an intelligence that was unmistakable and unnerving.

"Lots of death," Roosevelt repeated.

"Whose?"

"Ours."

Mungojerrie held my gaze.

Roosevelt said, "Cats know things."

"Not everything."

"Cats know," Roosevelt insisted.

The cat's eyes seemed to be full of sadness.

Roosevelt put Mungojerrie on one of the kitchen chairs so the cat wouldn't cut his paws on the splinters of broken china that still littered the floor. Although Mungojerrie is a Wyvern escapee, bred in the genetics labs, perhaps as smart as good Orson, certainly as smart as the average contestant on *Wheel of Fortune,* smarter than the majority of the policy advisers to the White House during most of the past century, he was nevertheless sufficiently catlike to be able to curl up and go instantly to sleep even though this was, by his prediction, doomsday eve and though we were unlikely to be alive by dawn. Cats may know things, as Roosevelt says, but they don't suffer from hyperactive imaginations or prickly-pear nerves like mine.

As for knowing things, Roosevelt himself knows more than a few. He knows football because he was, in the sixties and seventies, a major gridiron star, whom sportswriters dubbed the Sledgehammer. Now, at sixty-three, he's a successful businessman who owns a men's clothing store, a minimall, and half-interest in the Moonlight Bay Inn and Country Club. He also knows a lot about the sea and boats, living aboard the fifty-six-foot *Nostromo,* in the last berth of the Moonlight Bay marina. And, of course, he can talk to animals better than Dr. Dolittle, which is a handy talent to have here in Edgar Allan Disneyland.

Roosevelt insisted on helping us clear up the remaining

mess. Although it seemed peculiar to be doing housework side by side with a national monument and heir of Saint Francis, we gave him the vacuum cleaner.

Mungojerrie woke when the vacuum wailed, raised his head long enough to express displeasure with a quick baring of his fangs, and then appeared to go to sleep again.

My kitchen is large, but it seems small when Roosevelt Frost is in it, regardless of whether he's vacuuming. He stands six feet four, and the formidable dimensions of his neck, shoulders, chest, back, and arms make it difficult to believe that he was formed in anything as fragile as a womb; he seems to have been carved out of a granite quarry or poured in a foundry, or perhaps built in a truck factory. He looks considerably younger than he is, with only a few gray hairs at his temples. He succeeded big time in football not merely because of his size but because of his brains; at sixty-three he is nearly as strong as he ever was and—I'm guessing—even smarter, because he's a man who's always learning.

He also vacuums like a sonofabitch. Together, the three of us soon finished setting the kitchen right.

It would never again be entirely right, I'm afraid, not with only one shelf of Royal Worcester, Evesham pattern, remaining in the display cabinet. The empty shelves were a sad sight. My mother had loved those fine dishes: the soft colors of the hand-painted apples and plums on the coffee cups, the blackberries and pears on the salad plates. . . . My mother's favorite things were not my mother—they were merely her *things*—yet, though we like to believe that memories are as permanent as engravings in steel, even memories of love and great kindness are in fact frighteningly ephemeral in their details, and we remember best those that are linked to places and things; memory embeds in the form and weight and texture of real objects, and there it endures to be brought forth vividly with a touch.

There was a second set of dishes, the everyday stuff, and while Roosevelt set the kitchen table with cups and saucers, I brewed a pot of coffee.

In the refrigerator, Bobby discovered a large bakery box

crammed full of the pecan-cinnamon buns that are among my all-time-favorite things. *"Carpe crustulorum!"* he cried.

Roosevelt said, "What was that?"

I said, "Don't ask."

"Seize the pastry," Bobby translated.

I brought a couple of pillows from the living room and put them on one of the chairs, which allowed Mungojerrie—now awake—to sit high enough to be part of the gathering.

As Roosevelt was breaking off bits of a cinnamon bun and soaking them in the saucer of milk that he had poured for the cat, Sasha came home from whatever business she had been about. Roosevelt calls her *daughter,* the way he sometimes calls me and Bobby *son,* which is just his way, though he thinks so highly of Sasha that I suspect he would be pleased to adopt her. I was standing behind him when he lifted her and hugged her; as though she were a little girl, she entirely disappeared in his bearish embrace, except for one sneaker-clad foot, which dangled an inch off the floor.

Sasha brought the chair from her composition table in the dining room, positioning it between my chair and Bobby's. She fingered Bobby's sleeve and said, "Bitchin' shirt."

"Thanks."

"I've seen Doogie," Sasha said. "He's putting together a package of equipment, ordnance. It's now . . . just past three o'clock. We'll be ready to go as soon as it's dark."

"Ordnance?" Bobby asked.

"Doogie's got some really fine tech support."

"Tech support?"

"We're going to be prepared for contingencies."

"Contingencies?" Bobby turned to me. "Bro, are you sleeping with G.I. Jane?"

"Emma Peel," I corrected. To Sasha-Emma, I said, "We may need some ordnance. Manuel and two deputies were here, confiscated our weapons."

"Broke some china," Bobby said.

"Smashed some furniture," I added.

"Kicked the toaster around," Bobby said.

"We can count on Doogie," Sasha said. "Why the toaster?"

Bobby shrugged. "It was small, defenseless, and vulnerable."

We sat down—four people and one gray cat—to eat, drink, and strategize by candlelight.

"Carpe crustulorum," Bobby said.

Brandishing her fork, Sasha said, *"Carpe furcam."*

Raising his cup as if in a toast, Bobby said, *"Carpe coffeum."*

"Conspiracy," I muttered.

Mungojerrie watched us with keen interest.

Roosevelt studied the cat as the cat studied us, and said, "He thinks you're strange but amusing."

"Strange, huh?" Bobby said. "I don't think it's a common *human* habit to chase down mice and eat them."

Roosevelt Frost was talking to animals long before the Wyvern labs gave us four-legged citizens with perhaps more smarts than the people who created them. As far as I've seen, his *only* eccentric belief is that we can converse with ordinary animals, not just those that have been genetically engineered. He doesn't claim to have been abducted by extraterrestrials and given a proctological exam, doesn't prowl the woods in search of Big Foot or Babe the blue ox, isn't writing a novel channeled to him by the spirit of Truman Capote, and doesn't wear an aluminum-foil hat to prevent microwave control of his thoughts by the American Grocery Workers Union.

He learned animal communication from a woman named Gloria Chan, in Los Angeles, several years ago, after she facilitated a dialogue between him and his beloved mutt, Sloopy, now deceased. Gloria told Roosevelt things about his daily life and habits that she couldn't possibly know but with which Sloopy was familiar and which apparently the dog revealed to her.

Roosevelt says that animal communication doesn't require any special talent, that it isn't a psychic ability. He claims it's a sensitivity to other species that we all possess but have repressed; the biggest obstacles to learning the necessary techniques are doubt, cynicism, and preconceived notions about what is possible and what isn't.

After several months of hard work under Gloria Chan's tutelage, Roosevelt became adept at understanding the thoughts and concerns of Sloopy and other beasts of hearth and field. He's willing to teach me, and I intend to give it a shot. Nothing would please me more than gaining a better understanding of Orson; my four-footed brother has heard much from me over the last couple years, but I've never heard a word from him. Lessons with Roosevelt will either open a door on wonder—or leave me feeling foolish and gullible. As a human being, I'm intimately familiar with foolishness and gullibility, so I don't have anything to lose.

Bobby used to mock Roosevelt's tête-à-têtes with animals, though never to his face, attributing them to head injuries suffered on the football field; but lately he seems to have shoved his skepticism through a mental wood-chipper. Events at Wyvern have taught us many lessons, and one of them, for sure, is that while science can improve the lot of humankind, it doesn't hold all the answers we need: Life has dimensions that can't be mapped by biologists, physicists, and mathematicians.

Orson had led me to Roosevelt more than a year ago, drawn by a canine awareness that this was a special man. Some Wyvern cats and God knows what other species of lab escapees have also sought him out and talked his ear off, so to speak. Orson is the exception. He visits Roosevelt but won't communicate with him. Old Sphinx Dog, Roosevelt calls him, mute mutt, the laconic Labrador.

I believe that my mom brought Orson to me—for whatever reason—after falsifying the lab records to account for him as a dead puppy. Perhaps Orson fears being taken by force back to the lab if anyone realizes that he is one of their successes. Whatever the reason, he more often than not plays his I'm-just-a-good-old-dumb-dog game when he's around anyone other than Bobby, Sasha, and me. While he doesn't insult Roosevelt with that deception, Orson remains as taciturn as a turnip, albeit a turnip with a tail.

Now, sitting on a chair, raised on a pair of pillows, daintily eating milk-soaked bits of cinnamon bun, Mungojerrie made no pretense to being an ordinary cat. As we recounted the events of the past twelve hours, his green eyes followed the conversation with interest. When he heard something that surprised him, his eyes widened, and when he was shocked, he either twitched or pulled his head back and cocked it as if to say, *Man, have you been guzzling catnip cocktails, or are you just a congenital bullshit machine?* Sometimes he grinned, which was usually when Bobby and I had to reveal something stupid that we had said or done; it seemed to me that Mungojerrie grinned way too often. Bobby's description of what we glimpsed through the faceplate of Hodgson's bio-secure suit seemed to put the feline off his feed for a few minutes, but he was first and foremost a cat, with a cat's appetite and curiosity, so before we finished the tale, he had solicited and received from Roosevelt another saucer of milk-soaked *crustulorum*.

"We're convinced the missing kids and Orson are somewhere in Wyvern," I said to Roosevelt Frost, because I still felt weird about directly addressing the cat, which is peculiar, considering that I directly address Orson all the time. "But the place is just too big to search. We need a tracker."

Bobby said, "Since we don't own a reconnaissance satellite, don't know a good Indian scout, and don't keep a bloodhound hanging in the closet for these emergencies . . ."

The three of us looked expectantly at Mungojerrie.

The cat met my eyes, then Bobby's, then Sasha's. He closed his eyes for a moment, as if pondering our implied request, then finally turned his attention to Roosevelt.

The gentle giant pushed aside his plate and coffee cup, leaned forward, propped his right elbow on the table, rested his chin on his fist, and locked gazes with our whiskered guest.

After a minute, during which I tried unsuccessfully to recall the melody of the movie theme song from *That Darn Cat*, Roosevelt said, "Mungojerrie wonders if you were listening to what I said when we first arrived."

" 'Lots of death,' " I quoted.

"Whose?" Sasha asked.

"Ours."

"Who says?"

I pointed at the cat.

Mungojerrie managed to look like a swami.

Bobby said, "We know there's danger."

"He's not just saying it's dangerous," Roosevelt explained. "It's a . . . sort of prediction."

We sat in silence, staring at the cat, who favored us with an expression as inscrutable as that on the cats in Egyptian tomb sculptures, and eventually Sasha said, "You mean Mungojerrie's clairvoyant?"

"No," Roosevelt said.

"Then what *do* you mean?"

Still staring at the cat, who was now gazing solemnly at one of the candles as if reading the future in the sinuous dance of the flame upon the wick, Roosevelt said, "Cats know things."

Bobby, Sasha, and I looked at one another, but none of us could provide enlightenment.

"What, exactly, do cats know?" Sasha asked.

"Things," Roosevelt said.

"How?"

"By knowing."

"What is the sound of one hand clapping?" Bobby asked rhetorically.

The cat twitched its ears and looked at him as if to say, *Now you understand.*

"This cat's been reading too much Deepak Chopra," Bobby said.

Frustration pinched Sasha's face and voice. "Roosevelt?"

When he shrugged his massive shoulders, I could almost feel the cubic yard of displaced air wafting across the table. "Daughter, this animal-communication business isn't always like talking on the telephone. Sometimes it *is* just exactly as clear as that. But then sometimes there are . . . ambiguities."

"Well," Bobby said, "does this ball-bearing mousetrap

think we have *some* chance of finding Orson and the kids, then getting back here alive—any chance at all?"

With his left hand, Roosevelt gently scratched the cat behind the ears and stroked its head. "He says there's always a chance. Nothing is hopeless."

"Fifty-fifty chance?" I wondered.

Roosevelt laughed softly. "Mr. Mungojerrie says he isn't a bookmaker."

"So," Bobby said, "the worst that can happen is that we all go back there to Wyvern and we all die, get shredded and processed and packaged as lunchmeat. Seems to me, that's *always* been the worst that could happen, so nothing's changed. I'm up for it."

"Me too," said Sasha.

Obviously still speaking for the cat, which purred and leaned into his hand as he petted it, Roosevelt said, "What if these kids and Orson are somewhere we can't go? What if they're in The Hole?"

Bobby said, "Rule of thumb: Anyplace called The Hole can't be a good place."

"That's what they call the genetic research facility."

"They?" I asked.

"The people who work in it. They call it The Hole because . . ." Roosevelt tilted his head, as if listening to a small quiet voice. "Well, one reason, I guess, is that it's deep underground."

I found myself addressing the cat. "Then it's still functioning out there in Wyvern somewhere, like we've suspected, still staffed and operational?"

"Yes," Roosevelt said, stroking the cat under the chin. "Self-contained . . . secretly resupplied every six months."

"Do you know where?" I asked Mungojerrie.

"Yes. He knows. It's where he's from, after all," Roosevelt said, sitting back in his chair. "It's where he escaped from . . . that night. But if Orson and the children are in The Hole, there's no way to get to them or get them out."

We all brooded in silence.

Mungojerrie raised one forepaw and began to lick it,

grooming his fur. He was smart, he knew things, he could track, he was our best hope, but he was also a cat. We were entirely reliant on a comrade who, at any moment, might cough up a hairball. The only reason I didn't laugh or cry was that I couldn't do both at once, which was what I felt like doing.

Finally Sasha put the issue behind us: "If we have no chance of getting them out of The Hole, then we've just got to hope they're somewhere else in Wyvern."

"The big question is still the same," I said to Roosevelt. "Is Mungojerrie willing to help?"

The cat had met Orson only once, aboard the *Nostromo*, on the night my father died. They had seemed to like each other. They shared, as well, an origin in the intelligence-enhancement research at Wyvern, and if my mother was in some sense Orson's mother, because he was a product of her heart and mind, then this cat might feel that she was his lost mother, too, his creator, to whom he was in debt for his life.

I sat with my hands clasped tightly around my empty coffee cup, desperate to believe that Mungojerrie would not let us down, mentally listing reasons why the cat *must* agree to join our rescue effort, preparing to make the incredible and shameless claim that he was my spiritual brother, Mungojerrie *Snow*, just as Orson was my brother, that this was a *family* crisis to which he had a special obligation, and I couldn't help but remember what Bobby had said about this brave new smart-animal world being like a Donald Duck cartoon that for all its wackiness is nevertheless rife with fearsome physical and moral and spiritual consequences.

When Roosevelt said, "Yes," I was so feverishly structuring my argument against an expected rejection of our request that I didn't immediately realize what our friend the animal communicator had communicated.

"Yes, we'll help," Roosevelt explained in response to my dumb blinking.

We passed smiles, like a plate of *crustulorum,* around the table.

Then Sasha cocked her head at Roosevelt and said, " 'We'?"

"You'll need me along to interpret."

Bobby said, "The mungo man leads, we follow."

"It might not be that simple," Roosevelt said.

Sasha shook her head. "We can't ask you to do this."

Taking her hand, patting it, Roosevelt smiled. "Daughter, you aren't asking. I'm insisting. Orson is my friend, too. All these children are the children of my neighbors."

" 'Lots of death,' " I quoted again.

Roosevelt counter-quoted the feline's previous equivocation: "Nothing's hopeless."

"Cats know things," I said.

Now he quoted *me*: "Not everything."

Mungojerrie looked at us as if to say, *Cats know.*

I felt that neither the cat nor Roosevelt should finally commit to this dangerous enterprise without first hearing Leland Delacroix's disjointed, incomplete, at times incoherent, yet compelling final testament. Whether or not we found Orson and the kids, we would return to that cocoon-infested bungalow at the end of the night to set a purging fire, but I was convinced that during our search, we would encounter other consequences of the Mystery Train project, some potentially lethal. If, after hearing Delacroix's bizarre tale told in his tortured voice, Roosevelt and Mungojerrie reconsidered their commitment to accompany us, I would still try to persuade them to help, but I'd feel that I had been fair with them.

We adjourned to the dining room, where I replayed the original cassette.

The last words on the tape were spoken in that unknown language, and when they faded, Bobby said, "The tune's good, but it doesn't have a beat you can dance to."

Roosevelt stood in front of the tape player, frowning. "When do we leave?"

"First dark," I said.

"Which is coming down fast," Sasha said, glancing at the window blinds, against which the press of daylight was less insistent than when Bobby and I had first listened to Delacroix.

"If those kids are in Wyvern," Roosevelt said, "they might as well be at the gates of Hell. No matter what the risk, we can't leave them there."

He was wearing a black crewneck sweater, black chinos, and black Rockports, as though he had anticipated the covert action that lay ahead of us. In spite of his formidable size and rough-hewn features, he looked like a priest, like an exorcist grimly prepared to cast out devils.

Turning to Mungojerrie, who was sitting on Sasha's composition table, I said, "And what about you?"

Roosevelt crouched by the table, eye-to-eye with the cat.

To me, Mungojerrie appeared to be supremely disinterested, much like any cat when it's trying to live up to its species' reputation for cool indifference, mystery, and unearthly wisdom.

Apparently, Roosevelt was viewing this gray mouser through a lens I didn't possess or was listening to him on a frequency beyond my range of hearing, because he reported, "Mungojerrie says two things. First, he will find Orson and the kids if they're anywhere in Wyvern, no matter what the risks, no matter what it takes."

Relieved, grateful to the cat for its courage, I said, "And number two?"

"He needs to go outside and pee."

21

At twilight, I went into my bathroom, failed to throw up though the urge was there, and instead washed my face twice, once with hot water, once with cold. Then I sat on the edge of the bathtub, clasped my hands on my knees, and endured a siege of the shakes as violent as those that reportedly accompany malaria or an IRS audit.

I wasn't afraid that the mission into Fort Wyvern would result in the storm of death that our prescient pussycat had predicted—or that I would perish in the night ahead. Rather, I was afraid that I would live through the night but come home without the kids and Orson, or that I would fail in the rescue and also lose Sasha and Bobby and Roosevelt and Mungojerrie in the process.

With friends, this is a cool world; without friends, it would be unbearably cold.

I washed my face a third time, peed to show my solidarity with Mungojerrie, washed my hands (because my mom, would-be destroyer of the world, had taught me hygiene), and returned to the kitchen, where the others were waiting for me. I suspect that, with the exception of the cat, they had been through a ritual similar to mine, in other bathrooms.

Because Sasha—like Bobby—had noticed fishy types all over town and believed something major was soon to go down, she had anticipated that our house would be under surveillance by the authorities, if for no other reason than our connection with Lilly Wing. Therefore, she had arranged for us to meet Doogie Sassman at a rendezvous point far beyond prying eyes.

Sasha's Explorer, Bobby's Jeep, and Roosevelt's Mercedes were parked in front of the house. We would surely be tailed if we drove off in any of them; we would have to leave on foot and with considerable stealth.

Behind our house, beyond our backyard, is a hard-packed dirt footpath that separates our property and those flanking it from a grove of red-gum eucalyptus trees and, beyond the trees, the golf course of the Moonlight Bay Inn and Country Club, of which Roosevelt is half-owner. Surveillance probably extended to the footpath, and there was no chance that the watchers assigned to us could be bought off with invitations to Sunday brunch at the country club.

The plan was to travel backyard to backyard for a few blocks, risking the attention of neighbors and their dogs, until we were beyond the purview of any surveillance teams that might have been assigned to us.

Because of Manuel's confiscation celebration, Sasha possessed the only weapon, her .38 Chiefs Special, and two speedloaders in a dump pouch. She wouldn't relinquish the piece to Roosevelt or Bobby, or to me—not even to Mungojerrie. She announced, in a tone brooking no argument, that she would take the risky point position.

"Where do we meet up with Doogie?" I asked as Bobby stowed the sole remaining cinnamon bun in the refrigerator and I finished stacking cups and saucers in the sink.

"Out along Haddenbeck Road," Sasha said, "just beyond Crow Hill."

"Crow Hill," Bobby said. "I don't like the sound of that."

Sasha didn't get it for a moment. Then she did: "It's just a place. How could it have anything to do with those drawings?"

I was more concerned about the distance. "Man, that's seven, eight *miles*."

"Almost nine," Sasha said. "With all this new activity,

there's nowhere in town we could meet Doogie without drawing attention."

"It's going to take too long to cover that much ground on foot," I protested.

"Oh," she said, "we'll only go a few blocks on foot, just until we're able to steal a car."

Bobby smiled at me and winked. "This here is some moll you've got, bro."

"Whose car?" I asked her.

"Any car," she said brightly. "I'm not concerned about style, just mobility."

"What if we don't find a car with keys in it?"

"I'll hot-wire it," she said.

"You know how to hot-wire a car?"

"I was a Girl Scout."

"Daughter's got herself a car-theft merit badge," Roosevelt told Mungojerrie.

We locked the back door on the way out, leaving blinds drawn and some lights dialed low.

I didn't wear my Mystery Train cap. It no longer made me feel close to my mother, and it certainly didn't seem like a good-luck charm anymore.

The night was mild and windless, bearing a faint scent of salt air and decomposing seaweed.

An overcast as dark as an iron skillet hid the moon. Here and there, reflections of the town lights, like a rancid yellow grease, were smeared across the clouds, but the night was deep and nearly ideal for our purposes.

The silvered-cedar fence surrounding this property is as tall as I am, with no gaps between the vertical pales, so it's as solid as a wall. A gate opens onto the footpath.

We avoided the gate and went to the east side of the backyard, where my property adjoins that of the Samardian family.

The fence is extremely sturdy, because the vertical pales are fixed to three horizontal rails. These rails also would serve us well as a ladder.

Mungojerrie sprang up the fence as if he were lighter than

air. Standing with his hind paws on the uppermost rail, fore-paws on the top of the pales, he surveyed the backyard next door.

When the cat glanced down at us, Roosevelt whispered, "Looks like no one's home."

One at a time, and with relative silence, we followed the cat over the fence. From the Samardians' property, we crossed another cedar fence, into the Landsbergs' backyard. Lights were on in their house, but we passed unseen and stepped over a low picket fence into the Perez family's yard, from there moving steadily eastward, past house after house, with no problem except Bobo, the Wladskis' golden retriever, who isn't a barker but makes every effort to beat you into submission with his tail and then lick you to death.

We scaled a high redwood fence into the yard behind the Stanwyk place, leaving the thankfully barkless Bobo slobber-ing, wagging his tail with an air-cutting *whoosh-whoosh,* and dancing on his hind paws in bladder-straining excitement.

I had always thought of Roger Stanwyk as a decent man who had lent his talents to the Wyvern research for the no-blest of reasons, in the name of scientific progress and the advancement of medicine, much as my mother had done. His only sin was the same one Mom committed: hubris. Out of pride in his undeniable intelligence, out of misplaced trust in the power of science to resolve all problems and explain all things, he had unwittingly become one of the architects of doomsday.

That was what I'd always thought. Now I wasn't so sure of his good intentions. As Leland Delacroix's tape had re-vealed, Stanwyk was involved in both my mother's work and the Mystery Train. He was a darker figure than he had seemed previously.

All of us two-legged specimens dodged from shrub to tree across the Stanwyks' elaborately landscaped domain, hoping no one would be looking out a window. We reached the next fence before we realized that Mungojerrie wasn't with us.

Panicked, we doubled back, searching among the neatly trimmed shrubs and hedges, whispering his name, which isn't easy to whisper with a straight face, and we found him near the Stanwyks' porch. He was a ghostly gray shape on the black lawn.

We squatted around our diminutive team leader, and Roosevelt switched his brain to the Weird Channel to find out what the cat was thinking.

"He wants to go inside," Roosevelt whispered.

"Why?" I asked.

Roosevelt murmured, "Something's wrong here."

"What?" Sasha asked.

"Death lives here," Roosevelt interpreted.

"He keeps the yard nice," Bobby said.

"Doogie's waiting," Sasha reminded the cat.

Roosevelt said, "Mungojerrie says people in the house need help."

"How can he tell?" I asked, immediately knew the answer, and found myself repeating it with Sasha and Bobby in a whispered chorus: "Cats know things."

I was tempted to snatch up the cat, tuck him under my arm, and run away from here with him as if he were a football. He had fangs and claws, of course, and might object. More to the point, we needed to have his *willing* cooperation in the search ahead of us. He might be disinclined to cooperate if I treated him like a piece of sporting goods, even if I had no intention of drop-kicking him to Wyvern.

Forced to take a closer look at the Victorian house, I realized the place had a *Twilight Zone* quality. On the upper floor, windows revealed rooms brightened only by the flickering light of television screens, an unmistakable pulsing radiance. Downstairs, the two rooms at the back of the house—probably kitchen and dining room—were lit by the orange, draft-shaken flames of candles or oil lamps.

Our Tonto-with-a-tail sprang to his feet and sprinted to the house. He went boldly up the steps and disappeared into the shadows of the back porch.

Maybe Mr. Mungojerrie, phenomenal feline, has a well-honed sense of civic responsibility. Maybe his moral compass is so exquisitely magnetized that he cannot turn away from those in need. I suspected, however, that his compelling motivation was the well-known curiosity of his species, which so frequently leads to their demise.

The four of us remained squatting in a semicircle for a moment, until Bobby said, "Am I wrong to think this sucks?"

An informal poll showed a hundred percent agreement with the it-sucks point of view.

Reluctantly, stealthily, we followed Mungojerrie onto the back porch, where he was scratching persistently at the door.

Through the four glass panes in the door, we had a clear view of a kitchen so Victorian in its detail and bric-a-brac that I would not have been surprised to see Charles Dickens, William Gladstone, and Jack the Ripper having tea. The room was lit by an oil lamp on the oval table, as though someone within were my brother in XP.

Sasha took the initiative and knocked.

No one answered.

Mungojerrie continued to scratch at the door.

"We get the point," Bobby told him.

Sasha tried the knob, which turned.

Hoping to be thwarted by a dead bolt, we were dismayed to learn that the door was unlocked. It swung open a few inches.

Mungojerrie squeezed through the narrow gap and vanished inside before Sasha could have second thoughts.

"Death, much death," Roosevelt murmured, evidently communicating with the mouser.

I wouldn't have been surprised if Dr. Stanwyk had appeared at the door, dressed in a bio-secure suit like Hodgson, face seething with hideous parasites, a white-eyed crow perched on his shoulder. This man who had once seemed wise and kind—if eccentric—now loomed ominously in my imagination, like the uninvited party guest in Poe's "The Masque of the Red Death."

The Roger and Marie Stanwyk I had known for years were an odd but nonetheless happy and compatible couple in their early fifties. He sported muttonchops and a lush mustache, and was rarely seen in anything but a suit and tie; you sensed that he longed to wear wing collars and to carry a pocket watch on a fob, but felt these would be eccentricities in excess of those expected of a renowned scientist; nevertheless, he frequently allowed himself to wear quaint vests, and he spent an inordinate amount of time working at his Sherlockian pipe with tamp, pick, and spoon. Marie, a plump-cheeked matron with a rosy complexion, was a collector of antique ornamental tea caddies and nineteenth-century paintings of fairies; her wardrobe revealed a grudging acceptance of the twenty-first century, although regardless of what she wore, her longing for button-top shoes, bustles, and parasols was evident. Roger and Marie seemed unsuited to California, doubly unsuited to this century, yet they drove a red Jaguar, had been spotted attending excruciatingly stupid big-budget action movies, and functioned fairly well as citizens of the new millennium.

Sasha called to the Stanwyks through the open kitchen door.

Mungojerrie had crossed the kitchen without hesitation and had disappeared into deeper reaches of the house.

When Sasha got no answer to her third "Roger, Marie, hello," she drew the .38 from her shoulder holster and stepped inside.

Bobby, Roosevelt, and I followed her. If Sasha had been wearing skirts, we might have happily hidden behind them, but we were more comfortable with the cover provided by the Smith & Wesson.

From the porch, the house had seemed silent, but as we crossed the kitchen, we heard voices coming from the front room. They were not directed at us.

We stopped and listened, not quite able to make out the words. Quickly, however, when music rose, it became apparent that we were hearing not live voices but those on television or radio.

Sasha's entrance to the dining room was instructive and more than a little intriguing. Both hands on the gun. Arms out straight and locked. The weapon just below her line of sight. She cleared the doorway fast, slid to the left, her back against the wall. After she moved mostly out of view, I could still see just enough of her arms to know she swung the .38 left, then right, then left again, covering the room. Her performance was professional, instinctive, and no less smooth than her on-air voice.

Maybe she's watched a lot of television cop dramas over the years. Yeah.

"Clear," she whispered.

Tall, ornate hutches seemed to loom over us, as if tipping away from the walls, porcelain and silver treasures gleaming darkly behind leaded-glass doors with beveled panes. The crystal chandelier wasn't lit, but reflections of nearby candle flames winked along its strings of beads and off the cut edges of its dangling pendants.

In the center of the dining-room table, surrounded by eight or ten candles, was a large punch bowl half full of what appeared to be fruit juice. A few clean drinking glasses stood to one side, and scattered across the table were several empty plastic pharmacy bottles of prescription medication.

The lighting wasn't good enough to allow us to read the labels on the bottles, as they lay, and none of us wanted to touch anything. *Death lives here,* the cat had said, and maybe that was what had given us the idea, from the moment we entered the house, that this was a crime scene. Upon seeing the tableau on the dining-room table, we looked at one another, and it was clear that all of us suspected the nature of the crime, though we didn't speak its name.

I could have used my flashlight, but I might have drawn unwanted attention. Under the circumstances, any attention would be unwanted. Besides, the name of the medication wasn't important.

Sasha led us into the large living room, where the illumination came from a television screen nested in an ornate French cabinet with japanned panels. Even in the poor light, I could see that the chamber was as crowded as an automobile salvage yard, not with junked cars but with Victorian excess: deeply carved and intricately painted neo-rococo furniture; richly patterned brocade upholstery; wallpaper with Gothic-style tracery; heavy velvet drapes with cascades of braided fringe, capped with solid pelmets cut in elaborate Gothic forms; an Egyptian settee with beaded-wood spindles and damask seat cushions; Moorish lamps featuring black cherubs in gilded turbans supporting beaded shades; bibelots densely arranged on every shelf and table.

Amidst the layers on layers of decor, the cadavers almost seemed like additional decorative items.

Even in the flickery light of the television, we could see a man stretched out on the Egyptian settee. He was dressed in dark slacks and a white shirt. Before lying down, he'd taken off his shoes and placed them on the floor with the laces neatly tucked in, as though concerned about soiling the up-holstery on the seat cushions. Beside the shoes stood a drink-ing glass identical to those in the dining room—Waterford crystal, judging by appearance—in which remained an inch of fruit juice. His left arm trailed off the settee, the back of the hand against the Persian carpet, palm turned up. His other arm lay across his chest. His head was propped on two small brocade pillows, and his face was concealed beneath a square of black silk.

Sasha was covering the room behind us, less interested in the corpse than in guarding against a surprise assault.

The black veil over the face did not bellow or even flutter. The man under it was not breathing.

I knew that he was dead, knew what killed him—not a contagious disease, but a phenobarbital fizz or its lethal equiv-alent—yet I was reluctant to remove the silk mask for the same reason that any child, having pondered the possibility of a boogeyman, is hesitant to push back the sheets, rise up on his mattress, lean out, and peek under the bed.

Hesitantly, I pinched a corner of the silk square between thumb and forefinger, and pulled it off the man's face.

He was alive. That was my first impression. His eyes were open, and I thought I saw life in them.

After a breathless moment, I realized that his stare was fixed. His eyes appeared to be moving only because reflections of images on the TV screen were twitching in them.

The light was just bright enough to allow me to identify the deceased. His name was Tom Sparkman. He was an associate of Roger Stanwyk's, a professor at Ashdon, also a biochemist, and no doubt deeply involved in Wyvern business.

The body showed no signs of corruption. It couldn't have been here a long time.

Reluctantly, I touched the back of my left hand to Sparkman's brow. "Still warm," I whispered.

We followed Roosevelt to a button-tufted sofa with carved-wood rails at seat and crest, on which a second man lay, with hands folded across his abdomen. This one was wearing his shoes, and his drained glass lay on its side on the carpet, where he'd dropped it.

Roosevelt peeled back the square of black silk that concealed the man's face. The light was not as good here, the corpse not as close to the television as Sparkman, and I wasn't able to identify the body.

Two seconds after switching on my flashlight, I clicked it off. Cadaver number two was Lennart Toregard, a Swedish mathematician on a four-year contract to teach one class a semester at Ashdon, which was surely a front for his real work, at Wyvern. Toregard's eyes were closed. His face was relaxed. A faint smile suggested he was having a pleasant dream—or was in the middle of one when death claimed him.

Bobby slipped two fingers under Toregard's wrist, feeling for a pulse. He shook his head: nothing.

Batwing shadows swooped along one wall, across the ceiling.

Sasha spun toward the movement.

I reached under my jacket, but there was no shoulder holster, no gun.

The shadows were only shadows, sent flying through the room by a sudden flurry of action on the television screen.

The third corpse was slumped in a huge armchair, legs propped on a matching footstool, arms on the chair arms. Bobby stripped away the silk hood, I flashed the light on and off, and Roosevelt whispered, "Colonel Ellway."

Colonel Eaton Ellway had been second in command of

Fort Wyvern and had retired to Moonlight Bay after the base was closed. Retired. Or engaged in a clandestine assignment in civilian clothes.

With no additional dead men to investigate, I finally registered what was on the television. It was tuned to a cable channel that was running an animated feature film, Disney's *The Lion King*.

We stood for a moment, listening to the house.

Other music and other voices came from other rooms.

Neither the music nor the voices were made by the living.

Death lives here.

From the living room—a chamber grossly misnamed—we cautiously crossed the front hall to the study. Sasha and Roosevelt halted at the doorway.

A tambour door was open on an entertainment center incorporated into a wall of bookshelves, and *The Lion King* was on the television, with the volume low. Nathan Lane and company were singing "Hakuna Matata."

Inside, Bobby and I found two more members of this suicide club with squares of black silk over their heads. A man sat at the desk, and a woman was slumped in a Morris chair, empty drinking glasses near each of them.

I no longer had the heart to strip away their veils. The black silk might have been cult paraphernalia with a symbolic meaning that was comprehensible only to those who had come together in this ritual of self-destruction. I thought, however, that at least in part, it might be meant to express their guilt at being involved in work that had brought humanity to these straits. If they felt remorse, then their deaths had a degree of dignity, and disturbing them seemed disrespectful.

Before we had left the living room, I had once more covered the faces of Sparkman, Toregard, and Ellway.

Bobby seemed to understand the reason for my hesitancy, and he lifted the veil on the man at the desk, while I used the flashlight with the hope of making an identification. This was no one that either of us knew, a handsome man with a small, well-trimmed gray mustache. Bobby replaced the silk.

The woman reclining in the Morris chair was also a

stranger, but when I directed the light at her face, I didn't immediately switch it off.

With a soft whistle, Bobby sucked air between his teeth, and I muttered, "God."

I had to struggle to keep my hand from shaking, to keep the light steady.

Sensing bad news, Sasha and Roosevelt came in from the hall, and though neither of them spoke a word, their faces revealed all that needed to be said about their shock and revulsion.

The dead woman's eyes were open. The left was a normal brown eye. The right was green, and not remotely normal. There was almost no white in it. The iris was huge and golden, the lens a gold-green. The black pupil was not round but elliptical—like the pupil in the eye of a snake.

The socket encircling that terrifying eye was badly misshapen. Indeed, there were subtle but fearsome deformities in the entire bone structure along the right side of her once lovely face: brow, temple, cheek, jaw.

Her mouth hung open in a silent cry. Her lips were peeled back in a rictus, revealing her teeth, which for the most part appeared normal. A few on the right side, however, were sharply pointed, and one eyetooth seemed to have been in the process of reshaping itself into a fang.

I moved the beam of the flashlight down her body, to her hands, which were in her lap. I expected to see more mutation, but both her hands were normal. They were folded tightly together, and clasped in them was a rosary: black beads, silver chain, an exquisite little silver crucifix.

Such desperation was apparent in the posture of her pale hands, such pathos, that I switched off the light, overcome by pity. To stare at this grim evidence of her final distress seemed invasive, indecent.

Upon finding the first body in the living room, in spite of the black silk veils, I'd known that these people had not committed suicide solely out of guilt over their involvement in the research at Wyvern. Perhaps some felt guilty, perhaps all of them did, but they participated in this chemical hara-kiri primarily because they were becoming and because they were deeply fearful of *what* they were becoming.

To date, as the rogue retrovirus has transferred other species' DNA into human cells, the effects have been limited. They manifest, if at all, only psychologically, except for telltale animal eyeshine in the most seriously afflicted.

Some of the big brains have been confident that physical change is impossible. They believe that as the cells of the body wear out and are routinely replaced, new cells will not contain the sequences of animal DNA that contaminated the previous generation—not even if stem cells, which control growth throughout the human body, are infected.

This disfigured woman in the Morris chair proved that they were woefully wrong. Hideous physical change clearly can accompany mental deterioration.

Each infected individual receives a load of alien DNA different from the one that anybody else receives, which means that the effect is singular in every case. Some of the infected may not undergo any perceptible change, mentally or physically, because they receive DNA fragments from so many sources that there is no focused cumulative effect other than a general destabilization of the system, resulting in rapidly metastasizing cancers and deadly autoimmune disorders. Others may go mad, psychologically devolve into a subhuman condition, driven by murderous rages, unspeakable needs. Those who, in addition, suffer physical metamorphosis will be radically different from one another: a nightmare zoo.

My mouth seemed to be choked with dust. My throat felt tight and parched. Even my cardiac muscle seemed to have withered, for in my own ears, my heartbeat was juiceless, dry, and strange.

The singing and comic antics of the characters in *The Lion King* failed to fill me with magic-kingdom joy.

I hoped Manuel knew what he was talking about when he predicted the imminent availability of a vaccine, a cure.

Bobby gently draped the square of silk over the woman's face, concealing her tortured features.

As Bobby's hands came close to her, I tensed and found

myself repositioning my grip on the extinguished flashlight, as if I might use it as a weapon. I half expected to see the woman's eyes shift, to hear her snarl, to see those pointed teeth flash and blood spurt, even as she looped the rosary around his neck and pulled him down into a deadly embrace.

I am not the only one with a hyperactive imagination. I saw a wariness in Bobby's face. His hands twitched nervously as he replaced the silk.

And after we left the study, Sasha hesitated and then returned to the open door to check the room once more. She no longer gripped the .38 in both hands but nonetheless held it at the ready, as though she wouldn't have been surprised to discover that even a glassful of the Jonestown punch, their version of a Heaven's Gate cocktail, was not poisonous enough to put down the creature in the Morris chair.

Also on the ground floor were a sewing room and a laundry room, but both were deserted.

In the hallway, Roosevelt whispered Mungojerrie's name, because we had yet to see the cat since we'd entered the house.

A soft answering *meow* followed by two more, audible above the competing sound tracks of the Disney movie, drew us forward along the hall.

Mungojerrie was sitting on the newel post at the bottom of the stairs. In the gloom, his radiant green eyes fixed on Roosevelt, then shifted to Sasha when she quietly but urgently suggested that we get the hell out of here.

Without the cat, we had little chance of conducting a successful search of Wyvern. We were hostage to his curiosity—or to whatever it was that motivated him to turn his back to us on the newel post, sprint agilely up the handrail, spring to the stairs, and disappear into the darkness of the upper floor.

"What's he doing?" I asked Roosevelt.

"Wish I knew. It takes two to communicate," he murmured.

22

As before, Sasha took the point position as we ascended the stairs. I brought up the rear. The carpeted treads creaked a little underfoot, more than a little under Roosevelt's feet, but the movie sound track drifting up from the living room and study—and similar sounds coming from upstairs—effectively masked the noises we made.

At the top of the stairs, I turned and looked down. There weren't any dead people standing in the foyer, with their heads concealed under black silk. Not even one. I had expected five.

Six doors led off the upstairs hall. Five were open, and pulsing light came from three rooms. Competing sound tracks indicated that *The Lion King* was not the universal choice of entertainment for these condemned.

Unwilling to pass an unexplored room and possibly leave an assailant behind us, Sasha went to the first door, which was closed. I stood with my back to the wall at the hinged edge of the door, and she put her back to the wall on the other side. I reached across, gripped the knob, and turned it. When I pushed the door open, Sasha went through fast and low, the gun in her right hand, feeling for the light switch with her left.

A bathroom. Nobody there.

She backed into the hall, switching off the light but leaving the door open.

Beside the bathroom was a linen closet.

Four rooms remained. Doors open. Light and voices and music coming from three of them.

I emphatically am *not* a gun lover, having fired one for the first time only a month previously. I still worry about shooting myself in the foot, and would *rather* shoot myself in the foot than be forced ever again to kill another human being. But now I was seized by a desire for a gun that was probably only slightly down the scale of desperation from the urgency with which a half-starved man craves food, because I couldn't bear to see Sasha taking all the risks.

At the next room, she cleared the doorway quickly. When there was not an immediate outburst of gunfire, Bobby and I followed her inside, while Roosevelt watched the hall from the threshold.

A bedside lamp glowed softly. On the television was a Nature Channel documentary that might have been soothing, even elegiac, when it had been turned on to provide a distraction for the doomed as they drank their spiked fruit punch; but at the moment a fox was chewing the guts out of a quail.

This was the master bedroom, with an attached bath, and though it was a large chamber, with brighter colors than those downstairs, I felt suffocated by the determined, slathered-on, high-Victorian cheerfulness. The walls, the drapes, the spread, and the canopy on the four-poster bed were all of the same fabric: a cream background heavily patterned with roses and ribbons, explosions of pink, green, and yellow. The carpet featured yellow chrysanthemums, pink roses, and blue ribbons, lots of blue ribbons, so many blue ribbons that I couldn't help but think of veins and unraveling intestines. The painted and parcel-gilt furniture was no less oppressive than the darker pieces downstairs, and the room contained so many crystal paperweights, porcelains, small bronzes, silver-framed photographs, and other bibelots that, if considered ammunition, they could have been used to stone to death an entire mob of malcontents.

On the bed, atop the gay spread and fully dressed, lay a man and a woman with the de rigueur black silk face coverings, which now began to seem neither cultish nor symbolic but quite Victorian and proper, draped across the awful faces of the dead to spare the sensitivities of those who might discover them. I was sure that these two—on their backs, side by side, holding hands—were Roger and Marie Stanwyk, and when Bobby and Sasha pulled aside the veils, I was proved correct.

For some reason, I surveyed the ceiling, half expecting to see five-inch-long, fat cocoons spun in the corners. None hung over us, of course. I was getting my waking nightmares confused.

Struggling to resist a potentially crippling claustrophobia, I left the room ahead of Bobby and Sasha, joining Roosevelt in the hallway, where I was pleased—though surprised—to find there were *still* no walking dead people with black silk hoods covering their cold white faces.

The next bedroom was no less gonzo Victorian than the rest of the house, but the two bodies—in the carved mahogany half-tester bed with white muslin and lace hangings—were in a more modern pose than Roger and Marie, lying on their sides, face-to-face, embracing during their last moments on this earth. We studied their alabaster profiles, but none of us recognized them, and Bobby and I replaced the silks.

There was a television set in this room, too. The Stanwyks, for all their love of distant and more genteel times, were typical TV-crazed Americans, for which they were certainly dumber than they otherwise would have been, as it is well known and probably proven that for every television set in a house, each member of the family suffers a loss of five IQ points. The embracing couple on the bed had chosen to expire to a thousandth rerun of an ancient *Star Trek* episode. At the moment, Captain Kirk was solemnly expounding upon his belief that compassion and tolerance were as important to the evolution and survival of an intelligent species as were eyesight and opposable thumbs, so I had to resist the urge to switch the damn TV to the Nature Channel, where the fox was eating the guts of a quail.

I didn't want to judge these poor people, because I

couldn't know the angst and physical suffering that had brought them to this end point; but if I were becoming and so distraught as to believe that suicide was the only answer, I would want to expire not while watching the products of Empire Disney, not to an earnest documentary about the beauty of nature's bloodlust, not to the adventures of the starship *Enterprise*, but to the eternal music of Beethoven, Johann Sebastian Bach, perhaps Brahms, Mozart; or the rock of Chris Isaak would do, and do handsomely.

As you may perceive from my baroque ranting, by the time I returned to the upstairs hall, with the body count currently at nine, my claustrophobia was getting rapidly worse, my imagination was in full-on hyperdrive, my longing for a handgun had intensified until it was almost a sexual need, and my testicles had retracted into my groin.

I knew that we weren't all going to get out of this house alive.

Christopher Snow knows things.

I knew.

I *knew*.

The next room was dark, and a quick check revealed that it was used to store excess Victorian furniture and art objects. In two or three seconds of light, I saw paintings, chairs and more chairs, a column-front cellarette, terra-cotta figures, urns, a Chippendale-style satinwood desk, a breakfront—as if the Stanwyks' ultimate intention had been to wedge every room of the house so full that no human being could fit inside, until the density and weight of the furnishings distorted the very fabric of space-time, causing the house to implode out of our century and into the more comforting age of Sir Arthur Conan Doyle and Lord Chesterfield.

Mungojerrie, to all appearances unaffected by this surfeit of death and decor, was standing in the hallway, in the inconstant light that pulsed through the open door of the final room, peering intently past that last threshold. Then suddenly he became way *too* intent: His back was arched and his hackles were raised, as if he were a witch's familiar that had just seen the devil himself rising from a bubbling cauldron.

Though gunless, I was not going to let Sasha go through another doorway first, because I believed that whoever entered this next room in the point position would be blown away or chopped like a celery stalk in a Cuisinart. Unless the last four bodies had been mutated in ways concealed by clothing, we had not encountered another refugee from *The Island of Dr. Moreau* since the woman slumped in the Morris chair downstairs, and we seemed overdue for another close encounter of the bowel-loosening kind. I was tempted to pick up Mungojerrie and pitch him into the room ahead of me, to draw fire, but I reminded myself that if any of us survived, we would need the mouser to lead us through Wyvern, and even if he landed on his feet unscathed, in the great tradition of felines since time immemorial, he was likely thereafter to be uncooperative.

I moved past the cat and crossed the threshold with absolutely no cunning, ad-libbing and adrenaline-driven, hurtling headlong into a deluge of Victoriana. Sasha was close behind me, whispering my name with severe disapproval, as though it really ticked her off to lose her last best opportunity to be killed in this sentimental wonderland of filigree and potpourri.

Amidst a visual cacophony of chintz, in a blizzard of bric-a-brac, a television screen presented the cuddly cartoon creatures of the veld capering through *The Lion King.* The marketing mavens at Disney ought to turn this into a bonanza, produce a special edition of the film for the terminally distraught, for rejected lovers and moody teenagers, for stockbrokers to keep on the shelf against the advent of another Black Monday, package the videotape or DVD with a square of black silk, a pad and pencil for the suicide note, and a lyrics sheet to allow the self-condemned to sing along with the major musical numbers until the toxins kick in.

Two bodies, numbers ten and lucky eleven, lay on the quilted chintz spread, but they were less interesting than the robed figure of Death, who stood beside the bed. The Reaper, traveling without his customary scythe, was bending over the deceased, carefully arranging squares of black silk to conceal their faces, plucking at specks of lint, smoothing wrinkles in the fabric, surprisingly fussy for Hell's grim tyrant, as Alexander Pope had called him, although those who rise to the top of their professions know that attention to detail is essential.

He was also shorter than I had imagined Death would be, about five feet eight. He was remarkably heavier than his popular image, too, although his apparent weight problem might be illusory, the fault of the second-rate haberdasher who had put him in a loosely fitted robe that did nothing to flatter his figure.

When he realized that there were intruders behind him, he slowly turned to confront us, and he proved not to be Death, the lord of all worms, after all. He was merely Father Tom Eliot, the rector of St. Bernadette's Catholic Church, which explained why he wasn't wearing a hood; the robe was actually a cassock.

Since my brain is pickled in poetry, I thought of how Robert Browning had described Death—"the pale priest of the mute people"—which seemed to fit this lowercase reaper. Even here in the animated African light, Father Tom's face appeared to be as pale and round as the Eucharistic wafer placed upon the tongue during communion.

"I couldn't convince them to leave their mortal fate in God's hands," Father Tom said, his voice quavering, his eyes brimming with tears. He didn't bother to remark upon our sudden appearance, as if he had known that *someone* would catch him at this forbidden work. "It's a terrible sin, an affront to God, this turning away from life. Rather than suffer in this world any longer, they've chosen damnation, yes, I'm afraid that's what they've done, and all I could do was comfort them. My counsel was rejected, though I tried. I tried. Comfort. That was all I could give. Comfort. Do you understand?"

"Yes, we do, we understand," Sasha said with both compassion and wariness.

In ordinary times, before we had entered The End of Days, Father Tom had been an ebullient guy, devout without being stuffy, sincere about his concern for others. With his expressive and rubbery face, with his merry eyes and quick smile, he was a natural comedian, yet in times of tragedy he served as a reliable source of strength for others. I wasn't a member of his church, but I knew his parishioners had long adored him.

Lately, things hadn't gone well for Father Tom, and he himself hadn't been well. His sister, Laura, had been my mother's colleague and friend. Tom is devoted to her—and has not seen her for more than a year. There is reason to believe that Laura is far along in her becoming, profoundly changed, and is being held in The Hole, at Wyvern, where she is an object of intense study.

"Four of those here are Catholic," he said. "Members of my flock. Their souls were in my hands. My hands. The others are Lutheran, Methodist. One is Jewish. Two were atheists until . . . recently. All their souls mine to save. Mine to lose." He was talking rapidly, nervously, as if he were aware of a bomb clock relentlessly ticking toward detonation, eager to confess before being obliterated. "Two of them, a misguided young couple, had absorbed incoherent fragments of the spiritual beliefs of half a dozen American Indian tribes, twisting everything in ways the Indians would never have understood. These two, they believed in such a mess of things, such a jumble, they worshipped the buffalo, river spirits, earth spirits, the corn plant. Do I belong in an age where people worship buffalo and corn? I'm lost here. Do you understand? Do you?"

"Yes," Bobby said, having followed us into the room. "Don't worry, Father Eliot, we understand."

The priest was wearing a loose cloth gardening glove on his left hand. As he continued to speak, he worried ceaselessly at the glove with his right hand, plucking at the cuff, tugging at the fingers, as if the fit was not comfortable. "I didn't give them extreme unction, last rites, didn't give them the last rites," he said, voice rising toward a hysterical pitch and pace, "because they were *suicides*, but maybe I should have given unction, maybe I should have, compassion over doctrine, because all I did for them . . . the only thing I did for these poor tortured people was give comfort, the comfort of words, nothing but empty words, so I don't know whether their souls were lost because of me or in spite of me."

A month ago, the night my father died, I experienced a strange and unsettling encounter with Father Tom Eliot, of which I've written in a previous volume of this journal. He'd been even less in control of his emotions on that cruel night than he was here in the Stanwyk mausoleum, and I had suspected he was becoming, though by the end of our encounter, he had seemed to be racked not by anything uncanny but rather by a heart-crushing anguish for his missing sister and by his own spiritual despair.

Now, as then, I searched for unnatural yellow radiance in his eyes, but saw none.

The cartoon colors from the television patterned his face, so I seemed to be looking at him through a constantly changing stained-glass window depicting distorted animal shapes rather than saints. This inadequate and peculiar light flickered in his eyes, as well, but it couldn't have concealed more than the faintest and the most transient glimmer of animal eyeshine.

Still worrying at the glove, his voice as tight with stress as power lines taut and singing in a storm wind, sweat shining on his face, Father Tom said, "They had a way out, even if it was the wrong way, even if it was the worst sin, but I can't take their way, I'm too scared, because there's the soul to think about, there's always the immortal soul, and I believe in the soul more than in release from suffering, so there's no way out for me now. I have damning thoughts. Terrible thoughts. Dreams. Dreams full of blood. In the dreams, I feed on beating hearts, chew at the throats of women, and rape . . . rape small children, and then I wake up sickened but also, but also, also I wake up *thrilled*, and there's no way out for me."

Suddenly he stripped the glove off his left hand. The thing that slid out of the glove, however, wasn't a human hand. It was a hand in the process of becoming something else, still exhibiting evidence of humanity in the tone and the texture of the skin, and in the placement of the digits, but the fingers were more like finger-size talons, yet not talons precisely, because each appeared to be split—or at least to have begun to split—into appendages resembling the serrated pincers of baby lobster claws.

"I can only trust in Jesus," the priest said.

His face streamed with tears no doubt as bitter as the vinegar in the sponge that had been offered to his suffering savior.

"I believe. I believe in the mercy of Christ. Yes, I believe. I believe in the mercy of Christ."

Yellow light flared in his eyes.

Flared.

Father Tom came at me first, perhaps because I was between him and the doorway, perhaps because my mother was Wisteria Jane Snow. After all, though she gave us such miracles as Orson and Mungojerrie, her life's work also made possible the twitching thing at the end of the priest's left arm. Though the human side of him surely did believe in the immortal soul and the sweet mercy of Christ, it was understandable if some other, darker part of him placed its faith in bloody vengeance.

No matter what else he was, Father Tom was still a priest, and my folks had not raised me to take punches at priests, or at people insane with despair, for that matter. Respect and pity and twenty-eight years of parental instruction overcame my survival instinct—which made me a disappointment to Darwin—and instead of aggressively countering Father Tom's assault, I crossed my arms over my face and tried to turn away from him.

He was not an experienced fighter. Like a grade-school boy in a playground brawl, he threw himself wildly against me, using his entire body as a weapon, ramming into me with a lot more force than you would expect from an ordinary priest, even more than you'd expect from a Jesuit.

Driven backward, I slammed hard into a tall armoire. One of the door handles gouged into my back, just below my left shoulder blade.

Father Tom was hammering at me with his right fist, but I was more worried about that weird left appendage. I didn't know how sharp the serrated edges on those little pincers might be, but more to the point, I didn't want to be *touched* by that thing, which looked unclean. Not unclean in a sanitary sense. Unclean in the sense that the cloven hoof or the hairless pink corkscrew tail of a demon might look unclean.

As he pounded on me, Father Tom urgently repeated his statement of religious commitment: "I believe in the mercy of Christ, the mercy of Christ, the mercy, I believe in the mercy of Christ!"

His spittle sprayed my face, and his breath was disconcertingly sweet with the fragrance of peppermint.

This ceaseless chanting wasn't meant to persuade me or anyone else—not even God—of the priest's unshaken faith. Rather, he was trying to convince himself of his belief, to remind himself that he had hope, and to use that hope to seize control of himself once more. In spite of the malevolent sulfurous light in his eyes, in spite of the urge to kill that pumped uncanny strength into his undisciplined body, I could see the earnest and vulnerable man of God who struggled to suppress the raging savage within and to find his way back toward grace.

Shouting, cursing, Bobby and Roosevelt clutched at the priest, trying to tear him off me. Even as he clung fast to me, Father Tom kicked at them, drove his elbows backward into their stomachs and ribs.

He hadn't been a skilled fighter when he launched himself at me, seconds ago, but he seemed to be learning fast. Or perhaps he was losing the struggle to subdue his new becoming self, the savage within, which knew all about fighting and killing.

I felt something pulling at my sweater and was sure that it was the hateful claw. The pincer serrations were snagged in the cotton fabric.

With revulsion thick in my throat, I grabbed the priest's wrist to restrain him. The flesh under my hand was strangely hot, greasy, and as vile to the touch as might be a corpse in an advanced state of decay. In places, the meat of him was disgustingly soft, although in other places, his skin had hardened into what might have been patches of a smooth carapace.

Until now, our bizarre struggle had been desperate yet at least darkly amusing to me, something that you couldn't laugh at now but at which you knew you would laugh later, over a beer, on the beach: this roundhouse fight with a chubby clergyman in a chintz-choked bedroom, a Looney Tunes collaboration between Chuck Jones and H. P. Lovecraft. But suddenly a positive outcome didn't seem as assured as it had a moment ago, and it wasn't amusing anymore, not slightly, not even darkly.

His wrist joint was no longer like the wrist joint you study on a skeleton chart in a general-biology class, more like something you might see during advanced delirium tremens while drying out from a ten-bottle bourbon binge. The entire hand turned backward on the wrist, as no human hand could do, as if it operated on a ball joint, and the pincers snapped at my fingers, forcing me to let go before he had a chance to cut me.

Although I felt as though I had been struggling with the priest long enough to justify having his name tattooed on my biceps, he had been in this pummeling frenzy for no more than half a minute before Roosevelt tore him off me. Our usually gentle animal communicator communicated to the animal inside Father Tom by lifting him off the floor and throwing him as if he were no heavier than the real Death, who is, after all, nothing but bones in a robe.

Cassock skirt flaring, Father Tom crashed into the footboard of the bed, causing the pair of suicides to bounce as though with postmortem delight, springs singing under them. He toppled facedown to the floor, but instantly sprang to his feet with inhuman agility.

No longer chanting about his faith, now grunting like a boar, spitting, making strange strangled sounds of rage, he seized a walnut chair that featured tie-on cushions in a daffodil print and slip-on daffodil arm protectors, and for an instant it seemed that he would use it to smash everything around him, but then he pitched it at Roosevelt.

Roosevelt spun away just in time to take the chair across his broad back rather than in the face.

From the television came the mellifluous and emotional voice of Elton John, with full orchestral and choral accompaniment, singing "Can You Feel the Love Tonight?"

Even as the chair was cracking against Roosevelt's back, Father Tom threw a vanity bench at Sasha.

She didn't dodge quickly enough. The bench clipped her shoulder and knocked her over an ottoman.

As the furniture struck Sasha, the possessed priest was already firing items off the vanity at me, at Bobby, at Roosevelt, and though bestial sounds continued to issue from him, he also snarled a few broken but familiar words, with a vicious glee, to punctuate his attack: a silver hairbrush, an oval hand mirror with mother-of-pearl frame and handle—*"in the name of the Father"*—a heavy silver clothes brush—*"and the Son"*— a few decorative enamel boxes—*"and the Holy Spirit!"*—a porcelain bud vase that hit Roosevelt so hard in the face he dropped as if he'd been smacked with a ball-peen hammer, a silver comb. A perfume bottle sailed past my head and shattered against a distant hulk of furniture, flooding the bedroom with the fragrance of attar of roses.

During this barrage, ducking and dodging, protecting our faces with raised arms, Bobby and I tried to move toward Tom Eliot. I'm not sure why. Maybe we thought that together we could pin him down and hold the pitiable wretch until this seizure passed, until he regained his senses. If he had any senses left. Which seemed less likely by the second.

When the priest fired the last of the clutter from the arsenal atop the vanity, Bobby rushed him, and I went after him, too, just a fraction of a second later.

Instead of retreating, Father Tom launched himself forward, and when they collided, the priest lifted Bobby off the floor. He wasn't Father Tom at all anymore. He was something unnaturally powerful, with the strength and ferocity of a mad bull. He lunged across the bedroom, knocking over a chair, and slammed-jammed-crushed Bobby into a corner so hard that Bobby's shoulders should have snapped. Bobby cried out in pain, and the priest leaned into him, punching, clawing at his ribs, *digging* at him.

Then I was in the melee, too, on Father Tom's back, slipping my right arm around his neck, gripping my right wrist with my left hand. Got him in a chokehold. Jerked back on his head. Just about crushed his windpipe, trying to pull him away from Bobby.

He retreated from Bobby, all right, but instead of dropping to his knees and capitulating, he seemed not to need the air that I was choking out of him, or the blood supply to the brain that I pinched off. He bucked, trying to throw me over his head and off his back, bucked again and more furiously.

I was aware of Sasha shouting, but I didn't listen to what she was saying until the priest bucked a fourth time and nearly *did* pitch me off. My chokehold slipped, and he snarled as if sensing triumph, and I finally heard Sasha saying, "Get out of the way! Chris! Chris, get out of the way!"

Doing what she demanded took some trust, but then it's always about trust, every time, whether it's deadly combat or a kiss, so I released my faltering chokehold, and the priest threw me off even before I could scramble away.

Father Tom rose to his full height, and he appeared to be taller than before. I think that must have been an illusion. His demonic fury had attained such intensity, such blazing power, that I expected electric arcs to leap from him to any nearby metal object. Rage made him appear to be larger than he was. His radiant yellow gaze seemed brighter than mere eyeshine, as if inside his skull was not merely a new creature becoming but the elemental nuclear fire of an entire new universe aborning.

I retreated, gasping for breath, stupidly groping for the gun that Manuel had taken from me.

Sasha was holding a bed pillow, which she evidently had jerked out from under the head of one of the suicides. This seemed as crazy as everything else that was happening, as if she intended to smother Father Tom or to batter him into submission with a sack of goose down. But then, as she ordered him to back off and sit down, I understood that the pillow was folded around her .38 Chiefs Special, to muffle the report of the revolver if she was forced to use it, because this bedroom was at the front of the house, where the sound might carry to the street.

You could tell that the priest wasn't listening to Sasha. Maybe by this time he wasn't capable of listening to anything except to what was happening inside him, to the internal hurricane-roar of his becoming.

His mouth opened wide, and his lips skinned back from his teeth. An unearthly shriek came from him, then another, more chilling than the first, followed by squeals and cries and wretched groans, which alternately seemed to express pain and pleasure, despair and joy, blind rage and poignant remorse, as if there were multitudes within this one tortured body.

Instead of ordering Father Tom to desist, Sasha was now pleading with him. Maybe because she didn't want to be forced to use the gun. Maybe because she was afraid his crazed shouting would be heard in the street and draw unwanted attention. Her pleas were tremulous, and tears stood in her eyes, but I could tell that she would be able to do whatever needed to be done.

The shrieking priest raised his arms as if he were calling down the wrath of Heaven upon all of us. He began to shake violently, like one afflicted with Saint Vitus' dance.

Bobby was standing in the corner where Father Tom had left him, both hands pressed to his left flank, as though stanching the flow of blood from a wound.

Roosevelt blocked the hall door, holding one hand to his face, where he'd been hit by the bud vase.

I could tell from their expressions I wasn't alone in believing that the priest was building toward an explosion of violence far more fearsome than anything we had witnessed yet. I didn't expect Father Tom to metamorphose before our eyes, from minister to monster in one minute, like a shape-changing alien in a science-fiction movie, half basilisk and half spider, slashing-snapping-stinging-ripping its way through the four of us, then swallowing Mungojerrie as if the hapless cat were an after-dinner mint. Surely flesh and bone couldn't be transformed as quickly as popcorn kernels in a microwave oven. On the other hand, such a fantastic change, pastor to predator, would not have surprised me, either.

The priest *did* surprise me, however, surprised all of us, when he turned his rage against himself; though in retrospect, I realized I should have remembered the birds, the *veve* rats, and Manuel's words about psychological implosion. The cleric let out a wail that seemed to oscillate between rage and grief, and though it wasn't as loud as the preceding cries, it was even more terrifying because it was so devoid of hope. To this marrow-freezing lament, he repeatedly bashed himself in the face with his right fist, and also with the semblance of a fist that he was able to make with his deformed hand, striking such solid blows that his nose crunched and his lips split against his teeth.

Sasha was still pleading with him, though she must have realized that Father Tom Eliot was beyond her reach, beyond the help of anyone in this world.

As if trying to scourge the devil from himself, he began to claw his cheeks, digging his fingernails deep, and with those pincers, he went at his right eye as though to pluck it out of himself.

Feathers suddenly whirled through the air, spinning around the priest, and I was briefly confused, astonished, until I realized that Sasha had fired the .38. The pillow couldn't have entirely muffled the shot, but I'd heard nothing other than Father Tom's wail drilling my skull.

The priest jerked from the impact of the slug, but he didn't drop. He didn't bite off that skirling lament or stop tearing at himself.

I heard the second shot—*whump*—and the third.

Tom Eliot crumpled to the floor, lay twitching, briefly kicked his legs as if he were a dog chasing rabbits in his sleep, and then was motionless, dead.

Sasha had relieved him from his agony but had also saved him from the self-destruction that he believed would condemn his immortal soul to eternal damnation.

So much had happened since the priest had thrown the

chair at Roosevelt and the vanity bench at Sasha that I was surprised to hear Elton John still singing "Can You Feel the Love Tonight?"

Before dropping the pillow, Sasha turned toward the television and fired one more round, blowing out the screen.

As satisfying as it was to put an end to the inappropriately uplifting music and images of *The Lion King*, we were all alarmed by the total darkness that claimed the room following a shower of sparks from the terminated TV. We *assumed* that the becoming priest must be dead, because any of us would be worm food, for sure, with three .38 slugs in the chest, but as Bobby had noted the previous night, there were no rules here on the eve of the Apocalypse.

When I reached for my flashlight, it was no longer snugged under my belt. I must have dropped it during the struggle.

In my imagination, the dead priest had already self-resurrected and had become something that an entire division of marines couldn't kill.

Bobby switched on one of the nightstand lamps.

The dead man was still nothing more than a man, and still dead, a ruined heap that didn't bear close inspection.

Holstering the .38, Sasha turned away from the body and stood with her shoulders slumped, head hung, one hand covering her face, collecting herself.

The lamp featured a three-way switch, and Bobby clicked it to the lowest level of light. The shade was rose-colored silk, which left the room still mostly in shadow but bright enough to prevent us from succumbing to an attack of the brain twitches.

I spotted my flashlight on the floor, snatched it up, and jammed it under my belt again.

Trying to quiet my breathing, I went to the nearer of two windows. The drapes were a heavy tapestry, as thick as an elephant's hide, with a blackout liner. This would have suppressed the sound of gunfire almost as effectively as the plush pillow through which Sasha had fired the revolver.

I pulled aside one drape and peered out at the lamplit

street. No one was pointing or running toward the Stanwyk residence. No traffic had stopped in front of the house. In fact, the street appeared to be deserted.

As far as I can recall, none of us said anything until we were all the way downstairs and in the kitchen again, where the solemn cat was waiting for us in the light of the oil lamp. Perhaps we simply didn't say anything memorable, but I think that we did, indeed, make our way through the house in numbed silence.

Bobby stripped off his Hawaiian shirt and black cotton pullover, which were damp with blood. Along his left side were four slashes, wounds inflicted by the cleric's teratoid hand.

That was a useful word from my mom's world of genetic science. It meant something monstrous, described an organism or a portion of an organism deformed because of damaged genetic material. As a kid, I was always interested in my mother's research and theories, because she was, as she liked to put it, searching for God in the clockworks, which I thought must be the most important work anyone could do. But God prefers to see what we can make of ourselves on our own, and He doesn't make it easy for us to find Him on this side of death. Along the way, when we think we've located the door behind which He waits, it opens not on anything divine but on something teratoid.

In the half bath adjoining the kitchen, Sasha found first-aid supplies and a bottle of aspirin.

Bobby stood at the kitchen sink, using a fresh dishcloth and liquid soap to clean his wounds, hissing between clenched teeth.

"Hurt?" I asked.

"No."

"Bullshit."

"You?"

"Bruises."

The four cuts in his side weren't deep, but they bled freely.

Roosevelt settled into a chair at the table. He'd gotten

some ice cubes from the freezer and wrapped them in a dish towel. He held this compress to his left eye, which was swelling shut. Fortunately, the bud vase hadn't shattered when it hit him, because otherwise he might have had splinters of porcelain in his eye.

"Bad?" I asked.

"Had worse."

"Football?"

"Alex Karras."

"Great player."

"Big."

"He run you down?"

"More than once."

"Like a truck," I suggested.

"A Mack. This was just a damn vase."

Sasha saturated a cloth with hydrogen peroxide and pressed it repeatedly to Bobby's wounds. Every time she took the cloth away, the shallow cuts bubbled furiously with bloody foam.

I couldn't have ached in more places if I'd spent the past six hours tumbling around in an industrial clothes dryer.

I washed down two aspirin with a few sips of an Orange Crush that I found in the Stanwyks' refrigerator. The can shook so badly that I drizzled more soda over my chin and clothes than I managed to drink—suggesting that my folks had been misguided when they allowed me to stop wearing a bib at the age of five.

After several applications of the peroxide, Sasha switched to rubbing alcohol and repeated the treatment. Bobby wasn't bothering to hiss anymore; he was just grinding his teeth to dust. Finally, when he had ground away enough dental surface to be limited to a soft diet for life, she smeared the still-weeping wounds with Neosporin.

This extensive first aid was conducted without comment. We all knew why it was necessary to apply as many antibacteriological agents as possible to his wounds, and talking about it would only scare the crap out of us.

In the weeks and months to come, Bobby would be

spending more time than usual in front of a mirror, checking himself out, and not because he was vain. He'd be more aware of his hands, too, watching for something . . . teratoid.

Roosevelt's eye was swollen to a slit. Nevertheless, he still believed in the ice.

While Sasha finished wrapping Bobby's cuts with gauze bandages, I found a chalk message slate and pegboard beside the door connecting the kitchen to the garage. Sets of car keys hung on the pegs. Sasha wouldn't have to hot-wire a car, after all.

In the garage were a red Jaguar and a white Ford Expedition.

By flashlight, I lowered the rear seat in the Expedition to enlarge the cargo area. This would allow Roosevelt and Bobby to lie down, below window level. We might draw more attention as a group than Sasha would draw if she appeared to be alone.

Because Sasha knew exactly where we were going out on Haddenbeck Road, she would drive.

When Bobby entered the garage with Sasha and Roosevelt, he was wearing his pullover and Hawaiian shirt again, and moving somewhat stiffly.

"You be okay back here?" I asked, indicating the rear of the Expedition.

"I'll grab some nap time."

In the front passenger's seat, when I slumped below the window line in a classic fugitive-on-the-lam posture, I became acutely aware of every contusion, neck to toe. But I was alive. Earlier, I'd been sure we wouldn't all leave the Stanwyk house with beating hearts and brain activity, but I'd been wrong. When it comes to presentiments of disaster, perhaps cats know things, but Christopher Snow's hunches can't necessarily be trusted—which is comforting, actually.

When Sasha started the engine, Mungojerrie scrambled onto the console between the front seats. He sat erect, ears pricked, looking forward, like a misplaced hood ornament.

Sasha used a remote control to put up the electric garage door, and I said, "You okay?"

"No."

"Good."

I knew that she was physically unhurt and that her answer referred to her emotional state. Killing Tom Eliot, Sasha had done the only thing she could do, perhaps saving one or more of our lives while sparing the priest from a hideous frenzy of self-destruction, and yet the firing of those three shots had sickened her; now she was living under a grave weight of moral responsibility. Not guilt. She was smart enough to know that no guilt should attend what she'd done. But she also knew that even moral acts can have dimensions that scar the mind and wound the heart. If she had answered my question with a smile and assurances that she was fine, she would not have been the Sasha Goodall that I love, and I would have had reason to suspect that she was becoming.

We rode through Moonlight Bay in silence, each of us occupied with his or her own thoughts.

A couple miles from the Stanwyk house, the cat lost interest in the view through the windshield. He surprised me by stepping down onto my chest and peering into my eyes.

His green gaze was intense and unwavering, and I met it directly for an eerily long time, wondering what he might be thinking.

How radically different his thinking must be from ours, even if he shares our high level of intelligence. He experiences this world from a perspective nearly as unlike ours as our perspective would be unlike that of a being raised on another planet. He faces each day without carrying on his back the weight of human history, philosophy, triumph, tragedy, noble intentions, foolishness, greed, envy, and hubris; it must be liberating to be without that burden. He is both savage and civilized. He is closer to nature than we are; therefore, he has fewer illusions about it, knows that life is hard by design, that nature is beautiful but cold. And although Roosevelt says other cats of Mungojerrie's breed escaped from Wyvern, their numbers cannot be large; while Mungojerrie isn't as singular a specimen as Orson seems to be, and while cats by nature are more adaptable to solitude than dogs are, this small creature must at times know a profound loneliness.

When I began to pet him, Mungojerrie broke eye contact and curled up on my chest. He was a small, warm weight, and I could feel his heartbeat both against my body and under my stroking hand.

I am not an animal communicator, but I think I know why he led us into the Stanwyk house. We were not there to bear witness to the dead. We were there solely to do what needed to be done for Father Tom Eliot.

Since time immemorial, people have suspected that some animals have at least one sense in addition to our own. An awareness of things we do not see. A prescience.

Couple that special perception with intelligence, and suppose that with greater intelligence comes a more refined conscience. In passing the Stanwyk house, Mungojerrie might have sensed the mental anguish, the spiritual agony, and the emotional pain of Father Tom Eliot—and might have felt compelled to bring deliverance to that suffering man.

Or maybe I'm full of crap.

The possibility exists that I am both full of crap and right about Mungojerrie.

Cats know things.

23

Haddenbeck Road is a lonely stretch of two-lane blacktop that for a few miles runs due east, paralleling the southern perimeter of Fort Wyvern, but then strikes southeast, serving a score of ranches in the least populated portion of the county. Summer heat, winter rains, and California's most violent weather—earthquakes—have left the pavement cracked, hoved, and ragged at the edges. Skirts of wild grass and, for a short while here in early spring, an embroidery of wildflowers separate the highway from the sensuously rolling fields that embrace it.

When we had traveled some distance without encountering oncoming headlights, Sasha suddenly braked to a halt and said, "Look at this."

I sat up in full view, as did Roosevelt and Bobby, and surveyed the night around us in confusion as Sasha rammed the Expedition into reverse and backed up about twenty feet.

"Almost ran over them," she said.

On the pavement ahead of us, revealed by the headlights, were enough snakes to fill the cages of every reptile house in every zoo in the country.

Leaning forward into the front seat, Bobby whistled softly and said, "Must be an open door to Hell around here somewhere."

"All rattlers?" Roosevelt asked, taking the ice pack off his swollen eye, squinting for a better look.

"Hard to tell," Sasha said. "But I think so."

Mungojerrie stood with hind paws on my right knee, forepaws on the dashboard, head craned forward. He made one of those cat sounds that are half hiss, half growl, and all loathing.

Even from a distance of only twenty-five feet, it was impossible to make an accurate count of the number of serpents in the squirming mass on the highway, and I had no intention of wading in among them to take a reliable census. At a guess, there were as few as seventy or eighty, as many as a hundred.

In my experience, rattlesnakes are lone hunters and do not, as a matter of course, travel in groups. You'll see them in numbers only if you're unlucky enough to stumble into one of their nests—and few if any nests would contain this many individuals.

The behavior of these serpents was even stranger than the fact that they were gathering here in the open. They twined over and under and around one another, in a slowly seething sinuous mass, and from among these slippery braids, eight or ten heads rose at any one time, weaving two, three, four feet into the air, with jaws cracked, fangs bared, tongues flickering, then shrank back into the scaly swarm as new and equally wicked-looking heads rose from the roiling multitude, one set of sentinels replacing another.

It was as if the Medusa, of classic Grecian myth, were lying on Haddenbeck Road, napping, while her elaborate coiffure of serpents groomed itself.

"You going to drive through that?" I asked.

"Rather not," Sasha said.

"Close the vents, crank this buggy up to warp speed," Bobby said, "and take us for a ride on the rattlesnake road."

Roosevelt said, "My mama always says, 'Patience pays.' "

"The snakes aren't here because we are," I said. "They don't care about us. They aren't blocking us. We just happened to come through here at the wrong time. They'll move on, probably sooner than later."

Bobby patted my shoulder. "Roosevelt's mom is a lot more succinct than you are, dude."

Every snake that rose into sentry position from the churning host immediately focused its attention on us. Depending on the angle at which the headlamps caught them, their eyes brightened and flared red or silver, less often green, like small jewels.

I assumed that the light drew their interest. Desert rattlers, like most snakes, are nearly as deaf as dirt. Their vision is good, especially at night, when their slit-shaped pupils dilate to expose more of their sensitive retinas. Their sense of smell may not be as powerful as that of a dog, since they're seldom called upon to track down escaped prisoners or to sniff out dope in smugglers' luggage; however, in addition to a good nose, a snake has a second organ of smell—Jacobson's organ, consisting of two pouches lined with sensory tissue—located in the roof of the mouth. That's why a serpent's forked tongue flicks ceaselessly: It licks microscopic particles of odor from the air, conveying these clusters of molecules to the pouches in its mouth, to savor and analyze them. Now these rattlers were busily licking the air for our scents to determine if suitably delicious prey might be found behind the headlights.

I've learned a great deal about desert rattlesnakes, with which I share the earlier—and warmer—part of the night. In spite of their evil appearance, they possess a compelling beauty.

Weird became weirder when one of the weaving sentries abruptly reared back and struck at another that had risen beside it. The bitten rattler bit back; the two coiled around each other and then dropped to the pavement. The flexuous swarm closed over them, and for a minute, turmoil swept through the braided multitude, which writhed not languorously, as before, but in a frenzy, as supple and quick as lashing whips, twisting and coiling excitedly, as though the urge to bite their own had spread beyond the angry pair we'd seen strike each other, briefly sparking civil war within the colony.

As the slithery horde grew calmer again, Sasha said, "Do snakes usually bite one another?"

"Probably not," I said.

"Wouldn't think they'd be vulnerable to their own venom," said Roosevelt, returning the ice pack to his left eye.

"Well," Bobby said, "if we're ever condemned to live through high school again, maybe we can make a science project out of that question."

Again, one of the rearing rattlers, weaving above the rest and licking the air for prey, struck at another of the sentries, and then a third grew agitated enough to strike the first. The trio raveled down into the swarm, and another siege of spastic thrashing whipped through the undulant masses.

"It's the birds again," I said. "The coyotes."

"The folks at the Stanwyks'," Roosevelt added.

"Psychological implosion," Sasha said.

"I don't suppose a snake has much of a psyche to be logical about," Bobby said, "but yeah, it sure looks like part of the same phenomenon."

"They're moving," Roosevelt noted.

Indeed, the squirming legions were, so to speak, on the march. They began to move across the two-lane blacktop, across the narrow dirt shoulder, vanishing into the tall grass and wildflowers to the right of the highway.

The complete procession, however, consisted of more than the eighty or one hundred specimens that we had been watching. As scores of snakes disappeared into the grass beyond the right-hand shoulder, scores of others appeared out of the field to the left of Haddenbeck Road, as if they were pouring out of a perpetual-motion, snake-making machine.

Perhaps three or four hundred rattlers, increasingly quarrelsome and agitated, crossed into the southern wilds before the blacktop was clear at last. When they were gone, when not a single wriggling form remained on the highway, we sat in silence for a moment, blinking, as if we had awakened from a dream.

Mom, I love you, and I always will. But what the hell *were you thinking?*

Sasha shifted gears and drove forward.

Mungojerrie made that sound of loathing again. He changed positions in my lap, so his forepaws were on the door, and he gazed out the side window, at the dark fields into which the serpent horde had slithered toward whatever oblivion it was seeking.

A mile later, we reached Crow Hill, beyond which Doogie Sassman should be waiting for us. Unless the snakes had crossed his path before they crossed ours.

I don't know why Crow Hill is named Crow Hill. The shape of it in no way suggests the bird, nor do crows tend to flock there more than elsewhere. The name isn't in honor of a prominent local family or even a colorful scoundrel. Crow Indians are located in Montana, not California. No crowfoot grows there. And history has no record of braggarts regularly trekking to the top of this mound to gloat and boast.

At the crown of the hill, an enormous outcropping of rock rises from the surrounding gentle contours of the loamy land, a solitary gray-white knob like a partially exposed bone in the skeleton of a buried behemoth. Carved on one face of this monument is the figure of a crow, which is not, as I once thought, the source of the name. Crude but intriguing, this carving captures the cockiness of the bird yet somehow has an ominous quality, as though it is the totem of a murderous clan, a warning to travelers to find a route around their territory or risk dire consequences. On a July night forty-four years ago, the image of the crow was scored into the stone by a person—or persons—unknown. Until curiosity had led me to learn the origins of the carving, I'd assumed that it dated from another century, that perhaps it had been chiseled into the rock even before Europeans set foot on this continent. There is a disquieting aspect to the image of the crow, a quality that speaks to mystics, who have been known to travel considerable distances to view and touch it. Old-timers say this place has been called Crow Hill since at least the time of their grandparents, however, and references in time-yellowed public records confirm their claim. The carving seems to embody some primitive knowledge long lost to civilized man, yet the name of the hill predates it, and evidently the anonymous carver meant only to create a pictorial landmark sign.

This image was not like the bird on the message left with

Lilly Wing, except that both seemed to radiate malevolence. As Charlie Dai had described them, the crows—or ravens, or blackbirds—left at the scenes of the other abductions were also unlike this carving. Charlie would have remarked on the resemblance if there had been one.

Nevertheless, the coincidence was creepy.

As we approached the crest, the crow in the stone appeared to be watching us. The raised planes of the bird's body reflected white in the headlights, while shadows filled the deep lines that had been cut by the carver's tools. This was a colloidal stone, and chips of some shiny aggregate—perhaps nuggets of mica—were scattered through it. The carving had been artfully composed to position the largest of these chips as the eye of the bird, which was now filled with an imitation of animal eyeshine and with a peculiar quality that some visiting mystics insist is forbidden knowledge, although I've never understood how an inanimate hunk of rock can have knowledge.

I noticed that everyone in the Expedition, including the cat, regarded the stone crow with an uneasy expression.

As we drove past this figure, the shadows in the chiseled lines should have shrunk from us in the rapidly diminishing light, as the entire carving settled into darkness. But unless my eyes deceived me, for an instant the shadows elongated, violating the laws of physics, as if trying to follow the light. And as the crow disappeared into the night behind us, I could have sworn the shadow pulled loose of the stone and took flight as though it were a real bird.

As we headed down the eastern slope of Crow Hill, I restrained myself from remarking on the unnerving flight of the shadow, but Bobby said, "I don't like this place."

"Me neither," Roosevelt agreed.

"Ditto," I said.

Bobby said, "Humankind wasn't meant to travel this far from the beach."

"Yeah," Sasha said, "we're probably getting dangerously close to the edge of the earth."

"Exactly," Bobby said.

"You ever see any of those maps from the time when they thought the earth was flat?" I asked.

Bobby said, "Oh, I see, you're one of those round-earth kooks."

"The mapmakers actually showed the edge of the earth, the sea just cascading into an abyss, and sometimes they lettered a warning across the void: *'Here there be monsters.'*"

After a brief but deep group silence, Bobby said, "Bad choice of historical trivia, bro."

"Yeah," Sasha said, gradually slowing the Expedition as she peered into the dark fields north of Haddenbeck Road, evidently looking for Doogie Sassman. "Don't you know any amusing anecdotes about Marie Antoinette at the guillotine?"

"That's the stuff!" Bobby agreed.

Roosevelt darkened the mood by communicating what didn't need to be communicated: "Mr. Mungojerrie says the crow flew off the rock."

"With all due respect," Bobby said, "Mr. Mungojerrie is just a fuckin' cat."

Roosevelt seemed to listen to a voice beyond our hearing. Then: "Mungojerrie says he may be just a fuckin' cat, but that puts him two steps up the social ladder from a boardhead."

Bobby laughed. "He didn't say that."

"No other cat here," Roosevelt said.

"*You* said that," Bobby accused.

"Not me," Roosevelt said. "I don't use that kind of language."

"The cat?" Bobby said skeptically.

"The cat," Roosevelt insisted.

"Bobby's only a recent believer in all this smart-animal stuff," I told Roosevelt.

"Hey, cat," Bobby said.

Mungojerrie turned in my lap to look back at Bobby.

Bobby said, "You're all right, dude."

Mungojerrie raised one forepaw.

After a moment, Bobby caught on. His face bright with wonder, he extended his right hand across the back of my seat. He and the cat gave each other a gentle high five.

Good work, Mom, I thought. *Very nice. Let's just hope when all is said and done, we end up with more smart cats than crazed reptiles.*

"Here we are," Sasha said as we reached the bottom of the hill.

She shifted the Expedition into four-wheel drive and turned north off the highway, driving slowly because she had doused the headlights and was guided only by the much dimmer parking lights.

We crossed a lush meadow, wove through a stand of live oaks, approached the boundary fence surrounding Fort Wyvern, and stopped beside the largest sports utility vehicle I had ever seen. This black Hummer, the civilian version of the military's Humvee, had undergone customization after being driven off the showroom floor. It featured oversize tires and sat even higher on them than did a standard model, and it had been stretched by the addition of a few feet to its cargo space.

Sasha switched off the lights and the engine, and we got out of the Expedition.

Mungojerrie clung to me as though he thought I might put him down on the ground. I understood his concern. The grass was knee-high. Even in daylight, you'd have difficulty spotting a snake before it struck, especially considering how fast a motivated serpent can move. When Roosevelt reached out, I handed the cat to him.

The driver's door opened on the Hummer, and Doogie Sassman got out to greet us, like a steroid-hammered Santa Claus climbing out of a Pentagon-designed sleigh. He closed the door behind him to kill the cabin light.

At five feet eleven, Doogie Sassman is five inches shorter than Roosevelt Frost, but he is the only man I've ever known who can make Roosevelt appear to be petite. The sass man enjoys no more than a hundred-pound advantage on Roosevelt, but I've never seen a hundred pounds used to better effect. He seems to be not merely forty percent larger than Roosevelt, but *twice* as large, more than twice, and taller even though he isn't, a true leviathan on land, a guy who might discuss the techniques of city destruction over lunch with Godzilla.

Doogie carries his massive weight with unearthly grace and does not appear to be fat. All right, Doogie *does* look big, très mondo, mondo maximo, but he's not soft. You get the impression that he's made of animate concrete, impervious to arteriosclerosis, bullets, and time. There's something about Doogie that's every bit as mystical as the stone crow at the top of Crow Hill.

Maybe his hair and beard contribute to the impression that he's an incarnation of Thor, the god of thunder and rain once worshipped in ancient Scandinavia, where they now worship cheesy pop stars like everyone else. His untamed blond hair, so thick that it offends the sensibilities of Hare Krishnas, hangs to the middle of his back, and his beard is so lush and wavy that he couldn't possibly shave it off with anything less than a lawn mower. Great hair can radically enhance a man's aura of power—as witness those who have been elected to the presidency of the United States with no other qualifications—and I'm sure Doogie's hair and beard have more than a little to do with the supernatural impression that he makes, though the real mystery of him cannot be explained by hair, size, the elaborate tattoos that cover his body, or his gas-flame blue eyes.

This night he wore a zippered black jumpsuit tucked into black boots, which should have made him look like a Brobdingnagian baby in Dr. Denton pajamas. Instead, he had the presence of a guy who might be called down to Hell by Satan to unclog a furnace chimney choked with the gnarled and half-burnt contentious souls of ten serial killers.

Bobby greeted him: "Hey, sass man."

"Bobster," Doogie replied.

"Cool wheels," I said admiringly.

"It kicks ass," he acknowledged.

Roosevelt said, "Thought you were all Harleys."

"Doogie," Sasha said, "is a man of many conveyances."

"I am a wheel-o-maniac," he admitted. "What happened to your eye, Rosie?"

"In a fight with a priest."

The eye was better, still swollen but not to such a tight slit. The ice had worked.

"We ought to get moving," Sasha said. "It's weird out here tonight, Doogie."

He agreed. "I've been hearing coyotes like no coyotes I've ever heard before."

Bobby, Sasha, and I looked at one another. I recalled Sasha's prediction that we hadn't seen the last of the pack that had come out of the canyon beyond Lilly Wing's house.

The cathedral-quiet fields and hills lay under a shrouded sky, and the breeze from the west was as feeble as the breath of a dying nun. In the live oaks behind us, the leaves whispered only slightly louder than memory, and the tall grass barely stirred.

Doogie led us around to the back of the customized Hummer and opened the tailgate. The interior light was not as bright as usual, because half the fixture was masked with electrician's black tape, but even the reduced illumination was a beacon in these star-denied, moon-starved grasslands.

Just inside the tailgate were two shotguns. They were pistol-grip, pump-action Remingtons even sweeter than the classic Mossberg that Manuel Ramirez had confiscated from Bobby's Jeep.

Doogie said, "I don't think either of you boardheads is likely to shoot a hole in a silver dollar with a handgun, so these suit you better. I know you're shotgun-familiar. But you'll be using magnum loads, so be prepared for the kick. With this punch and spread, you buckaroos don't have to worry about aiming, and you'll stop just about anything."

He handed one shotgun to Bobby, the other to me, and also gave each of us a box of ammunition.

"Load up, then distribute the rest of the shells in your jacket pockets," he said. "Don't leave any in the box. The last shell can be the one that saves your ass." He looked at Sasha, smiled, and said, "Like Colombia."

"Colombia?" I asked.

"We did some business there once," Sasha said.

Doogie had lived in Moonlight Bay six years, and Sasha had been here two. I wondered if this business trip had been recent or before either of them settled in the Jewel of the Central Coast. I had been under the impression that they had met at KBAY.

"Colombia, the country?" Bobby asked.

"Not the record company," Doogie assured him.

"Tell me not drugs," Bobby said.

Doogie shook his head. "Rescue operation."

Sasha's smile was enigmatic. "Interested in the past, after all, Snowman?"

"Right now, just the future."

Turning to Roosevelt, Doogie said, "I didn't realize you'd be coming, so I don't have a weapon for you."

"I've got the cat," Roosevelt said.

"Killer."

Mungojerrie hissed.

The hiss reminded me of the snakes. I looked around nervously, wondering if the loco reptiles we had seen earlier would give us the courtesy of a warning rattle.

Closing the tailgate, Doogie said, "Let's rock."

In addition to the cargo area just inside the tailgate—which contained a pair of five-gallon fuel cans, two cardboard boxes, and a well-stuffed backpack—the customized Hummer provided seating for eight. Behind the pair of bucket-style front seats were two bench seats, each capable of accommodating three grown men, although not three as well grown as Doogie.

Thor Incarnate drove, and Roosevelt rode shotgun, figuratively speaking, holding our long-tailed tracker in his lap. Immediately behind them, I sat with Bobby and Sasha on the first bench seat.

"Why aren't we going into Wyvern by the river?" Bobby wondered.

"The only way to get down to the Santa Rosita," Doogie said, "is on one of the levee ramps in town. But tonight the town's crawling with a bad element."

"Anchovies," Bobby translated.

"We'd be spotted and stopped," Sasha said.

With the way illuminated only by its parking lights, the Hummer passed through a huge hole in the fence, where the ragged edges of the flanking panels of chain-link were as snarled as masses of string left with a playful kitten.

"You cut this open all by yourself?" I asked.

"Shaped charge," Doogie said.

"Explosives?"

"Just a little boom plastic."

"Didn't that draw attention?"

"Shape the charge in a thin line, where you want the links to pop, and you're using so little it's like one really big beat on a bass drum."

"Even if someone's close enough to hear," Sasha said, "it's over so quick, he'd never get a fix on the direction."

Bobby said, "Radio engineering requires way more cool skills than I thought."

Doogie asked where we were headed, and I described the cluster of warehouses in the southwest quadrant of the base, where I had last seen Orson. He seemed familiar with the layout of Fort Wyvern, because he needed few directions.

We parked near the big roll-up door. The man-size door beside the larger entrance stood open, as I had left it the previous night.

I got out of the Hummer, carrying my shotgun. Roosevelt and Mungojerrie joined me, while the others waited in the vehicle in order not to distract the cat in his efforts to pick up the trail.

Pooled with shadows, smelling vaguely of oil and grease, home to weeds that sprouted from fissures in the blacktop, littered with empty oil cans and with assorted paper trash and leaves deposited by the previous night's wind, surrounded by the corrugated-steel facades of the hulking warehouses, this serviceway had never been a festive place, not a prime venue for a royal wedding, but now the atmosphere was downright sinister.

Last night, the stocky abb with the close-cropped black hair, aware that Orson and I were close behind him in the

Santa Rosita, must have used a cell phone to call for assistance—perhaps from the tall, blond, athletic guy with the puckered scar on his left cheek, who had snatched the Stuart twins only hours before. He had handed Jimmy off to someone, anyway, and then had led Orson and me into the warehouse, with the intention of killing me there.

From an inside jacket pocket, I withdrew the tightly wadded top of Jimmy Wing's cotton pajamas, with which the abb had confused the scent trail. To be fair to Orson, who had been briefly baffled but never entirely misled, I was the one suckered into the warehouse by odd noises and a muffled voice.

The garment seemed so small, almost like doll's clothing.

"I don't know if this helps," I said. "Cats aren't bloodhounds, after all."

"We'll see," Roosevelt said.

Mungojerrie sniffed the pajama top delicately but with interest. Then he took a tour of the immediate area, smelling the pavement, an empty oil can, which made him sneeze, and the tiny yellow flowers on a weed, which made him sneeze again and more vigorously. He returned for a brief inhalation of the garment, and then he tracked a scent along the pavement once more, moving in a widening spiral, from time to time lifting his head to savor the air, all the while appearing suitably quizzical. He padded to the warehouse, where he raised one leg and relieved himself against the concrete foundation, sniffed the deposit he had made, returned for another whiff of the pajama top, spent half a minute investigating an old rusted socket wrench lying on the pavement, paused to scratch behind his right ear with one paw, returned to the weed with the yellow flowers, sneezed, and had just risen to the top of my List of People or Animals I Most Want to Choke Senseless, when he suddenly went rigid, turned his green eyes toward our animal communicator, and hissed.

"He's got it," Roosevelt said.

Mungojerrie hurried along the serviceway, and we set out after him. Bobby joined us on foot, armed with his shotgun, while Doogie and Sasha followed in the Hummer.

Taking a different route from the one I'd chosen the previous night, we proceeded along a blacktop road, across an athletic field gone to weeds, across a dusty parade ground, between ranks of badly weathered barracks, through a residential neighborhood of Dead Town that I had never explored, where the cottages and bungalows were identical to those on other streets, and overland again, to another service area. After more than half an hour at a brisk pace, we arrived at the last place I wanted to go: the huge, seven-story, Quonset-roofed hangar, as large as a football field, that stands like an alien temple above the egg room.

As it became clear where we were headed, I decided it wouldn't be wise to drive up to the entrance, because the Hummer's engine was noticeably less quiet than the mechanism of a Swiss watch. I waved Doogie toward a passageway between two of the many smaller service buildings that surrounded the giant structure, about a hundred yards from our ultimate destination.

When Doogie killed the engine and the parking lights, the Hummer all but vanished in this nook.

As we gathered behind the vehicle to study the enormous hangar from a distance, the dead night began to breathe. A few miles to the west, the Pacific had exhaled a cool breeze, which now caused a loose sheet-metal panel to vibrate in a nearby roof.

I recalled Roosevelt's words, relayed from Mungojerrie, outside the Stanwyk house: *Death lives here.* I was getting identical but much stronger vibes from the hangar. If Death lived at the Stanwyk place, that was only his pied-à-terre. Here was his primary residence.

"This can't be right," I said hopefully.

"They're in that place," Roosevelt insisted.

"But we were here last night," Bobby protested. "They weren't in the damn place last night."

Roosevelt scooped up the cat, stroked the furry head, chucked the mungo man under the chin, murmured to him, and said, "They *were* here then, the cat says, and they're here now."

Bobby scowled. "This reeks."

"Like a Calcutta sewer," I agreed.

"No, trust me," Doogie said. "A Calcutta sewer is in a class all by itself."

I decided not to pursue the obvious question.

Instead, I said, "If these kids were snatched just to be studied and tested, snatched because their blood samples indicate they're somehow immune to the retrovirus, then they must have been taken to the genetics lab. Wherever that may be, it isn't here."

Roosevelt said, "According to Mungojerrie, the lab he came from is far to the east, in what appears to be open land, where they once had an artillery range. It's very deep underground, hidden out there. But Jimmy, at least, is here. And Orson."

After a hesitation, I said, "Alive?"

Roosevelt said, "Mungojerrie doesn't know."

"Cats know things," Sasha reminded him.

"Not this thing," Roosevelt said.

As we stared at the hangar, I'm sure each of us was remembering Delacroix's audiotape testimony about the Mystery Train. Red sky. Black trees. *A fluttering within* . . .

Doogie removed the backpack from the Hummer, slipped it over his shoulders, closed the tailgate, and said, "Let's go."

During the brief time that the cargo-hold light was on, I saw the weapon he was carrying. It was a wicked-looking piece.

Aware of my interest, he said, "Uzi machine pistol. Extended magazine."

"Is that legal?"

"It would be if it wasn't converted to full automatic fire."

Doogie headed toward the hangar. With the breeze stirring his blond mane and wavy beard, he looked like a Viking warrior leaving a conquered village, heading toward a longboat with a bag of plundered valuables on his back. All he needed to complete the image was a horned helmet.

Into my mind's eye came an image of Doogie in a tuxedo

and such a helmet, leading a supermodel through a perfect tango in a dance competition.

There are two faces to the coin of my rich imagination.

The man-size door, inset in one of the forty-foot-high steel hangar doors, was closed. I couldn't remember whether Bobby and I had shut it on our way out the night before. Probably not. We hadn't been in a clean-up-after-yourself, turn-out-the-lights-and-close-the-door mood when we'd fled this place.

At the door, Doogie extracted two flashlights from jump-suit pockets and gave them to Sasha and Roosevelt, so that Bobby and I would have both hands free for the shotguns.

Doogie tried the door. It opened inward.

Sasha's crossing-the-threshold technique was even smoother than her on-air patter at KBAY. She moved to the left of the door before she switched on the light and swept the beam across the cavernous hangar, which was too large to be entirely within the reach of any flashlight. But she didn't shoot at anyone, and no one shot at her, so it seemed likely that our presence was not yet known.

Bobby followed her, shotgun at the ready. With the cat in his arms, Roosevelt entered after Bobby. I followed, and Doogie brought up the rear, quietly closing the door behind us, as we had found it.

I looked expectantly at Roosevelt.

He stroked the cat and whispered, "We've got to go down."

Because I knew the way, I led the group. Second star to the right, and straight on till morning. Watch out for the pirates and the crocodile with the ticking clock inside.

We crossed the vast room under the tracks that once supported a mobile crane, past the massive steel supports that held up these rails, moving cautiously around the deep wells in the floor, where hydraulic mechanisms had once been housed.

As we progressed, swords of shadow and sabers of light leaped off the elevated steel crane rails and silently fenced with one another across the walls and the curved ceiling. Most of the high clerestory windows were broken out, but reflections flared in the remaining few, like white sparks from clashing blades.

Suddenly I was halted by a sense of wrongness I can't adequately describe: a change in the air too subtle to define; a mild tingle on my face; a quivering of the hairs in my ear canals, as if they were vibrating to a sound beyond my range of hearing.

Sasha and Roosevelt must have felt it, too, because they turned in circles, searching with their flashlights.

Doogie held the Uzi pistol in both hands.

Bobby was near one of the cylindrical steel posts that supported the crane tracks. He reached out, touched it, and whispered, "Bro."

As I moved to his side, I heard a ringing so faint that I could not hold fast to the sound, which repeatedly came and went. When I put my fingertips against the post, I detected vibrations passing through the steel.

Abruptly, the air temperature changed. The hangar had been unpleasantly cool, almost cold; but from one instant to the next, it became fifteen or twenty degrees warmer. This would have been impossible even if the building had still contained a heating plant, which it did not.

Sasha, Doogie, and Roosevelt joined Bobby and me, instinctively forming a circle to guard against a threat from any direction.

The vibrations in the post grew stronger.

I looked toward the east end of the hangar. The door by which we had entered was about twenty yards away. The flashlights were able to reach that far, though they couldn't chase away all the shadows. In that direction, I could see to the end of the shorter length of the overhead crane tracks, and all seemed as it had been when we'd first come into the building.

The flashlights were not able to probe to the west end of the structure, however; it lay at least eighty and perhaps as much as a hundred yards away. As far as I *could* see, there was nothing out of the ordinary.

What bothered me was the unyielding blackness in the last twenty or thirty yards. Not seamless blackness. Many shades of black and deepest grays, a montage of shadows.

I had an impression of a large, looming object concealed in that montage. A towering and complex shape. Something black and gray, so well camouflaged in the gloom that the eye couldn't quite seize upon the outline of it.

Bobby whispered, "Sasha, your light. Here."

She directed it where he pointed, at the floor.

The light gleamed off one of the inch-thick steel angle plates anchored to the concrete, where heavy machinery had once been mounted. These prickled up from the floor at many points in the room.

I didn't understand why Bobby had called our attention to this unremarkable object.

"Clean," he said.

Then I understood. When we had been here last night—in fact, on every occasion that I had passed through this hangar—these angle plates and the bolts holding them down had been smeared with grease and caked with dirt. This one was shiny, clean, as though someone had recently done maintenance on it.

Holding the cat in one arm, Roosevelt moved his light across the floor, up the steel post, across the tracks above us.

"*Everything's* cleaner," Doogie murmured, and he meant not since last night but just since we had entered the hangar.

Though I'd taken my hand off the post, I knew the vibrations in the steel had increased, because I could hear that faint ringing coming from the entire double colonnade that flanked us and from the tracks that the columns supported.

I looked toward the far, dark end of the building, and I swore that something immense was moving in the gloom.

"Bro!" Bobby said.

I glanced at him.

He was gaping at his wristwatch.

I checked mine and saw the digital readouts racing backward.

Sudden fear, like cold rain, washed through me.

A strange muddy red light rose throughout the hangar, evenly distributed, with no apparent source, as if the very molecules of the air had become radiant. Perhaps it was a dangerous light to an XPer like me, but this seemed the least of my troubles at the moment. The red air shimmered, and though the darkness retreated across the entire building, visibility hardly improved. This odd light cloaked as much as it revealed, and I felt almost as if I were underwater, in a drowned world . . . in water tinted with blood.

The flashlight beams were no longer effective. The light that they produced seemed to be trapped behind the lenses, pooling there, rapidly growing brighter and brighter, but unable to pass beyond the glass and penetrate the red air.

Here and there beyond the colonnades, dark forms began to quiver into existence where there had been nothing but bare floor. Machines of some kind. They looked real and yet not real, like objects in a mirage. Phantom machines at the moment . . . but becoming real.

The vibrations were getting louder, and their tone was changing, growing deeper, more ominous. A rumbling.

At the west end of the room, where there had been a troubling darkness, there was now a crane atop the tracks, and hanging from the boom was a massive . . . *something*. An engine, perhaps.

Though I could see the shape of the crane in the dire red light, as well as the object that it was lifting, I could also see *through* them, as if they were made of glass.

In the low rumbling that had grown out of the faint high-pitched ringing in the steel, I recognized the sound of train wheels, steel wheels revolving, grinding along steel tracks.

The crane would have steel wheels. Guide wheels above the track, upstop wheels below to lock it to the rails.

". . . out of the way," Bobby said, and when I looked at him, he was moving, as if in slo-mo, out from beneath the tracks, sliding around a support post with his back pressed to it.

Roosevelt, as wide-eyed as the cat he held, was on the move.

The crane was more solid than it had been a moment ago, less transparent. The big engine—or whatever the crane was transporting—hung from the end of the boom, below the tracks; this payload was the size of a compact car, and it was going to sweep through the space where we were standing as the crane rolled past overhead.

And here it came, moving faster than such a massive piece of equipment could possibly move, because it wasn't really physically coming toward us; rather, I think that time was running backward to the moment when we and this equipment would be occupying the same space at the same instant. Hell, it didn't matter whether it was the crane moving or time moving, because either way the effect would be the same: Two bodies *can't* occupy the same place at the same time. If they tried, either there would be a fierce release of nuclear energy in a blast heard at least as far away as Cleveland, or one of the competing bodies—me or the car-size object dangling from the crane—would cease to exist.

Although I started to move, grabbing at Sasha to pull her with me, I knew that we had no hope of getting out of harm's way in time.

Time.

As we reeled toward a moment in the past when the hangar had been filled with functional equipment, just as the oncoming crane appeared about to click into total reality . . . the temperature suddenly dropped. The muddy red light faded. The rumble of big steel wheels became a higher-pitched ringing.

I expected the crane to retreat, to roll back toward the west end of the building as it grew less substantial. When I looked up, however, it was passing over us, a shimmering mirage of a crane, and the burden that it carried, which was once more as transparent as glass, hit Sasha, then hit me.

Hit isn't the correct word. I don't really know what it did to me. The ghost crane swept past overhead, and the ghost payload enveloped me, passed through me, and vanished on the other side of me. A cold wind briefly shook me. But it didn't even stir my hair. It was entirely internal, an icy breath whistling between my very cells, playing my bones as if they were flutes. For an instant I thought it would blow apart the bonds among the molecules of which I'm composed, dispersing me as though I'd never been anything but dust.

The last of the red light vanished, and the pent-up beams sprang out of the flashlights.

I was still alive, glued together both physically and mentally.

Sasha gasped: "Raw!"

"Killer," I agreed.

Shaken, she leaned against one of the track-support columns.

Doogie had been standing no more than six feet behind me. He had watched the ghost payload pass through us and vanish before it reached him.

"Time to go home?" he wondered only half jokingly.

"Need a glass of warm milk?"

"And six Prozac."

"Welcome to the haunted laboratory," I said.

Joining us, Bobby said, "Whatever was going on in the egg room last night, it's affecting the entire building now."

"Because of us?" I wondered.

"We didn't build the place, bro."

"But did we start it up last night, by energizing it?"

"I don't think, just because we used two flashlights, we're major villains here."

Roosevelt said, "We've got to move fast. The whole place is . . . coming apart."

"Is that what Mungojerrie thinks?" Sasha asked.

In ordinary times, Roosevelt Frost could fix you with a solemn look that any undertaker would envy. With one eye still full of dark amazement at what he had just seen, and with the other eye swollen half shut and shot through with blood, he made me think I'd better pack my bags and get ready to meet that glory-bound train.

He said, "It's not what Mr. Mungojerrie thinks. It's what he *knows*. Everything here is going to . . . come apart. Soon."

"Then let's go down and find the kids and Orson."

Roosevelt nodded. "Let's go down."

24

In the southwest corner of the hangar, the empty elevator shaft was as it had been the previous night. But the stainless-steel jamb and threshold at the stairhead doorway—over-looked by salvagers—were free of grease and dust, which they had not been at any time since I first explored this structure, nearly a year earlier. In the beam from Sasha's flashlight, the first several steps were not covered in dust any longer, and the dead pill bugs were gone.

Either a kindly gnome was preceding us, making the world more pleasing to the eye, or the phenomena that Bobby and I had witnessed in the egg room, one night before, were leaching beyond the walls of that mysterious chamber. My money was not on the gnome.

Mungojerrie stood on the second step, peering down the concrete stairwell, sniffing the air, ears pricked. Then he descended.

Sasha followed the cat.

The stairs were wide enough for two people to walk abreast, with room to spare, and I stayed at Sasha's side, relieved to be sharing the point-position risk with her. Roosevelt followed, then Doogie with the Uzi. Bobby was our tail gunner, keeping his back to one wall, crabbing sideways down the stairs, to make sure no one crept in behind us.

Aside from being suspiciously clean, the first flight of steps was as it had been on my previous visit. Bare concrete on all sides. Evenly spaced core holes in the ceiling, which had once been the end points of electrical chaseways. Painted iron pipe attached to one wall, as a handrail. The air was cold, thick, redolent with the scent of lime that leached from the concrete.

When we reached the landing and turned toward the second flight, I put one hand on Sasha's arm, halting her, and to our feline scout I whispered, "Whoa, cat."

Mungojerrie halted four steps into the next flight and, with an expectant expression, looked up at us.

The ceiling ahead was fitted with fluorescent fixtures. Because these lights weren't switched on, they posed no danger to me.

But they hadn't been here before. They had been torn out and carted away when Fort Wyvern shut down. In fact, this particular structure might have been scoured to the bare concrete long *before* the base was closed, when the Mystery Train ran off the tracks and scared its designers into the realization that their project had been pursued with a truly *loco* motive.

Time past and time present existed here simultaneously, and our future was here, too, though we could not see it. All time, said the poet T. S. Eliot, is eternally present, leading inexorably to an end that we believe results from our actions but over which our control is mere illusion.

At the moment, that bit of Eliot was too bleak for me. While I studied the fluorescent lights, trying to imagine what might wait ahead of us, I mentally recited the initial couplet of the first-ever poetry about Winnie-the-Pooh—"A bear, however hard he tries / Grows tubby without exercise"—but A. A. Milne failed to drive Eliot from my mind.

We could no more retreat from the dangers below, from this eerie confusion of past and present, than I could return to my childhood. Nevertheless, how lovely it would be to crawl under the covers with my own Pooh and Tigger, and pretend that the three of us would be friends, still, when I was a hundred and Pooh was ninety-nine.

"Okay," I told Mungojerrie, and we continued our descent.

When we reached the next landing, which was at the doorway to the first of the three subterranean levels, Bobby whispered, "Bro."

I looked back. The fluorescent-light fixtures above the steps behind us had vanished. The concrete ceiling featured only cored holes from which the fixtures and the wiring had been stripped.

Time present was again more present than time past, at least for the moment.

Scowling, Doogie murmured, "Give me Colombia anytime."

"Or Calcutta," Sasha said.

On behalf of Mungojerrie, Roosevelt said, "Got to hurry. Going to be blood if we don't hurry."

Led by the fearless cat, we slowly descended four more flights, to the third and final level beneath the hangar.

We found no additional indications of hobgoblins or bugaboos until we reached the bottom of the stairwell. As Mungojerrie was about to lead us into the outer corridor that encircles this entire oval-shaped level of the building, the muddy red light that we had first seen on the ground floor of the hangar pulsed beyond the doorway. It lasted only an instant and then was replaced by darkness.

A general dismay rose from our little group, mostly expressed in whispered expletives, and the cat hissed.

Other voices echoed from somewhere in this sub-subbasement, deep and distorted. They were like the voices on a tape played at too slow a speed.

Sasha and Roosevelt switched off their flashlights, leaving us in gloom.

Beyond the doorway, the bloody glow pulsed again, and then several more times, like the revolving emergency beacon on a police cruiser. Each pulse was longer than the one before it, until the darkness in the hallway retreated entirely and the eerie luminosity finally held fast.

The voices were growing louder. They were still distorted, but almost intelligible.

Curiously, not one scintilla of the malign red light in the

corridor penetrated to the space at the bottom of the stairs, where we huddled together. The doorway appeared to be a portal between two realities: utter darkness on this side, the red world on the other side. The line of bloody light along the floor, at the threshold, was as sharp as a knife edge.

As in the hangar upstairs, this radiance brightened the space it filled but did little to illuminate what it touched: a murky light, alive with phantom shapes and movement that could be detected only from the corner of the eye, creating more mysteries than it resolved.

Three tall figures passed the doorway, darker maroon shapes in the red light, perhaps men but possibly something even worse. As these individuals crossed our line of sight, the voices grew louder and less distorted, then faded as the figures moved out of view along the hall.

Mungojerrie padded through the doorway.

I expected him to flare as if sizzled by a death ray, leaving no trace behind except the stink of scorched fur. Instead, he became a small maroon shape, elongated, distorted, not easily identifiable as a cat even though you could tell that he had four feet, a tail, and attitude.

The radiance in the hall began to pulse, now darker than blood, now red-pink, and with each cycle from dark to bright, a throbbing electronic hum swelled through the building, low and ominous. When I touched the concrete wall, it was vibrating faintly, as the steel post had vibrated in the hangar.

Abruptly, the corridor light flashed from red to white. The pulsing stopped. We were looking through the doorway at a hall blazingly revealed under fluorescent ceiling panels.

Instantaneously with the change of light, my ears popped, as if from a sudden decrease in air pressure, and a warm draft gusted into the stairwell, bringing with it a trace of the crisp ozone scent that lingers on a rainy night in the wake of lightning.

Mr. Mungojerrie was in the corridor, no longer a maroon blur, gazing at something off to the right. He was standing not on bare concrete but on clean white ceramic floor tiles that had not been there before.

I peered up the dark stairs behind us, which appeared to be firmly anchored in our time, in the present rather than the past. The building was not phasing entirely in and out of the past; the phenomenon occurred in a crazy-quilt pattern.

I was tempted to sprint up the steps as fast as I could, into the hangar and from there into the night, but we were past the point of no return. We had passed it when Jimmy Wing was kidnapped and Orson disappeared. Friendship required us to venture off the map of the known world, into areas that ancient cartographers couldn't have imagined when they had inked those words *Here there be monsters.*

Squinting, I withdrew my sunglasses from an inside jacket pocket and slipped them on. I had no choice but to risk letting the light bathe my face and hands, but the glare was so bright that it would have stung tears from my eyes.

When we moved cautiously into the corridor, I knew beyond doubt that we had stepped into the past, into a time when this facility had not yet been shut down, before it had been stripped of all evidence. I saw a grease-pencil scheduling chart on one wall, a bulletin board, and two wheeled carts holding peculiar instruments.

The throbbing hum had not fallen silent with the disappearance of the red light. I suspected that it was the sound of the egg room in full operation. It seemed to pierce my eardrums, penetrate my skull, and vibrate directly against the surface of my brain.

Metal doors had appeared on the previously doorless rooms that opened off the inner wall of the curving hallway, and the nearest of these was wide open. In the small chamber beyond, two swivel chairs were unoccupied in front of a complex control board, not unlike the mixing board that any radio-station engineer uses. On one side of this board stood a can of Pepsi and a bag of potato chips, proving that even the architects of doomsday enjoy a snack and a refreshing beverage now and then.

To the right of the stairs, sixty or eighty feet farther along the corridor, three men were moving away from us, unaware that we were behind them. One wore jeans and a white shirt, sleeves rolled up. The second was in a dark suit, and the third wore khakis and a white lab coat. They were walking close together, heads bent, as if conferring, but I couldn't hear their voices over the pulsing electronic hum.

These were surely the three maroon figures that had passed the stairwell in the murky red light, so blurry and distorted that I had not been able to tell whether they were, in fact, human.

I glanced to the left, worrying that someone else might appear and, seeing us, raise an alarm. Currently, however, that length of the corridor was deserted.

Mungojerrie was still watching the departing trio, apparently unwilling to lead us farther until they had rounded the curve in the long racetrack-shaped corridor or entered one of the rooms. This straightaway was five hundred feet long, from curve to curve, and at least a hundred fifty feet remained ahead of the three men before they would turn out of sight.

We were dangerously exposed. We needed to retreat until the Mystery Train staffers were gone. Besides, I was already nervous about the quantity of light that was hammering my face.

I caught Sasha's attention and gestured toward the stairwell.

Her eyes widened.

When I followed her gaze, I saw that a door blocked access to the stairs. From inside the stairwell, there had been no door; we had seen straight through to the red—and then to the fluorescent-drenched—hallway. We had passed directly from there to here without obstruction. From this side, however, the barrier existed.

I went quickly to the door, yanked it open, and almost crossed the threshold. Fortunately, I hesitated when I sensed a *wrongness* about the darkness beyond.

Sliding my sunglasses down my nose, peering over the frames, I expected concrete-walled gloom with steps leading up. Instead, before me was a clear night sky, necklaces of stars, and a pendant moon. This skyscape was the *only* thing out there where the stairs had been, as though this door now opened high above the earth's atmosphere, in interplanetary space, a long way from the nearest doughnut shop. Or perhaps it opened into a time when the earth no longer existed. No floor lay beyond the threshold, nothing but empty space jeweled with more stars, a cold and infinite drop from the bright corridor in which I stood.

Sharky.

I closed the door. I gripped the shotgun fiercely in both hands, not because I expected to use it but because it was *real*, solid and unyielding, an anchor in this sea of strangeness.

Sasha was now immediately behind me.

When I turned to face her, I could tell that she had seen the same celestial panorama that had rocked me. Her gray eyes were as clear as ever, but they were darker than before.

Doogie hadn't glimpsed the impossible sight, because he was holding the Uzi at the ready and watching the three departing men.

Frowning, standing with his fists balled tightly at his sides, Roosevelt studied the cat.

From his position, Bobby couldn't have seen through the doorway, either, but he knew something was wrong. His face was as solemn as that of a rabbit reading a cookbook recipe for hare soup.

Mungojerrie was the only one of us who didn't appear to be about to blow out snarled springs like an overwound cuckoo clock.

Trying not to dwell on what I'd seen beyond the stairwell door, I wondered how the cat could find Orson and the kids if they were in a present-time place while we were stuck here in the past. But then I figured that if we could pass from one time period to another, be caught up in the time shifts taking place around us, so could my four-footed brother and the children.

Anyway, from every indication, we hadn't actually traveled back in time. Rather, the past and present—and perhaps the future—were occurring simultaneously, weirdly pressed together by whatever force or force field the engines of the egg room had generated. And perhaps it was not only one night from the past that was bleeding into our present time; maybe we were experiencing moments from different days and nights when the egg room had been in operation.

The three men were still walking away from us. Ambling. Taking their sweet time.

The rhythmic swell and recession of the electronic sound began to have an odd psychological effect. A mild vertigo overcame me, and the corridor—this entire subterranean floor—seemed to be turning like a carousel.

My grip on the shotgun was too fierce. Unwittingly, I was exerting dangerous pressure on the trigger. I hooked my finger around the trigger guard instead.

I had a headache. It wasn't a result of being knocked around by Father Tom at the Stanwyk house. I was sustaining a brain bruise from pondering time paradoxes, from trying to make sense of what was happening. This required a talent for mathematics and theoretical physics; but although I can balance my checkbook, I haven't inherited my mother's love of math and science. In the most general sense, I understand the theory of leverage that explains the function of a bottle opener, why gravity makes it a bad idea to leap off a high building, and why running headlong into a brick wall will have little effect on the bricks. Otherwise, I trust the cosmos to run itself efficiently without my having to understand it, which is also pretty much my attitude toward electric razors, wristwatches, bread-baking machines, and other mechanical devices.

The only way to deal with these events was to treat them as supernatural occurrences, accept them as you might accept poltergeist phenomena—levitating chairs, hurtling knick-knacks, doors slammed by invisible presences—or the spectral appearance of a moldering and semitransparent corpse glimpsed on a midnight stroll in a graveyard. Thinking too much about time-bending force fields and time paradoxes and reality shifts, straining to grasp the logic of it, would only make me crazy, when what I desperately needed to be was cool. Calm. Therefore, this structure was just a haunted house. Our best hope of finding our way through its many rooms and back to the safer side of the spook zone was to remember that ghosts can't hurt you unless you yourself give them the power to harm you, unless you feed their substance with your fear. This is the classic theory, well known to spirit channelers and ghostbusters all over the world. I think I read it in a comic book.

The three ghosts were just fifty feet from the turn that would finally take them out of sight, around one arc of the long racetrack corridor.

They stopped. Stood with their heads together. Talking above the throbbing noise that flooded the building.

The specter in the jeans and white shirt turned to a door and opened it.

Then the other two wraiths—the one in the suit, the one in the khakis and lab coat—continued toward the end of the hall.

As he opened the door, the first spook must have registered us in his peripheral vision. He swung toward us, as though *he* had seen ghosts.

He took a couple steps in our direction but then halted, maybe because he noticed our guns.

He shouted. His words weren't clear, but he wasn't suggesting a tour and complimentary lunch in the cafeteria.

Anyway, he wasn't calling to us but to the pair of phantasms strolling toward the turn in the corridor. They spun around and gaped at us as though they were stunned sailors gazing at the ghost ship *Marie Celeste* gliding silently past in a light fog.

We had spooked them as much as they had spooked us.

The one in the suit evidently wasn't merely a well-tailored scientist or a project bureaucrat, and certainly not a Jehovah's Witness pushing *Watchtower* magazine in a tough territory, because he drew a handgun from a holster under his jacket.

I reminded myself that ghosts couldn't hurt us unless we gave them power by feeding them with our fear—and then I wondered if this rule applied to haunts packing heat. I wished that I could remember the name of the comic book in which I'd chanced upon this wisdom, because if the information had been in *Tales from the Crypt*, it might be true, but if it was from an issue of Donald Duck adventures, then I was screwed.

Instead of opening fire on us, the armed apparition pushed past his two phantom friends and disappeared through the door that the one in jeans had opened.

He was probably running for a telephone, to call security. We were about to be crunched, swept up, bagged, and put out for garbage collection.

Around us, the corridor *rippled*, and things changed.

The white ceramic floor tiles quickly faded beneath us, leaving us standing on bare concrete, although I felt nothing move underfoot. Here and there along the hall, patches of tile remained, the edges not sharply defined, feathering into the concrete, as though these were widely scattered puddles of time past that hadn't yet evaporated from the floor of time present.

The rooms opening along the inner wall of the corridor no longer had doors.

Shadows swarmed as the fluorescent panels began to disappear from the ceiling. Yet, in an irregular pattern, a few fixtures remained, brightening widely separated sections of the corridor.

I took off my sunglasses and pocketed them as the grease-pencil scheduling chart dissolved from the wall. The bulletin board still hung unchanged.

One of the wheeled carts faded away before my eyes. The other cart remained, though a few of the odd instruments racked on it were becoming transparent.

The ghost in blue jeans and the ghost in a lab coat really looked like spirits now, mere ectoplasmic entities that had congealed out of a white mist. They started hesitantly toward us, then began to run, perhaps because we were fading from their view just as they were disappearing from ours. They covered only half the ground between us before they vanished.

The suit with the gun returned to the hallway from the office, having raved to security about Vikings in jumpsuits and invading cats, but he was now the weakest of revenants, a shimmering wraith. As he raised his weapon, he departed time present without a trace.

The throbbing electronic noise was less than half as loud as it had been at full power, but like some of the lights and floor tiles, it didn't fade altogether.

None of us was relieved by this reprieve. Instead, as the past receded into the past where it belonged, we were seized by a greater urgency.

Mr. Mungojerrie was dead right: This place was coming apart. The residual effect of the Mystery Train was gathering power, feeding on itself, extending beyond the egg room, rapidly seeping throughout the structure. The ultimate effect was unknowable but sure to be catastrophic.

I could hear a clock ticking. This wasn't the timepiece in Captain Hook's omnivorous crocodile, either, but the reliable clock of instinct telling me that we were on a short countdown to destruction.

With the ghosts gone, the cat sprang into action, padding to the nearby elevator shaft.

"Down," Roosevelt translated. "Mungojerrie says we have to go farther down."

"There's nothing below this floor," I said, as we all gathered at the elevator. "We're on the lowest level."

The cat fixed its luminous green eyes on me, and Roosevelt said, "No, there're three levels beneath this one. They required an even higher security clearance than these floors, so they were concealed."

During my explorations, I'd never thought to look into the shaft to see if it served hidden realms that couldn't be accessed by the stairs.

Roosevelt said, "The lower levels can be approached . . . from some other building on the base, through a tunnel. Or by this elevator. The steps don't go down as far."

This development posed a problem, because the elevator shaft wasn't empty. We couldn't simply climb down the service ladder and go where Mungojerrie directed. Like the scattered floor tiles, like the few remaining fluorescent panels, and like the softer but still ominous electronic hum that throbbed through the building, the past maintained tenacious control of the elevator. A pair of stainless-steel sliding doors covered the shaft, and most likely a cab waited beyond them.

"We'll be quashed if we hang around here," Bobby predicted, reaching out to press the elevator call button.

"Wait!" I cautioned, stopping his hand before he could do the deed.

Doogie said, "Bobster's right, Chris. Sometimes fortune favors the foolhardy."

I shook my head. "What if we get in the elevator, and when the doors close, the damn thing just totally vanishes under us like the floor tiles did?"

"Then we fall to the bottom of the shaft," Sasha guessed, but that prospect didn't seem to give her pause.

"Some of us might break our ankles," Doogie predicted. "Not all of us, necessarily. It's probably only about forty feet or so, a mean drop but survivable."

Bobby, a Road Runner cartoon freak, said, "Bro, we could have ourselves a full-on Wile E. Coyote moment."

"We've got to move," Roosevelt warned, and Mungojerrie scratched impatiently at the stainless-steel doors, which remained stubbornly solid.

Bobby pressed the call button.

The elevator whined toward us. With the oscillating electronic hum continuing to pulse through the building, I couldn't determine whether the cab was descending or ascending.

The corridor *rippled*.

The floor tiles began to reappear under my feet.

The elevator doors slowly, slowly slid open.

Fluorescent panels reappeared on the corridor ceiling, and I narrowed my eyes against the glare.

The cab was full of muddy red light, which probably meant the interior of the shaft occupied a different point in time from the place—or places—that we occupied. There were passengers, a lot of them.

We stepped back from the door, expecting the crowd in the elevator to give us trouble.

In the corridor, the throbbing sound grew louder.

I could discern several blurry, distorted, maroon figures inside the cab, but I couldn't see who or what they were.

A gunshot cracked, then another.

We were under fire not from the elevator but from the end of the corridor where, earlier, the sonofabitch in the suit had drawn down on us with a handgun.

Bobby took a bullet. Something peppered my face. Bobby rocked backward, the shotgun flying out of his hands. He was still dropping as if in slow motion when I realized that hot blood had sprayed my face. Bobby's blood. Jesus, God. Even as I was swiveling toward the source of the gunfire, I discharged my shotgun and immediately chambered another shell.

Instead of the guy in the dark suit, there were two guards we had never seen before. Uniforms, but not army. No service that I recognized. Project cops. Mystery Train security. Too far away to be anything other than annoyed by my shotgun fire.

Another piece of the past had solidified around us, and Doogie triggered the Uzi as Bobby hit the floor and bounced. The machine pistol settled the dispute totally and abruptly.

Sickened, I looked away from the two dead guards.

The elevator doors had closed before anyone stepped out of the crowded cab.

The gunfire was sure to draw more security.

Bobby lay on his back. Blood was spattered on the white ceramic tile around him. Too much blood.

Sasha stooped at his left side. I knelt at his right.

She said, "Hit once."

"Got biffed," Bobby said, *biffed* meaning smacked hard by a wave.

"Hang in there," I said.

"Totally thrashed," he said, and coughed.

"Not totally," I insisted, more terrified than I had ever been before, but determined not to show it.

Sasha unbuttoned the Hawaiian shirt, hooked her fingers in the bullet-punctured material of Bobby's black pullover, and ripped the sweater to expose the wound in his left shoulder. The hole was too low in the shoulder, too far to the right, something you would have to call a chest wound, not a shoulder wound, if you were going to be honest, which I was by God *not* going to be.

"Shoulder wound," I told him.

The throbbing electronic sound dwindled, the ceramic tiles faded under Bobby, taking the spatters of blood with them, and the overhead fluorescent panels began to vanish, though not all of them. Time past was surrendering to time present again, entering another cycle, which might give us a minute or two before more uniformed abbs with guns showed up.

Rich blood, so deeply red that it was almost black, welled out of the wound. We could do nothing to stop this type of bleeding. Neither a tourniquet nor a compress would help. Neither would hydrogen peroxide, rubbing alcohol, Neosporin, and gauze bandages, even if we'd had any of those things.

"Woofy," he said.

The pain had washed away his perpetual tan, leaving him not white but jaundice-yellow. He looked bad.

The hallway had fewer lingering fluorescents and the oscillating hum was quieter than during the previous cycle.

I was afraid the past was going to fade entirely out of the present, leaving us with an empty elevator shaft. I wasn't confident that we could carry Bobby up six flights of stairs without causing him further damage.

Getting to my feet, I glanced at Doogie, whose solemn expression infuriated me, because Bobby was going to be all right, damn it.

Mungojerrie scratched at the elevator doors again.

Roosevelt was either doing as the cat wished or following my own track of reasoning, because he repeatedly jammed his thumb against the call button.

The indicator board above the doors showed only four floors—G, B-1, B-2, and B-3—though we knew there were seven. The cab was supposedly up at the first level, *G* for *ground,* which was the hangar above this subterranean facility.

"Come on, come on," Roosevelt muttered.

Bobby tried to lift his head to reconnoiter, but Sasha gently pressed him back, with one hand on his forehead.

He might go into shock. Ideally, his head should be lower than the rest of him, but we didn't have any means to elevate his legs and lower body. Shock kills as surely as bullets. His lips were slightly blue. Wasn't that an early symptom of shock?

The cab was at B-1, the first basement under the hangar floor. We were on B-3.

Mungojerrie was staring at me as if to say, *I warned you.*

"Cats don't know shit," I told him angrily.

Surprisingly, Bobby laughed. It was a weak laugh, but it was a laugh nonetheless. Could he be dying or even slipping into shock if he were laughing? Maybe everything would be okay.

Just call me Pollyanna Huckleberry Holly Golightly Snow.

The elevator reached B-2, one floor above us.

I raised the shotgun, in case passengers were in the elevator, as there evidently had been before.

Already, the pulsing hum of the egg room engines—or whatever infernal machines made the noise—grew louder.

"Better hurry," Doogie said, because if the wrong moment of the past flowed into the present again, it might wash some angry, armed men with it.

The elevator whined to a stop at B-3, our floor.

The corridor around me grew steadily brighter.

As the elevator doors began to slide open, I expected to see the murky red light in the cab, and then I was suddenly afraid I'd be confronted with that impossible vista of stars and cold black space I'd seen beyond the stairwell door.

The elevator cab was just an elevator cab. Empty.

"Move!" Doogie urged.

Roosevelt and Sasha already had Bobby on his feet, virtually carrying him between them, while trying to minimize the strain on his left shoulder.

I held the elevator door, and as they took Bobby past me,

his face twisted with agony. If he had been about to scream with pain, he repressed it and instead said, *"Carpe cerevisi."*

"Beer later," I promised.

"Beer now, party boy," he wheezed.

Slipping off his backpack, Doogie followed us into the big elevator, which could probably carry fifteen passengers. The cab briefly swayed and jiggled as it adjusted to his weight, and we all tried not to step on Mungojerrie.

"Up and out," I said.

"Down," Bobby disagreed.

The control panel had no buttons for the three floors that were supposedly below us. An unlabeled slot for a magnetic card indicated how someone with the proper security clearance could reprogram the existing control buttons to gain access to lower realms. We didn't have a card.

"There's no way to get farther down," I said.

"Always a way," Doogie demurred, rummaging in his backpack.

The corridor was bright. The loud throbbing sound grew louder.

The elevator doors rolled shut, but we didn't go anywhere, and when I reached toward the *G* button, Doogie slapped my hand as though I were a child reaching for a cookie without having asked permission.

"This is nuts," I said.

"Radically," Bobby agreed.

He sagged against the back wall of the cab, supported by Sasha and Roosevelt. He was gray now.

I said, "Bro, you don't have to be a hero."

"Yeah, I do."

"No, you *don't!*"

"Kahuna."

"What?"

"If I'm Kahuna, I can't be a chickenshit."

"You aren't Kahuna."

"King of the surf," he said. When he coughed this time, blood bubbled on his lips.

Desperate, I said to Sasha, "We're getting him up and out of here, right now."

A crack and then a creak sounded behind me. Doogie had picked the lock on the control panel and had swung the cover aside, exposing the wiring. "What floor?" he asked.

"Mungojerrie says all the way down," Roosevelt advised.

I protested: "Orson, the kids—we don't even know if they're alive!"

"They're alive," Roosevelt said.

"We don't *know*."

"We know."

I turned to Sasha for support. "Are you as crazy as the rest of them?"

She said nothing, but the pity in her eyes was so terrible that I had to look away from her. She knew that Bobby and I were as tight as friends can get, that we were brothers in all but blood, as close as identical twins. She knew that a part of me was going to die when Bobby died, leaving an emptiness even she would never fill. She saw my vulnerability; she would have done anything, anything, *anything,* if she could have saved Bobby, but she could do nothing. In her helplessness, I saw my own helplessness, which I couldn't bear to contemplate.

I lowered my gaze to the cat. For an instant I wanted to *stomp* Mungojerrie, crush the life out of him, as if he were responsible for our being here. I had asked Sasha if she was as crazy as the rest of them; in truth, I was the one who was kooking out, shattered by even the prospect of losing Bobby.

With a lurch, the elevator started down.

Bobby groaned.

I said, "Please, Bobby."

"Kahuna," he reminded me.

"You're not Kahuna, you kak."

His voice was thin, shaky: "Pia thinks I am."

"Pia's a dithering airhead."

"Don't dis my woman, bro."

We stopped on the seventh and final level.

The doors opened on darkness. But it wasn't that view of starry space, merely a lightless alcove.

With Roosevelt's flashlight, I led the others out of the elevator, into a cold, dank vestibule.

Down here, the oscillating electronic hum was muffled, almost inaudible.

We put Bobby on his back, to the left of the elevator doors. We laid him on my jacket and Sasha's, to insulate him from the concrete as much as possible.

Sasha fiddled in the control wiring and temporarily disabled the elevator, so it would be here when we returned. Of course, if time past phased completely out of time present, taking the elevator with it, we'd have to climb.

Bobby couldn't climb. And we could never carry him up a service ladder, not in his condition.

Don't think about it. Ghosts can't hurt you if you don't fear them, and bad things won't happen if you don't think them.

I was grasping at all the defenses of childhood.

Doogie emptied stuff out of the backpack. With Roosevelt's help, he folded the empty bag and wedged it under Bobby's hips, elevating his lower body at least slightly, though not enough.

When I put the flashlight at Bobby's side, he said, "I'll probably be way safer in the dark, bro. Light might draw attention."

"Switch it off if you hear anything."

"You switch it off before you leave," he said. "I can't."

When I took his hand, I was shocked at the weakness of his grip. He literally didn't have the strength to handle the flashlight.

There was no point leaving him a gun for self-defense.

I didn't know what to say to him. I had never been seriously speechless with Bobby before. I seemed to have a mouth full of dirt, as if I were already lying in my own grave.

"Here," Doogie said, handing me a pair of oversize goggles and an unusual flashlight. "Infrared goggles. Israeli military surplus. Infrared flashlight."

"What for?"

"So they won't see us coming."

"Who?"

"Whoever's got the kids and Orson."

I stared at Doogie Sassman as if he were a Viking from Mars.

Bobby's teeth chattered when he said, "The dude's a ballroom dancer, too."

A rumbling noise rose, like a freight train passing overhead, and the floor shook under us. Gradually, the sound diminished, and the shaking stopped.

"Better go," Sasha said.

She, Doogie, and Roosevelt were wearing goggles, with the lenses against their foreheads rather than over their eyes.

Bobby had closed his eyes.

Frightened, I said, "Hey."

"Hey," he replied, looking at me again.

"Listen, if you die on me," I said, "then you're king of the assholes."

He smiled. "Don't worry. Wouldn't want to take the title away from you, bro."

"We'll be back fast."

"I'll be here," he assured me, but his voice was a whisper. "You promised me a beer."

His eyes were inexpressibly kind.

There was so much to be said. None of it could be spoken. Even if we'd had plenty of time, none of what was in my heart could have been spoken.

I switched off his flashlight but left it at his side.

Darkness was usually my friend, but I hated this hungry, cold, demanding blackness.

The fancy eyewear featured a Velcro strap. My hands were so unsteady that I needed a moment to adjust the goggles to my head, and then I lowered the lenses over my eyes.

Doogie, Roosevelt, and Sasha had switched on their infrared flashlights. Without the goggles, I had not been able to see that wavelength of light, but now the vestibule was revealed in various shades and intensities of green.

I clicked the button on my flashlight and played the beam over Bobby Halloway.

Supine on the floor, arms at his sides, glowing green, he might already have been a ghost.

"Your shirt really pops in this weird light," I said.

"Yeah?"

"Bitchin'."

The freight-train rumble rose again, louder than before. The steel and concrete bones of the structure were grinding together.

The cat, with no need for goggles, led us out of the vestibule. I followed Roosevelt, Doogie, and Sasha, who might have been three green spirits haunting a catacomb.

The hardest thing I'd ever had to do in my life—harder than attending my mother's funeral, harder than sitting by my father's deathbed—was to leave Bobby alone.

25

From the vestibule, a sloping tunnel, ten feet in diameter, descended fifty feet. After reaching the bottom, we followed an entirely horizontal but wildly serpentine course, and with every turn, the architecture and engineering progressed from curious to strange to markedly alien.

The first passageway featured concrete walls, but every tunnel thereafter, while formed of reinforced concrete, appeared to be lined with metal. Even in the inadequately revelatory infrared light, I detected sufficient differences in the appearances of these curved surfaces to be confident that the type of metal changed from time to time. If I'd lifted the goggles and switched on an ordinary UV flashlight, I suspect that I would have seen steel, copper, brass, and an array of alloys that I couldn't have identified without a degree in metallurgy.

The largest of these metal-lined tunnels were about eight feet in diameter, but we traveled some that were half that size, through which we had to crawl. In the walls of these cylindrical causeways were uncounted smaller openings; some were two or three inches in diameter, others two feet; probing them with the infrared flashlight revealed nothing more than could have been seen by peering into a drainpipe or a gun barrel. We might have been inside an enormous, incomprehensibly elaborate set of refrigeration coils, or exploring the plumbing that served all the palaces of all the gods of ancient myths.

Unquestionably, something had once surged through this colossal maze: liquids or gases. We passed numerous tributaries, in which were anchored turbines with blades that must have been driven by whatever had been pumped through this system. At many junctions, various types of gigantic electrically controlled valves stood ready to cut off, restrict, or redirect the flow through these Stygian channels. All the valves were in open or half-open positions; but as we passed each block point, I worried that if they snapped shut, we would be imprisoned down here.

These tubes had not been stripped to the concrete, as had all the rooms and corridors in the first three floors under the hangar. Consequently, as there were no apparent lighting sources, I assumed that workmen servicing the system had always carried lamps.

Intermittently, a draft stirred along these strange highways, but for the most part the atmosphere was as still as that under a bell jar. Twice, I caught a whiff of smoldering charcoal, but otherwise the air carried only a faint astringent scent similar to iodine, though not iodine, which eventually left a bitter taste and caused a mild burning sensation in my nasal membranes.

The trainlike rumble came and went, lasting longer with each occurrence, and the silences between these assaults of sound grew shorter. With every eruption, I expected the ceiling to collapse, burying us as irrevocably as coal miners are occasionally entombed in veins of anthracite. Another and utterly chilling sound spiraled along the tunnel walls from time to time, a shrill keening that must have had its source in some machinery spinning itself to destruction, or else crawling these byways was a creature that I had never heard before and that I hoped never to encounter.

I fought off attacks of claustrophobia, then induced new bouts by wondering if I were in the sixth circle of Hell or the seventh. But wasn't the seventh the Lake of Boiling Blood? Or did that come *after* the Fiery Desert? Neither the blood lake nor the great burning sands would be green, and everything here was relentlessly green. Anyway, Lower Hell couldn't be far away, just past the luncheonette that serves only spiders and scorpions, around the corner from the men's shop that offers bramble shirts and shoes with razor-blade in-cushions. Or maybe this wasn't Hell at all; maybe it was just the belly of the whale.

I think I went a little nuts—and then recovered—before we reached our destination.

For sure, I lost all track of time, and I was convinced that we were ruled by the clock of Purgatory, on which the minute and hour hands turn without ever advancing. Days later, Sasha would claim we had spent less than fifteen minutes in those tunnels. She never lies. Yet, when eventually we prepared to return the way we had come, if she had tried to convince me that retracing our route would require only a quarter of an hour, I would have assumed we were in whatever circle of Hell was reserved for pathological liars.

The final passage—which would lead us to the kidnappers and their hostages—was one of the larger tunnels, and when we entered it, we discovered that the abbs we were seeking—or at least one of them, anyway—had posted a neatly arranged gallery of perverse achievement. Newspaper articles and a few other items were taped to the curved metal wall; the text was not easily readable by the infrared flashlights, but the headlines, subheads, and some of the pictures were clear enough.

We played our lights over the various items, quickly absorbing the exhibition, trying to understand why it was here.

The first clipping was from the *Moonlight Bay Gazette,* dated July 18, forty-four years earlier. Bobby's grandfather had been the publisher in those days, before the paper had passed to Bobby's mother and father. The headline screamed, BOY ADMITS TO KILLING PARENTS, and the subhead read, 12-YEAR-OLD CAN'T BE TRIED FOR MURDER.

The headlines on several additional clippings from the *Gazette,* dating to that same summer and the following autumn, described the aftermath of these murders, which apparently had been committed by a disturbed boy named John Joseph Randolph. Ultimately, he had been remanded to a juvenile detention center in the northern part of the state, until he achieved the age of eighteen, by which time he would have been psychologically evaluated; if declared criminally insane, he would subsequently be hospitalized for long-term psychiatric care.

The three pictures of young John showed a towheaded boy, tall for his age, with pale eyes, slim but athletic-looking. In all the shots, which appeared to be family photographs taken prior to the homicides, he had a winning smile.

That July night, he'd shot his father in the head. Five times. Then he hacked his mother to death with an ax.

The name John Joseph Randolph was unnervingly familiar, though I couldn't think why.

On one of the clippings, I spotted a subhead that referred to the arresting police officer: Deputy Louis Wing. Lilly's father-in-law. Jimmy's grandfather. Lying now in a coma in a nursing home, after suffering three strokes.

Louis Wing will be my servant in Hell.

Evidently, Jimmy had not been abducted because his blood sample, given at preschool, had revealed an immune factor protecting him from the retrovirus. Instead, old-fashioned vengeance was the motivation.

"Here," Sasha said. She pointed to another clipping, where the subhead revealed the name of the presiding judge: George Dulcinea. Great-grandfather to Wendy. Fifteen years in the grave.

George Dulcinea will be my servant in Hell.

No doubt, Del Stuart or someone in his family had crossed John Joseph Randolph somewhere, sometime. If we knew the connection, it would expose a motive for vengeance.

John Joseph Randolph. The strangely familiar name continued to worry me. As I followed Sasha and the others along the gallery, I seined my memory but came up with an empty net.

The next clipping dated back thirty-seven years and dealt with the murder-dismemberment of a sixteen-year-old girl in a San Francisco suburb. Police, according to the subhead, had no leads.

The newspaper had published the dead girl's high-school photo. Across her face, someone had used a felt-tip marker to print four slashing letters: MINE.

It occurred to me that if he hadn't been diagnosed criminally insane prior to turning eighteen, John Joseph Randolph might have been released from juvenile detention that year—with a handshake, an expunged record, pocket money, and a prayer.

The following thirty-five years were chronicled by thirty-five clippings concerning thirty-five apparently unsolved, savage murders. Two-thirds had been committed in California, from San Diego and La Jolla to Sacramento and Yucaipa; the rest were spread over Arizona, Nevada, and Colorado.

The victims—each photo defaced with the word MINE—presented no easily discernible pattern. Men and women. Young and old. Black, white, Asian, Hispanic. Straight and gay. If all these were the work of the same man, and if that man was John Joseph Randolph, then our Johnny was an equal-opportunity killer.

From a cursory examination of the clippings, I could see only two details linking these numerous murders. First: the horrendous degree of violence with which they had been committed, whether with blunt or sharp instruments. The headlines used words like BRUTAL, VICIOUS, SAVAGE, and SHOCKING. Second: None of the victims was sexually molested; Johnny's only passions were bashing and slashing.

But only one event per calendar year. When Johnny indulged in his annual murder, he *really* let himself go, burnt off all his excess energy, poured out every drop of pent-up bile. Nonetheless, for a lifelong serial killer with such a prodigious career, his three hundred and sixty-four days of self-restraint for every single day of maniacal butchery were surely without precedent in the annals of sociopathic homicide. What had he been *doing* during those days of restraint? Into what had all that violent energy been directed?

In less than two minutes, as I quickly scanned this montage of mementos from Johnny's scrapbook, my claustrophobia had been pressed out of me by a more fundamental, more visceral terror. The faint but constant electronic hum, the trainlike rumble, and the less frequent but fearsome keening combined to mask any sounds that we made as we approached the killer's lair, but the same cacophony might screen the sounds that Johnny made as he crept up on us.

I was the last in our procession, and each time I glanced back the way we had come—which was about every ten seconds—I was certain old Johnny Randolph would be there, about to strike at me, slithering snakelike on his belly or crawling spiderlike across the ceiling.

Evidently, he had been a brutal killer all his life. Was he now *becoming*? Was that why he snatched these kids and squirreled them away in this weird place—in addition to the desire for revenge on those who had proved he'd killed his parents and had locked him away? If a good man like Father Tom could spiral so far down into madness and savagery, how much farther into the heart of darkness could John Randolph descend? What unthinkable beast might he become, considering where he'd started?

In retrospect, I realize that I was *encouraging* my imagination to spin even further out of control than usual, because as long as it was feverishly conjuring crawly fears of bizarro Johnny, it wasn't able to taunt me with images of Bobby Halloway alone and helpless, bleeding to death in the elevator alcove.

Following Sasha, Doogie, and Roosevelt, I swiftly played the infrared beam over the final cluster of clippings.

Two years ago, the frequency of these killings increased. Judging by the presentation on this wall, they were occurring every three months. The headlines roared of sensational mass murders, not of solitary victims anymore: three to six souls per pop.

Perhaps this was when Johnny had decided to bring in a partner: the stocky charmer who had so earnestly endeavored to give me some skull exercise in the hallway under the warehouse. Where do tandem killers meet? Probably not at church. How do they decide to divide the labor, or do they just take turns sweeping up after?

With a fun partner, perhaps, Johnny had expanded his territory, and the clippings showed him venturing as far as Connecticut and then south to sunny Georgia. On to Florida. A jaunt over to Louisiana. A long ride up to the Dakotas. Travelin' man.

Johnny's weapons of choice had changed: no more hammers, no lengths of iron pipe, no knives, no meat cleavers, no ice picks, no hatchets, not even any labor-saving chain saws or power drills. These days the lad favored fire.

And these days his victims fit a clear, consistent profile. For the past two years, they had all been children.

Were they all the children or grandchildren of people who had once crossed him? Or perhaps until these latest abductions, he'd been motivated solely by the thrill of it.

I was more than ever frightened for the four kids now in John Joseph Randolph's hands. I took some cold comfort from the knowledge that, according to the clippings in this demonic gallery, when he committed these atrocities against groups of victims, he destroyed them all at once, in a single fire, as if making a burnt offering. Therefore, if one of the kidnapped children was alive, then all were probably still alive.

We had assumed that the disappearances of Jimmy Wing and the other three were related to the gene-swapping retrovirus and to the events at Wyvern. But not all the evil in the world arises directly from my mom's work. John Joseph Randolph had been busy prepping for Hell from at least his twelfth year, and perhaps what I'd suggested to Bobby last night was true: Randolph might have imprisoned these children here for no other reason than that he had stumbled upon the place and enjoyed the atmosphere, the satanic architecture.

The gallery ended with two startling items.

Taped to the wall was a sheet of art paper bearing the likeness of a crow. *The* crow. The crow on the rock at the top of Crow Hill. This was an impression that had been made by pressing the paper over the incised stone and rubbing it with graphite until the image appeared.

Beside the crow was a Mystery Train patch of the kind that we'd seen on the breast of William Hodgson's spacesuit.

Already, then, Wyvern was back in the picture. There *was* a connection between Randolph and top-secret research conducted on the base, but the link might not be my mother or her retrovirus.

A rock of truth was visible in this sea of confusion, and I strove to get a grip on it, but my mind was exhausted, weak, and the rock was slippery.

John Joseph Randolph wasn't merely becoming. Maybe he wasn't becoming at all. His connection to Wyvern was more complex than that.

I dimly remembered a story about a wacko kid killing his folks in a house on the edge of town, out along Haddenbeck Road, a lot of years ago, but if I'd ever known his name, I'd long forgotten it. Moonlight Bay was a conservative community, assiduously well groomed for tourists; the citizens preferred to talk up the fine scenery and the seductively easy lifestyle, while playing down the negatives. Johnny Randolph, self-made orphan, would never have been featured in the chamber of commerce literature or written up in the *Mobil Guide* under local historical figures.

If he'd returned to Moonlight Bay as an adult, long before the recent child snatchings, to work or live here, *that* would have been major news. The past would have been dredged up, and I would have known all the gossip.

He might, of course, have come back under a new name, having legally changed from John Joseph Randolph with the sanction of the doting therapists at the facility where he'd been incarcerated, in the interest of putting his troubled past behind him and starting his life anew, with a healed heart and enhanced self-esteem and blah-blah-blah. Fully grown, no longer recognizable as the infamous dad-blasting, mom-chopping twelve-year-old, he might have walked unknown on the streets of his hometown. He might have gone to work at Fort Wyvern in some capacity associated with the Mystery Train.

John Joseph Randolph.

The name still gnawed at me.

Now, as Mungojerrie led us along the final length of this tunnel, which appeared to be a dead end, I took one last look at the gallery—and thought I grasped the purpose of it.

Initially it had seemed to be a bragging wall, the equivalent of a star athlete's trophy case, a display that would make Johnny tuck his thumbs in his armpits, puff out his chest, and strut. Homicidal sociopaths are proud of their handiwork but can seldom risk opening their scrapbooks and grisly souvenir collections for the admiration of family and neighbors; they are forced to preen privately.

Then I had thought the gallery was nothing more than pornography to titillate a radically twisted mind. To this freak, the newspaper headlines might be the equivalent of obscene dialogue. The victim and crime-scene photographs might get him off more readily than any triple-X adult film ever made.

But now I saw that the display was an offering. His whole life was an offering. The murder of his parents, the single killing every twelve months, his three hundred sixty-four days of stern self-denial each year, and recently the storm of child murders. *Burnt offerings.* As I studied the vile gallery, I didn't know to whom these terrible gifts were made, or for what purpose; although even at that point, I would have been willing to hazard a guess.

The tunnel ended at a fully deployed, eight-foot-diameter gate valve, which had once been operated by an electric motor.

When Doogie set aside his machine pistol and hooked his fingers into a groove on the face of the valve, without the aid of a motor he was able to roll the barrier aside almost as easily as he would have retracted a sliding door. Although unused for more than two years, it traveled in its recessed tracks with only a little noise, which was, in any case, lost in the increasingly ominous sounds that rumbled and squealed through these drained guts of the "temporal relocator."

Oddly enough, I thought of the awestricken, shipwrecked seamen who had been rescued by Captain Nemo in *20,000 Leagues Under the Sea* and then given a tour of the labyrinthine mechanical bowels of the megalomaniac's *Nautilus*. Eventually they might have felt enough at home aboard that leviathan of a submarine to break out the hornpipe, play a tune, and dance a sprightly jig; but even the most gregarious and adaptable of folks, left to prowl the seemingly endless metal intestines here below the egg room, would forever feel that they were in alien and hostile territory.

Although Doogie opened the doorlike valve only three feet, lamplight poured through from a space beyond, flaring with blinding power in my infrared lenses.

I raised the goggles to my brow, switched off the infrared flashlight and jammed it under my belt. The lamplight wasn't as bright as I had expected; the lenses had exaggerated it, because they weren't meant to function in the ultraviolet spectrum. The others pulled up their goggles, too.

Beyond the gate valve was a fourteen- or sixteen-foot length of tunnel, clad in seamlessly butted sleeves of brushed stainless steel, terminating in a second valve, identical to the first. This one was already open approximately as far as Doogie had opened the first; the goggle-defeating UV light issued from the room beyond.

Sasha and Roosevelt remained at the first valve. Armed with the .38, Sasha would make sure that no one came along behind us to block what might be our only exit. Roosevelt, whose left eye was swelling again, stayed with her because he wasn't armed and because he was our essential link to the cat.

The mouser hung with Sasha and Roosevelt, keeping safely out of the forward action. We hadn't dropped a trail of bread crumbs on the way in, and we weren't a hundred percent certain that we could find the route back to Bobby and the elevator without feline guidance.

I followed Doogie to the inner gate valve.

After peering into the space beyond the gate, he raised two fingers to suggest that there were only two people in there about whom we needed to worry. He indicated that he would go first, moving immediately to the right after entering, and that I should follow, going to the left.

As soon as he cleared the doorway, I slipped into the room, with the shotgun thrust in front of me.

The Twilight-of-the-Gods rumble, rattle, bang, and skreek that shook down through the entire facility, from roof to bedrock, was muffled here, and the only light came from an eight-battery storm lamp sitting on a card table.

This chamber was similar in shape to the egg room three floors overhead, though this was much smaller, about thirty feet long and fifteen feet in diameter at its widest point. The curving surfaces were sheathed not in that glassy, gold-flecked substance but in what appeared to be ordinary copper.

My heart soared when I saw the four missing children sitting with their backs to the wall in the shadows at one end of the room. They were exhausted and frightened. Their small wrists and ankles were bound, and their mouths were covered with strips of cloth tape. They were not visibly injured, however, and their eyes widened with amazement at the sight of Doogie and me.

Then I spotted Orson, lying on his side, near the kids, muzzled and restrained. His eyes were open, and he was breathing. *Alive.* Before my vision could blur, I looked away from him.

In the center of the room, frozen by Doogie's gun, two men sat in padded folding chairs, facing each other across the card table that held the storm lamp. In this stark tableau, they reminded me of characters in a stripped-down stage set from one of those stultifying minimalist plays about boredom, isolation, emotional disconnection, the futility of modern relationships, and the sobering philosophical implications of the cheeseburger.

The guy on the right was the abb who had tried to brain me with a two-by-four under the warehouse. He was wearing the same clothes he'd been wearing then, and he still had those tiny white teeth, although his smile was considerably more strained than it had been previously, as though he had just discovered a corn worm among that mouthful of white kernels.

I wanted to pump one shot into his mug, because I

sensed not just smugness in the geek, but also vanity. After he took a magnum round at such close range, the only word adequate to describe his face would also spur on a dogsled team.

The man on the left was tall, blond, with pale green eyes and a puckered scar, in his mid-fifties. He was the one who had snatched the Stuart twins—and his smile was as winning as it had been when he was a boy of twelve with the blood of his parents on his hands.

John Joseph Randolph was unnervingly self-possessed, as if our arrival neither startled nor concerned him. "How're you doing, Chris?"

I was surprised he knew my name. I'd never seen him before.

Whispery echoes of his voice were conducted like a current along the copper walls, one word overlaying the next: "Your mother, Wisteria—she was a great woman."

I couldn't understand how he knew my mother. Instinct told me that I didn't want to know. A shotgun blast would silence him, and scour that smile off his face—the smile with which he charmed the innocent and the unwary—turning it into a lipless death's-head grin.

"She was deadlier than Mother Nature," he said.

Renaissance men ponder, brood, and analyze the complex moral consequences of their actions, preferring persuasion and negotiation to violence. Evidently, I'd forgotten to renew my membership in the Renaissance Man Club, and they had repossessed my principles, because all I wanted to do was blow away this butchering creep—and with extreme prejudice.

Or maybe I'm just becoming.

It's the rage these days.

With my heart made brittle by bitterness, I might have pulled the trigger if the kids hadn't been there to witness the carnage. I was also inhibited because the copper skin on the curved walls was guaranteed to spin deadly ricochets in all directions. My soul was saved not by the purity of my morals but by circumstances, which is a humbling confession.

With the barrel of the Uzi, Doogie gestured at the playing

cards in the two men's hands. "What's the game?" His voice echoed tinnily around the curved copper walls.

I didn't like these two men's watchful calm. I wanted to see fear in their eyes.

Now Randolph turned his hand of cards faceup on the table and replied to Doogie's question with too much dry amusement. "Poker."

Before Doogie decided how best to restrain the card-players, he needed to determine, if he could, whether they had guns. They were wearing jackets that could conceal shoulder holsters. With nothing to lose, they might do something reckless—like take wild shots at the kids, rather than at us, before they themselves were cut down, hoping to kill one more tender victim just to go out on a final thrill.

With four children in the room, we didn't dare make a mistake.

"If not for Wisteria," Randolph said, addressing me, "Del Stuart would have pulled the plug on my financing long before he did."

"Your financing?"

"But when she screwed up, they needed me. Or thought they did. To see what the future held."

Sensing a pending revelation of an ugly truth, I said, "Shut up," but I spoke in little more than a murmur, perhaps because I knew I needed to hear whatever he had to tell me, even if I'd no *desire* to hear it.

To Doogie, Randolph said, "Ask me what the stakes are."

The word *stakes* spiraled around the ovoid room, still whispering back to us even as Doogie dutifully asked, "What are the stakes?"

"Conrad and I play to see who gets to soak each of these tykes in gasoline."

Conrad mustn't have been in possession of a gun in the warehouse the previous night. If he'd had one, he would have shot me dead the moment that I touched his face in the dark.

Moving his hands as if dealing imaginary cards, Randolph said, "Then we play to see who gets to light the match."

Looking as if he might shoot first and worry about ricochets later, Doogie said, "Why haven't you killed them already?"

"Our numerology tells us there should be five in this offering. Until recently, we thought we had only four. But now we think . . ." He smiled at me. "We think the dog is special. We think the dog makes five. When you interrupted, we were playing cards to see who lights the mutt boy."

I didn't think that Randolph had a firearm, either. As far as I could remember from my hasty scan of his gallery of hellish achievement, his father was the only victim he'd dispatched with a gun. That was forty-four years ago, probably the first murder he'd committed. Since then, he preferred to have more personal involvement, to get right into the wet of the work. Hammers and knives and the like were his weapons of choice—until he started to make his burnt offerings.

"Your mother," he said, "was a dice woman. Rolled the dice for the whole human race, and crapped out. But I like cards."

Pretending to deal cards again, Randolph had moved one hand close to the storm lamp.

"Don't," Doogie said.

But Randolph did. He snapped the lamp switch, and suddenly we were blind.

Even as the light went off, Randolph and Conrad were on the move. They got to their feet so fast that they knocked their chairs over, and these hard noises rattled repeatedly around the room like the sharp rat-a-tat produced by a running boy dragging a stick along a picket fence.

I was instantly on the move, too, following the curve of the room toward the children, trying to stay out of Conrad's way, since he was the one closest to me and would most likely go hard and fast for the place where I had been when the lights went out. Neither he nor Randolph was the type to run for the exit.

As I sidled toward the kids, I slipped the infrared goggles off my forehead, over my eyes. I yanked the special flashlight from my belt, clicked it on, and swept the room where Conrad might be.

He was closer than I'd expected, having intuited my attempt to shield the children. He held a knife in one hand, slashing blindly at the air around him, hoping to get lucky and cut me.

How very strange it is to be a man with sight in the kingdom of the blind. Watching Conrad seeking without finding, flailing in mindless rage, seeing him so confused and frustrated and desperate, I knew one percent of what God must feel like when He watches us at our furious game of life.

I quickly circled Conrad as he ambitiously but ineffectively sought to disembowel me. Employing a technique sure to elicit the righteous indignation of the American Dental Association, I gripped the butt of the flashlight between my teeth, to free both hands for the shotgun, and I slammed the stock of the gun into the back of his head.

He went down and stayed down.

Apparently, neither one-name Conrad nor the inimitable John Joseph Randolph had realized that our goggles were part of infrared sets, because Doogie was almost literally dancing around the most successful serial killer of our time—excluding politicians, who generally hire out the wet work—and beating the crap out of him with a natural-born enthusiasm and with a skill honed as a bouncer in biker bars.

Perhaps because he had a greater concern for dental safety and oral hygiene than I did, or perhaps just because he didn't like the taste of the flashlight handle, Doogie had simply placed the infrared light on the card table and then herded Randolph into the primary path of the beam with a relentless series of judiciously delivered pokes, punches, and chops with his fists and with the barrel and butt of the Uzi.

Randolph went down twice and got up twice, as though he really believed that he had a chance. Finally he dropped like a load from a dinosaur: prepared to lie there until he fossilized. Doogie kicked him in the ribs. When Randolph didn't move, Doogie administered the traditional Hell's Angel first aid, kicking him again.

Unquestionably, Doogie Sassman was a Harley-riding maniac, a man of surprising talents and accomplishments, a true mensch in many ways, a source of valuable if arcane knowledge, perhaps even a font of enlightenment. Nevertheless, no one was likely to structure a new religion around him anytime soon.

Doogie said, "Snowman?"

"Hey."

"Handle some real light?"

Slipping off my goggles, I said, "Fade me in."

He switched on the storm lamp, and the copper-lined room was filled with rust-colored shadows and shiny-penny light.

The pre-cataclysmic rumbles, cracks, squeals, and groans that shook through the vast building continued to be muffled here, more like the embarrassing noises of digestive distress. But we didn't need a fifty-page directive from the Occupational Safety and Health Administration to know that we should vacate the premises as soon as possible.

We quickly determined that the children were not merely bound with rope or shackled. Their wrists had been wired together, as had their ankles. The wires were drawn cruelly tight, and I winced at the sight of bruised skin and dried blood.

I checked Orson. He was breathing, but shallowly. His forepaws were wired together, his hind legs, too. A makeshift muzzle of wire clamped his jaws shut, so he was able to issue only a thin whine.

"Easy, bro," I said shakily, stroking his flank.

Doogie stepped to the gate valve and shouted along the tunnel to Sasha and Roosevelt: "We got 'em. All alive!"

They whooped with delight, but Sasha also urged us to hurry.

"We're shakin' and bakin'," Doogie assured her. "Keep your guard up." After all, there might be worse than Randolph and Conrad in this labyrinth.

A couple of satchels, backpacks, and a Styrofoam cooler were stacked near the card table. Under the assumption that this gear belonged to the tandem killers, Doogie went in search of pliers or any other tool with which we could free the kids, because the wires had been braided and knotted with such obsessive care that we couldn't easily unwind them.

I gently pulled the tape off Jimmy Wing's mouth, and he said he needed to pee-pee, and I told him that I did, too, but that we would both have to hold it for a little while, which shouldn't be any trouble because we were both brave guys with the right stuff, and this earned his solemn expression of agreement.

The six-year-old Stuart twins—Aaron and Anson—thanked me politely when I untaped their mouths. Anson informed me that the two unconscious kooks on the floor were bad men. Aaron was blunter and less clean-spoken than his brother, calling them "shitheads," and Anson warned him that if he used that forbidden word in front of their mother, he would be toast.

I had expected tears, but these weeds had cried all they were going to cry, at least over this weird experience. There's a natural toughness in most kids that we seldom acknowledge, because we usually view childhood through glasses of nostalgia and sentimentality.

Wendy Dulcinea was, at seven, a glorious reflection of her mother, Mary, from whom I'd been unable to learn the piano but with whom I'd once been in deep puppy love. She wanted to give me a kiss, and I was happy to receive it, and then she said, "The doggie is really thirsty—you should give him a drink. They let us drink, but they wouldn't give him anything."

The corners of Orson's eyes were crusted with white matter. He looked sick and weak, because with his mouth wired shut, he had not been able to perspire properly. Dogs sweat not through pores in their skin but largely through their tongues.

"Gonna be okay, bro," I promised him. "Gonna get out of here. Hold on. Going home. We're going home. You and me. Out of here."

Returning from a search of the killers' gear, Doogie stooped by my side and, using lineman's pliers with sharp side cutters, snipped the bonds between my brother's paws, pulled them off, and threw them aside. Cutting the wires around Orson's jaws required more care and time, during which I continued to babble that everything was going to be cool, primo, sweet, stylin'; and in less than a minute, the hateful muzzle was gone.

Doogie moved to the kids, and though Orson made no effort to sit up, he licked my hand. His tongue was rough and dry.

Empty assurances had poured glibly from me. Now I wasn't able to speak, because everything I had to say was important and so deeply felt that if I started to let it out, I would be laid low by my own words, emotionally wrecked, and with all the obstacles that remained in the way of our escape and survival, I couldn't afford tears now, maybe not even later, maybe not ever.

Instead of saying anything, I pressed my hand against his flank, feeling the too-fast but steady beat of his great, good heart, and I kissed his brow.

Wendy had said that Orson was thirsty. His tongue had felt dry and swollen against my hands. Now I saw that his flews, scored from the pressure lines left by the muzzling wire, appeared to be chapped. His dark eyes were slightly filmy, and I saw a weariness in them that scared me, something close to resignation.

Although reluctant to leave Orson's side, I went to the large Styrofoam cooler beside the card table. It was half full of cold water in which floated a few chips of ice. The killers appeared to be health conscious, because the only drinks they had brought with them were bottles of V8 vegetable juice and Evian water.

I took one bottle of water to Orson. In my absence, he had struggled off his side and was lying on his belly, though he seemed not to have the strength to raise his head.

Cupping my left hand, I poured some Evian into it. Orson lifted his head barely enough to be able to lap the water from my palm, at first listlessly but soon with enthusiasm.

As I repeatedly replenished the water, I reviewed the physical damage he had endured, and my increasing anger ensured that I'd be able to hold back my tears. The cartilage of his left ear appeared to be crushed, and the fur was matted with a lot of dried blood, as though he had sustained a blow to the head with a club or a length of pipe. Blunt instruments were one of Mr. John Joseph Randolph's specialties. In his left cushion, half an inch from his nose, was a blood-caked cut. A couple of the nails in his right forepaw were broken off, and his toes were sheathed in hardened blood. He had put up a good fight. The pasterns on all four legs were chafed from the wire, and two were bleeding, though not seriously.

Doogie had finished snipping the wires that bound the kids and had moved on to Conrad, who was still out cold. Using a spool of the killers' wire, he had shackled the man's feet. Now he was using more wire to cuff his wrists behind his back.

We couldn't risk taking the two men with us, back through the maze. Because crawling was required in some of the tunnels, we wouldn't be able to bind even their hands, and without restraints, they would be completely uncontrollable. We would have to send the police back here for them—assuming the entire structure didn't collapse from the stresses of the time-shifting phenomena occurring overhead.

Although I might have changed my mind later, at that moment I wanted to immobilize them, seal their mouths shut with tape, put a bottle of water where they could see it, and leave them here to die painfully of thirst.

Orson had finished the Evian. He struggled to his feet, wobbly as a baby, and stood panting, blinking the filminess out of his eyes, looking around with interest.

"Poki akua," I told him, which is Hawaiian for *dog of the gods.*

He chuffed weakly, as though pleased by the compliment.

A sudden *pong,* followed by a nerve-jangling squeal, as of metal torquing violently, passed through the copper room. Both Orson and I looked at the ceiling, then around at the walls, but there was no evident distortion of the smooth metal surfaces.

Tick, tick, tick.

I dragged the heavy cooler across the floor to Orson and opened the lid. He looked in at the icy water sloshing among the bottles of Evian and vegetable juice, and he happily began to lap it up.

On his side, curled in the fetal position, Randolph was groaning but not yet conscious.

Doogie clipped off a few feet of wire, all he needed to finish binding Conrad, and passed the spool to me.

I rolled Randolph facedown and hurriedly wired his wrists together behind his back. I was tempted to cinch the bonds as tight as those on the children and Orson, but I controlled myself and made them only tight enough to ensure that he could not free himself.

After securing his ankles, I looped wire from the shackles at his feet to those at his wrists, further limiting his ability to move.

Randolph must have awakened as I began to apply this final restraint, because when I finished, he spoke with a clarity not characteristic of someone just regaining consciousness: "I've won."

I moved out from behind him and hunkered down to look at his face. His head was turned to the side, left cheek against the copper floor. Lips split and bleeding. His right eye was pale green and bright, but I saw no evidence of animal eyeshine.

Curiously, he appeared to be in no distress. He was at peace, as if he weren't trussed and helpless but were merely resting.

When he spoke, his voice was calm, even slightly euphoric, like that of someone coming out of a light Demerol sleep. I would have felt better if he'd ranted, snarled, and spat. His relaxed demeanor seemed to support his unnerving contention that he had won in spite of his current circumstances. "I'll be on the other side before the night is gone. They stripped out the engine. That wasn't a mortal wound. This is a sort of . . . organic machine. In time, it has healed. Now it powers itself. You can feel it. Feel it in the floor."

Those rumblings, like passing trains, were louder than

before, and the spells of calm between were shorter. Although the effect in this room had been less than elsewhere in the structure, the noise and the vibrations in the floor were at last gaining power here, too.

Randolph said, "Powers itself with the littlest help. A storm lamp in the translation chamber two hours ago—that's all it took to get it running again. This is no *ordinary* machine."

"You worked on this project?"

"Mine."

"Dr. Randolph Josephson," I said, suddenly remembering the name of the project leader I'd heard on Delacroix's tape. John Joseph Randolph, boy killer, had become Randolph Josephson. "What does it do, where does it . . . go?"

Instead of answering me, he smiled and said, "Did the crow ever appear to you? It never appeared to Conrad. He said it did, but he lies. The crow appeared to *me*. I was sitting by the rock, and the crow rose out of it." He sighed. "Formed out of the solid rock that night, in front of my eyes."

Orson was with the children, accepting their affection. He was wagging his tail. Everything was going to be all right. The world wasn't going to end, at least not here, at least not tonight. We would get out of here, we would survive, we would live to party, ride the waves again, it was guaranteed, it was a sure thing, it was a done deal, because right here was the omen, the sign of good times coming: Orson was wagging his tail.

"When I saw the crow, I knew I was someone special," Randolph said. "I had a destiny. Now I've fulfilled it."

Once more, the fearsome twang of torquing metal punctuated the rumble of the ghost train.

"Forty-four years ago," I said, "you're the one who carved the crow on Crow Hill."

"I went home that night, fully alive for the first time ever, and did what I'd always wanted to do. Blew my father's brains out." He said this as if reporting an achievement that filled him with quiet pride. "Cut Mother to pieces. Then my *real* life began."

Doogie was sending the kids out of the room, one after the other, along the tunnel to where Sasha and Roosevelt waited.

"So many years, so much hard work," Randolph said with a sigh, as though he were a retiree pleasantly contemplating well-earned leisure. "So much study, learning, striving, *thinking*. So much self-denial and restraint through so many years."

One killing every twelve months.

"And when it was *built*, when success was at hand, the cowards back in Washington were scared by what they saw on the videotapes from the unmanned probes."

"What did they see?"

Instead of answering, he said, "They were going to shut us down. Del Stuart was ready right then to pull the plug on my funding."

I thought I knew why Aaron and Anson Stuart were in this room. And I wondered if the other kids who had been snatched and killed all over the country were related somehow to other people on the Mystery Train project who had disappointed this man.

"Then your mother's bug got loose," Randolph said, "and they wanted to know what the future held, whether there would even be a future."

"Red sky?" I asked. "Strange trees?"

"That's not the future. That's . . . *sideways*."

From the corner of my eye, I saw the copper wall buckle.

Horrified, I turned toward where the concave curve had seemed to become convex, but there was no sign of distortion.

"Now the track is laid," Randolph said contentedly, "and no one can tear it up. The border is breached. The way is open."

"The way to where?"

"You'll see. We're all going soon," he said with disconcerting assurance. "The train is already pulling out of the station."

Wendy was the fourth and last child through the gate

valve at the entrance to the chamber. Orson followed her, still tottering a little.

Doogie motioned urgently to me, and I rose to my feet.

Randolph's pale green eye fixed on me, and he gave me a bloody, broken-toothed, eerily affectionate smile. "Time past, time present, time future, but most important . . . time *sideways*. Sideways is the only place I ever wanted to go, and your mother gave me the chance."

"But where is sideways?" I asked with considerable frustration as the building shook around us.

"My destiny," he said enigmatically.

Sasha cried out, and her voice was so full of alarm that my heart jolted, raced.

Doogie looked down the tunnel, aghast, and then shouted, "Chris! Grab one of those chairs!"

As I snatched up one of the collapsed folding chairs and then my shotgun, John Joseph Randolph said, "Stations on a track, out there sideways in time, like we always knew, always knew but didn't want to *believe*."

I had been right when I'd suspected that truths were hidden in his strange statements, and I wanted to hear him out and understand, but staying there any longer would have been suicidal.

As I joined Doogie, the half-closed gate valve, which was the door of the chamber, began to slide all the way shut.

Cursing, Doogie gripped the valve and put all his muscle against it, the arteries in his neck bulging from the effort, slowly forcing the steel disc back into the wall.

"Go!" Doogie said.

Because I'm the kind of guy who knows good advice when he hears it, I squeezed past the mambo king and sprinted along the sixteen-foot section of tunnel between the two enormous valves.

Above a thundering and a windlike shrieking worthy of the final storm on doomsday, I could hear John Joseph Randolph shouting, not with terror but with joy, with passionate conviction: "I *believe*! I *believe*!"

Sasha, the kids, Mungojerrie, and Orson had already

passed through to the next section of tunnel beyond the outer gateway.

Roosevelt was wedged into the breach, to prevent the valve from sealing Doogie and me in here. I could hear the motor grinding in the wall, trying to drive the steel disc into the fully closed position.

I jammed the metal folding chair into the gap, above Roosevelt's head, bracing the valve open.

"Thanks, son," he said.

I followed Roosevelt through the gate.

The others were waiting beyond, with an ordinary flashlight. Sasha looked far more beautiful when she wasn't green.

The gap in the gateway was a tight fit for the sass man, but he popped through, too, and then he wrenched the chair out of the gap, because we were likely to need it again.

We passed the Mystery Train patch and the image of the crow. No draft currently moved through this tunnel. None of the newspaper clippings ahead of us stirred at all. And yet the large sheet of art paper, which featured the graphite rubbing of the carved-stone bird, was fluttering as if a gale-force wind were tearing at it. The loose ends of the paper curled and flapped vigorously. The crow seemed to be pulling angrily at the pieces of tape that fixed it to the curved steel surface, determined to break out of the paper as, according to Randolph, it had once arisen out of rock.

Maybe I was hallucinating this business with the crow, sure, and maybe I was born to be a snake charmer, but I wasn't going to hang around to see if a real bird morphed out of the paper and took flight, any more than I was going to lie down in a nest of cobras and hum show tunes to entertain them.

On a hunch that I might want proof of what I'd seen down here, I tore a few newspaper clippings from the wall and stuffed them in my pockets.

With the faux crow flapping furiously against the wall behind us, we hurried on, keeping our group together, doing what any sane person would do when the world was coming apart around him and death loomed at every side: We followed the cat.

I tried not to think about Bobby. The first problem was just getting to him. If we got to him, everything would be okay. He would be waiting for us—cold and sore and weak, but waiting by the elevator where we had left him—and he would remind me of my promise by saying, *Carpe cerevisi, bro.*

The faint iodine odor that had been with us all the way through the labyrinth was sharper now. Threaded through it were whiffs of charcoal, sulfur, rotting roses, and an indescribable, bitter scent unlike anything I had smelled before.

If the time-shifting phenomena were spreading down here into the deepest realms of the structure, we were at greater risk than at any moment since we had entered the hangar. The worst possibility wasn't that our escape would be delayed or even cut off by the motor-driven valves. Worse, if the wrong moment of the past intersected with the present, as had happened more than once upstairs, we might suddenly be inundated by whatever oceans of liquid or toxic gas had pumped through these tubes, whereupon we would either drown or suffocate in poisonous fumes.

26

One cat, four kids, one dog, one deejay-songwriter, one animal communicator, one Viking, and the poster child for Armageddon—that's me—ran, crawled, squirmed, ran, fell, got up, ran some more, along the dry beds of steel rivers, brass rivers, copper creeks, one white light flaring off curved walls, brightly spiraling, feathery darkness whirling like wings everywhere that the light didn't reach, with the rumble of invisible trains all around, and a shrill shrieking like the whistles of locomotives, the iodine smell now chokingly heavy, but now so faint it seemed the previous density had been imagined, currents of the past washing in like a mushy tide, then ebbing out of the present. Terrified by a periodic sound of rushing water, water or something worse, we came at last to the sloping concrete tunnel, and then into the alcove by the elevator, where Bobby lay as we had left him, still alive.

While Doogie reconnected the wires in the elevator control panel, and while Roosevelt, carrying Mungojerrie, shepherded the kids into the cab, Sasha, Orson, and I gathered around Bobby.

He looked like Death on a bad hair day.

I said, "Lookin' good."

Bobby spoke to Orson in a voice so weak that it barely carried over the sounds of clashing times, clashing worlds, which I guess is what we were hearing. "Hey, fur face."

Orson nuzzled Bobby's neck, sniffed his wound, then looked worriedly at me.

"You did it, XP Man," Bobby said.

"It was more a Fantastic Five caper than a one-superhero gig," I demurred.

"You got back in time to make your midnight show," Bobby told Sasha, and I had the sickening feeling that, in his way, he was saying goodbye to us.

"Radio is my life," she said.

The building shook, the train rumble became a roar, and concrete dust sifted down from the ceiling.

Sasha said, "We have to get you in the elevator."

But Bobby looked at me and said, "Hold my hand, bro."

I gripped his hand. It was ice.

Pain cramped his face, and then he said, "I screwed up."

"You never."

"Wet my pants," he said shakily.

The cold seemed to come out of his hand and up my arm, coiling in my heart. "Nothing wrong with that, bro. Urinophoria. You've done it before."

"I'm not wearing neoprene."

"So it's a *style* issue, huh?"

He laughed, but the tattered laughter frayed into choking.

Doogie announced, "Elevator's ready."

"Let's move you," Sasha suggested, as tiny chips of concrete joined the fall of dust.

"Never thought I'd die so *inelegantly*," Bobby said, his hand tightening on mine.

"You're not dying," I assured him.

"Love you . . . bro."

"Love you," I said, and the words were like a key that locked my throat as tight as a vault.

"Total wipeout," he said, his voice fading until the final syllable was inaudible.

His eyes fixed on something far beyond us, and his hand went slack in mine.

I felt a whole great slab of my heart slide away, like the shaling face of a cliff, down into a hateful darkness.

Sasha put her fingertips to his throat, feeling for a pulse in his carotid artery. "Oh, God."

"Gotta get out of here *now*," Doogie insisted.

In a voice so thick I didn't recognize it as my own, I said to Sasha, "Come on, let's get him in the elevator."

"He's gone."

"Help me get him in the elevator."

"Chris, honey, he's gone."

"We're taking him with us," I said.

"Snowman—"

"We're taking him with us!"

"Think of the kids. They—"

I was desperate and crazy, crazy-desperate, a dark whirlpool of grief churning in my mind, sucking away all reason, but I was not going to leave him there. I would die with him, beside him, rather than leave him there.

I grabbed him by the shoulders and started dragging him into the elevator, aware that I was probably frightening the kids, who must already be scared shitless, no matter how contemporary and cool and tough they were. I couldn't expect them to clap their hands with glee at the prospect of taking an elevator ride up from Hell with a corpse for company, and I didn't blame them, but that was the way it had to be.

When they saw that I wasn't going anydamnwhere without Bobby Halloway, Sasha and Doogie helped me drag him into the elevator.

The rumbling, the banshee shrieking, the snap-cracklepop that seemed to indicate imminent structural implosion all faded suddenly, and the drizzle of concrete chips stopped, but I knew this had to be temporary. We were in the eye of the time hurricane, and worse was coming.

Just as we got Bobby inside, the elevator doors started to close, and Orson slipped in with so little time to spare that he almost caught his tail.

"What the hell?" Doogie said. "I didn't press a button."

"Somebody called it, someone upstairs," Sasha said.

The elevator motor whined, and the cab rose.

Already crazy-desperate, I became crazier when I realized that my hands were slick with Bobby's blood, and more desperate as I was overcome by the idea that there was something I could do to change all this. The past and the present are present in the future, and the future is contained in the past, as T. S. Eliot wrote; therefore, all time is unredeemable, and what will be will be. What might have been—that's an illusion, because the only thing that could have happened is what *does* happen, and there's not anything we can do to change it, because we're doomed by destiny, fucked by fate, though Mr. Eliot hadn't put it in exactly those words. On the other hand, Winnie-the-Pooh, much less of a broody type than Mr. Eliot, believed in the possibility of all things, which might be because he was only a stuffed bear with a head full of nothing, but it also might be the case that Mr. Pooh was, in fact, a Zen master who knew as much about the meaning of life as did Mr. Eliot. The elevator rose—we were at B-5—and Bobby lay dead on the floor, and my hands were slick with blood, and there was nevertheless hope in my heart, which I didn't understand at all, but as I tried to see clearly the *why* of my hope, I reasoned that the answer was in combining Mr. Eliot's insights and those of Mr. Pooh. As we reached B-4, I glanced down at Orson, whom I'd thought was dead but was now alive again, resuscitated just as Tinker Bell had been after she'd drunk the cup of poison to save Peter Pan from the murderous schemes of the homicidal Hook. I was beyond crazy, caught in a wave of totally macking lunacy, sick with terror, sicker with despair, sickest with hope, and I could not stop thinking about good Tink being saved by sheer *belief,* by all the dreaming kids in the world clapping their small hands to proclaim their belief in fairies. Subconsciously, I must have known where I was going, but when I snatched the Uzi out of Doogie's hands, I had no conscious idea what I intended to do with it, though judging by the expression on the waltz wizard's face, I must have looked even crazier than I felt.

B-3.

The elevator doors opened on B-3, and the corridor beyond was filled with muddy red light.

In this mysterious radiance were five tall, blurry, distorted maroon figures. They might have been human, but they might have been something even worse.

With them was a smaller creature, also a maroon blur, with four legs and a tail, which might have been a cat.

In spite of all the *might-have-beens,* I didn't hesitate, because only precious seconds remained in which to act. I stepped out of the elevator, into the muddy red glow, but then the corridor was full of fluorescent light when I crossed into it.

Roosevelt, Doogie, Sasha, Bobby, Mungojerrie, and I— me, myself, Christopher Snow—stood in the corridor, facing the elevator doors, looking as if they—we—expected trouble.

A minute ago, down on B-6, just as we had loaded Bobby's corpse into the elevator, someone *up here* had pushed the call button. That someone was Bobby, a living Bobby from earlier in the night.

In this strangely afflicted building, time past, time present, and time future were all present here at once.

With my friends—and I myself—gaping at me in astonishment, as if I were a ghost, I turned right, toward the two oncoming security men that the others hadn't yet seen. One of these guards had fired the shot that killed Bobby.

I squeezed off a burst from the Uzi, and both guards were cut down before they fired a shot.

My stomach twisted with revulsion at what I'd done, and I tried to escape my conscience by taking refuge in the fact that these men would have been killed by Doogie, anyway, after they had shot Bobby. I had only accelerated their fate while changing Bobby's altogether, for a net saving of one life. But perhaps excuses of that sort make excellent paving stones for the road to Hell.

Behind me, Sasha, Doogie, and Roosevelt rushed into the corridor from the elevator.

The astonishment among all these doppelgängers was as

thick as the peanut butter on the banana sandwiches that had ultimately killed Elvis.

I didn't understand how this could be happening, because it had not happened earlier. We had never met ourselves in this hallway on our way down to find the children. But if we were meeting ourselves *now*, why didn't I have a memory of it?

Paradox. Time paradox, I guess. You know me and math, me and physics. I'm more a Pooh guy, an Eliot guy. My head ached. I had changed Bobby Halloway's fate, which was, to me, a pure miracle, not mere mathematics.

The elevator was full of muddy red light and the blurry maroon figures of the kids. The doors began to slide shut.

"Hold it!" I shouted.

Present-time Doogie blocked the door, half in the fluorescent corridor and half in the murky red elevator.

The throbbing electronic sound swelled louder. It was fearsome.

I remembered John Joseph Randolph's pleasurable anticipation, his confidence that we would all be going to the other side soon, to that sideways place he wouldn't name. The train, he'd said, was already beginning to pull out of the station. Suddenly I wondered if he'd meant the whole building might make that mysterious journey—not just whoever was in the egg room, but everyone within the walls of the hangar and the six basements below it.

With a renewed sense of urgency, I asked Doogie to look in the elevator and see if Bobby was there.

"I'm here," said the Bobby in the hall.

"In there, you're a pile of dead meat," I told him.

"No way."

"Way."

"Ouch."

"Maximum."

I didn't know why, but I thought it wouldn't be a good idea to return upstairs to the hangar, beyond this zone of radically tangled time, with *both* Bobbys, the live one and the dead one.

Still holding the door, present-time Doogie stepped into the elevator, hesitated, then returned to the corridor. "There's no Bobby in there!"

"Where'd he go?" asked present-time Sasha.

"The kids say he just . . . *went*. They're jazzed about it."

"The body's gone because he wasn't shot here, after all," I explained, which was about as illuminating as describing a thermonuclear reaction with the words *it go boom*.

"You said I was dead meat," the past-time Bobby said.

"What's happening here?" the past-time Doogie demanded.

"Paradox," I said.

"What's that mean?"

"I read *poetry*," I said with super-mondo frustration.

"Good work, son," said both Roosevelts in perfect harmony, and then looked at each other in surprise.

To Bobby, I said, "Get in the elevator."

"Where are we going?" he asked.

"Out."

"What about the kids?"

"We got them."

"What about Orson?"

"He's in the elevator."

"Cool."

"Will you *move* your ass?" I demanded.

"A little crabby, aren't we?" he said, stepping forward, patting my shoulder.

"You don't know what I've been through."

"Wasn't *I* the one who died?" he asked, and then disappeared into the murky red elevator, becoming another maroon blur.

The past-time Sasha, Doogie, Roosevelt, and even the past-time Chris Snow looked confused, and the past-time Chris said to me, "What are we supposed to do?"

Addressing myself, I said, "You disappoint me. I'd expect you, at least, to figure it out. Eliot and Pooh, for God's sake!"

As the oscillating thrum of the egg-room engines grew

louder and a faint but ominous rumble passed through the floor, like giant train wheels beginning to turn, I said, "You've got to go down and save the kids, save Orson."

"You already saved them."

My head was spinning. "But maybe *you* still have to go down and save them, or it'll turn out that *we* didn't."

The past-time Roosevelt picked up the past-time Mungojerrie and said, "The cat understands."

"Then just follow the damn cat!" I said.

All of us present-time types who were still in the corridor—Roosevelt, Sasha, me, Doogie holding the elevator door—stepped back into the red light, but when we were in the cab with the kids, there was no red light at all, just the incandescent bulb in the ceiling.

The corridor, however, was now flooded with red murk, and our past-time selves, minus Bobby, were maroon blurs once more.

Doogie pressed the button for the ground floor, and the doors closed.

Orson squeezed between me and Sasha, to be close to my side.

"Hey, bro," I said softly.

He chuffed.

We were cool.

As we started upward at an excruciatingly slow pace, I looked at my wristwatch. The luminous LED digits weren't racing either forward or backward, as I had seen them do previously. Instead, pulsing slowly across the watch were curious squiggles of light, which might have been distorted numbers. With growing dread, I wondered if this meant we were beginning to move sideways in time, heading toward the other side that Randolph was so eager to visit.

"You were dead," Aaron Stuart said to Bobby.

"So I heard."

"You don't remember being dead?" Doogie asked.

"Not really."

"He doesn't remember dying because he never died," I said too sharply.

I was still struggling with grief at the same time that a wild joy was surging in me, a manic glee, which was a weird combination of emotions, like being King Lear and Mr. Toad of Toad Hall at the same time. Plus my fear was feeding on itself, growing fatter. We weren't out of here yet, and we had more than ever to lose, because if one of us died now, there was no chance that I'd be able to pull another rabbit out of a hat; I didn't even *have* a hat.

As we ground slowly up, still short of B-2, a deep rumbling rose through the elevator shaft, as if we were in a submarine around which depth charges were detonating, and the lift mechanism began to creak.

"If it was me, I'd sure remember dying," Wendy announced.

"He didn't die," I said more calmly.

"But he *did* die," insisted Aaron Stuart.

"He sure did," said Anson.

Jimmy Wing said, "You peed your pants."

"I never," Bobby denied.

"You told us you did," said Jimmy Wing.

Bobby looked dubiously at Sasha, and she said, "You were dying, it was excusable."

On my wristwatch, the luminous squiggles were twisting across the readout window faster than before. Maybe the Mystery Train was pulling out of the station, gathering speed. Sideways.

As we reached B-2, the building began to shake badly enough to cause the elevator cab to rattle against the walls of the shaft, and we grabbed at the handrails and at each other to keep our balance.

"My pants are dry," Bobby noted.

"Because you didn't die," I said tightly, "which means you never wet your pants, either."

"He did too," said Jimmy Wing.

Sensing my state of mind, Roosevelt said, "Relax, son."

Orson put one paw on my shoe, as if to indicate that I should listen to Roosevelt.

Doogie said, "If he never died, why do we remember him dying?"

"I don't know," I said miserably.

The elevator seemed to have gotten stuck at B-2, and abruptly the doors opened, though Doogie had pressed only the *G* button.

Maybe the kids weren't able to see past us to what lay beyond the cab, but those of us in the front row had a good look, and the sight froze us. A corridor, either stripped to the bare concrete or equipped as it had been in years gone by, should have waited out there past the threshold, but we were facing a panoramic landscape instead. A smoldering red sky. Oily black fungus grew in gnarled, vaguely treelike masses, and thick rivulets of vile dark syrup oozed from puckered pustules on the trunks. From some limbs hung cocoons like those we had seen in the Dead Town bungalow, glossy and fat, pregnant with malignant life.

For a moment, as we stood stunned, no sound or odor issued from this twisted landscape, and I dared to hope it was more a vision than a physical reality. Then movement at the threshold drew my eye, and I saw the red-and-black-mottled tendrils of a ground-hugging vine, as beautiful and evil-looking as a nest of baby coral snakes, questing at the sill of the door, growing as fast as plants in a nature film run at high speed, wriggling into the cab.

"Shut the door!" I urged.

Doogie pressed a button labeled *close door* and then pushed the *G* button again, for the ground floor.

The doors didn't close.

As Doogie jammed his thumb against the button again, something loomed in that otherworldly place, no more than two feet away from us, crossing from the left.

We brought up our guns.

It was a man in a bio-secure suit. *Hodgson* was stenciled across the brow of his helmet, but his face was that of an ordinary man, not crawling with parasites.

We were in the past *and* on the other side. Chaos.

The writhing tendrils of the black-and-red vine, the diameter of earthworms, lapped at the elevator carpet.

Orson sniffed them. The tendrils rose like swaying cobras, as if they would strike at his nose, and Orson twitched
away from them.

Cursing, Doogie pounded the side of his fist against *close
door*. Then against *G*.

Hodgson could see us. Amazement pried open his eyes.

The unnatural silence and stillness were broken when
wind gusted into the cab. Hot and humid. Reeking of tar and
rotting vegetation. Circling us and blowing out again, as if it
were a living thing.

Careful to avoid stepping on the vine tendrils, afraid they
would bore through the sole of my shoe and then through the
sole of my foot, I tugged frantically at the door, trying to pull
out the sliding panel on the left. It wouldn't budge.

With the stench came a faint but chilling sound like
thousands of tortured voices, issuing from a distance—and
threaded through those screams, also distant, was an inhuman
shriek.

Hodgson turned more directly toward us, pointing for
the benefit of another man in a bio-secure suit, who hove into
view.

The doors began to close. The vine tendrils crunched
between the sliding panels. The doors shuddered, almost retreated, but then pinched the vines off, and the cab rose.

Oozing yellow fluid and the bitter scent of sulfur, the
severed tendrils curled and twisted with great agitation—and
then dissolved into an inert mush.

The building shook as if it were the home of all thunder,
the foundry where Thor forged his lightning bolts.

The vibrations were affecting either the elevator motor or
the lift cables, perhaps both, because we were rising more
slowly than before, grinding upward.

"Mr. Halloway's pants are dry now," Aaron Stuart said,
picking up the conversation where it had left off, "but I
smelled the pee."

"Me too," said Anson, Wendy, and Jimmy.

Orson woofed agreement.

"It's a paradox," Roosevelt said solemnly, as though to save me the trouble of explaining.

"There's that word again," Doogie said. His brow was furrowed, and his gaze remained riveted on the indicator board above the door, waiting for the B-1 bulb to light.

"A time paradox," I said.

"But how does that work?" Sasha asked.

"Like a toaster oven," I said, meaning *who knows?*

Doogie pressed his thumb against *G* and kept it there. We didn't want the door to open on B-1. B for *bedlam*. B for *bad news*. B for *be prepared to die squishily*.

Aaron Stuart said, "Mr. Snow?"

I took a deep breath: "Yes?"

"If Mr. Halloway didn't die, then whose blood is on your hands?"

I looked at my hands. They were sticky-damp with Bobby's blood, which had gotten on them when I'd dragged his body into the elevator.

"Weird," I admitted.

Wendy Dulcinea said, "If the body went poof, why didn't the blood on your hands go poof?"

My mouth was too dry, my tongue too thick, and my throat too tight to allow me to answer her.

The shuddering elevator briefly caught on something in the shaft, tore loose with a ripping-metal sound, and then we groaned to B-1. Where we stopped.

Doogie leaned on *close door* and on the button for the ground floor.

We didn't ascend any farther.

The doors slid inexorably open. Heat, humidity, and that fetid stench rolled over us, and I expected the vigorous alien vegetation to grow into the cab and overwhelm us with explosive force.

In our slice of time, we'd risen one level, but William Hodgson was still out there in neverland, where we had left him. Pointing at us.

The man beyond Hodgson—*Lumley,* according to his helmet—also turned to look at us.

Shrieking, something flew out of that baleful sky, among the black trees: a creature with glossy black wings and whip-like tail, with the muscular, scaly limbs of a lizard, as if a gargoyle had torn itself loose of the stone high on an ancient Gothic cathedral and had taken flight. As it swooped down on Lumley, it appeared to spit out a stream of objects, which looked like large peach pits but were something deadlier, something no doubt full of frenzied life. Lumley twitched and jerked as though he had been hit by machine-gun fire, and several perfectly round holes appeared in his spacesuit, like those we had seen in poor damn Hodgson's suit in the egg room the previous night.

Lumley screamed as though he were being eaten alive, and Hodgson stumbled backward in terror, away from us.

The elevator doors began to close, but the flying thing abruptly changed directions, streaking straight toward us.

As the doors bumped shut, hard objects rattled against them, and a series of dimples appeared in the steel, as if it had been hit by bullets with *almost* enough punch to penetrate to the interior of the cab.

Sasha's face was talcum white.

Mine must have been whiter still, to match my name.

Even Orson seemed to have gone a paler shade of black.

We ascended toward the ground floor through crashes of thunder, the grinding rumble of steel wheels on steel track, harsh whistles, shrieks, and the throbbing electronic hum, but in spite of all those sounds of worlds colliding, we also heard another noise, which was more intimate, more terrifying. Something was on the roof of the elevator cab. Crawling, slithering.

It could have been nothing but a loose cable, which might have explained our quaking, jerky progress toward the ground floor. But it wasn't a loose cable. That was wishful thinking. This thing was alive. Alive and purposeful.

I couldn't imagine how anything could have gotten into the shaft with us after the doors had shut, unless the intermingling of these two realities was nearly complete. In which case, at any moment, might not the thing on the roof pass through the ceiling and be among us, like a ghost passing through a wall?

Doogie remained focused on the indicator board above the doors, but the rest of us—animals, kids, and adults—turned our faces up toward the menacing sounds.

In the center of the ceiling was an escape hatch. A way out. A way *in*.

Borrowing the Uzi from Doogie once more, I aimed at the ceiling. Sasha also covered the trapdoor with her shotgun.

I wasn't optimistic about the effectiveness of gunfire. Unless I was misremembering, Delacroix had suggested that at least some of the expedition members were heavily armed when they went to the other side. Guns hadn't saved them.

The elevator groaned-rattled-squeaked upward.

This side of the three-foot-square hatch featured neither hinges nor handles. There was no latch bolt, either. To escape, you had to push the panel up and out. To enable rescue workers to pull it open from the other side, there would be a handle or a recessed groove in which fingers could be hooked.

The flying gargoyle had hands, thick talonlike fingers. Maybe those huge fingers wouldn't fit in a groove handle.

A hard, frantic scraping noise. Something clawing busily at the steel roof, as if trying to dig through. A creak, a hard pop, a rending sound. Silence.

The kids clutched one another.

Orson growled low in his throat.

So did I.

The walls seemed to press closer to one another, as though the elevator cab were reshaping itself into a group coffin. The air was thick. Each breath felt like sludge in my lungs. The overhead light began to flicker.

With a metallic squeal, the escape hatch sagged toward us as though a great weight were pressing on it. The frame in which it sat would not allow it to open inward.

After a moment, the weight was removed, but the panel didn't return entirely to normal. It was distorted. Steel plate.

Bent like plastic. More force had been required for that task than I cared to think about.

Sweat blurred my vision. I wiped at my eyes with the back of my hand.

"Yes!" Doogie said, as the *G* bulb lit on the indicator board.

The promise of release was not immediately fulfilled. The doors didn't open.

The cab began to bob up and down, rising and falling as much as a foot with each sickening bounce, as though the hoist cables and the limit switches and the roller guides and the pulleys were all about to crack apart and send us plunging to the bottom of the shaft in a mass of mangling metal.

On the roof, the gargoyle—or something worse—yanked on the escape hatch. Its prior efforts had tweaked the panel in the frame, and now the trap was wedged shut.

The elevator doors were still shut, too, and Doogie angrily punched the button labeled *open doors*.

With a shrill bark, the badly distorted rim of the steel trap stuttered in the frame, as the creature above furiously pulled on it.

At last the elevator doors opened, and I spun toward them, sure that we were now *surrounded* by neverland, that the predator on the roof would have been joined by others.

We were at the ground floor. The hangar was noisier than a New Year's Eve party in a train station with howling wolves and a punk band with nuclear amplifiers.

But it was recognizably the hangar: no red sky, no black trees, no slithering vines like nests of coral snakes.

Overhead, the warped escape hatch screeched, rattled violently. The surrounding frame was coming apart.

The elevator bobbed worse than ever. The floor of the cab rose and fell in relation to the hangar floor, the way a dock slip moves in relation to a boat deck in choppy seas.

I gave the Uzi to Doogie, snatched up my shotgun, and followed the sass man into the hangar, jumping across the shifting threshold, with Bobby and Orson close behind me.

Sasha and Roosevelt hurried the kids out of the elevator,

and Mungojerrie came last, after a final curious glance at the ceiling.

As Sasha turned to cover the cab with her shotgun, the escape hatch was torn out of the ceiling. The gargoyle came down from the roof. The leathery black wings were folded as it dropped, but then they spread to fill the cab. The muscles bulged in the beast's sleek, scaly limbs as it tensed to spring forward. The tail whipped, lashing against the cab walls. Silver eyes flashed. Its raw mouth appeared to be lined with red velvet, but its long forked tongue was black.

I remembered the seedlike projectiles that it had spat at Lumley and at Hodgson, and as I cried out to Sasha, the gargoyle shrieked. She squeezed off a round from the shotgun, but before she could be riddled with squirming parasites, the elevator broke apart and the cab plunged out of sight with the screaming creature still aboard, trailing cables and counterweights and pulleys and steel beams.

Because the beast had wings, I expected it to rise out of the ruins and soar up the shaft, but then I realized that the shaft no longer existed. Instead, I was looking into the starry void that I had glimpsed earlier in the night, where the stairwell should have been.

Crazily, I thought of a magical wardrobe serving as a doorway to the enchanted land of Narnia, mirrors and rabbit holes leading to a bizarre kingdom ruled by a playing-card queen. This was only a transient madness.

Recovering, I did the Pooh thing and gamely accepted all that I had seen—and was still seeing. I led our intrepid band across the hangar, where super-weird and maximum-sharky stuff was happening, across this neverland of past, present, future, and sideways time, saying *hello* to a startled ghost workman in a hard hat, brandishing the shotgun at three ghosts that looked as if they would give us trouble, while trying as best I could not to put us in the same space that was about to be occupied by an object materializing from another time, and if you think all that was easy, you're a kak.

At times we were in a dark and abandoned warehouse, then we were in the murky red light of a time shift, but ten steps later, we were walking through a well-lighted and bustling place populated by busy ghosts as solid as we were. The worst moment was when we passed through a red fog and, though still far from the exit door, found ourselves beyond the warehouse, in a landscape where black masses of fungus rose with vaguely treelike forms and clawed at a red sky in which two dim suns burned low on the horizon. But an instant later, we were among the workmen ghosts again, then in darkness, and finally at the exit.

Nothing and no one followed us into the night, but we kept running until we had nearly reached the Hummer, where at last we stopped and turned and stared at the hangar, which was caught in a time storm. The concrete base of the structure, the corrugated steel walls, and the curve of the Quonset-style roof were pulsing with that red radiance. From the high clerestory windows came white beams as intense as those from a lighthouse, jabbing at the sky, carving bright arcs. Judging by the sound, you would have thought that a thousand bulls were smashing through a thousand china shops inside the building, that tanks were clashing on battlefields, that mobs of rioters were screaming for blood. The ground under our feet was trembling, as though from an earthquake, and I wondered if we were at a safe distance.

I expected the structure to explode or burst into flames, but instead it began to unravel. The red glow faded, the searchlights spearing from the high windows went dark, and we watched while the huge building flickered as though two thousand days and nights were passing in just two minutes, moonglow alternating with sunshine and darkness, the corrugated walls appearing to flutter in the strobing light. Then suddenly the building began to dismantle itself, as if it were unraveling into time past. Workmen swarmed over its surface, all moving backward; scaffolding and construction machinery appeared around it; the roof vanished, and the walls peeled down, and trains of trucks sucked the concrete *out* of the foundation, back into their mixers, and steel beams were craned out of the ground, like dinosaur bones from a paleontological dig, until all six subterranean floors must have been deconstructed, whereupon a blinding fury of massive dump trucks and excavators replaced the earth that they had once removed, and then after a final crackle of red light passed across the site and winked out, all was still.

The hangar and everything under it had ceased to exist.

The spectacle left the kids ecstatic, as if they had met E.T. and ridden on the back of a brontosaurus and taken a quick trip to the moon all in one evening.

"It's over?" Doogie wondered.

"As if it never was," I suggested.

Sasha said, "But it *was*."

"The residual effect. A runaway residual effect. The whole place imploded into . . . the past, I guess."

"But if it never existed," Bobby said, "why do I remember being inside the place?"

"Don't start," I warned him.

We packed ourselves into the Hummer—five adults, four excited kids, one shaky dog, and a smug cat—and Doogie drove to the bungalow in Dead Town, where we had to deal with Delacroix's rotting cadaver and the ceilings festooned with frankfurter-size cocoons. An exorcist's work is never done.

On the way, Aaron Stuart, the troublemaker, reached a solemn conclusion about the blood on my hands. "Mr. Halloway must be dead."

"We've *done* this," I said impatiently. "He's not dead anymore."

"He's dead," Anson agreed.

"I may be dead," Bobby said, "but my pants are dry."

"Dead," Jimmy Wing agreed.

"Maybe he *is* dead," Wendy brooded.

"What the *hell* is wrong with you kids?" I demanded, turning in my seat to glare at them. "He's not dead, it's a paradox, but he's not dead! All you've got to do is believe in fairies, clap your hands, and *Tinker Bell will live*! Is that so hard to understand?"

"Ice it down, Snowman," Sasha advised me.

"I'm cool."

I was still glaring at the kids, who were in the third and final seat. Orson was in the cargo space behind them. He cocked his burly head and looked at me over the kids' heads, as if to say *Ice it down.*

"I'm mellow," I assured him.

He sneezed a sneeze of disagreement.

Bobby had been dead. As in *dead and gone.* As in *deader than dead.* All right. Time to get over it. Here in Wyvern, life goes on, occasionally even for the deceased. Besides, we were more than half a mile from the beach, so anything that happened here couldn't be *that* important.

"Son, the Tinker Bell thing makes perfect sense," Roosevelt said, either to placate me or because he had gone stark, raving mad.

"Yeah," said Jimmy Wing. "Tinker Bell."

"Tinker Bell," the twins said, nodding in unison.

"Yeah," Wendy said. "Why didn't I think of that?"

Mungojerrie meowed. I don't know what that meant.

Doogie drove over the curb, across the sidewalk, and parked on the front lawn at the bungalow.

The kids stayed in the vehicle with Orson and Mungojerrie.

Sasha, Roosevelt, and Doogie took positions around the Hummer, standing guard.

At Sasha's suggestion, Doogie had included two cans of gasoline in the provisions. With the criminal intention of destroying still more government property, Bobby and I carried these ten gallons of satisfyingly flammable liquid to the bungalow.

Going back into this small house was even less appealing than submitting to extensive gum surgery, but we were manly men, and so we climbed the steps and crossed the porch without hesitation, though quietly.

In the living room, we set down the gasoline cans with care, as though to avoid waking a quarrelsome sleeper, and I switched on a flashlight.

The cocoons that had been clustered overhead were gone.

At first I thought the residents of those silky tubes had

chewed free and were now loose in the bungalow in a form that was sure to prove troublesome. Then I realized that not even one wisp of gossamer filament remained in any corner, and none floated on the floor.

The lone red sock, which might once have belonged to one of the Delacroix children, lay where it had been previously, still caked with dust. In general, the bungalow was as I remembered it.

No cocoons hung in the dining room. None were to be found in the kitchen, either.

Leland Delacroix's corpse was gone, as were the photographs of his family, the votive-candle glass, the wedding ring, and the gun with which he had killed himself. The ancient linoleum was still cracked and peeling, but I could see no biological stains that would have indicated that a dead body had been rotting here recently.

"The Mystery Train was never built," I said, "so Delacroix never went to . . . the other side. Never opened the door."

Bobby said, "Never got infected—or possessed. Whatever. And he never infected his family. So they're all alive somewhere?"

"God, I hope so. But *how* could he not be here when he was here and we remember it?"

"Paradox," Bobby said, as if he himself were entirely satisfied with that less than illuminating explanation. "So what do we do?"

"Burn it, anyway," I concluded.

"To be safe, you mean?"

"No, just because I'm a pyromaniac."

"Didn't know that about you, bro."

"Let's torch this dump."

As we emptied the gasoline cans in the kitchen, dining room, and living room, I repeatedly paused because I thought I heard something moving inside the bungalow walls. Every time I listened, the elusive sound stopped.

"Rats," Bobby said.

This alarmed me, because if Bobby heard something, too,

then the furtive noises weren't the work of my imagination. Furthermore, this wasn't the scuttling-scratching-squeaking of rodents; it was a liquid slithering.

"Humongous rats," he said with more force but less conviction.

I fortified myself with the argument that Bobby and I were just woozy from gasoline fumes and, therefore, couldn't trust our senses. Nevertheless, I expected to hear voices echoing inside my head: *Stay, stay, stay, stay.* . . .

We escaped the bungalow without being munched.

Using the last half gallon of gasoline, I poured a fuse across the front porch, down the steps, and along the walkway.

Doogie pulled the Hummer into the street, to a safer distance.

Moonlight mantled Dead Town, and every silent structure seemed to harbor hostile watchers at the windows.

After setting the empty fuel can on the porch, I hurried out to the Hummer and asked Doogie to back it up until one of the rear tires was weighing down the manhole. The monkey manhole.

When I returned to the front yard, Bobby lit the fuse.

As the blue-orange flame raced up the walkway and climbed the front steps, Bobby said, "When I died . . ."

"Yeah?"

"Did I scream like a stuck pig, blubber, and lose my dignity?"

"You were cool. Aside from wetting your pants, of course."

"They're not wet now."

The fuse flame reached the gasoline-soaked living room, and a firestorm blew through the bungalow.

Basking recklessly in the orange light, I said, "When you were dying . . ."

"Yeah?"

"You said, *I love you, bro.*"

He grimaced. "Lame."

"And I said it was mutual."

"Why did we have to do that?"

"You were dying."

"But now here I am."

"It's awkward," I agreed.

"What we need here is a custom paradox."

"Like?"

"Where we remember everything else but forget my dying words."

"Too late. I've already made arrangements with the church, the reception hall, and the florist."

"I'll wear white," Bobby said.

"That would be a travesty."

We turned away from the burning bungalow and walked out to the street. Harried by the witchy firelight, twisted tree shadows capered across the pavement.

As we drew near the Hummer, a familiar angry squeal tortured the night, followed by a score of other shrill voices, and I looked left to see the troop of Wyvern monkeys, half a block away, loping toward us.

The Mystery Train and all its associated terrors might be gone as if they had never been, but the life's work of Wisteria Jane Snow still had its consequences.

We piled into the Hummer, and Doogie locked all the doors with a master switch on the console, just as the rhesuses swarmed over the vehicle.

"Go, move, woof, meow, get outta here!" everyone was shouting, though Doogie needed no encouragement.

He floored the accelerator, leaving part of the troop screaming in frustration as the rear bumper slipped from under their grasping hands.

We weren't in the clear yet. Monkeys were clinging tenaciously to the luggage rack on the roof.

One nasty specimen was hanging by its hind legs, upside down at the tailgate, shrieking what must have been simian obscenities and furiously slapping its hands against the window. Orson snarled to warn it away, face-to-face at the glass, while struggling to stay on his feet as Doogie resorted to slalom maneuvers to try to shake the primates loose.

Another monkey slid down from the roof, directly in front of the windshield, glaring in at Doogie, blocking his view. With one hand it gripped the armature of one windshield wiper, to keep from tumbling off the Hummer, and in its other hand was a small stone. It hammered the stone against the windshield, but the glass didn't break, so it swung again, and this time the stone left a starburst scratch.

"Hell with this," Doogie said, switching on the wipers.

The moving armature pinched the monkey's hand, and the whisking blade startled it. The beast squealed, let go, tumbled across the hood, and fell off the side of the Hummer.

The Stuart twins cheered.

In the front seat, forward of Sasha, Roosevelt rode shotgun, sans shotgun but with cat. Something cracked against the window beside him, loud enough to make Mungojerrie yelp with surprise.

A monkey was hanging there, too, also upside down, but this one had a combination wrench in its right hand, gripping it by the box end, using the open end as a hammer. It was the wrong tool for the job, but it was a lot better than the stone, and when the precocious primate swung it again, the tempered glass crazed.

As thousands of tiny fissures laid an instant crackle glaze across the side window, Mungojerrie sprang out of Roosevelt's lap, onto the backrest of the front seat, onto the seat between Bobby and me, up and over and into the third row, taking refuge with the kids.

The cat moved so fast that it was landing among the children even as the sparking, gummy sheet of tempered glass collapsed onto Roosevelt's lap. Doogie needed both hands for the wheel, and none of the rest of us could take a shot at the invader without blowing off our animal communicator's head, which seemed counterproductive. Then the monkey was inside, swarming across Roosevelt, snapping its teeth at him and swinging the wrench when he tried to seize it, so fast that it might have been a cat, out of the front seat and into the middle seat, where I was sitting between Sasha and Bobby.

Surprisingly, it went for Bobby, perhaps because it mistook him for the boychick of Wisteria Jane Snow. Mom was its creator, which in monkey circles made me the son of Frankenstein. I heard the wrench ring dully off the side of Bobby's skull, though not a fraction as hard as the rhesus would have liked, because it hadn't been able to get in a good, solid swing as it was leaping.

Then somehow Bobby had it by the neck, both hands around its small throat, and the beast let go of the wrench to pry at Bobby's choking hands. Only an extremely reckless monkey hater would have attempted to use a gun in these close quarters, and so as Doogie continued to slalom from curb to curb, Sasha put down the window at her side, and Bobby held the invader toward me. I slipped my hands around its neck, under Bobby's hands, and got a strangulation grip as he let go. Though this all happened fast, too fast to think about what we were doing, the snarling-gagging-spitting rhesus made its presence felt, kicking and thrashing with surprising strength, considering that it wasn't getting any breath and the blood supply to its brain was zero, twenty-five pounds of pissed-off primate, grabbing at our hair, determined to gouge our eyes, tear off our ears, lashing its tail, twisting fiercely as it tried to pull free. Sasha turned her head aside, and I leaned across her, trying to choke the monkey senseless but, more important, trying to shove it out of the Hummer, and then it was through the window, and I let it go, and Sasha cranked the glass up so fast that she almost pinched my hands.

Bobby said, "Let's not do that again."

"Okay."

Another screeching fleabag swung down from the roof, intending to enter through the broken window, but Roosevelt whacked it with a sledgehammer-size fist, and it flew away into the night as though it had been fired out of a catapult.

Doogie was still putting the Hummer through quick serpentine maneuvers, and at the tailgate, the monkey hanging upside down from the roof rack swung back and forth across the unbroken window, as if it were a clock pendulum. Orson tumbled off his feet but sprang up at once, snarling and snapping his teeth to remind the rhesus of the price it would pay if it tried to get inside.

Looking beyond the tick-tock monkey, I saw that the rest of the troop continued to give chase. Doogie's slalom trick, while shaking loose some of the attackers, had slowed us down, and the bright-eyed nasties were gaining on us.

Then the sass man stopped swerving, accelerated, and rounded a corner so fast that he almost stood us on end when he had to jam the brake pedal to the floorboard to avoid plowing through a pack of coyotes.

The monkey at the tailgate shrieked at either the sight or the smell of the pack. It dropped off the Hummer and ran for its life.

The coyotes, fifty or sixty of them, parted like a stream and flowed around the vehicle.

I was afraid they would try to come through the broken window. With their wicked teeth, they would be harder to hold off than mere monkeys. But they showed no interest in canned people meat, racing past, closing ranks again behind us.

The pursuing troop rounded the corner and met the pack. Monkeys shot into the air with such surprise that you would have thought they were on a trampoline. Being smart monkeys, they retreated without hesitation, and the coyotes went after them.

The kids turned backward in their seats, cheering the coyotes.

"It's a Barnum and Bailey world," Sasha said.

Doogie drove us out of Wyvern.

The clouds had cleared while we'd been underground, and the moon hung high in the sky, as round as time.

27

With midnight still ahead of us, we took each of the kids home, and that was totally fine. Tears are not always bitter. As we made our rounds, the tears on the faces of the children's parents were as sweet as mercy. When Lilly Wing looked at me, with Jimmy in her arms, I saw in her eyes something that I had once yearned to see, but now what I saw was less fulfilling for me here in time present than it might have been in time past.

When we got back to my house, Sasha, Bobby, and I were prepared to party, but Roosevelt wanted to get his Mercedes, drive home to his handsome Bluewater cruiser at the marina, and craft a pirate's patch out of filet mignon to cover his swollen eye. "Children, I'm getting old. You go celebrate, and I'll go sleep."

Because he was off duty at the radio station, Doogie had made a midnight date, as if he'd never doubted that he would come back from neverland and feel like dancing. "Good thing I have time to shower," he said. "I think I smell like monkey."

While Bobby and Sasha loaded my and Sasha's surfboards into her Explorer, I washed my bloodstained hands. Then Mungojerrie and Orson and I went into the dining room, now Sasha's music room, to listen to the tape that I had heard twice before. Leland Delacroix's testament.

It was not in the machine where I had left it when I'd

played it for Sasha, Roosevelt, and Mungojerrie. Apparently, it had vanished like the building that had housed the Mystery Train. If Delacroix had never killed himself, had never worked on the train, had never gone to the other side, then no tape had ever been made.

I went to the rack in which Sasha stores audiotapes of all her compositions. The dupe of Delacroix's testament, labeled "Tequila Kidneys," was where I had put it.

"It'll be blank," I said.

Orson regarded me quizzically. The poor battered boy needed to be bathed, treated with antiseptics, and bandaged. Sasha was probably one step ahead of me, already packing a first-aid kit into the truck.

Mungojerrie was waiting at the tape player when I returned with the cassette.

I popped it into the machine and pressed the *play* button.

The hiss of magnetic tape. A soft click. Rhythmic breathing. Then ragged breathing, weeping, great miserable sobs. Finally, Delacroix's voice: *"This is a warning. A testament."*

I pressed *stop*. I could not understand how the original tape could cease to exist, while this copy remained intact. How could Delacroix be making this testament if he'd never ridden the Mystery Train?

"Paradox," I said.

Orson nodded in agreement.

Mungojerrie looked at me and yawned, as if to say that I was full of crap.

I switched the machine on and fast-forwarded until I came to the place on the tape at which Delacroix listed as many of the personnel on the project as he'd known, citing their titles. The first name was, as I had remembered, Dr. Randolph Josephson. He was a civilian scientist—and head of the project.

Dr. Randolph Josephson.

John Joseph Randolph.

On leaving juvenile detention at the age of eighteen, Johnny Randolph had surely become Randolph Josephson. In this new identity, he had acquired an education, apparently one hell of an education, driven to fulfill a destiny that he had imagined for himself after seeing a crow emerge from solid rock.

Now, if you want, you can believe that the devil himself paid a visit to twelve-year-old Johnny Randolph, in the form of a talking crow, urging him to kill his parents and then develop a machine—the Mystery Train—to open the door between here and Hell, to let out the legions of dark angels and demons who are condemned to live in the Pit.

Or you can believe that a homicidal boy read a similar scenario in, oh, say it was a moldering comic book, and then borrowed the plot for his own pathetic life, built it into a grand delusion that motivated him to create that infernal machine. It might seem unlikely that a slashing-chopping-hacking sociopath could become a scientist of such stature that billions of dollars in black-budget government money would be lavished on his work, but we know he was an unusually self-controlled sociopath, who limited his killings to one a year, pouring the rest of his murderous energy into his career. And, of course, most of those who decide how to spend black-budget billions are probably not as well balanced as you and I. Well, not as well balanced as you, since anyone reading these volumes of my Moonlight Bay journal will be justified in questioning my balance. The keepers of our communal coffers often seek out insanely ambitious projects, and I would be surprised if John Joseph Randolph—aka Dr. Randolph Josephson—was the only raving lunatic who was showered with our tax money.

I wondered if Randolph could be dead back there in Fort Wyvern, buried alive under the thousands of tons of earth that, in the manic reversal of time, had been returned by dump trucks and excavators to the hole where the egg room and associated chambers had once existed. Or had he never gone to Wyvern in the first place, never developed the Mystery Train? Was he alive elsewhere, having spent the past decade working on another—and similar—project?

The three-hundred-ring circus of my imagination abruptly set up its tent, and I became convinced that John

Joseph Randolph was at the dining-room window, staring at me this very moment. I spun around. The pleated shade was down. I crossed the room, grabbed the pull cord, yanked the shade up. Johnny wasn't there.

I listened to a little more of the tape. The eighteenth name on Delacroix's list was Conrad Gensel. No doubt he was the stocky bastard with the cropped black hair, yellow-brown eyes, and doll's teeth. Perhaps he was one of the temponauts who had traveled to the other side, one of the few who had come back alive. Maybe he had glimpsed a destiny of his own in that world of the red sky, or had been driven quietly mad by what he'd seen and had found himself self-destructively drawn to that nightmare place. In any case, he and Randolph hadn't met at a church supper or a strawberry festival.

The skin was still crawling on the nape of my neck. Although the Mystery Train building had been deconstructed down to the last chip of concrete and the final scrap of steel, I didn't feel that we'd reached closure in this matter.

John Joseph Randolph hadn't been at the window; however, now I was sure Conrad Gensel had his nose pressed to the pane. Because I had lowered the blind after checking for mad Johnny, I crossed the room again. Hesitated. Yanked up the shade. No Conrad.

The dog and the cat were watching me with interest, as if they were being highly entertained.

"The big question," I said to Mungojerrie and Orson, as I led them into the kitchen, "is whether the door Johnny opened was really a door into Hell or a door to somewhere else."

He wouldn't have submitted a grant application with the promise of building a bridge to Beelzebub. He'd have been more discreet. I'm sure the cloak-and-dagger financiers believed that they were funding research and experiments in time travel; and because they are all comfortable in their lunacy, *that* seemed rational.

As I took a package of frankfurters out of the freezer, I said, "And from what he was ranting in that copper room, I guess it must have been time travel of a sort. Forward, back—but mostly what he called *sideways*."

I stood pondering the problem, holding the frozen hot dogs.

Orson started pacing in circles around me.

"Suppose there *are* worlds out there in time streams that flow *beside* ours, parallel worlds. According to quantum physics, an infinite number of shadow universes exist simultaneously with ours, as real as ours. We can't see them. They can't see us. Realities never intersect. Except maybe at Wyvern. Where the Mystery Train, like a giant blender, whipped realities together for a while."

Mungojerrie was now pacing around me, too, following Orson.

"Isn't it possible that one of those shadow universes is so terrible that it might as well be Hell? For that matter, maybe there's a parallel world so glorious we couldn't distinguish it from Heaven."

The pacing pooch and the pacing cat were so focused on the hot dogs, in such a solid trance, that if Orson had suddenly stopped, Mungojerrie would have walked halfway up his butt before realizing where he was.

I cut open the package of frankfurters, spread the sausages on a plate, headed for the microwave oven, but stopped in the middle of the room, pondering the imponderable.

"In fact," I said, "isn't it possible that some people—genuine psychics, mystics—have actually at times looked through the barrier between time streams? Had visions of these parallel worlds? Maybe that's where our concepts of the afterlife come from."

Bobby had entered the kitchen from the garage as I'd launched into my latest monologue. He listened to me for a moment, but then he fell in behind Mungojerrie and Orson, pacing circles around me.

"And what if we *do* move on from this world when we die, sideways into one of those parallel to us? Are we talking religion or science here?"

"*We're* not talking anything," Bobby said. "You're talking

your head off about religion and science and pseudoscience, but we're just thinking hot dogs."

Taking the hint, I put the plate in the microwave. When the hot dogs were warm, I gave two to Mungojerrie. I gave six to Orson, because when I had lifted the cut chain-link and urged him to enter Wyvern the previous night, I had promised him frankfurters, and I always keep my promises to my friends, just as they always keep their promises to me.

I didn't give any to Bobby, because he'd been a smartass.

"Look what I found," he said, as I was washing the frankfurter grease from my hands.

My fingers were dripping when he gave me the Mystery Train cap.

"This can't exist," I said.

If the entire building that housed the project had unraveled from existence, why would the cap have been made in the first place?

"It doesn't exist," he said. "But something else does."

Baffled, I turned the cap in my hands, to look at the words above the bill. The ruby-red stitching didn't form *Mystery Train* anymore. Instead, the two words were *Tornado Alley*.

"What's Tornado Alley?" I asked.

"You find it a little . . ."

"Not uncreepy?"

"Yeah."

"Maximo weird," I said.

Maybe Randolph and Conrad and others were out there in Wyvern or some other part of the world, working on the same project, which now had a different name. No closure.

"Gonna wear it?" Bobby asked.

"No."

"Good idea."

"Another thing," he said. "What *did* happen to the dead me?"

"Here we go again. He ceased to exist, that's all."

"Because I didn't die."

"I'm no Einstein."

He frowned. "What if I wake up some morning, and beside me in bed is that dead me, all rotting and oozing slime?"

"You'll have to buy new sheets."

When we were packed and ready to party, we drove out to the point of the southern horn of the bay, on which Bobby's cottage—a beautiful structure of weathered teak and glass—is the only residence.

On the way, Sasha stopped at a pay phone, disguised her voice by doing a Mickey Mouse imitation—God knows why Mickey Mouse, when any of the characters from *The Lion King* would have been more apt—and tipped the police to the scene at the Stanwyk house.

When we were on the move again, Bobby said, "Bro?"

"Yo."

"Who left that Mystery Train cap for you in the first place? And who slipped Delacroix's security badge under the windshield wiper on the Jeep last night?"

"No proof."

"But a suspicion?"

"Big Head."

"You serious?"

"I think it's way smarter than it looks."

"It's some mutant freak," Bobby insisted.

"So am I."

"Good point."

At Bobby's place, we changed from street clothes into wet suits, then loaded a cooler full of beer and a variety of snacks into the Explorer.

Before we could party, however, we needed to resolve one issue—so we could stop glancing nervously at the windows, looking for the crazy conductor of the Mystery Train.

The oversize video displays at the computer workstations in Bobby's home office were ablaze with colorful maps, bar graphs, photos of the earth taken from orbit only minutes ago, and flow charts of dynamic weather conditions worldwide. Here—and with the help of his employees in the Moonlight Bay offices of Surfcast—Bobby predicted surf conditions for subscribers in over twenty countries.

As I am not computer compatible, I stood back while Bobby settled into one of the workstations, rattled his fingers across the keyboard, went on-line, and searched a database listing all the leading American scientists of our time. Logic insisted that a mad genius obsessed with the possibility of time travel, determined to prove that parallel worlds existed alongside our own and that these lands could be reached by a lateral movement *across* time, would have to become a physicist, and a damned good one, enormously well funded, if he had any hope of applying his theories effectively.

Bobby found Dr. Randolph Josephson in three minutes. He was associated with a university in Nevada, and he lived in Reno.

Mungojerrie sprang onto the workstation to peer intently at the data on the screen. There was even a photo. It was our mad scientist, all right.

In spite of the widespread base closures that had followed the end of the Cold War, Nevada had been left with a few sprawling facilities. It was reasonable to assume that on at least one of them, top-secret research projects in the Wyvern vein were still being undertaken.

"He might have moved up there to Reno after Wyvern closed," Sasha said. "That doesn't mean he's still alive. He could have come back here to snatch these kids—and died when that building . . . came apart."

"But maybe he never worked at Wyvern at all. If the Mystery Train never happened, then maybe he's been up there in Reno all along—building Tornado Alley or something else."

Bobby called directory assistance in Reno and obtained a listed number for Dr. Randolph Josephson. With a felt-tip pen, he jotted it on a notepad.

Though I knew my imagination was to blame, the ten digits seemed to have an evil aura, as if this was the phone number at which soul-selling politicians could reach Satan twenty-four hours a day, seven days a week, holidays included, collect calls accepted.

"You're the only one of us who's heard his voice," Bobby said. He rolled his chair aside, so I could reach the telephone at the workstation. "I've got caller-ID block and trace-call block, so if you make him curious, he can't find us."

When I picked up the handset, Orson put his forepaws on the workstation and gently clamped his jaws around my wrist, as if to suggest that I should put the phone down without making the call.

"Got to do it, bro."

He whined.

"Duty," I told him.

He understood duty, and so he released me.

Although the fine hairs on the back of my neck were dueling with one another, I keyed in the number. As I listened to it ring, I told myself that Randolph was dead, buried alive in the hole where that copper-lined room had been.

He answered on the third ring. I recognized his voice at once, from the single word *hello*.

"Dr. Randolph Josephson?" I asked.

"Yes?"

My mouth was so dry that my tongue stuck to my palate almost as securely as Velcro to Velcro.

"Hello? Are you there?" he asked.

"Is this the Randolph Josephson formerly known as John Joseph Randolph?"

He did not answer. I could hear him breathing.

I said, "Did you think your juvenile record was expunged? Did you really think you could kill your parents and have the facts erased forever?"

I hung up, dropping the handset so fast that it rattled in the cradle.

"Now what?" Sasha asked.

Getting up from the workstation chair, Bobby said, "Maybe in this version of his life, the kook didn't get funding for his project as quickly as he found it at Wyvern, or maybe not enough funding. He might not yet have started up another model of the Mystery Train."

"But if that's true," Sasha said, "how do we stop him? Drive over to Reno and put a bullet in his brain?"

"Not if we can avoid it," I said. "I tore some clippings off the wall of his murder gallery, in that tunnel under the egg room. They were still in my pockets when I got home. They hadn't just vanished like . . . Bobby's corpse. Which must mean those are killings Randolph's still committed. His annual thrill. Maybe tomorrow I should make anonymous calls to the police, accusing him of the murders. If they look into it, they might find his scrapbook or other mementos."

"Even if they nail him," Sasha said, "his research could go on without him. The new version of the Mystery Train might be built, and the door between realities might be opened."

I looked at Mungojerrie. Mungojerrie looked at Orson. Orson looked at Sasha. Sasha looked at Bobby. Bobby looked at me and said, "Then we're doomed."

"I'll tip the cops tomorrow," I said. "It's the best we can do. And if the cops can't convict him . . ."

Sasha said, "Then Doogie and I will drive over to Reno one day and waste the creep."

"You have a way about you, woman," Bobby said.

Time to party.

Sasha drove the Explorer across the dunes, through shore grass silvered with moonlight, and down a long embankment, parking on the beach of the southern horn, just above the tideline. Driving this far onto the strand isn't legal, but we had been to Hell and back, so we figured we could survive virtually any punishment meted out for this violation.

We spread blankets on the sand, near the Explorer, and fired up a single Coleman lantern.

A large ship was stationed just beyond the mouth of the bay, north and west of us. Although the night shrouded it, and though the porthole lights were not sufficient to entirely define the vessel, I was sure that I had never seen anything quite like it in these parts. It made me uneasy, though not uneasy enough to go home and hide under my bed.

The waves were tasty, six to eight feet from trough to crest. The offshore flow was just strong enough to carve them into modest barrels, and in the moonlight, the foam glimmered like mermaids' pearl necklaces.

Sasha and Bobby paddled out to the break line, and I took the first watch on shore, with Orson and Mungojerrie and two shotguns. Though the Mystery Train might not exist any longer, my mom's clever retrovirus was still at work. Perhaps the promised vaccine and cure were on the way, but people in Moonlight Bay were still becoming. The coyotes couldn't have crunched up the entire troop; a few Wyvern monkeys, at least, were out there somewhere, and not feeling kindly about us.

Using the first-aid kit that Sasha had brought, I gently cleaned Orson's abraded pasterns with antiseptic and then coated the shallow cuts with Neosporin. The laceration on his left cushion, near his nose, was not as bad as it had first looked, but his ear was a mess. In the morning, I would have to try to get a vet to come to the house and give us an opinion about the possibility of repairing the broken cartilage.

Although the antiseptic must have stung, Orson never complained. He is a good dog and an even better person.

"I love you, bro," I told him.

He licked my face.

I realized that, from time to time, I was looking left and right along the beach, half expecting monkeys but even more prepared for the sight of Johnny Randolph strolling toward me. Or Hodgson in his spacesuit, face churning with parasites. After reality had been so thoroughly cut to pieces, perhaps it could never again be stitched back together in the old, comfortable pattern. I couldn't shake the feeling that, from now on, *anything* could happen.

I opened a beer for me and one for Orson. I poured his into a bowl and suggested he share some of it with Mungojerrie, but the cat took one taste and spat with disgust.

The night was mild, the sky was deep with stars, and the rumble of the point-break surf was like the beating of a mighty heart.

A shadow passed across the fat moon. It was only a hawk, not a gargoyle.

That creature with black leather wings and a whiplike tail had also been graced with two horns, cloven hooves, and a face that was hideous largely because it was human, too human to have been plugged into that otherwise grotesque form. I'm pretty sure drawings of such creatures can be found in books that date back as far as books have been printed, and under most if not all of those drawings, you will find the same caption: *demon.*

I decided not to think about that anymore.

After a while, Sasha came out of the surf, panting happily, and Orson panted back at her as though he thought she was trying to converse.

She dropped on the blanket beside me, and I opened a beer for her.

Bobby was still thrashing the night waves.

"See that ship out there?" she asked.

"Big."

"We paddled a little farther out than we needed to. Got just a little closer look. It's U.S. Navy."

"Never saw a battleship anchored around here before."

"Something's up."

"Something always is."

A chill of premonition passed through me. Maybe a cure and a vaccine were forthcoming. Or maybe the big brains had decided the only way to cover up the fiasco at Wyvern and obscure the source of the retrovirus was to scrub the former base and all of Moonlight Bay off the map. Scrub it away with a thermonuclear brush that even viruses couldn't survive. Might the wider public believe, if properly prepared, that any nuclear event obliterating Moonlight Bay was the work of terrorists?

I decided not to think about that anymore.

"Bobby and I are going to set a date," I said. "Gotta get married now, you know."

"Mandatory, once he said he loved you."

"That's the way we feel."

"Who's the bridesmaid?" she asked.

"Orson," I said.

"We're deep into gender confusion."

"Want to be best man?" I asked.

"Sure, unless, when the time comes, I'm up to my ass in angry monkeys or something. Take some waves, Snowman."

I got to my feet, picked up my board, said, "I'd leave Bobby standing at the altar in a minute, if I thought you'd marry me instead," and headed for the surf.

She let me get about six steps before she shouted, "Was that a proposal?"

"Yes!" I shouted.

"Asshole!" she shouted.

"Is that an acceptance?" I called back to her as I waded into the sea.

"You don't get off that easy. You owe me a lot of romancing."

"So it was an acceptance?" I shouted.

"Yes!"

With surf foaming around my knees, I turned to look back at her as she stood there in the light of the Coleman lantern. If Kaha Huna, goddess of the surf, walked the earth, she was here this night, not in Waimea Bay, not living under the name Pia Klick.

Orson stood beside her, sweeping his tail back and forth, obviously looking forward to being a bridesmaid. But then his tail abruptly stopped wagging. He trotted closer to the water, raised his head, sniffed the air, and gazed at the warship anchored outside the mouth of the bay. I could see nothing different about the vessel, but some change evidently had drawn Orson's attention—and concern.

The waves, however, were too choice to resist. *Carpe diem. Carpe noctem. Carpe aestus*—seize the surf.

The night sea rolled in from far Tortuga, from Tahiti, from Bora Bora, from the Marquesas, from a thousand sun-drenched places where I will never walk, where high tropical skies burn a blue that I will never see, but all the light I need is here, with those I love, who shine.

About the Author

DEAN KOONTZ is the author of a dozen #1 *New York Times* bestsellers, including *Sole Survivor* and *Intensity*. He lives in southern California.

Correspondence for the author should be addressed to:
Dean Koontz
P.O. Box 9529
Newport Beach, CA 92658

On the heels of his critically acclaimed *New York Times* bestsellers *Fear Nothing* and *Seize the Night*, Dean Koontz stuns readers with a deeply sinister and endlessly surprising tale of a rare and terrifying phobia: autophobia—fear of oneself.

DEAN KOONTZ

FALSE MEMORY

Available December 28, 1999, wherever hardcover books are sold.

Turn the page for a special advance preview of *False Memory*, the new novel from Dean Koontz, acclaimed by *Rolling Stone* as "America's most popular suspense novelist," with, as *People* put it, "the power to scare the daylights out of us."

Autophobia is a real personality disorder. The term is used to describe three different conditions: 1) fear of being alone; 2) fear of being egotistical; 3) fear of oneself. The third is the rarest of these conditions.

1

On that Tuesday in January, when her life changed forever, Martine Rhodes woke with a headache, developed a sour stomach after washing down two aspirin with grapefruit juice, guaranteed herself an epic bad-hair day by mistakenly using Dustin's shampoo instead of her own, broke a fingernail, burnt her toast, discovered ants swarming through the cabinet under the kitchen sink, eradicated the pests by firing a spray can of insecticide as ferociously as Sigourney Weaver wielded a flamethrower in one of those old extraterrestrial-bug movies, cleaned up the resultant carnage with paper towels, hummed Bach's *Requiem* as she solemnly consigned the tiny bodies to the trash can, and took a telephone call from her mother, Sabrina, who still prayed for the collapse of Martie's marriage three years after the wedding. Throughout, she remained upbeat—even enthusiastic—about the day ahead, because from her late father, Robert "Smilin' Bob" Woodhouse, she had inherited an optimistic nature, formidable coping skills, and a deep love of life in addition to blue eyes, ink-black hair, and ugly toes.

Thanks, Daddy.

After convincing her ever hopeful mother that the Rhodes marriage remained happy, Martie slipped into a leather jacket and took her golden retriever, Valet, on his morning walk. Step by step, her headache faded.

Along the whetstone of clear eastern sky, the sun sharpened scalpels of light. Out of the west, however, a cool onshore breeze pushed malignant masses of dark clouds.

The dog regarded the heavens with concern, sniffed the air warily, and pricked his pendant ears at the hiss-clatter of palm fronds stirred by the wind. Clearly, Valet knew a storm was coming.

He was a gentle, playful dog. Loud noises frightened him, however, as though he had been a soldier in a former life and was haunted by memories of battlefields blasted by cannon fire.

Fortunately for him, rotten weather in southern California was seldom accompanied by thunder. Usually, rain fell unannounced, hissing on the streets, whispering through the foliage, and these were sounds that even Valet found soothing.

Most mornings, Martie walked the dog for an hour, along the narrow tree-lined streets of Corona Del Mar, but she had a special obligation every Tuesday and Friday that limited their excursion to fifteen minutes on those days. Valet seemed to have a calendar in his furry head, because on their Tuesday and Friday expeditions, he never dawdled, finishing his toilet close to home.

This morning, only one block from their house,

on the grassy sward between the sidewalk and the curb, the pooch made water while in a discreet squat. He had been trained not to lift a leg, and he was, in any event, too shy to do so.

Half a block farther, he was preparing to conclude the second half of his morning business when a passing garbage truck backfired, startling him. He huddled behind a queen palm, peering cautiously around one side of the tree bole and then around the other, convinced that the terrifying vehicle would reappear.

"No problem," Martie assured him. "The big bad truck is gone. Everything's fine. This is now a safe-to-poop zone."

Valet was unconvinced. He remained wary.

Martie was blessed with Smilin' Bob's patience, too, especially when dealing with Valet, whom she loved almost as much as she might have loved a child if she'd had one. He was sweet-tempered and beautiful: light gold, with gold and white feathering on his legs, soft snow-white flags on his butt, and a lush tail.

Of course, when the dog was in a doing-business squat, like now, Martie never looked at him, because he was as self-conscious as a nun in a topless bar. While waiting, she softly sang Jim Croce's "Time in a Bottle," which always relaxed the pooch.

As she began the second verse, a sudden chill climbed the ladder of her spine, causing her to fall silent. She was not a woman given to premonitions, but as the icy quiver ascended to the back of her neck, she was overcome by a sense of impending danger.

Turning, she half expected to see an approaching

assailant or a hurtling car. Instead, she was alone on this quiet residential street.

Nothing rushed toward her with lethal purpose. The only moving things were those harried by the wind. Trees and shrubs shivered. A few crisp brown leaves skittered along the pavement. Garlands of tinsel and Christmas lights, from the recent holiday, rustled and rattled under the eaves of a nearby house.

Still uneasy, but feeling foolish, Martie let out the breath that she'd been holding. When the exhalation whistled between her teeth, she realized that her jaws were clenched.

She was probably still spooked from the dream that awakened her after midnight, the same one she'd had on a few other recent nights. The man made of dead, rotting leaves. Whirling, raging.

Then her gaze dropped to her elongated shadow, which stretched across the close-cropped grass, draped the curb, and folded onto the cracked concrete pavement. Inexplicably, her uneasiness swelled into alarm.

She took one step backward, then a second, and of course her shadow moved with her. Only as she retreated a third step did she realize that this very silhouette was what frightened her.

Ridiculous. More absurd than her dream. Yet something in her shadow was not right: a jagged distortion, a menacing quality.

Her heart knocked as hard as a fist on a door.

In the severe angle of the morning sun, the houses and trees cast distorted images, too, but she saw nothing fearsome in their stretched and buckled shadows—only in her own.

She recognized the absurdity of her fear, but this

awareness did not diminish her anxiety. Terror courted her, and she stood hand-in-hand with panic.

The shadow seemed to throb with the thick slow beat of its own heart. Staring at it, she was overcome with dread.

Martie closed her eyes and tried to get control of herself.

For a moment, she felt so light that the wind seemed strong enough to sweep her up and carry her inland, with the relentlessly advancing clouds, toward the steadily shrinking band of cold blue sky. As she drew a series of deep breaths, however, weight gradually returned to her.

When she dared to look again at her shadow, she no longer sensed anything unusual about it. She let out a sigh of relief.

Her heart continued to pound, powered not by irrational terror anymore, but by an understandable concern as to the cause of this peculiar episode. She'd never previously experienced such a thing.

Head cocked quizzically, Valet was staring at her.

She had dropped his leash.

Her hands were damp with sweat. She blotted her palms on her blue jeans.

When she realized that the dog had finished his toilet, Martie slipped her right hand into a plastic pet-cleanup bag, using it as a glove. Being a good neighbor, she neatly collected Valet's gift, turned the bright blue bag inside out, twisted it shut, and tied a double knot in the neck.

The retriever watched her sheepishly.

"If you ever doubt my love, baby boy," Martie said, "remember I do this every day."

Valet looked grateful. Or perhaps only relieved.

Performance of this familiar, humble task restored her mental balance. The little blue bag and its warm contents anchored her to reality. The weird incident remained troubling, intriguing, but it no longer frightened her.

DEAN KOONTZ

FALSE MEMORY

On sale December 28, 1999

Fear for your mind.

DEAN KOONTZ, called by *Rolling Stone* "America's most popular suspense novelist," invites you to meet Christopher Snow and enter the strange and wondrous world he inhabits in Moonlight Bay, California...

When you are different from everyone else, the night is not your enemy, the darkness is not intimidating, the shadows are not terrifying. And if you're different enough, you...

FEAR NOTHING

"*Fear Nothing* will make you fear almost everything."—*San Francisco Examiner*

"*Fear Nothing* demonstrates a master of darkness's continuing power to scare the daylights out of us."
—*People*

__57975-4 $7.99/$10.99